MURDER IN A SCOTTISH GARDEN
"In her second Scottish Shire mystery, Hall capably juggles multiple story lines and vividly evokes the Scottish backdrop."
—*Booklist*

MURDER AT A SCOTTISH SOCIAL
"Witty characters match the well-crafted plot. . . . Cozy fans will want to see a lot more of the compassionate Paislee."
—*Publishers Weekly*

MURDER AT A SCOTTISH WEDDING
"Down-to-earth characters and two mysteries to solve add up to a solid read."
—*Kirkus Reviews*

"Intriguing. . . . Fans of all things Scottish will have fun."
—*Publishers Weekly*

MURDER AT A SCOTTISH CHRISTMAS
"This latest adventure of a charming Scottish family is perfect for readers who like thorny mysteries and puppies."
—*Kirkus Reviews*

Books by Traci Wilton

MRS. MORRIS AND THE GHOST

MRS. MORRIS AND THE WITCH

MRS. MORRIS AND THE GHOST OF CHRISTMAS PAST

MRS. MORRIS AND THE SORCERESS

MRS. MORRIS AND THE VAMPIRE

MRS. MORRIS AND THE POT OF GOLD

MRS. MORRIS AND THE WOLFMAN

MRS. MORRIS AND THE MERMAID

MRS. MORRIS AND THE VENOMOUS VALENTINE

MRS. MORRIS AND THE DAY OF THE DEAD

And writing as Traci Hall

MURDER IN A SCOTTISH SHIRE

MURDER IN A SCOTTISH GARDEN

MURDER AT A SCOTTISH SOCIAL

MURDER AT A SCOTTISH WEDDING

MURDER AT A SCOTTISH CASTLE

MURDER AT A SCOTTISH CHRISTMAS

MURDER AT THE SCOTTISH GAMES

Published by Kensington Publishing Corp.

Murder
at the
Scottish
Games

TRACI HALL

Kensington Publishing Corp.
kensingtonbooks.com

ISBN: 978-1-4967-5468-4 (ebook)
ISBN: 978-1-4967-5467-7

First Kensington Trade Edition: December 2025

10 9 8 7 6 5 4 3 2 1

Printed in the United States of America

The authorized representative in the EU for product safety and compliance
is eucomply OU, Parnu mnt 139b-14, Apt 123
Tallinn, Berlin 11317, hello@eucompliancepartner.com

This book is dedicated to readers everywhere! It has been my joy to meet so many in the past few years who share my love of stories. Whether it's been on social media, or in person, the author-reader connection means the world. Thank YOU!

Evelyn McCauley was the winner at the Loch Norman Highland Games in North Carolina, where I had the privilege of speaking for their thirtieth anniversary at Rural Hill. Evelyn chose Aibreann as a character name, which I think is very pretty. It was wonderful to see the many clans perform throughout the day, from the caber toss, to duck herding, which is where I got the idea for the scene in *Murder at the Scottish Games*.

My thanks to Stacy Phillips at Rural Hill Centre of Scottish Heritage for being so welcoming. If you live close to the area, I highly recommend the annual event.

Chapter 1

Friday afternoon, Cashmere Crush was busy with tourists snapping up tams, scarves, or cardigans. Summer to others from warmer countries meant hot weather, but here in Nairn, it was sixty-five degrees on this August day. Toasty enough for Paislee Shaw's coastal blood, but tourists were often chilled, and she had a selection of bespoke items to comfort them.

It was a boon to Paislee's cash register to get her through the slower winter months in addition to her growing side business at Ramsey Castle where she sold luxury cashmere goods. She couldn't keep the Grant tartan coin purses in stock.

With a thankful glance at the ceiling and the memory of her angelic Gran, Paislee bagged a wool cardigan vest, in gray, with pockets and wooden buttons, adding a crocheted flower keychain with the receipt, which had her business information printed on it.

"I've tried to knit, but I'm all thumbs. I just love everything in your shop." The young woman's accent was Canadian. Brunette, in her early twenties, she wore a Nairn putting stone T-shirt. The fabled stone had its own lore to rival the stone in Inverness.

"Thank you," Paislee said. "You're here for the Highland Games?"

"Yes. From Nova Scotia. My husband's parents raved about a

magical holiday they had in Nairn, so we came last year for our honeymoon, not realizing it was the same weekend as the games. We've decided to make it an annual tradition."

"That's splendid. Where did you stay?"

The woman grinned, brown eyes sparkling. "The Muthu Newton, of course. I'm Dania MacNeal."

The hotel helped put Nairn on the map thanks to Charlie Chaplin's family staying there for summer holidays where they rented the second floor. "Nice tae meet you. I'm Paislee Shaw." They shook hands and Paislee walked with the woman toward the front door. "Happy anniversary."

Dania left, holding the door open for a person Paislee knew well—her bestie, Lydia Barron-Smythe.

"Lyd!" Her best friend in the world was tall, gray-eyed, slim, and currently sporting silver hair in a shag style that Paislee could only envy and never pull off. She wore designer jeans in black, high-heeled silver boots, and a short-sleeved cashmere top Paislee had made for her several Christmases ago. They hugged and stepped back, smiling at one another. "And what are you doing here?"

They'd just spent the prior Thursday evening at her weekly Knit and Sip event. Lydia didn't knit, but she loved to sip and create divine snacks. She kept the gossip going as well as the plates filled.

"What a welcome!" Rhona Smythe, Paislee's newest hire, giggled. She was a Smythe cousin to Lydia's husband Corbin and all of nineteen. Though wealthy, her parents had decided a dose of reality was in order after the teenager's second speeding ticket. They'd garaged the car and insisted Rhona get a job to pay back the fines they'd paid for the tickets, since she wasn't going to university.

The teen was a bubbly addition to the crew. Grandpa worked alternate afternoons and some Saturdays, and Amelia Henry, currently away at Tulliallan for police officer training, normally filled in on Saturdays. Cashmere Crush was closed on Sundays.

"Bumped intae Meri, completely overwhelmed, at the petrol station. She gave me tasks." Lydia's lips twitched as she held back laughter. Their mutual friend Meri McVie was a judge for the annual bagpipe contest in September and had joined their knitting group on Thursdays. She believed in taking part in her community. Like many leaders, she could be . . . assertive. This year Meri was chairman of the board for the Nairn Highland Games, which trickled down to Paislee also being on the volunteer committee. Lydia and her husband had been in Germany, studying wine. "I have another thing for you too."

"What is it?" Paislee had sponsored the eight-hundred-meter sprint because Brody was running in the race, though he was giving her grief about going. He'd turned thirteen and was taller now than her and almost to Grandpa's six feet. Grandpa teased that his shoes could be used for canoes, his feet had grown so big.

Paislee and Lydia stepped to the side as another customer entered the yarn shop. Rhona greeted them with an enthusiastic hello.

"Something tae do with the new dog-herding event." Lydia scrolled through her mobile. "She asked if Brody might help. And how is my godson?"

Paislee shrugged. For Brody, the summer break from school had brought with it the news that Jenni just wanted to be friends and Edwyn Maclean, Brody's best mate, was quitting football. Change was a four-letter word in the Shaw household these days.

"Could be better." Brody's summer had been split between playing video games, football camp, and dog-sitting Snowball, a white Pomeranian, for Amelia at their house. He spent a lot of time in the back garden perfecting his football skills with Wallace, their black Scottish terrier. Dogs were a boy's best friend and Snowball fit right in, though she was a mere eight pounds to Wallace's sturdy eighteen.

Paislee tried to be encouraging but missed the days of easy hugs. Especially, when compared to living with the prickly young man with acne who didn't understand that this teenage awkwardness would pass. Had she ever thought so when puberty had hit her? She longed to help, but she was the last person her son wanted around. "You remember how awful it was tae be thirteen."

Lydia shuddered. "I do."

"We had your mum, at least, who was easy tae talk tae."

"And each other. How's Angus?" Lydia glanced around the shop, but the only silver head belonged to Elspeth Booth, her other part-timer, a few years beyond seventy and retired from her clerical position for Father Dixon at the church. She and Grandpa had a sweet flirtation, though Grandpa's heart belonged to Paislee's granny. Elspeth was also frustrated by Grandpa's lack of care regarding his cough from his fall in the River Nairn almost three weeks before.

"He's a stubborn Scot and won't go tae the doctor." Grandpa and Brody loved to fish, which was how her grandfather had slipped into the river, where he'd caught a cold instead of haddock. He insisted his cough would pass. Nothing sleep and a whisky couldn't cure. It hurt Paislee physically to hear him cough.

"Puir man," Lydia said with concern, before she brightened. "What does he ken aboot herding sheep?"

"He's never mentioned it, but I'll ask him. Why?"

"A judge Meri had contacted for sheepherding is a mibbe. She's anxious that something will go wrong and she'll end up with egg on her face."

One of the committee members had pushed back against the new event, but Meri had stood her ground, believing it would broaden the opportunities for competitors and add to the entrance fees, which brought in money for the shire. "It's her first time being in charge so I don't blame her." Paislee scanned the busy shop. "I can't think of anyone tae step in."

Rhona rang up the customer she'd been chatting with, adding the flower keychain with interlocking letter Cs for Cashmere Crush and purchase receipt for a tam and matching scarf. Elspeth straightened skeins on the shelves, turning toward the door when it opened again.

Paislee loved summer in Nairn and all the wonderful tourists!

"Welcome," Elspeth said, while Rhona waved goodbye to the customer she'd just rung up.

"There's more tae Meri's list," Lydia said. "She wants us tae be there at six in the morning. As you ken, I am allergic tae six in the morning on a Saturday."

Paislee shared an understanding laugh with Lydia. "Why six? I thought the volunteers didn't have tae be there until eight."

"Right? The participants dinnae need tae be at the park until nine tae check in." Rhona joined them at the tail end of the conversation. The teen watched three customers browsing, ready to jump in if anybody needed assistance. Paislee didn't subscribe to the hovering salesperson style.

"The parade with the marching band starts at ten and will reach the arena at ten thirty. Lord Cawdor will announce the games at eleven, and the first events start at eleven fifteen." Paislee had the schedule memorized.

Meri had a whiteboard on the wall at the town hall meeting room and wasn't afraid to use it.

"Meri noticed my, em, lack of enthusiasm, and offered tae pick you up so Angus can have the Juke, since we'd planned tae carpool." Lydia touched her wedding ring. "Corbin loves tae make breakfast in bed for us."

They were the perfect pair—Lydia baked like a dream and created phenomenal appetizers but didn't cook. Corbin had almost as much skill in the kitchen as Grandpa.

"That's fine with me. What else is on Meri's list?" Paislee asked.

Lydia tapped the screen on her phone and pulled up her notes app. "Ask aboot sheepherding—check. Early morning, check. Meri wants us tae pick up the placement ribbons from the printer, and since I willnae be getting up at the crack of dawn, I'll bring them at a reasonable hour of eight."

Rhona looked at Lydia with admiration in her deep brown eyes. The Smythe clan had a tendency toward brown eyes and velvety brown hair. The Smythe nose, which could be termed as strong, wasn't present on her oval face. "I'm coming with Mum and Da at nine. I tried tae convince them tae let me have my car back early so they dinnae have tae stay all day." Her shoulders slumped.

"How's that going?" Lydia had a lead foot of her own, so could relate.

The first time, the police officer had given Rhona a verbal warning. The second time, a ticket and a fine, and the third, an even larger fine, to a total of five thousand pounds. Her folks had paid the fines to keep her from going to court, and Paislee was impressed that they'd taken the car away until the fines were paid off.

Rhona happened to be a hard worker—a girl couldn't keep up her dance schedule and her studies without proper effort—but the cute sportscar she'd gotten for completion of secondary had given her freedom previously untasted on the Highland roads.

"Slow," Rhona lamented. "I cannae help it—me and Aibreann adore shopping. I'm afraid I'll be working for Paislee forever."

Paislee placed her hand on the teen's shoulder. "I wouldn't mind, but I think you're destined for greater things. The thrill of your own paycheck will wear off eventually."

"I want tae be a professional dancer someday and specialize in the Highland Fling," Rhona said. "I'll need tae join a troupe in order tae make decent money. Right now, I just want tae have fun. Artie says he doesnae mind driving me around, and I always have my bike."

"Artie is a sweetie," Lydia said.

"He is!" Rhona sighed besottedly, as she thought of her boyfriend of six months. They'd met at the golf course, where Artie worked as a caddy and Rhona had been playing a round of golf with her dad, McDermot Smythe. Paislee had no interest in the sport, and Brody, so far, was settled on football.

"Is Artie ready for tomorrow's games?" Paislee asked.

Rhona scrunched her nose. "He's verra confident aboot the hammer throw but nervous that the caber he's worked so hard on, training for the caber toss, will somehow fail. I dinnae see how, with all of his practice. He wants tae make his da proud."

Lydia exuded empathy. Artie's older brother, Cam, on his way to being a professional strongman, had died in a car accident two years back. "Artie doesnae enjoy it for himself?"

"It's complicated," the teen announced. Then a woman glanced around with an armful of yarn, and Rhona stepped her way. "Och, let me help you with that."

"Thanks," the woman said. Together they carried the skeins to the counter. "I'm making an infinity scarf." She held the yarn to her cheek. "This is so soft. Is it cashmere?"

"Nah—this is a blend of Merino and Shetland wool Paislee's been trying because of its texture."

"I'm curious tae see how it will hold up," the woman said.

"You live around here?" Rhona deposited the yarn on the counter.

"I do. Well, in Elgin, anyway, so near enough. Why do you ask?"

"Paislee hosts a Thursday night Knit and Sip group with like-minded knitters if you're interested?"

"Too bad! I work on Thursdays until nine. Great idea, though."

"She's brilliant," Rhona assured the woman.

Paislee blushed and hoped that Rhona wouldn't introduce her, but it was too late, and Rhona pointed to the high-top counter where Paislee and Lydia stood. Her bestie chuckled.

"And right there!" Rhona rang up the woman. "Do you have everythin' you need? I hate when I get home and dinnae have all my supplies."

The woman waved at Paislee and then nodded at Rhona. "I need a sewing needle, actually. I dinnae suppose . . ."

"We carry a selection on the side of the counter." Rhona walked around and pointed to an assortment of needles, scissors, sewing tape, and thimbles, as well as knitting needles or crochet hooks. There even were hoops and fabric for needlepoint projects.

"I'm glad you mentioned it—and I'd better get another pair of scissors too. I swear my sofa eats them."

Paislee smiled as Rhona then walked with the woman toward the exit.

"Are you sairy you gave Rhona a chance?" Lydia asked.

Paislee had been hesitant when Lydia asked her to employ one of Corbin's cousins for a favor, but Rhona was a true gem. "Not even a little bit. I don't know how I'll replace her when she realizes she can do better than stock yarn here."

"You pay Rhona over minimum wage, and she's learning a valuable skill, so she's lucky tae have the opportunity. She's not keen on university and wants tae dance for her career."

"From Rhona's videos she's shown me, she's very good. I'm worried about Artie though—that caber is twice the size he is," Paislee murmured. His muscles were the lean variety, rather than bulky. She'd met him when he'd come in to pick Rhona up after work. She also knew Aibreann Laird, Rhona's best friend. She was twenty to Rhona's nineteen and had an added maturity that grounded Rhona.

"It's only recently that Rhona decided she didnae want tae dance as a hobby. I think graduation came as a surprise—she did her schoolwork well, and her dance, and now what?" Lydia sighed. "She'd be a wonderful salesperson but isnae interested in real estate. I asked."

"She should be 'interested' in paying her bills," Paislee remarked without heat. "Then again, we had tae do so, which puts us in a different category." Lydia was wealthy now, of her own accord—before marrying uber rich Corbin Smythe—but hadn't been born to riches.

"True." Lydia read the notes on her phone again. "Last item. Meri needs someone at the toddler race."

"What about Blaise? I don't think Meri has tapped the O'Connors with anything besides sponsorship for a grand prize." Blaise and Shep O'Connor had moved to Nairn from Inverness, and had a daughter Suzannah, who was nine. Shep was the golf pro at Nairn Golf Course, and Blaise part of their Knit and Sip group.

"They're hosting the local craftsman beer tent," Lydia said. "The Smythes are sponsoring one of the whisky tents."

Paislee shook her head as she imagined the cost. "I know what I paid for a single event—it's nice of you tae do a whole tent with alcohol."

"It's in the Smythe budget, so no worries." Lydia noted the time. "And Shep's backed by the Nairn golf course. I cannae believe it's four already. I have a closing at five, so I must run. Will you text Meri and let her ken that we're all on the same page?"

"I will. See you tomorrow!"

Elspeth went home at six, and Rhona at six thirty. The teen cleaned as Paislee counted the money in the register and put it in the small safe, setting up the cash for the next day. Artie dashed inside to pick up Rhona.

"Hi, Paislee!" Artie's friendly features split into a smile that reached his blue eyes. A lock of shaggy dark blond hair flopped over his forehead. "Ready, Rhona?" He picked Rhona up as if she weighed nothing and lifted her over his head. He was much stronger than he looked.

"Put me doon!" Rhona squeaked, not actually upset. She patted his broad shoulders and leaned up to kiss his cheek. "What's the plan?"

"We're meeting with Foster at his flat tae grill steaks." Artie patted his flat stomach. "Gotta feed the tank for tomorrow."

"Can we invite Aibreann?" Rhona asked. Her best friend had a wee crush on Artie's best friend, but Foster was oblivious.

"Let's call her from the truck," Artie suggested.

"Okay—bye, Paislee. See you tomorrow!" Rhona said, dancing out the back door and down the steps.

Artie waved at Paislee and followed Rhona, equally besotted.

Paislee then stayed until seven, taking inventory of the sweaters and accessories she'd have to replace. Another grand day.

Before leaving, she texted Grandpa to ask if he needed anything from the market. He answered right away that a casserole was in the oven and ready to eat when she got there. She sent a quick thank-you message back.

Singing along to her favorite song on the radio, Paislee reached home and parked under the carport. Though after seven, the evening sky was a light subdued blue. Once the song was over, she turned off the engine and exited the Juke.

She went inside, where Wallace and Snowball greeted her with excitement. The back door was open and the telly on in the living room. Spices wafted down the hall.

"Hey, family!" Paislee put her handbag on the hook by the door and her keys in a small ceramic dish Brody had made last year in one of his electives. She loved it, even if it had an uneven rim.

Grandpa, an oven mitt on his hand, leaned out of the kitchen. His black-framed glasses were fogged with steam, his silver hair mussed.

Paislee hurried toward him. "How can I help?"

"I've got this!" Grandpa said, using his hip to close the oven door. "Brody, lad, time tae eat."

"Finally. I'm starvin'," Brody said from the living area. Lydia had redesigned the interior space so well that it felt like a brand-new home.

Stainless-steel appliances, the washer-dryer combo tucked out of sight behind a door under a long counter, and best of all, the new window over the sink that allowed the daylight in. Soft ivory paint, gray accents, and her round table refinished and polished to last another hundred years. The "wall" of plants by the back door created a partition without darkness. The couch was re-covered, the armchairs by the fire inviting. Of course, the telly was the center of the lounge, but they all enjoyed their movie nights.

Brody shuffled toward her, his face morphing before her eyes into that of the man he would become. His auburn hair was darkening, his brown eyes flashed with golden hues surrounded by thick lashes. His smile, when he bothered to use it, was broad and filled with strong white teeth. Yes, he had some acne, but that would pass with time. Hormones wreaked havoc with complexions. He seemed to be embarrassed by it, and Paislee was at a loss on how to handle it.

Answers for everything could be found on the Internet, and one site she followed suggested open communication. She and Brody had a relationship based on honesty, so when he moped and complained about the acne, even though it might be painful, she replied with facts and solutions, like buying special face wash. Grandpa helped immensely, reiterating that it was part of growing up and didn't last forever.

"How was your day?" Paislee asked. She would love her son until her last breath, even if he was crabbit.

"My last day of freedom before school starts again?" Brody asked on a squeak. His voice was changing as well.

"You have Monday off too," Paislee replied. "After six weeks of holiday. But aye. How was it?"

"Boring," Brody said.

Grandpa placed the casserole in the center of the round table. "I asked if you, me lad, wanted tae go tae the movies, but you said no."

Brody sat down at the table. Wallace paced nearby, sniffing the air. Snowball stayed near Grandpa. The casserole had cheesy potatoes and crumbled sausage, smelling divine.

"You turned down going tae the movies?" Paislee asked in surprise.

Brody shrugged. "I was playing video games with Sam and Ryan."

Edwyn had spent the summer with his grandparents in London,

so wasn't around to hang out. Sam and Ryan were both on the same recreational football team as Brody while Edwyn took a break from the sport.

"Your choice," Grandpa said. His cheeks were ruddy, and his chest wheezed.

Not wanting to nag, Paislee washed up. "Everyone have something tae drink?" She scanned the table. Grandpa had set out glasses of water for them all and a side of steamed green beans to go with the casserole. "We were so busy that my lunch wore off hours ago."

They said a prayer of thanks before digging in. Paislee couldn't stop a smile at Grandpa as Brody went for seconds. Meals around this old table with loved ones were worth all the heartache of this kitchen.

"What's the plan for later?" Brody asked after he'd slowed down.

"Tomorrow is going tae be a big day so we should rest." Paislee had rarely missed attending the Nairn Highland Games throughout the years, but this was her first time behind the scenes. "Don't suppose either of you know anything about sheepherding?"

Grandpa snorted. "No. Dinnae they require a special dog or something?"

"Nope." Brody laughed. "Why?"

"Meri added dog-herding tae encourage more participants and one of the judges might not make it. Grandpa, I know you and Elspeth are working, but Brody, maybe you could help with the toddler race instead? It's the cutest."

"I dinnae want tae go, Mum. I told you."

"You already signed up, so you don't get tae quit. If you don't want tae participate next year, that's fine but we don't back out on our commitments."

"You made me do it. I dinnae want tae volunteer either."

Paislee locked eyes with her son. "It's important tae give back tae our community—you know this. Coach Harris will be there."

Brody's eyes flicked with angst. "I didnae ask him tae come."

"He's competing in the half marathon, so will be there anyway." Brody's event was a sprint rather than a longer run. "Would you prefer tae do that next year? Now that you're thirteen, this is the last time you'll compete in this category."

"I ken how old I am, Mum." His voice cracked. "This is so embarrassing."

That last sentence broke her heart, and she reached across the table to pat his hand. "Hey, is there something besides the race going on? You can talk tae me."

Brody stood and scooted back from the table, knocking the chair over. His cheeks flushed red. "I just dinnae feel guid." He ran outside, Wallace at his heels. Snowball stayed where the food was likely to fall by the table.

Paislee looked at Grandpa. "I don't know what tae do. Is this normal guy stuff?"

"It is. Best thing for him tae do is stay active," Grandpa said. "Give the lad some slack—he doesnae ken what end is up."

Paislee rose and righted the chair. Brody had climbed the tall chestnut tree and had his back to the house. "How long?" Months, or worse, a year?

"Until he's eighteen?" Grandpa laughed at her crestfallen expression. "Just kidding. He'll discover girls and cars long before then."

"Not helping." Paislee gathered the dishes and rinsed them, keeping an eye on Brody as he climbed even higher. She sensed that if she told him to come down it would be an argument. "I'll keep Doc Whyte on speed dial."

"Guid idea." Grandpa rose too quickly and started to cough.

"You can see him too," Paislee said.

"Isnae he a pediatrician?"

"Yes, but he might make an exception for you—acting like a child afraid of a jab at the clinic." Paislee loaded the dishes into the dishwasher and turned to face her grandfather. His skin was flushed from the effort of trying to control his cough.

"No thanks." Grandpa shook his head. "I'm fine."

"I'm dealing with two stubborn Scots." Paislee pressed the start button on the heavenly machine.

"I'm going tae watch telly," Grandpa said. "Join me?"

"I will later." Paislee flipped on the electric kettle for tea and then pulled a stool from under the counter closer to the sink and window. "I've got more coin purses tae do for Ramsey Castle. Would you like some tea?"

"Aye," Grandpa said. "I'll add a wee bit of whisky tae calm my chest."

"I'll bring it tae you." Paislee chose two mugs, her attention on the tree outside. She relaxed as Brody came down a bit lower, though he stayed in the leafy branches.

She texted Meri that she'd be ready at six in the morning and Lydia would bring the printed participation ribbons at eight. Neither Brody nor Grandpa knew about sheepherding to fill in as a judge.

Meri sent a thumbs-up emoji.

Paislee brought Grandpa tea with an inch of room and then took her mug outside to the back porch with her knitting and her phone, playing music on low. Wallace climbed the steps to the porch and lay beside her, as did Snowball. Brody came down and practiced his football drills. The ball seemed to be an extension of his foot as he dribbled and controlled it.

As she watched her son, she acknowledged that though things were difficult now, it would be all right. It had to be. Paislee wasn't one to shy away from hard work to make it so.

After watching a movie together, popcorn with extra butter, and everyone in a good mood, Paislee locked up her house and went upstairs to bed.

Something woke her at midnight.

She went downstairs and opened the door to see Brody coming in the front door. Her racing pulse slowed to a stop. What on earth was he doing outside at this time of night?

Brody was so busted.

"What're you doing outside at this hour?" Paislee shouted. She didn't mean to shout, but it was a natural response that came from fear. Yes, Nairn was safe, but Brody was a child. He'd snuck out without her knowledge. What if something had happened to him?

"I had so much energy that I went for a run." Brody slid by her into the foyer and started toward the steps up to his room.

Was this the first time he'd done so? Paislee caught his arm. "No, son. You are not going tae bed until we have a conversation." She gestured him down the hall to the kitchen table. "Where's Wallace?"

"In my room with Snowball."

She turned on the kitchen light and eyed the tea kettle as well as the clock. Twelve fifteen. Tea might keep her awake, but she needed to do something with her hands so that she didn't shake her belligerent child by the shoulders. Herbal, then.

With a flick of a switch, the kettle perked on.

Paislee poured a glass of water for Brody and fixed a mug of tea for herself, then sat down opposite him. She reached out and swiped his fringe from his forehead. "Please look at me."

Brody peered up with reluctance.

Her heart squeezed. How could she take his pain and uncertainty to lighten the load? "Want tae talk about it?"

"There's nothin' tae say," Brody said.

"Is this about Jenni?"

"No."

"Edwyn?"

"Naw."

"The games tomorrow?"

Brody hesitated, eyes flicking to the side of the table before he shrugged. "Aye."

"You're very fast, and the sprint should be no problem," Paislee said. "Were you out practicing?"

He shook his head.

"Is this the first time you've done this?"

"No."

"Please don't do it anymore." Her stomach tightened. "I know you're tired of me saying this, but it's your last year that you'll be able tae compete as a youth." The cutoff was thirteen and under.

"I came in second. Edwyn was first."

Paislee breathed in the scent of chamomile from her tea, feeling like they might be closer to the point. "Hmm."

Brody drank his water in a gulp. "Coach thinks I should take Edwyn's position now that Edwyn isnae playing on the rec team."

She tilted her head. "Really?" Brody was clearly uncertain about it. In his mind, Edwyn had always been a little bit better—not that Paislee could tell—and they had made an incredible duo on the field. Change.

"Yeah. Coach Harris wants me tae play center forward. He thinks I can do it, but my legs hurt from growing. I trip over my feet all the time." Brody stomped the soles of his trainers to the floor. "It's embarrassing."

Paislee's eyes welled at the hurt her son was feeling that she couldn't do anything about. "You're going tae grow intae your body, and it will be okay."

Brody scowled at Paislee. "By tomorrow?"

Oh.

"You ken what I pray for, Mum?"

"What?"

"I want tae be a pro footballer, but how can I if I'm so uncoordinated? Two bloody left feet."

"Brody, love, you've got tae be patient. I bet if you ask your coach if he ever went through something like this, he'd reassure you that it's normal and will pass. Grandpa says so—we can talk tae Corbin, or Hamish, or,"

"Are ye tryin' tae kill me, Mum? I dinnae need any more humiliation!" With that, Brody darted up the stairs to his room. She didn't have the emotional resources to call him back.

Her mother had been around during puberty, but working; Paislee had Lydia, and Lydia's mum, to find out information. She recalled how Lydia had shot up in height and how her bones had ached. She'd been teased for being a giraffe at school. Sophie Barron had recommended warm baths. She'd do the same for Brody and check in with Doc Whyte on Monday, just to be sure there wasn't anything else to be done.

Paislee dragged herself up from the chair and put her mug in the sink, checking the locks on the doors and windows before heading up the stairs, avoiding the third and fifth out of habit, and falling into her bed to sleep.

Five thirty in the morning was a cruel time to wake up, and Paislee was so tempted to call Meri and meet her at the park later, but she'd agreed, and that was that. The games were a single day of events. The fair would be in town. Maybe Brody would want to do that on their Sunday Funday, and she could sleep in.

A brisk shower had her alert as she stumbled to her room to get dressed for the day—jeans and a light blue T-shirt that said NAIRN HIGHLAND GAMES on the front and VOLUNTEER across the back. Brody would wear his brand-new Shaw kilt, and she'd created a rosette for her name tag and a matching head band in the Shaw colors of blue and green.

Grabbing a granola bar from the pantry and a to-go mug of strong Brodies tea, she was out the door at six, just as Meri arrived. The piping judge drove a black SUV and pulled to a stop at the curb. Paislee hopped in the passenger side, her bag at her feet. She'd chosen a larger tote today to put in a water bottle, a sweatshirt, and sunscreen.

"Mornin'," Meri said with a bright smile at odds with Paislee's lack of sleep. Now who was the crabbit one? Her friend had a wise narrow face, orange hair, and an intelligent brown gaze behind silver-framed glasses that probably noticed the shadows under Paislee's eyes.

"Morning!" Paislee replied. Her hair was slightly damp from her shower, the sky lightening with dawn.

"I'm glad we're going tae be early," Meri said, waiting for Paislee to buckle up. Meri's stainless-steel mug smelled of coffee and vanilla. "The judge that was on the fence canceled—puir dear has a summer cold and doesnae want tae spread it. Kind in theory, but it leaves me shorthanded. When we get tae the office, I'd like you tae scan our volunteer lists tae see if any have sheepherding dog experience."

"I can do that."

"I ken I can count on you, Paislee." Meri pulled away from the curb and drove toward the town hall, where the members of the volunteer committee for the Nairn Highland Games met monthly for eight months of the year, with weekly meetings closer to and after the event.

"Happy tae help," Paislee said, cautiously sipping her strong tea.

"I brought assorted pastries from Tesco." Meri jerked her thumb toward the back of the SUV. "Bagels, croissants, and sweet rolls."

"Much better than the granola bar I dropped in my bag."

"You have common sense. It's appalling tae me how many people lack that simple attribute." Meri stopped at a light and studied Paislee. "You okay, dear?"

"Fine!" She didn't want to get into poor Brody's hormones with a woman who hadn't had children—by choice.

The light turned green, and within moments, they'd arrived at the town hall. Meri parked in front, as nobody else was there yet. Later today, this quiet dawn on the firth would be difficult to imagine due to the crowd of thousands.

Meri didn't get out of the car but studied Paislee with concern.

"What is it?" Paislee's stomach clenched. What could be so bad the morning of the annual games? Surely nothing to stop them from proceeding.

Pursing her lips, Meri said solemnly, "We had an anonymous tip that there might be steroid use today at the games, which, as you ken, is highly illegal and against the rules."

That would do it.

Chapter 2

"Should we call the police?" Paislee searched Meri's face for a clue as to how her friend, the chairman for the games, wanted to proceed. These events were for amateur athletes to participate within the spirit of competition and as a triumph for their personal best. In the old days, the win had been for the clan's honor.

"I hate cheaters," Meri said. It had been a problem in the last piping competition that Meri had judged, but the council was cracking down because of Meri's efforts. "And I dinnae appreciate a coward with a tip that may not be true. It would tarnish the reputation of the games if word got oot that steroids were tolerated."

"What are our options?"

"There are tests athletes could be required tae take the day of the competition, but they're expensive, and we dinnae have the budget," Meri said. "I called Simon last night tae get his thoughts, but our hands are tied unless we actively see someone using steroids, which is not likely." Simon Sinclair was the previous chairman from the prior year and a close friend of Lord Cawdor's.

"I'll be on the lookout for shady dealings," Paislee promised. Meri unlocked the doors, and they slid out of the car.

To the far left were the fairground rides, resembling giant skeletons in the gray dawn. The carnival company had arrived yesterday and would stay through Monday evening, as Monday was a holiday, to pack up and depart Tuesday morning. The rides were like dead creatures without the lights flashing and music blaring.

"They're creepy," Paislee said aloud.

Meri noted where Paislee was staring and nodded. "People love the rides, though. They make me queasy, but I'm a fair shot at the duck hunt. Last year I won a teddy bear as big as me. Nairn gets a percentage of the ticket sales, which is a boost tae our economy."

The committee for the Nairn Highland Games believed it was important to build Nairn as a tourist destination even better than it had been a hundred years ago, consequently bringing in money for the local businesses to prosper; a fact she'd seen herself at Cashmere Crush. Community mattered, and her personal beliefs aligned with the goal for the future.

It hadn't been that long ago when she might have been more vocal against progress, preferring the old to the new, but for the community to thrive, certain things had to change. Growing pains. Like Brody was suffering, though in the end, the economy would be stronger, as would her son. If the next generation was to soar, Paislee and her generation had to manage things in a way that was conscious of the future.

Paislee couldn't be responsible for all the plastics in the ocean, but she was accountable for her utilization; they recycled, and she minimized her usage with bamboo toothbrushes, garbage bags of recycled plastic, and no plastic water bottles—not even at the football games.

A door opened on a long caravan in the car park of the fairground, allowing loud music to escape from inside.

"Someone else is up besides us," Paislee said, with a laugh.

"Probably never went tae bed," Meri mused. "There are two caravans for the fair employees tae stay in on the property. I had a cousin who joined the carnival as a kid, and the stories he told us opened my eyes. Not the life I'd want."

"What happened tae your cousin?"

"He enlisted in the military and straightened himself up. Used tae joke that he'd traded one carnival for another. Retired now, with a small croft. Dogs." Meri's eyes widened, but then her expression fell. "Not herding dogs. We need someone knowledgeable aboot border collies."

"You're that worried?"

"Aye. Lachlan wants me tae fail in a big way, as we'd butted heads aboot his idea tae raise prices tae see the games. Nairn is the last Highland Games around that offers free seating ootside the arena so everyone can watch them. He's against adding this event, which is on a trial basis, tae get even."

Paislee recalled the meeting three months ago when Lachlan had suggested a nominal fee for seating outside the arena. Meri had immediately given reasons why it wasn't good for Nairn to charge, but then had brought up the idea of the dog-herding category that many other Highland Games venues offered, which could bring in money.

Forty-five-year-old Lachlan Felling owned a successful lumber-yard and construction company that sold cabers. He was on the Highland Council and didn't like being refused. "He won't get backing," Paislee assured Meri. "Nobody agreed with his motion tae start charging."

"He's sneaky and devious. I dinnae like people like that. He and Dyana are too cozy for my liking. She could be persuaded tae change her mind, for the right incentive." Meri rubbed her fingers together with her thumb in the universal sign for money. "She's on and on aboot her healthy green juice, but between you and me, Paislee, it tastes like seaweed."

Dyana Barclay was forty-two and between husbands. She'd been the ladies shot put champion for years and was now selling a superjuice that was supposed to give you energy and help you lose weight. She was the secretary for the committee.

"What can you do?" Paislee asked.

"Be on guard, I guess. Sandi received the anonymous tip last night aboot the doping." Sandi Peckett was head of the volunteers, while Paislee did marketing and helped Meri.

Lachlan and Dyana both had a sales mentality that made them successful. Lachlan had excelled in the heavy events for all of his twenties, but now he was a judge and on the cabertoss committee, where he offered his expertise behind the scenes.

"Sandi didn't support the idea of charging," Paislee said. The retired strongwoman, who headed the volunteer committee, had been vocal about her belief that there should be space for those who wanted to view the games for free.

"She is a loyal member of this board and has been a part of the Nairn games since she was in the toddler races." Meri laughed and unlocked the door to the town hall. "If anybody hates cheating as much as I do, it's Sandi."

Sandi was an emergency room nurse, and her position required the calm personality she was known for in order to deal with the chaos of the games. She'd hung up her weights at forty and was now forty-three. Paislee liked working with her because she knew the task would get done.

As Meri had noted earlier, it was difficult to find reliable volunteers.

When they arrived at the meeting room, Meri, the box of breakfast treats in one arm, unlocked the door and they went inside.

Paislee placed her to-go mug of tea on the oval table that could seat up to twenty people. Her stomach rumbled.

"You'd better eat now," Meri advised. "It's going tae be crazy. You've done the games before?"

"Only as a sponsor, not on the committee," Paislee said. "It's very different experiences."

"You dinnae compete?"

"They don't have a knitting competition," Paislee said with a straight face, only partially kidding. Her survival left little time for hobbies not related to her business.

Meri took the top off the box. "Help yerself."

Paislee chose a croissant and put it on a napkin. "Thanks."

"You dinnae play any sport, or any instrument?" Meri asked in disbelief.

"No. Brody didn't get his agility from me that's for sure. Wants tae be a pro footballer."

Meri didn't bring up Brody's father, as Paislee never discussed him. Brody belonged to her, and that was that. "It can be an exciting sport tae watch."

Paislee put a bite of flaky crust in her mouth and nodded. She was on the edge of her seat whenever Brody played and often standing on the sidelines, her camp chair forgotten. "I just want him tae be happy."

"What time will he be coming in? Nine tae check in?"

"Yes. I'm not sure if he'll volunteer. It's the end of summer, and he'd rather be with his mates."

"At the fairground, riding rides."

It occurred to Paislee at that moment that Brody was at an age to just go and spend the day with possibly Ryan and Sam by themselves. She sipped her tea to get the suddenly dry croissant down her esophagus.

"You might be right about that." Paislee cleared her throat. "Now, where were the papers you wanted me tae go through?"

Meri went to the file cabinet, unlocked it with a tiny metal key hanging on the side of the cabinet, and took out a sheaf of applications. There had to be hundreds. "Anybody with collies or who has sheepherding experience. If not, mibbe Brody can step in, just tae be an extra body?"

"Brody doesn't know anything about either." She swallowed the response that he was only thirteen. She was filled with doubts that she was doing a good job—should she make him volunteer or was it enough that he showed up for his event?

A knock sounded on the door and Meri opened it. Sandi Peckett stood there with a cardboard box of coffee and a sleeve of hot cups.

"Thank you!" Meri said. "I dinnae suppose you ken anything aboot border collies?"

"What's wrong?" Sandi asked. Her tone was measured as she entered the room and placed the coffee on a side table with cream and sugar, next to the towering cups.

"A judge called oot sick. Paislee's going through the volunteers tae see if any have experience."

"Let me have half, love, and we'll get through it quicker." Sandi held out her hand, accepted the stack from Paislee, and sat down with a coffee and a sprinkled donut.

"Nothing stands out here," Paislee realized within fifteen minutes. Most of the volunteers were locals with friends or family competing, but she'd just remembered Jerry and his girlfriend, Freya. "I know someone who works on a farm, and she might be able tae help."

Sandi patted her stack she'd gone through. "None here either."

"Who?" Meri asked.

"Jerry McFadden's girlfriend," Paislee said. "You know him from the piping competition circuit. Well, Freya works at JoJo's."

Paislee texted Jerry, hoping she didn't wake him, to ask about Freya at, she gulped, seven. She explained the problem. He texted back that Freya was with him, and she'd be happy to judge as she knew all about border collies. Freya and Jerry would both arrive before nine. Jerry planned to compete in the piping contest and take part in the parade, and now Freya would step in as a judge with the sheepherding event.

"Guid job," Meri said when Paislee explained they had a stand in. She walked to the whiteboard, crossed out the previous judge's name, and put in Freya's.

"Freya Duncan," Paislee supplied, and wiped her brow theatrically. "What's next?"

"I've already separated T-shirts intae sizes." Sandi gestured to the boxes stacked against the wall, clearly marked S, M, L, XL, and XXL. Each participant would get one in dark blue when they registered. The volunteers had special shirts of light blue. "I'll work on the lanyards. We have three hundred people registered! I remember when it wasnae so big. Lord Cawdor has done wonders for bringing awareness tae our Highland Games."

Meri placed her hand on Paislee's shoulder. "Want tae prep the volunteer clipboards?"

"Sure!" Paislee didn't mind the simple task of attaching a map of the events along with a schedule and a list of mobile phone numbers for Meri, Sandi, and Donnie who were the contact points with the public.

Lydia arrived at eight on the dot. "Guid morning, friends!" She carried several boxes from the printing office and put them on the table. "First place, second place, and third. Also, another for participation that Jeb tossed in at no cost."

"Jeb is a love," Meri declared. "Super guid contact, Paislee."

"Thanks." Paislee had called each local business, and Jeb's Printing had the best prices and reviews. The ribbons would be handed out before the big trophies for overall winners at six. She set the last clipboard aside and sipped her tea. "And thank you, Lydia, for picking them up."

"No problem." Lydia wore a one-piece sheath in blue-and-green squares with black-and-red striping. The clans had many options for tartans, and it was no surprise to Paislee that Lydia would embrace her husband's Smythe tartan with style. "Where's Brody?"

"He doesn't want tae march in the parade or compete in the one event he signed up for, let alone volunteer. He's having a very tough go," Paislee murmured. She shared what had happened last night when he'd left the house to go for a midnight run. "And it wasn't his first time! I wish I could make things easier for him."

"Saying that it will pass doesnae help, does it?" Lydia had gone through a period when she'd been gangly and awkward, though you'd never know she had felt out of place from her confidence today. "Mum and Da gave me love, which you do for Brody. It's all we can do."

"Should I let him out of the race?" It felt wrong to allow him to back out of a commitment.

"Let's check how he's feeling. Could be Brody has a wee injury before the event," Lydia suggested slyly. "What time is he performing?"

"One."

"We'll see," Lydia said, and Paislee felt wonderful to know she had an ally. While she couldn't suggest an evasive action, Aunt Lydia could and get away with it.

At eight thirty, Meri, who had changed from jeans to her red-and-white-checked kilt for Clan McVie, raced into the office with Lachlan behind her. He kept his light brown hair trimmed within an inch of his scalp, his face clean-shaven. He wore his kilt with an Oxford and tie instead of his volunteer shirt. His overconfidence grated on Paislee's nerves.

"Lord Cawdor is here," Lachlan said. "He'll officiate and present the trophies with Drake. Where are the ribbons?—oh, there." He smiled at Lydia and then smirked at Meri. "I heard there was a problem with the new event? It's more hassle than it's worth."

"Not anymore. We have another judge tae replace the one who is sick," Meri said. Her light-blue volunteer T-shirt was tucked into her kilt, her figure trim. She wore a lanyard around her neck with her name easy to read. Lachlan didn't give off the same ask-me vibe.

Dyana Barclay entered with a wide grin. Blunt chestnut bangs hovered over thick brown brows and hazel eyes. Her yellow-and-black-checked kilt showed off her sculpted legs. She'd patented the healthy organic green drink Meri thought tasted like seaweed. "The car park is already full! This is sure tae be the best year yet."

"That would be great," Simon Sinclair said, arriving at that moment. He was good mates with Lord Cawdor and the pair often made the paper for their philanthropic endeavors. His thick auburn hair and beard were neatly trimmed. He'd just turned fifty. "It will bring in cash tae build the new miniature golf course—creating fun for tourists and jobs for locals."

"Fun for locals too. Miniature golf is amazing," Krissie Stewart said, coming in after Simon and batting her ultra long fake lashes at him. Her blond hair was in a loose twist. She chose half of a bagel with cream cheese as well as a lanyard with a badge that read JUDGE. She was twenty-seven and held the title in the sprint races, earning her wage as a clerk at the Delphin Hotel, though she planned to be a coach once she no longer competed. She wore a Stewart tartan and her dark blue participant shirt, as she was competing today as well as judging in a different event.

Donnie Weber, heavyweight judge and competitor, pushed into the meeting room and went straight for the coffee. Handsome, with thick, long dark brown hair and green eyes, he bartended at The Bandstand. His style included T-shirts molded to his biceps and sandalwood cologne. He filled a paper cup with dark roast and added a splash of almond milk. "Sandi, these the bamboo cups I told you aboot?"

"They are—the lids are recycled plastic too," Sandi said. "I've brought them intae the hospital where I work because they are so durable. Where did you find oot aboot them?"

"One of the regulars at the bar invested in the project and made a ton," Donnie said. "He invited me in on it, but that's not where me head is at right now. I've got tae concentrate on winning at the local strongman competitions."

"That would've been a grand opportunity," Sandi said, "but I concede your point. You're in your physical prime."

"Hundred percent." Donnie took the compliment as his due. He leaned his hip against the oval table and looked down at the boxes of ribbons. "What are these?"

"The prize ribbons for all of the events," Lydia said. "Jeb was a dream tae work with."

"Because you're a dream," Donnie teased with a wink.

Krissie rolled her eyes. "Eejit." She pulled a rainbow ribbon for participation from one of the boxes and arched a brow. "Really?"

"Why not?" Sandi asked. "The games are supposed tae be for fun." Her expression tightened, and Paislee thought the nurse might share about the doping accusation, but she didn't, so Paislee also didn't mention it.

Lachlan's phone rang, and he answered quickly. "Aye, we'll be there." He ended the call. "McNichols is ready tae get the parade participants rounded up. Said herding cats would be easier."

Drake McNichols was the convener for the Nairn Highland Games and had been for ten years. He did such a terrific job that nobody wanted him to step down.

Jerry and Freya arrived at eight thirty. "Hey!" Freya spoke cheerily as Jerry, hand on her back, entered behind her.

"You're a doll for filling in," Sandi said to Freya. "Let's get you a volunteer T-shirt."

Freya smiled. "Thanks. Do you have a medium?"

Sandi went through the boxes of shirts sorted by size. "Here's one."

Freya accepted the light blue T-shirt. "I'll go put it on and wander around with Jerry before he leaves with the parade. Where should I be?"

Meri offered Freya a map along with the list of events and times. "Dog-herding isnae until twelve thirty, so you have plenty of time tae be in the parade with Jerry, if you'd like."

"I might tag along, then," Freya said. "My parents are marching too. It's a beautiful day tae be ootside."

"If you have any questions, I'll be at the volunteer table by the first-aid station." Sandi's muscles had softened since she no longer trained or competed, but she was still quite strong, and had no problem lifting two bins of shirts and lanyards with name badges. "Thank you again."

"It's my pleasure," Freya assured everyone. "I grew up with border collies and Shetland sheep."

Jerry and Freya followed Sandi out of the crowded office.

Meri checked her watch. "It's quarter till nine, but it will take that long tae get everyone sorted. It's a boon tae have so many people involved."

"And just imagine if we could charge them all," Lachlan said snarkily. He hurried out of the office, followed by Simon, who wore an annoyed expression.

Meri peered at Paislee. "Do ye see what I mean?"

"He's just mad aboot the dog-herding." Krissie shrugged. "He'll get over it. How many extra entries did we have because of it?"

Meri thinned her mouth. "We'll ken for sure later today. Tuesday night's meeting will be the proof in the pudding one way or the other." She eyed those around the table: Paislee, Lydia, Donnie, Dyana, and Krissie. "Am I wrong tae try and broaden our appeal?"

"No," Dyana said with confidence. She sipped her green drink out of a clear glass tumbler. "Most everyone loves dogs and weans."

Agreement rounded the oval table.

"Everyone, please help yourself tae the jugs of the green juice. I cannae tell you what a difference the organic herbs have made tae my energy level." Dyana pointed to glass pitchers on the counter of what appeared to be sludge.

A smattering of polite conversation to try it later arose yet everyone remained seated.

"Oh!" Meri said. "Paislee, do we have someone tae assist the toddlers?"

"I thought I'd ask Blaise or Mary Beth," Paislee said. Meri knew them well from their Thursday night Knit and Sip meetings at Cashmere Crush.

"Guid." Meri swiped her hands together. "I willnae worry aboot it anymore. I'll go check with Drake tae make sure we're on time. Eleven o'clock for Lord Cawdor's speech. I love how much he cares for Nairn. Coming?"

"Not yet. I'm waiting for Brody who should be here at nine," Paislee said. Lydia hooked her arm through Paislee's.

"I'll join you, Meri!" Dyana clutched her tumbler.

"Me too," Krissie said. Donnie went out last, choosing a pastry from the depleted box, biting into it and suggestively licking the sugar from his lips.

Lydia cringed as Donnie swaggered out, overconfident in his prowess. His love for himself dinged the appeal.

Sandi entered for two more bins of shirts. "There's nothing like the energy of Game Day. Just think what it was like hundreds of years ago, when the clan chieftain would choose his best warriors? I would've wanted tae win too. Take me place in a shield wall."

"I can easily imagine the gorgeous men, bare chested and in kilts," Lydia admitted, "but I'd rather coordinate strategy from the safety of the tent than join the danger on the field."

Chuckling, Sandi brought the boxes closer to the table and lowered her voice, "Fair point. Hey, I overheard Lachlan and Dyana conspiring against Meri. Lachlan will collaborate with Dyana with the caveat that she votes against Meri regarding the pricing structure."

"That's not fair," Paislee said. "We'll have tae tell Meri and warn her."

"I was hopin' you would," Sandi said. "You ken Meri better than I do."

"What does Lachlan gain?" Lydia asked.

"Lachlan wants tae run for chairman of the committee next year and oust Meri." Sandi shifted the heavy boxes in her arms without breaking a sweat. "He's angry aboot the dog-herding event—probably because he didnae think of it himself. Anyway, if

Meri was willing tae do that, then why not change the fee structure? He thinks she's blocking him just tae flex her power."

"Meri isn't like that!" Paislee said.

"I ken it," Sandi agreed. "I love that we're the last free games in
the Highlands tae offer seating ootside the arena. Lachlan thinks he's
a big deal, and mibbe he used tae be in his prime, but he's like me
now, thicker around the middle. Hard tae believe we used tae be
champions."

"In what event?" Lydia asked.

Sandi placed the boxes on the floor and straightened, curling
her biceps. The effect wasn't as dramatic with the plumpness of her
arms. "Any of the heavy events for women, but I excelled in the
hammer throw." She blushed. "Not enough tae go pro. There were
no agents sniffing around ready tae sign me. Lachlan, for all his blus-
ter, didnae have what it took either. We were big fish in a small
pond." The strongwoman laughed self-deprecatingly as she patted
her round stomach.

"I like that it's an amateur competition. I think it would be
closer tae what it might've been like in the past tae prove yourself
tae your clan chief." Lydia sipped water from her metal tumbler.
Nobody had taken Dyana up on her offer of the organic juice.

"Aye! Exactly. Meri said she told you aboot the tip that some of
the players might be doping." Sandi placed her hand to her heart.
"There's no pride in oneself if you cheat. It makes me verra mad.
Though you cannae tell now, my body was pure muscle. I've got
pictures somewhere."

"I want tae see them!" Lydia glanced at Paislee, who hadn't had
time to share with Lydia about the rumor, and then Sandi. "You
deserve tae be proud."

"I'll show you later," Sandi said. "Doping takes away the glory
of hard work for results. Why sully that for others by causing doot?"

"Cannae you test the athletes?" Lydia asked.

"Aye. The kits are expensive, and we have the right tae test, but we dinnae have enough for all the competitors." Sandi shrugged. "I could get some from the hospital I work at. I ken who I'd choose, but he's not competing today."

"Who?" Paislee asked.

Sandi tapped her temple. She had big pink sunglasses on her head like a headband. "I'd rather not say, but trust me ladies, I'll be watching."

"I never realized how much goes on behind the scenes for one big day," Paislee said.

"Right?" Sandi hefted the boxes. "See you oot there."

"Okay." Paislee stood, as did Lydia.

"That was interesting." Lydia waggled her brows. She loved a good blether. "Who is Sandi talking aboot?"

"I don't know. We'll have tae watch her, watching the crowd." Paislee picked up her clipboard with the list of events and the map, grabbing extras. "Want one?"

"No clipboard for me, but I'll take a schedule," Lydia said. "And the scoop aboot the doping."

"That's all I know." Paislee's phone dinged with a message from Brody. "Brody's here—he caught a ride tae the shop with Grandpa and walked over." It was less than half a mile and probably easier than Grandpa having to manage traffic to get Brody closer.

"Mibbe have him go tae the Smythe canopy where Corbin is waiting. I think Rhona is here with her parents already too."

After sending the text to Brody, Paislee braced herself for the crowd. Lydia thrived on people and chaos, while Paislee preferred her chaos in smaller doses.

"Ready?" Lydia asked.

"Ready!"

The pair left the room, Paislee making sure the door was locked, as there was personal information in the file cabinets, and went outside.

Paislee followed Lydia across the car park and inside the arena.

As a volunteer, she didn't have to pay the small fee, neither did participants, though one had to register and check in at the entrance.

Covered seating wasn't provided, but for a cost and a sponsorship, one could have some amenities. There was a Cawdor canopy, and another for the judges. They passed the O'Connors as Blaise, her husband, Shep, and their daughter, Suzannah, set out tables and chairs beneath a canopy provided by the golf course where Shep was a pro and somewhat of a celebrity.

"Hey, O'Connor family!" Paislee said. Suzannah and Blaise wore matching dresses and Shep had on a kilt in the O'Connor tartan: green, black, and blue with white stripes.

"Hi!" Blaise greeted them with hugs. Her reddish-brown hair was loose to her shoulders, her amber eyes sparkling with joy.

"Suz, you look adorable," Paislee said. Blaise's daughter was her mini, though her hair had streaks of Shep's blond and was in pigtails with curly ribbon.

"Thank you, Paislee." Suzannah, at nine, grinned with big white teeth she had yet to grow into. "Why arenae you dressed nice?"

"Suz!" Shep cried in alarm, having heard his daughter's words.

"Out of the mouths of babes." Paislee was not at all offended. "I'm working, Suz, so I didn't want tae get my nice things dirty and opted for jeans. I'm wearing the Shaw colors in my headband." She patted the rosette pinned to her lanyard, which also matched Brody's kilt. "Blaise, I have a favor—could you please help us fill in at the toddler race?"

"That's right!" Lydia said. "Our last task on Meri's list."

"I think so," Blaise said, always happy to pitch in. "What does it require?"

"Making sure the race starts on time and then handing out ribbons for participation." Paislee smiled at Suzannah. "In fact, it would be wonderful if you had a helper, like Suz."

Suzannah bounced up and down on her toes. "I want tae do it!"

"I guess we're in," Blaise said. "What time?"

Paislee checked the schedule that she carried on her clipboard. "It starts at twelve. I love the toddler races. The bairns are so cute with their plump cheeks."

"What do I need tae do?" Blaise asked.

"I'll introduce you tae Sandi. She's in charge of the volunteers and can give you the exact instructions."

"I wanna come with you!" Suz clasped Lydia's hand. "I like your dress, Lydia."

"Thank you, sweetie. Your ootfit is verra pretty too."

The ladies went in search of Sandi, walking toward the volunteer table near the first-aid station. As it was early, there wasn't anyone there yet.

To Paislee's surprise, Sandi shoved a muscled man just a little taller than herself backward. "I ken what the hell yer up tae, and I willnae have it, Joseph, do you understand me? Do ye?"

"You're loony," the man she'd called Joseph replied and stepped into Sandi's space.

The strongwoman shoved him again, drawing a small group of folks.

Blaise looked at Paislee with alarm. Lydia understood quickly and sidestepped, taking Suz with her, to show the little girl a picture on her mobile. "Do you like pink flowers or purple better?"

Paislee stepped toward Sandi, but Drake McNichols interceded, his broad shoulders and deep voice commanding. "Sandi." Paislee stopped in surprise as the convener wended around the first-aid table from the judge's tent near the entrance toward the strongwoman and Joseph. "Can I talk tae you, *now*?"

Sandi's rosy cheeks paled as she realized she had an audience. Joseph brushed the front of his chest with exaggeration. He was solidly built with closely cropped brown hair and angry eyes. "Watch yourself, Sandi." He stalked off.

"Are you okay, Sandi?" Paislee asked.

The convener turned to Paislee and Blaise. Drake dipped his head toward Paislee and Lydia, whom he'd recognized from being on the committee. "Ladies!"

Paislee worried that Sandi might be in trouble and hurried to intervene. "I wanted tae talk with Sandi. Sandi, this is Blaise O'Connor, and she can help you with the toddler race."

The convener realized that his talk (reprimand?) would have to wait. Drake melted back toward the judge's tent.

"Thanks, Paislee. I'm sairy—that was Joseph Whittle." Sandi took the pink sunglasses from the top of her head and put them on to cover moisture in her eyes.

"Related tae Artie Whittle?" Paislee asked. Artie was taller and blond.

"You ken him?" Sandi asked.

Lydia stepped up with Suz now that the altercation had passed. "He's dating a Smythe cousin, Rhona."

"I ken Rhona—she's dancing in the Highland Fling today." Sandi gathered herself and blew out a calming breath. "Thank you for helping." She smiled at Suz, who hadn't noticed anything wrong. "Hey, bonnie lass. Are ye goin' tae dance today?"

"Naw, I'm helping Mum watch the toddlers."

Paislee's phone dinged. Brody was at the Smythe tent with Corbin. Looking up, she said, "Are you fine if we head tae the Smythe canopy?"

Blaise, Suz, and Sandi all nodded.

Blaise said to Sandi, "Suz hasnae started dance classes, but she can if she wants."

"Yay!" Suzannah clapped and bounced on her toes.

"Another babe drawn intae pointe shoes and leotards," Lydia expressed to Paislee as they walked away.

Paislee and Lydia had each been in various dance classes through their primary years, but neither had liked it enough to take it further, as Rhona and her best friend, Aibreann, wanted to do.

They reached the canopy as Corbin was handing Brody an Irn-Bru in a can. "Hello!" Paislee said to the group on chairs or standing near tables with snacks. She didn't see Rhona or her parents. "How's it going, son?"

"Awful. My bones ache." It was now ten, and Brody didn't have to compete until one. The parade performers would be back soon, and Lord Cawdor, with Drake and Simon, would officially start the games at eleven.

Paislee noted the length of the kilt she'd had made for Brody, as he'd outgrown the one from last year—this fit perfectly. He wore a dark blue Nairn Highland Games T-shirt. "Your Aunt Lydia grew practically overnight, remember, Lyd?"

"Aye, I do." Lydia stood next to Brody, who was taller than her now too. "It was agony."

"Really?" Brody studied Lydia in a different way—she was five eight, to Paislee's five four.

"Your mum gave you baths with Epsom salts tae make you feel better," Paislee said.

"It worked," Lydia said. "Though it was temporary, and my bones throbbed within the hour. I often wished we'd had a hot tub."

"I'm not faking," Brody said, glancing at Paislee.

"I never said you were!" Paislee exclaimed.

"I understand completely," Lydia said.

"I believe you, Brody!" Paislee said. "I want tae help you feel better."

"Then dinnae make me perform today! I ken ye think I should do it, but I dinnae want tae," Brody said. "If I fall during my sprint, I'll make a fool of meself in front of me coach. He willnae want me on the team."

"I've been thinking about that." Paislee held his gaze. "I trust you tae do what is right for you and your body."

Brody perked up, having expected an argument. "Really?"

"Yes." Now how to get out of it? She gave Lydia a tiny nod. "I'm going tae track down Artie and Rhona, and ask about his dad, Joseph. Maybe get his side of the story of what happened with Sandi. You can hang out here for a bit, and I'll be right back."

She hoped the gaze she sent her best friend would get the message across. A small white fib just this once. Brody wasn't a complainer, and he had a reason for wanting to bow out—he couldn't trust his legs and his feet to cooperate. Puberty was a legit excuse that didn't fit on a score sheet. Oh, the angst of being thirteen.

"Artie and Rhona went tae greet the parade," Corbin said. Lydia's husband had the same ebony hair and dark brown eyes as the rest of the Smythe clan and also wore a kilt with a snug black T-shirt. He was as handsome as he was kind, and he loved Lydia with all his heart. After a terrible mix-up, the couple decided to legally hyphenate both of their last names: Lydia and Corbin Barron-Smythe.

Paislee left the shaded canopy and headed toward the field where the parade would end up, searching for Rhona's dark hair and Artie's tall, thin figure with a blond mop. Before she found them, she heard her name being called by two young voices—the Mulholland twins!

She turned and grinned. They couldn't be cuter if they tried. Matching braids and costumes, with Iona (slightly taller) in purple and Anna in pink. They exuded excitement. They were now ten, soon to be eleven. Mary Beth and Arran stood behind their daughters.

"Paislee," Arran said. "They were so excited tae dance today that they were up way too early."

"Which meant we were up way too early," Mary Beth said. Her eyes twinkled with good humor, the same cornflower blue as her girls.

"What time is your performance?" Paislee asked.

"Two. Will you watch us?" Anna asked.

"Of course—I'll cheer you on!"

"Yay!"

"Why weren't you marching in the parade?" Paislee asked.

"Daddy didnae want tae," Anna said. "He said we could have an extra ride at the fair later if we didnae make him do it."

Mary Beth snickered. "Outed, Arran." She observed her husband with love. Paislee understood making deals for good behavior, with parents dallying treats. It seemed this bargain meant the girls got to have more fun later so long as Arran didn't have to walk the parade.

The glaring sound of the rides beginning clashed with the drums and pipes as the parade returned to the field.

It was now ten minutes to eleven.

"Have you seen Rhona and Artie?" Paislee asked.

"We did, at the entrance," Mary Beth said. "She told the girls tae break a leg, and we had tae explain that meant guid luck and Rhona isnae being mean. This is the first year they're competing."

"Her performance is at eleven thirty," Paislee said. "At the seaside stage." She pointed toward the Moray Firth.

"How many stages are there?" Arran asked.

Paislee took an extra schedule from her clipboard and gave it to them. "Here you go. We have two stages and then the heavy events will be on the field. The times are listed here—with Lord Cawdor tae make his announcement at eleven, by the bandstand."

"We'll come back, but we promised the girls a lemonade," Mary Beth said. "See you in a bit!"

Paislee hurried toward the entrance, smiling in welcome and grateful for the clipboard that conveyed a sense of purpose as she strode by people in costume waiting for Lord Cawdor to announce the beginning of the games.

Neil Masterson, band major, had arrived with his parade participants, and everyone was in wonderful cheer.

Rhona and Artie stood with Joseph and a woman that Paislee

hadn't met but recognized from pictures as Artie's mother, Gemma Whittle. A very handsome man about thirty-five was with them and talking earnestly to the young couple.

She wouldn't interrupt.

"Paislee!" She turned at the frantic call of her name to see Freya.

"Hi! What is it?"

"Jerry tweaked his back in the parade, those Great Highland Bagpipes are no joke tae play and march with. I'm worried that he should go tae hospital, but he willnae." Freya's eyes filled with concern.

"Good luck with that," Paislee said. "Scots pride won't allow more than a dram or two of whisky tae mask the pain," she added in a semi-joking tone.

"There will be plenty of that, I'm sure," Freya said. "I've offered tae drive him, but he refuses. We've argued. I hate tae upset him." She blinked tears from her eyes. "I guess I was hoping you'd convince him, but I realize that perhaps I've worrit too much."

It was very sweet, Paislee thought. This was their first big love for each of them, proving that cupid could strike at any age. "We have a first-aid station here," Paislee suggested. "Maybe they can advise?"

"Paislee, Freya." Jerry walked toward them, his mouth beneath his thick mustache in a grim line as he winced with each step. "I've stashed the pipes in the truck."

"Guid!" Freya studied his face. "Hospital?"

"It's a twinge. Whisky," Jerry countered.

Freya held out her hand. "Keys."

They stared at one another before Jerry finally handed them over as he said, "We have time yet. The dog-herding isnae until twelve thirty."

"I've met some of the dogs, and they are gorgeous," Freya said. "Only one participant hasnae checked in yet, but I've met the other four trainers. They're stoked to practice with the pups and didnae have a complaint aboot the entrance fees."

"That's great information. Thanks again for helping us out," Paislee said.

"Isnae she lovely?" Jerry asked.

"She is!"

The couple linked arms and ambled toward the whisky tent. It wouldn't open until after Lord Cawdor's announcement, happening at that moment. She hated to be late!

Chapter 3

Paislee cringed at the screech of the microphone from the closest stage, the bigger of the two.

"Welcome tae Nairn Highland Games! We are proud tae be the last free games in the Highlands." Lord Cawdor fixated on Lachlan at the foot of the stage. Lachlan was helping with the electrics as his construction company had provided both stages at a discount. "And I intend tae keep it that way."

Lachlan's shoulders bowed as lines in the sand were drawn.

After much applause, the games began, and Paislee hustled all over the field to keep an eye on things as well as to answer questions. Her T-shirt with VOLUNTEER on the back meant that she was pulled in a million directions.

At eleven thirty, she watched Rhona and Aibreann perform the Highland Fling. The lasses did amazing. Paislee couldn't imagine kicking so high or being so in tune with another. They were sure to place and have a second performance at three. Fern McElroy and her partner Delilah also danced very well. Each team encouraged the others in the spirit of sportsmanship.

Paislee walked back to the Smythe canopy with Rhona, who mopped her brow and sipped her water. "They're the dance team tae beat," the teen said. "Fern is sweet. She used tae date Artie's brother Cam, but they broke up before he died."

"Where is Artie?" Paislee asked. "I saw him watching your performance, but then he was gone."

"Cheering on Foster, his best friend, at the hammer throw."

Lydia saw Paislee scanning the shaded interior for her tall son and laughed. "Brody is on the fence aboot the race—guid parenting tae give the decision back tae him. He's mulling on the rocks by the dunes."

Rhona finished her water. "Let's go find Aibreann and Foster. They'd be the most brilliant couple."

"Besides you and Artie," Lydia said. "Where are ye going, Paislee?"

Paislee lifted the clipboard with her schedule. "Toddler race at noon, then wandering around in case anyone needs help, but I'll be at the dog-herding event at twelve thirty."

"Meet you there!" Lydia read her printout. "Seaside stage."

"I want tae come too," Corbin said. "Collies are a guid investment if you have sheep."

When Paislee thought of dogs, she imagined sparkling eyes, soft fur, and the desire for belly rubs—which proved she didn't have an "investment" mindset.

At noon, she joined Blaise and Suzannah on the field where parents had their toddlers, bairns four and under, at the starting line, ready to dash fifty feet to the next ribbon at the blast of the whistle. Folks cheered on either side. Blaise and Suz waited at the other end, giving each young participant a rainbow ribbon as they crossed to the finish.

They were so cute, but Paislee was glad that Brody wasn't a wean anymore, though he'd been just as adorable as these dolls. There was a professional photographer at the games, and he was taking plenty of photos.

At twelve thirty, Paislee made her way across the lawn to the seaside stage and the coned area marked off for the dog-herding event. Freya and another judge, a collie breeder from Inverness, gathered the contestants. Meri was there, and Lachlan too. Corbin and Lydia watched from camp chairs they'd brought from the Smythe canopy. Paislee joined them.

Four dogs in the classic black-and-white color herded a group of five sheep. The fifth participant, the late arrival, was a woman name Myrna. Her dog was an older collie, with the black-and-white coloring of the others. She pulled a wagon behind her. Each collie's owner had brought their own sheep. They weren't penned in their groups of five but guarded by the trained dogs.

"I'm so sairy for being late," Myrna called, frustration clear in her voice. "Got lost, and then the ducks didnae want tae cooperate."

"Ducks?" Freya queried in surprise.

The collie breeder from Inverness shook her head in confusion. "Dogs herd sheep, or goats."

"Not ducks!" Meri said. Paislee imagined the committee chair clarifying the rules for next year.

Lachlan, on the edges of the group, gave a snicker.

"I can explain." The herder stopped the wagon she'd been pulling behind her. Sure enough, the sound of quacking could be heard through the tall wooden slats with a shaded top.

"This isnae in the rules," another dog owner said.

"Rules? Well, you tell that tae my sweet collie, Rascal. Rascal is a champion with blue ribbons galore. Purebred. She's twelve and didnae want tae retire, but sheep were getting tae be too much for the puir dear." Myrna shrugged. "So, I decided why not teach her tae herd ducks?"

Everyone watched in amazed silence.

Rascal, her muzzle white with age, waited at Myrna's command, her eyes sharp and intelligent.

"Are ducks so different than sheep?" Lydia asked, her curiosity piqued.

"I think we're aboot tae find oot," Corbin said, lips twitching.

Within moments, Myrna's assistant, her son, going by the clear resemblance, a lad of sixteen or so, had set out a trail with a nylon tunnel in bright orange, a three-foot bridge, and a plastic kiddie pool with an inch of water.

A crowd was growing as rumor spread of the woman about to herd ducks with her border collie.

The Nairn photographer was also there, next to Simon, Lord Cawdor, and Lachlan. Sandi, Krissie, and the Mulholland family were in attendance too. The twins loved animals. Rhona and Artie were watching from a distance. His event of the caber toss was at one fifteen, after Brody's possible sprint at one. She was disappointed that Brody wasn't here.

Her son loved dogs too, and this was a new event to Nairn. Would Wallace make a good herd dog? Not the point—she didn't have sheep, or ducks, for that matter.

Myrna opened the gate on the wagon, which turned into a ramp leading to the grass. The ducks streamed down it as Myrna blew a series of commands on her whistle.

Rascal ran the ducks like a pro. Up and over the bridge, into the kiddie pool where they splashed and then toward the nylon tunnel, which was maybe two feet high and two feet across.

The ducks balked, but Rascal rounded them up to try again. Quacking protests, the ducks still went through it.

"I'm more than a wee bit impressed," Corbin said.

Paislee clapped along with the others.

Meri seemed pleased, as did Lord Cawdor and Simon. Until a dog barked on the sideline, startling the ducks. This bark was not their Rascal.

One duck split off toward the crowd. Rascal wrangled it back but the other four had now broken into four other directions.

Lachlan was bent over double, laughing.

Myrna blew her whistle, but the ducks were in rebellion mode and frantic. Rascal caught one and had it penned with its herder's gaze. Myrna's son captured two and put them in the wagon leaving two in the crowd barreling, wings out and heads down, right toward Lord Cawdor.

Simon showed swift reflexes as he caught one duck under each arm, to the roar of approval from the crowd.

The photographer captured the victory on film.

Brody's coach, Pierce Harris, ran toward her, his face concerned. Of Nigerian descent, he was in his thirties and claimed football was in his blood. He'd acquired the rec team last year, intent of taking them to championships. "Paislee, come with me. Brody slipped on the rocks, and he's hurt."

All mirth left Paislee in a whoosh as she ran after him, Lydia and Corbin on her heels. It wasn't far, toward the sand dunes by the beach. Brody's auburn hair rustled in a breeze as he clambered from the rocks.

"Sairy Mum! I'm so clumsy." Coach Harris supported Brody on one side and Corbin took the other, helping Brody to the field.

Paislee gave Lydia a raised brow. This wasn't a fake injury but true klutziness. Blood and gravel mixed with scraped skin. "Does it need stitches?"

"I dinnae think so," Coach Harris said. "Send him tae the first-aid station tae get it cleaned up and bandaged." The coach checked his watch. "I've got me own races tae complete, so I cannae stay. I just happened tae be stretching and saw Brody's head one minute, and then he wasnae there anymore. Can ye move your leg?"

Brody winced but had full mobility.

"You're all right, lad. Lucky ye didnae break anything." Coach Harris smiled encouragingly.

"I've got two left feet," Brody lamented.

Coach Harris chuckled. "It's part of growing up—you'll outgrow it and get yer balance back. I need you in tip-top shape for practice, when school starts next week."

"I'll be ready." Brody's chin jutted.

"I'll tell the judges you cannae participate, since I'm headed that way anyway." Coach Harris waved to them and jogged off.

"Thanks, Coach," Brody called to his retreating back.

Paislee sighed. "Let's get you settled with Aunt Lydia and Uncle Corbin on a chair in the shade. Oh, Brody."

"I was going tae try, Mum," Brody said. "Watching Coach stretch made me feel like I should do me best, like you always say, and then I slipped."

Corbin helped Brody hop across the field to the Smythe canopy. "Some ice on it will feel guid," Lydia said. "Puir lamb."

Paislee found a camp chair not in use and set it at the edge of the shade with a view of the field. Rhona was waiting at the tent for them.

"What happened, Brody?" Rhona asked with concern.

"Slipped. Klutzy." Brody shrugged as if it was not a big deal, but she could tell he was in pain. He'd had a sprained arm over Christmas.

"That's awful. I was going tae ask how your race went," Rhona said.

"I missed it. It was at one." Brody sighed. It was now five minutes after.

Paislee had some pain reliever in her handbag, so she shook out two tablets and found an Irn-Bru. The cold drinks in the cooler were all gone as was the ice. His second soda of the day, but this was an emergency. Her water bottle was also empty. She'd need to refill it at the hydration station, which provided free water if you had your own bottle.

Brody chugged the tablets down with a grimace. If they'd been at home, he would have made a bigger deal, but because they were in company, he choked them down without acting like he was gagging.

Lydia handed Paislee a first-aid kit with a sanitizer wipe and antibiotic cream. Brody hissed, but they were done in minutes.

"Well done, Brody," Lydia said.

"You should stay here and rest a while," Paislee said.

Rhona's parents, Petra and McDermot, returned from where

they'd been watching the events. Neither had participated, but they were there to support Rhona, who was scheduled for her second dance, with Aibreann, at three.

"I'm ready tae cheer Artie on," Rhona said, antsy. "He's on in five minutes for the caber toss. He did well with the hammer throw, but his da is so . . . intense. I dinnae think Joseph likes me verra much. I get along with his mum pretty guid though. Come with me, will you, Paislee? We can fill our water bottles."

The hydration station was near the first-aid table, where Paislee could get an ice pack for Brody, since the cooler of ice at the Smythe canopy had melted.

"Okay. I'll be right back, Brody."

"He'll be fine," Lydia promised. "And not going anywhere."

Paislee and Rhona exited the canopy and crossed the field to where the heavy events were performed.

"Wasnae it so funny aboot the ducks being herded by the auld collie?" Rhona asked. "Lord Cawdor was close tae getting pelted by a duck beak, but Simon swooped in tae save him. I feel bad for Meri—here she is trying tae add a new event, and it didnae go so well."

"Simon tae the rescue, at least," Paislee said. There would be no moving forward with the event if Lord Cawdor had been injured.

"Look!" Rhona grasped Paislee's arm. "There's my Artie. Isnae he cute?"

Artie Whittle was attractive—tall and strong like the caber he was going to toss. He blew his shaggy blond hair from his eyes, his dark blue T-shirt, stretched over his muscles at chest and biceps, was tucked into a blue kilt. The training he'd done showed as he flexed to warm up.

Gemma and Joseph Whittle sat in camp chairs on the side of the field. The handsome man who'd been conversing with Artie and Rhona earlier had a seat next to Joseph. His fitted black T-shirt was tucked into a black-and-red checked kilt.

"Who is that?" Paislee asked.

"He's cute too, but kinda old. Like, thirty-five, I think." Rhona scrunched her nose. "I could introduce you. It's Ross McCrumb, the talent agent Joseph wants Artie tae impress so bad."

Paislee choked on the response that thirty-five wasn't old. She'd just turned thirty last year and would be thirty-one come November.

"I wish Joseph wouldnae pressure Artie so much. It just makes him nervous. Some people respond tae pressure by being tougher, but that's not my Artie." Rhona crossed the field until they reached Gemma and Joseph.

Gemma gave them a polite smile, but Joseph scowled at Rhona. Gemma had blond hair like Artie and wore a cap to shade her face. Paislee got the impression of a woman around forty wearing bright pink lipstick.

"Artie's got tae concentrate," Joseph told Rhona. "If you sit here with us, you need tae haud yer wheesht."

Ross and Gemma exchanged a look. Ross gave an apologetic shrug at Joseph's rude comment for her to shut up and stood. "Hi, Rhona." His gaze went to Paislee. "I'm Ross McCrumb—verra nice tae meet you."

"And you, I'm Paislee Shaw."

"She's my boss at the yarn shop," Rhona said brightly.

"Sh!" Joseph removed his cap and squished the brim in annoyance, revealing his cropped hair. His eyes were covered in black sunglasses. He'd changed from his gray T-shirt to a sleeveless tank top that read FORGE FITNESS, with cargo shorts instead of a kilt.

"You know what? I think I'd rather watch from over there." Paislee tugged Rhona with her. "We can see better and cheer as loud as we want."

Rhona smiled gratefully at Paislee, and they moved to midfield where the caber would land instead of the starting point on the grass. Sandi hadn't liked Joseph, and Paislee understood why.

The caber toss was an event where a competitor lifted a smooth log of about sixteen feet, balanced it as they stepped forward, and then flipped the log into the air, hoping that the caber would land in the twelve-o'clock position. It was an awkward task that required strength and agility.

"Artie's gotten it nearly perfect for the last several practices. Some of his mates have lucky cabers, can ye imagine? He created his from scratch." Rhona clasped her hands together in a prayer formation as Artie lifted the log.

Struggling to pick it up, Artie only managed five steps forward before releasing the caber. He shook his hands in confusion.

Donnie watched smugly from the end of the field at the starting point. His lanyard with JUDGE on it glinted in the sunshine. There were two judges of the event, one at the beginning and the other that walked with the competitor as they went down the length of the field. "Everything all right, Whittle?" His tone held a dig that Paislee didn't understand.

Lachlan and Dyana watched intently, as did Krissie and Fern. Though Krissie was several years older than Fern, they knew each other from dance classes and many competitions. The games were a celebration of individual strength as well as community.

Foster spoke with Artie and clapped his shoulder. "You got this." Foster nodded at Donnie as if to tell the judge to mind himself and then hustled off the field to stand next to Joseph, Ross, and Gemma. Joseph made a disparaging comment.

"Isn't it over?" Paislee sipped from her water bottle, but it was empty.

"No," Rhona said. "Artie has two more tries tae toss the caber. He's got tae be so disappointed, but it's the best of three attempts."

"Where do they get the cabers?" Paislee asked.

"Artie made his with his da, but you can buy them. Luckily the Whittles live close tae an empty field where they can practice tossing. They have a gym set up inside their house too, because Cam was training tae be a strongman champion," Rhona said with an edge.

Before Artie's second try, Joseph jumped up and gave him a jar of ointment that Artie applied to his hands, then dropped the container next to the camp chair. Joseph returned to the sidelines, his cap back on.

"What's that?" Paislee asked.

"Tree resin for grip," Rhona said. "It's allowed by the judges. Part of creating a caber is removing all of the bark on the log and making it smooth, which can be slippery."

"Concentrate, Artie!" Joseph yelled.

Ross leaned forward intently, his hands clasped. Artie must have shown promise if the agent was interested in his career. Had Cam been agented?

This time, Artie managed to both lift the log and gain speed enough to launch the caber, but it didn't flip over.

"Puir Artie." Rhona's shoulders bowed. "He's been nailing those flips during practice, Paislee."

"Last time, loser," Joseph said, as his son studied the caber before his third attempt to flip it. "Dinnae blame the log for your shortcomings."

Donnie gave Joseph a warning look. Gemma stared at her lap instead of encouraging her son. Dyana and Lachlan paced up and down the sidelines, conferring, though neither were judges in this event.

"Ready?" Donnie asked.

Artie rubbed his hands together and nodded.

Rhona whistled her encouragement. Joseph glared at her. Ross focused on Artie. Though the young man was lean, he was surprisingly strong. The caber weighed well over a hundred pounds, maybe even ten stone.

Artie struggled with the caber. From far away, Paislee could see he clutched the log so hard his face reddened. His biceps bulged, and he gained traction as well as speed. The toss was going to be good! He pitched the timber, and it launched, only to flip sideways, nowhere near the twelve-o'clock position.

Donnie shouted a warning to move as the caber narrowly missed the camp chairs where the agent sat with Artie's mother and father. Artie dropped to his knees in disbelief, hands fisted on his thighs.

Paislee and Rhona hurried across the grass. Ross and Joseph conversed in terse tones. Reaching down, Joseph clasped his son's elbow to pull him up. Rather than query if Artie was all right, Joseph's words were cold as ice. "You'd better get yer shite together or Ross willnae add you tae his roster. You'll be oot of the house, because I willnae support a deadbeat loser. Got it?"

Joseph was so overcome with anger that he didn't seem to realize he'd been overheard. He looked around at the spectators of his ill-treatment of his son and released Artie's wrist.

"I willnae be Cam," Artie said, eyes narrowed as he faced his father. Joseph emanated primal strength that caused Artie, despite being taller and thick with muscle, to avert his gaze.

"You can never compare to Cam." Joseph stomped away from where Gemma and Ross remained on the chairs. Gemma clasped the arms of her chair and whispered to Ross, who took off after Joseph.

"What does he mean by that?" Donnie questioned. "Is he talking aboot yer brother?"

"Never mind," Artie said in a bitter tone. He swiped his palms down the front of his kilt. Gemma remained in her chair alone.

Krissie eyed the scene with a speculative gaze, nodded at Rhona, and strode back to Fern, who waited for her with Delilah and Aibreann. Donnie studied the caber and made notes on his clipboard. Donnie was also in other heavy activities such as the Nairn stone put event that wasn't until three thirty. Artie had already done the hammer throw and heavyweight for distance event. He'd signed up for the Nairn stone put too.

"Are you okay?" Paislee asked the young man. Clearly, he was not.

"I'm fine." Artie seemed embarrassed more than anything and didn't look at Rhona, or Paislee.

Lachlan arched a brow at Artie and kicked the caber. "Broken. Waste of Scots pine," he stated derisively.

"Was it cracked before?" Donnie asked with suspicion.

"Of course, the caber wasnae cracked!" Artie replied with indignation. "I debarked it myself."

"There's a reason I dinnae sell tae Whittles," Lachlan said, sounding as smug as Donnie earlier.

"We dinnae need your bleedin' timber," Artie said. He knelt to inspect the log before straightening with a confused expression.

"Mine wouldnae have split," Lachlan said.

"It shouldnae have—I treated it with linseed oil and let it dry. There wasnae even a hint of a crack this morning." Artie showed his palms, shiny with oil. "That wasnae tree resin in me jar either."

Donnie reached over to sniff Artie's hands. "Linseed oil? No wonder you couldnae hold it. Let me see the container."

"Da has it."

"Uh-huh," Donnie said. He rolled his eyes.

"Is it possible tae have mixed the wrong thing?" Paislee asked. She recalled how carelessly Joseph had dropped the tin. She glanced back at the sidelines. Gemma hadn't budged from her seat.

"No," Artie said miserably.

Sandi arrived like an ill wind. "What's goin' on? Joseph just stormed past me."

Red-faced, Artie said, "I'm a disappointment, that's all. I was set up."

"Dinnae squall when you were caught breaking the rules," Lachlan said. "I bet you were trying tae make that caber lighter in some way, and that's why it cracked."

Donnie rubbed his chin as he perused Artie. "Are ye trying tae cheat?"

"I wouldnae be surprised at all," Lachlan decreed.

"I did not," Artie said, disgusted. He shifted toward his mother. Gemma wore a look of concern, but maintained her grip on her chair. If their roles were reversed and it was Brody on the field being harassed, Paislee would be right in the middle of things.

Paislee felt bad for Artie and "accidentally" bumped into Lachlan. She wouldn't abide a bully. "What can we do?"

Donnie gestured from the broken caber to the crowded car park. "That's for kindling, I guess—it needs tae be off the lawn. This is an amateur event, and there is no need tae cheat."

"I didnae," Artie repeated. "Somebody set me up."

Lachlan snickered, as more of Artie's mates joined them.

"We'll move the caber," Foster said. He'd competed in the sprint events and had the lean body type of a runner.

"I'll help," Aibreann said, her tone flirty as she curled her biceps in her Highland Dance costume. "I'm stronger than I look."

"You'll get your dress dirty," Foster said. "We've got this." Two other guys joined Foster and Artie.

"Thanks," Artie said.

"We'll be careful," Rhona said.

Artie and Rhona took one end, then Foster, then Aibreann and then two other guys. "Tae the truck!" The young athletes hustled the ruined caber off the grass to the car park.

Gemma stood and craned her neck until they were out of sight and then sank back to her chair, bringing out her mobile. Donnie and Lachlan groused about the Whittles and didn't bother to hide it.

"I willnae sell tae the Whittles—they arenae worth my pine." So saying, Lachlan glanced toward Gemma, alone on the sidelines, before hurrying off.

Paislee scowled at his broad back and turned to Donnie. "You can't accuse someone of cheating like that without proof."

"He's not so innocent, Paislee. In fact, Rhona should take care around the Whittles," Donnie said, not apologizing. "I knew Cam verra well, and the Whittles arenae trustworthy." He strode in the direction of the next caber toss competitor waiting on the lawn.

During this past year at the Highland Games committee meetings, she'd found Donnie to be arrogant, though she acknowledged he had skills. He was not competing in the caber toss as he was a judge, but he'd done it many times before. Could Joseph Whittle, on Artie's behalf, have cheated and it went wrong somehow?

Harmful gossip that Paislee wouldn't subscribe to without proof. She turned her attention to Gemma. She felt bad that the woman was all alone. Luckily, Rhona and the others returned quickly.

"Where's Da?" Artie asked, noting the two empty chairs. Paislee scanned the grass for the tin of ointment but didn't see it.

"I dinnae ken," Gemma said.

"Join us under the canopy where there is shade," Rhona invited, already folding up one of the lightweight chairs. "It will be nice tae get tae ken you better."

"That's a guid idea, Mum," Artie said, collapsing the other chair. "Dad and Ross can find us if they want tae."

It amazed Paislee that Artie was still so good-natured despite being reamed in public by his father.

Lydia and Corbin welcomed the Whittles into their space, which was already packed with a long table and Rhona's dance gear, Rhona's parents, and a few other cousins who were competing. Brody and one of the teenage Smythe boys were talking video games and lamenting they had to be at the field when the fair was so close by. Brody's knee was better, the scrape covered by a bandage.

The ten-by-ten canopy was cramped, but they made room. Rhona's parents had met the Whittles in passing, and this was a good opportunity to mingle. Joseph was not around. "He's probably at the whisky tent," Gemma said. "I texted him, so he knows where we are."

Paislee knew that Brody was feeling better, because when she left to watch the Mulholland twins dance at two, he came with her.

They went to the seaside stage where Arran and Mary Beth were giving the girls a pep talk.

"Just have fun!" Mary Beth said. They high-fived all around.

"Good luck!" Paislee called.

Brody clapped and cheered them on. After the dance, her son patted the top of Paislee's head with a mischievous chuckle. She would never get used to him being taller than her, would she?

"I'm starving," Brody said.

Paislee checked her watch. Twenty minutes past two and she hadn't had lunch. "I have time for a bite." They headed away from the fair toward the car park, where there were six different food kiosks.

"Sausages, shepherd's pie, or burgers?" Paislee asked.

"A cheeseburger and curry chips," Brody said, rubbing his flat stomach.

To save time, and because she didn't really care, Paislee opted for the burger line as well. It moved quickly, and by the time it was their turn, her mouth was watering. She went with the smaller burger and chips with gravy.

"I forgot my water bottle," Paislee lamented, as they carried their food to a bench just as it was vacated by an older couple.

Exchanging smiles with them, Paislee and Brody sat down. She placed her mobile beside her and offered a pocket hand sanitizer to Brody, then used it when he was done.

He bit into his cheeseburger, and it was gone in five bites. She offered him half of hers and concentrated on her chips and savory gravy.

"Thanks, Mum." Brody swiped his last chip through the curry sauce.

"I hope that will tide you over until dinner," Paislee said. "I promised Rhona I'd watch her and Aibreann dance at three. Want tae come?"

"Nah. Can we go tae the fair?"

"Not now, Brody. I'm working here."

"Tomorrow?"

"Maybe. No promises. I was hoping tae be able tae sleep in."

"It doesnae open until eleven. I checked."

"We'll see." Paislee pulled cash from her pocket. "If you still want something more, why not find a treat?"

"Thanks, Mum!" Brody turned to the donut cart. "I ken exactly what tae get. Want one?" He took the trash from Paislee.

"No thanks, love. I'll see you at the canopy later."

They went in separate directions, Brody tossing the trash on the way to buy a donut that Paislee thought smelled delicious. She observed the various events as she walked, making her way to the seaside stage by three.

Paislee joined Krissie, who was there to cheer on Fern and her dance partner, Delilah. Fern and Delilah were twenty-four years old to Rhona and Aibreann's nineteen and twenty. They were in their prime and very equally matched. Krissie, judging the women's heavy events, would perform in the solo competition after the pairs. The judge was a woman named Letti Cornwall, who had been a champion Highland Fling dancer in her day but was now retired and ran a dance studio.

Dyana passed out free samples of her green juice to performers for added hydration and energy, directing them to a booth where she sold bigger bottles.

"You look worn oot, Paislee," Dyana said, offering Paislee a small cup of the moss green juice. "Trust me, this will put a pep in your step."

She couldn't politely decline and wasn't fast enough to hide her grimace as she swallowed it down.

Dyana burst out laughing. "That was priceless—but I promise it's worth it tae have all those lovely organic vitamins coursing through your bluid." She continued through the throng with her tray of samples, still chuckling.

Paislee waved to Lydia and Corbin on her way from the canopy, her water bottle in hand. She needed to hydrate and get the icky taste out of her mouth. The boys were all playing video games on their phones in the shade, even Brody. She was tempted to send him home, but she hoped that he'd have fun at the ceilidh after the awards. Simon had hired a popular musical trio who would play from seven to eleven.

The last event, the famed Nairn stone put, had been pushed back to four. The line for the stone was long, as everyone wanted a chance to give it a toss. Meri, Lachlan, Sandi, Dyana, Drake, and Simon were busy adding scores so that the winners could be announced at six. This had been the best Nairn games yet.

At quarter past five, Paislee noticed folks still in line for the stone put. The younger entrants had already performed, and now it was the older heavyweight athletes. Artie and his friends had signed up, as had Donnie. Paislee saw Joseph in line for the contest as well. She hadn't realized he'd registered. Ross murmured tips to Artie and the others.

Donnie spoke just loud enough so the others could hear, "Those who cannae do, teach, right, Ross?"

"Rude," Krissie said. She raised her brow at Donnie as if surprised by his arrogant remarks, but Paislee didn't believe it out of character for the full-of-himself athlete.

"Dinnae be jealous because I didnae choose tae take you on as a client from the Forge Fitness days, Donnie," Ross said. "It's not becoming of an athlete."

"Amateur," Joseph remarked.

One of the judges read his list of entrants registered for the event and tapped Joseph on the shoulder. "You didnae sign up, Mr. Whittle. You'll have tae try again next year."

Joseph blustered, his face red.

Dyana whispered in his ear, and Joseph calmed down.

The judge called out fifteen names, ladies first, then the men. The point of the stone put competition was to see how far a competitor could throw the Nairn stone, which was 16.5 pounds rather than the 18 that was the most common.

Sandi had returned from the town hall office and watched the competitors toss the stone. "I used tae be quite brilliant at this. I once held the women's record."

"I would be terrible," Paislee said, having watched the three women compete. Because everyone wanted to use the iconic Nairn stone, you just had to have registered for the event. Twelve men were left. "It seems complicated."

"The board is called a trig," Sandi explained. "Let's watch Foster. He's verra, verra fast. I wonder if he's got the strength?"

Each person had three tries to throw it the farthest. Foster had a decent showing, and Artie went after him. Rhona cheered him on. Joseph shouted instructions on form. To Paislee's surprise, he lobbed the stone farther than Foster on the first try, and kept beating his own mark by the third go. "I've got first, second, and third," Artie joked.

Foster clapped him on the shoulder and laughed. Ross nodded, impressed.

As last year's champion, Donnie wanted to throw the final put. He had an eagle eye on Artie and Joseph on the sidelines. It wasn't until Leland, a muscled competitor from Edinburgh, here with his brother Jason, threw that Artie was beat, but Artie could still place. Jason went next. His best throw almost tied with Artie, but Artie's was an inch farther.

Donnie came up to the trig. He rubbed his hands together and lifted the stone. He'd done well in the hammer throw and weight for distance. His team had won in the tug-of-war. He was fierce and strong, his muscles glowing to a sheen. He had to beat Leland, Artie, and Jason.

"I want all three."

Despite his cockiness, his first throw fell short. Joseph hooted and teased him. If Donnie failed, Artie would be in second place, his only ribbon of the day. He'd been edged out of the hammer toss by Donnie, into fourth. If Donnie's next two turns beat out the others, he could place in first and second, knocking out Artie and Jason.

On the second lob Donnie was still short, though very close.

Paislee hoped Artie would keep the lead so that Joseph would back off.

Donnie closed his eyes and seemed to call on some inner power, for when he opened them again, he was ready to throw and resembled a pro as he arced his arm and released the stone down the field.

"Textbook form," Sandi whispered.

It knocked Leland out of first to second but at least Artie got to keep third place. Rhona cheered so loud it might as well have been first.

"Congratulations!" Paislee said to Donnie, Leland, and Artie.

Suddenly the screeching of the microphone on the main stage brought the attention away from the Nairn stone, as Drake called for everyone to join him for trophies and winner announcements.

It was six o'clock.

Drake, as convener, ran the show, while Meri had organized volunteers into several committees. It helped when people like Sandi had been around for years. Simon was another who had ten years under his belt, like Drake. Meri had been on the committees before, but this was her first year as chairman.

Paislee was proud of how well her friend had managed everything, right down to herding ducks. Ribbons having been handed out, now Meri, Krissie, Simon, and Lord Cawdor alternated with the trophies for the big winners, such as the winners of the individual games, before taking on the overall winners for ladies and men.

The trophies were gold-plated and had a space for the name plate to be engraved later. Paislee, Brody, Lydia, and Corbin joined Arran and Mary Beth to whistle and applaud when Iona and Anna won the Highland Fling dance for their age group. Rhona and Aibreann placed third and second, with Fern taking first. Krissie had missed a step in her solo dance and the mistake had cost her, putting her in fifth.

Artie stuffed his ribbon into the sporran on his kilt. "Who's that bloke with Fern? Looks like trouble."

Fern held her trophy and the guy, with long black hair and tattoos, cheered, kissing her right on the lips.

"She just met him at the fair," Delilah said with a mean snicker. She hadn't won or placed in her dance events today. "His name is Kev and he's a carny worker. Runs the Twister ride."

Brody's eyes widened. "For real?"

"Yep. Not the career I suggest you aspire tae," Delilah said.

"I want tae be a footballer."

Delilah tossed her skirt with approval. "*Do* you?"

Lydia stepped in front of Delilah, blocking her connection with Brody. "Rhona! Congrats."

When it was over, Lord Cawdor gave a final word on Nairn and how proud he was of the shire, with promises of the new mini golf course to come—maybe before the next Highland Games.

Everyone whistled and applauded.

Simon took the microphone next, explaining that the ceilidh would start exactly at seven. He told everyone to get food, whisky, and a safe ride home.

The field was cleared within fifteen minutes. The Smythe canopy had a view of the main stage and was about a hundred feet away. The bells and whistles from the fairgrounds were like background music.

"I'm hungry, Mum," Brody said. "Can we get more burgers?"

"I'd rather have a chicken sandwich." She gave him cash. "But get what you like!"

He pocketed the cash with a grin. "You're the best."

Paislee smiled, wishing she could relax, but she was on duty until eleven, when the trio of drum, electric bagpipes, and a bass ended for the night and they'd clean up.

Paislee had texted with her grandfather, who said they'd had a wonderful day of sales, and he was home with his feet up. He offered to pick her up when she was ready despite the late hour. She would let him know.

Brody returned with food, and they all ate. Before she knew it, the Smythe mates he'd made wanted to go to the fair. Lydia nodded that she thought it would be fine.

"Please, Mum? It's my last Saturday before school!"

His summer had been a quiet one, so Paislee agreed he could go. "But back here at ten—you have your mobile?"

"Aye."

Corbin pulled out his wallet. "Who is going tae the fair?" Six kids lined up, and Corbin gave them each cash for the entrance fee and rides.

"Thank you," they shouted in pure joy.

"Stay together," one of the mums said.

And like that, they were gone.

Lydia laughed at Paislee's disgruntled expression. "They'll be fine."

She had to trust that he'd make good choices. Was she sure? Not really.

"Let's get you a cider," Lydia said. "Lighten up. When was the last time you've danced?"

"Does my kitchen count?" Paislee joked. "I'm a rock star in the shower."

"I hear you, Paislee," Petra Smythe said. Rhona's mother was blond and a yoga fanatic. Like Lydia, she wore a sheath in the Smythe tartan. "When I sing in the car McDermot always turns it up tae drown me oot."

"No, I dinnae." McDermot's brown hair was loose to his shoulders, and he had a trim beard. His kilt matched his wife's sleeveless dress. "That would be Rhona. Our daughter can be critical of her parents. We both lack the cool factor."

Gemma Whittle joined them to watch the dancing. Like Paislee, she'd opted for a hard cider rather than spirits. "Cam was judgmental that way too. Mibbe it's first-born syndrome," she said softly. "Do you have other kids?"

"Just Rhona," Petra said. She glanced at Gemma. "I'm sairy for the loss of your son."

"It's a parent's worst nightmare. I have so many questions that have no answers." Gemma sipped and stared out at the dancing green where everyone danced together, though there were some couples, like Jerry and Freya, and Rhona and Artie. "Artie is an extra guid lad, taking it in stride. I couldnae be prouder of him. Joseph can be, well, tough."

Tough? Paislee bit her tongue. Joseph could be a real numpty. And from the way he was dancing with Dyana, he wasn't done.

Chapter 4

Joseph and Dyana shimmied together, laughing loudly, their movements very familiar. They weren't strangers. Artie bumped into his dad and glared at Dyana. Dyana had the grace to blush and dance with Donnie and then Lachlan.

Krissie and Fern danced with Kev, who must have been on a break from his job at the fair. He was good-looking but hard. His innocence was long gone, and Paislee wondered if he'd ever been a boy. Aibreann and Foster danced together. Donnie switched partners and then danced with three girls at a time, loving the attention.

Gemma finished her drink as if nothing was wrong, as if her husband wasn't a doaty bampot, though by nine she was ready to go. "Artie, love, will you take me home? You can come back, if ye like."

Artie, also not in a good mood, agreed. "I'll stay with you, Mum." He and Rhona had been whispering back and forth, texting each other, though they sat next to one another so as not to be overheard. It was way better than passing notes like she and Lydia had done in school.

Paislee recalled Donnie's derisive remarks. Could Artie have cheated and been called out? There was nothing in Artie's character that screamed trickster.

The older she got, the more she realized how different people could be at their core. Lydia used to tease her about her rose-colored glasses and how she'd viewed the world through optimism and joy—seeing Dyana flirt so brazenly with Joseph, under Gemma and Artie's nose, made her feel ill. Joseph *would* cheat.

"We're leaving, Da," Artie said. His tone was sharp and confrontational.

"I'll get a ride from someone," Joseph said, not turning around.

Two thirds of the Whittle family left. Rhona, sad, joined Paislee. Lydia and Corbin were dancing now with Petra and McDermot. The Smythe men were clearly friends as well as cousins.

"I feel terrible for Gemma and Artie. Has their family always been like that?" Paislee asked Rhona.

"No. Things changed after Cam died. Artie feels completely buried under his older brother's shadow. Their house is full of pictures of Cam's competitions. Joseph's blue ribbons and trophies are everywhere too."

Ross seemed to have forgiven Donnie his rude remark as they chatted between songs. Kev and Fern were getting very close as they danced. Was he ditching work to be with the very pretty Fern? The music was in Paislee's blood too, though she stayed on the sidelines.

At one point the tempo went so fast that Kev bumped into folks—too much to drink, probably. He'd have a sore head tomorrow, which couldn't be good with the noise of the rides.

Mary Beth and Arran stopped by the Smythe canopy to say their goodbyes. They were headed to the carnival to play some of the games and get the girls some candy floss before heading home.

"Congratulations on your win." Paislee gave the lasses hugs. "Brody and his mates are over there already."

"The big kids get tae do the roller coasters," Anna said.

"We dinnae like roller coasters," Iona declared. "Do you?"

"I used tae love them, but it's been a while since I've ridden one." These days, Paislee was more concerned with boring things like inventory at her shop than a wild, out-of-control ride at the fair. Usually, Brody went with Edwyn and Edwyn's dad, Bennett.

"Just like Mum and Dad," Anna said.

"We're old now." Arran shrugged. "One wrong wrench on the ride will mess up my golf swing."

"Is that right?" Mary Beth asked with a roll of her eyes. "The all-important golf game."

Arran looked around, then snapped his fingers. "The O'Connors have already gone home otherwise I'd have an ally."

Paislee smiled. "Yes, they left before the ceilidh started tae get Suz tae bed."

"She's not as big as us," Iona said.

"She's only nine," Anna said.

Rhona danced by the twins but stopped to smile at them and their trophies. They each had a first-place trophy since they'd danced as a team.

"Congratulations!" Rhona said. "Your dance was really guid."

"It was!" Aibreann seconded her. "But you ken, girls, if you ever want tips, you can just ask us any time."

"Thanks," they mumbled, suddenly shy at the attention of the older lasses.

The Mulhollands left for the fairgrounds with very happy daughters.

"How's Artie?" Paislee asked Rhona, as Aibreann danced away with Leland, Foster, Kev, and Fern. The other boys weren't as thrilled with Kev's attendance.

Rhona's smile slipped as she glared at Joseph, who had his hand on Dyana's hip. "He could be better. I didnae realize how mean his da could be. He's never said so before. Probably embarrassed."

Families were complicated—Paislee was the first to acknowledge that. Her mum was still in America and that was fine with Paislee, though they messaged and sent letters. She wasn't opposed to including her mother, but she guarded her underbelly.

Lydia pulled Paislee and Rhona out to dance with her and Corbin, as Rhona's parents went for drinks. "What are you guys whispering aboot?" Lydia danced them around to see Joseph and Dyana brushing hands. "That? Puir Gemma." She whirled them again.

"It's tragic. Artie didnae say anything tae me, but I ken he saw it. Why else did he push him? Mibbe he'll tell me later. He wasnae in the mood tae talk aboot anything tonight." Rhona sighed.

Krissie and Donnie were dancing together. Krissie had the confidence to be a partner to Donnie rather than a fan girl, even though she wasn't yet thirty. He probably wouldn't value her expertise. He kept flirting with Delilah, barely in her twenties.

Sandi was sitting next to Meri at the judge's canopy, the ladies each drinking from a Nairn Highland Games metal tumbler. Water stands were everywhere around the field for people to fill their containers rather than use plastic bottles. Knowing Meri, it could be whisky in that tumbler, and the woman deserved it.

Her phone dinged at two minutes to ten—Brody, asking if he could be out until eleven, like the other guys. She sighed but answered yes—and not to be late. He sent a thumbs-up emoji.

Though Grandpa had offered to pick her up, she wondered if Meri would mind if they could both ride home with her so that her grandfather could sleep.

Meri and Sandi were having an intense conversation when she arrived. "Sorry tae interrupt," Paislee said.

"You're not interrupting," Meri assured her.

Sandi scoffed. "It's important tae me, Meri." The volunteer coordinator rose in a huff and stalked off.

Meri raised a palm to Paislee. "It's okay—let her cool doon a bit. Did you see the altercation Sandi had with Joseph Whittle?"

That seemed like a lifetime ago. "Yes."

"Did she lose her temper, say, using bad language in front of a wean?"

Paislee thought back to the situation, where she'd been worried for Joseph—before realizing he was a weasel. "I was there, yes. Hell, it wasn't anything nobody hasn't heard."

"Were you offended?"

"No, not in the slightest." It was the truth that Scotland was home to very vocal and inventive cursing, but her Gran hadn't approved, so she'd never been in the habit.

"Well, we've had several complaints aboot what happened." Meri took off her glasses, putting them on the table next to the tumbler.

"Complaints?"

"Aye. Lachlan wants us tae let Sandi go and not use her volunteer services again for next year." Meri reached for her drink, clearly upset. "The woman has been a part of things since she was a toddler."

Paislee remembered Sandi saying so. "That punishment seems extreme. Everyone has a bad day."

"But tae have a bad day in front of witnesses." Meri slipped her glasses back on, then stood and stretched. "There's got tae be more tae the story, and it will take a vote for her tae be relieved of her position."

"That sounds more fair than a simple dismissal."

"If only life were fair." Meri sighed. "Lachlan has gained supporters for his idea tae charge."

"But Lord Cawdor said no!"

"True." Meri leaned toward Paislee to murmur, "He's been talking with Drake—"

"Break it up now!" Lachlan shouted behind them, loud enough to be heard over the music and the noise from the fairground.

Paislee and Meri hurried toward the circle where Kev and Leland were holding Joseph back from Donnie. Dyana and Krissie were on either side of the men.

"There's no call for that," Krissie shouted. She was angry, her body trembling with her temper.

"What happened?" Meri demanded. Though diminutive, her

voice held authority. Sandi glared at her regarding what had happened but had no explanation for the current situation. Meri's gaze skimmed the crowd and landed on Fern, next to Kev.

Fern broke. "We heard Joseph say rude things tae Krissie. Called her a slut."

Meri shifted to Joseph with an arched brow. "We dinnae condone violence. Joseph and Donnie, either shake hands or go home. Your choice."

Joseph sneered at the younger man. "I'd rather choke on mud than shake Donnie's hand." Dyana groaned. Donnie shook off Kev and Leland like fleas on a dog.

Meri stood in front of Donnie and crossed her arms to keep him from going around her to punch Joseph. She turned to Joseph. "In that case, Joseph Whittle, you are expelled from the Nairn Highland Games. I am very tempted tae ban you from further games until you learn the spirit of sportsmanship."

"Piss off, Meri. I wouldnae come back tae these games if it was my last breath on earth."

Kev, Lachlan, and every clansman in the ceilidh swarmed forward. Nobody dared talk to Meri that way! Paislee feared that Joseph was about to learn some respect the hard way.

Suddenly there was an official police whistle, and all parties froze. Sandi had called Constable Payne from the Nairn Police Station at the first sign of trouble.

"What seems tae be the problem?" Constable Payne asked. He was one of Paislee's favorites at the station, with laugh lines etched into his dark-skinned face. He'd encouraged Amelia Henry to pursue police training, which was why Brody was dog sitting Snowball.

"No problem, Constable," Ross said. "Joseph and I were just leaving, right, Joe?"

Joseph expelled a breath. "Aye. That's right."

Dyana also appeared relieved. "You'll take him home, then, Ross?"

"I will. You're really going tae owe me, Joe," the agent chuckled. "Saved you from two scraps in one night: Donnie—and Gemma."

Mindful of the constable's presence, Joseph didn't comment but ambled off with his friend.

"What did that mean?" Constable Payne asked.

Sandi snorted. "Ask Dyana."

"Mind your business," Dyana said sweetly. "We were just dancing."

Constable Payne checked the time on his watch. "When is this over?"

It was almost eleven. "Five minutes," Meri said.

Brody and the Smythe cousins were there, not asking for more time, which was a miracle. "Last song!" the dancers cried. And like that the attendees at the games let go of any anger to get just one more dance in before the games were over until next year.

Meri dropped Paislee and Brody off, the chairman distracted, though trying hard not to show it, as she thanked them for a fine day. It was midnight, and they'd done a good job of tidying. A professional crew would have the park cleaned up by noon the next day, keeping the bandstand beautiful.

"Thanks for your help today," Meri said to Paislee. "Night, Brody."

"Night!" Brody replied, as they exited the car.

They entered the house, the foyer dimly lit with a soft light. Wallace met them with a wagging tail and sleepy eyes. He liked to sleep in the cozy dog bed by the back door when they were gone because it had a view of the entrance. Snowball drowsed on the rug in the kitchen, not sure she wanted to get up.

Brody let Wallce and Snowball outside and waited on the back porch. Paislee stepped out too, eyeing the moon in the sky, shoulder to shoulder with Brody.

"Did you have fun?"

"Yeah, the rides were a blast."

"What was your favorite?"

"The Dragon Drop. It lifts you fast and drops you. I did it three times." Brody put his hand to his stomach. "My belly's whirling, but I didnae boke, like Max. He hurled."

"Gross." And because she was a mum she asked, "Is Max okay now? And where did it happen?" She imagined unsuspecting people below getting soaked by fair food vomit and her own stomach clenched.

Brody laughed at her expression. "In a bin. I guess so. We did the roller coaster after."

"That would have been game over for your mum, but I'm glad you had fun."

"Thanks for being brilliant and letting me decide aboot competing, and for not being weird aboot me going with them."

"You're welcome?"

He smiled at her, brown eyes glinting in a way that would always melt her heart. "You ken what I mean."

Sadly, she did. His being a teenager had her on guard as she waited for his other giant foot to drop. He couldn't help growing fast, or his other bodily changes. She didn't want to be either not sensitive enough or oversensitive—to push him away.

She bumped her shoulder to his, saved by Wallace and Snowball racing up the porch steps. "So does this mean that since you went tae the fair tonight, we don't have tae go tomorrow?"

"I'll never get tired of the rides," Brody promised.

Paislee would rather sleep, but it was Sunday Funday, and it looked like she'd be spending the day with her son. Sounded just fine.

"All right—Sunday Funday."

His sunny demeanor dimmed. "Last one before summer holiday is over."

"Let's hit the sack." She didn't say to not go for a midnight run but conveyed it with her arched brow, then locked the back door.

He raced up the stairs with Wallace and Snowball. Grandpa's door remained firmly closed, and Paislee went upstairs—crashing with dreams of Joseph and Dyana, too close to the edge. Coughing. No, that was her grandfather.

Sunday morning, Paislee enjoyed sleeping in until eight—when she got a text, from Meri, asking if she was up and could chat.

Paislee went downstairs to make tea and greeted Grandpa with a hug. "How are you feeling? It's awful that you had tae work yesterday when you should have been resting."

"I'm fine!" Grandpa insisted. "What's the plan for the day?"

"The fair is in town, so I told Brody we could go."

"That's not for me, lass."

Thank God he'd come to that decision on his own. "No? Well, whatever you decide." She took her phone to the back porch. "I have tae call Meri."

"Should I make breakfast?"

"I'll have porridge in a bit, and tea. You relax." Paislee stepped outside and breathed in the warm summer air, knowing this was heaven but that she couldn't stop the minutes from passing.

She called Meri.

"Sorry tae bother you!" Meri said.

"You aren't. What's wrong?"

"I cannae get Gemma Whittle oot of my mind. Losing a son is tragic, and her husband is an eejit."

"Is that what has you up?"

"No. It's Sandi. Her . . . altercation with Joseph is so oot of character. You know she works at the hospital, in the ER?"

"Yes."

"When we were talking last night Sandi shared that she was on call when Cam was brought in. While she couldnae go intae details, she seems tae harbor resentment toward Joseph."

"I don't know what happened tae Cam," Paislee said, the hair on her nape lifting with apprehension.

"A car accident. I did some research online aboot it—erratic driving, and his car went intae a tree."

"A tree?" Paislee asked in horror.

"That was all I could find—no details, but I'm thinking I might invite Sandi tae a cup of clam chowder at the Lion's Mane today. . . ."

Paislee gave a low laugh. "Good luck getting information—and share what you can, will you? I'm taking Brody tae the fair."

"Have fun! And dinnae forget Tuesday night's committee meeting tae recap the games. We can discuss ways tae better them for next year. Bye, now!"

Paislee entered the kitchen and placed her phone on the kitchen counter by the tea station.

"Already made you a mug," Grandpa said. "And your porridge is ready too."

"Thank you! I'm spoiled." She sat at the table. "Do you know anyone named Joseph Whittle by chance, or Cam Whittle?"

"No, why?"

"Well, our Rhona's dating Artie Whittle, and Cam was his brother, who died two years ago." She added cream and brown sugar.

"Tragic," Grandpa said. "How?"

"He died in a car accident. Gemma, Artie's mum, said last night that there were a lot of unanswered questions about it. I think that would be the worst, not knowing what happened."

"When I didnae ken what happened with Craigh, you saw how it affected me. Does Gemma want tae find oot more?" Grandpa had the paper out but wasn't reading it yet.

"I don't know." Paislee blew on a spoonful of porridge. "They had Cam's body, so not quite the same."

Grandpa coughed, and that small cough led to his gasping for breath. Paislee jumped up to rub his back.

"Leave me be, Paislee," Grandpa cautioned. "A hot shower will see me right as rain."

At that, they silently resumed eating their breakfasts, each mired in their own thoughts.

Paislee cleaned up the kitchen while Grandpa showered. He went into his room to rest, and Paislee was able to knit more coin purses on the back porch until Brody woke up at ten. They were at the car park for the fair by eleven, and it was packed.

Normally this would be something he'd do with Edwyn, but he was stuck with her, so they'd make the best of it.

"We have tae do the Dragon Drop," Brody said, as she paid for their entrance fee and tickets, then went inside the low-fenced area.

The smell of sausages and buttery popcorn overpowered the scent of the nearby sea. "I'm not doing any rides now."

"Mum!"

"Two," she conceded. "No roller coasters or Dragon Drop."

"What about the Twister?"

Paislee studied her options—she wasn't doing any Dragon Drop or roller coaster, which left the fun house, the Twister, the bumper cars, or the swings.

"Paislee!" She turned just in time to be embraced by Fern. The dancer was in jeans and a tank top. "Hi, Brody!"

"Hey, Fern." Her son seemed embarrassed to be with Paislee at the fair.

"What rides are you going tae do?" Fern asked. "I love the Twister. Kev got me on free last night after the games were over."

"Brilliant," Brody said.

"Delilah should be here any minute." Fern shielded her eyes and peered toward the entrance, and then the rides behind them. "There's Kev. Come on!"

Paislee and Brody were caught up in her enthusiasm like guppies in a net.

Kev appeared a little worse for wear, as if he hadn't had much sleep after a long night, his long black hair in a man bun.

Fern kissed him. "Hey, Kev. Remember Paislee and Brody from the games yesterday?"

"Yeah. Hey," Kev murmured. He glanced around and said, "I cannae do free rides for everyone."

"Oh! We weren't asking." Paislee held up the ride tickets to Kev. "We're still deciding what is the best."

"The Dragon Drop is the wildest," Kev said.

"I did that last night," Brody said. "Perfect."

Paislee gave Brody a stack of tickets. "I don't mind if you want tae do that one now. There's not much of a line yet."

Brody nodded. "Cool!" He took the stack and bolted.

Fern laughed. "He's so adorable!"

"I can't believe that he just shot up in height overnight," Paislee said.

"Catch ya later," Kev said, heading toward his station and the line of people waiting for him to start the ride.

"See you soon!" Fern and Paislee stayed talking as Fern was waiting for Delilah. A pretty gold bracelet shone around her wrist.

"Kev's cute," Paislee said, inviting conversation.

"He's all right—he's fun, and gets me on the rides. It's not serious."

"Artie mentioned that you'd dated his brother Cam. Was that serious?"

"Yeah. We dated in secondary, and off and on afterward. I thought he was the one, you ken?"

"Sure," Paislee said, though she had never been in love like that. "What happened?"

"He got too wild for me. Like, I understand training tae be the best you can be as an athlete—dancers work hard, not that we get much credit—anyway, Cam was really getting built and was thinking aboot going pro as a strongman."

"What perks come with that?"

"Paid sponsorships, for one, and being paid tae compete rather than having tae pay entry fees, which add up. You have tae become a personality, like a celebrity," Fern's nose scrunched, "and that meant he had girls hanging oot with him all the time. I knew he was messing around, even though he told me he wasnae."

Paislee put her arm around Fern's shoulder. "I'm sorry."

"It was a long time ago. Ancient history."

"Were you still friends when he died?"

"Sorta," Fern said. "He'd get pished and call me, beg me tae take him back. That was a big mistake. I'm an idiot, and it took a few tries for me to realize Cam was using me for sex."

"You loved him."

"Yeah."

"How did he die, Fern?"

"Car accident. He was driving too fast and rammed intae a tree."

"Were you surprised it happened?"

"No. Surprised it didnae happen sooner, actually. There are lots of times I prayed for me life when he was behind the wheel."

"His poor family!"

"Artie's great. Gemma is all right, but Joseph?" Fern shook her head. "He's a real arse. Cam idolized him. His dad could've gone pro in the heavy events, but something happened, and he was supposedly cheated oot of a brilliant career. Nobody will tell you how, but that's the family story."

Before Paislee could ask more questions, Fern squealed, "Delilah!" and raced toward the entrance.

To Paislee's amazement, she and Brody had an incredible day at the fair. She won a Loch Ness stuffie popping balloons with the dart game, but her son won a giant superhero poster for his wall with his football kick.

"I've never had so much fun at the fair," Paislee said that night at dinner, sitting with Grandpa and Brody around their kitchen table. "I always wondered what the fuss was." She'd been a very young mother, and the fair wasn't in the budget.

"Your face when we did the Dragon Drop was the best!" Brody agreed. "Next year? Roller coaster. You gotta, Mum."

"We will see," Paislee said, her heart full that Brody'd had such a good time.

Later, they watched movies until Paislee was falling asleep on the couch and she had to drag herself to bed. Though she'd checked her phone messages from Meri, there had been not a peep about her possible lunch with Sandi.

"Night, guys," she said. It was on the tip of her tongue to say something about the last weekend, but she wisely kept her counsel.

Monday morning, Paislee arrived at Cashmere Crush, parking next to Jerry McFadden's lorry in the alley behind the shop. She exited and pocketed her keys. The August sky could not be any bluer, the coastal breeze carrying the slightest hint of brine.

Jerry delivered her yarn on Tuesdays, but that day he was bringing a special box of daisy yellow for an online order she'd gotten on Friday.

"What a games!" Jerry said as he climbed down from his truck.

"Some of the best I've seen. I have tae admit I didn't have tae work as hard when I just sponsored Brody's event."

"Being on the committee or in charge of things can ruin the magic. I was in my final year of secondary, studying photography, when we had tae form teams. I was picked tae be lead and hated every second. I never cared aboot cameras again."

"You have a point," Paislee said. "It was so sweet of Freya tae jump in. What a surprise about the ducks though!"

"She's still laughing aboot that," Jerry said. "I'll never forget the shock on Simon's face as he scooped up the charging ducks before they attacked Lord Cawdor."

Paislee went up the steps and unlocked the back door, waiting for Jerry to bring up a box of yarn. Yellow had been very popular this summer.

"After you," she said.

"Thanks." Jerry passed her and went inside the shop, placing the cardboard box on the counter by her register.

Paislee loved Cashmere Crush. The smell of the wool, the polished cement floor, the shelves of brightly colored yarn, the racks of bespoke items, from jumpers to scarves—this was her second home.

She left the back door open for the fresh air and peered into the box, counting the skeins before writing Jerry a check. "Here you are. Thanks for coming an extra day this week."

Jerry pocketed the slip of paper. "My pleasure, Paislee. How is Hamish?"

"I told you—he's visiting his mum over the summer. We are just friends. Why do you ask?"

"He has a girlfriend, did ye ken?"

Her stomach clenched and she busied herself taking out the skeins. Twenty of bright daisy yellow. "Does he?"

She'd wondered if that had panned out but hadn't been brave enough to ask, and Paislee wasn't one to troll someone on social media, not that Hamish was one to post on social media—being a headmaster at a primary school.

"A nice lady. Bree Wellington. Paislee?"

Paislee schooled her thoughts and looked at Jerry. "Hmm?"

"Should we hate Bree?" Jerry offered.

"What? No! I've never met the woman, and I've told you before that Hamish and I were only friends." Friends who had kissed and been deluged by waterpipes in her kitchen, and then he'd suggested they go away for a romantic weekend together and that—well, that was not anything Paislee was willing to do. She'd put him off and then, when he'd told her about meeting an old friend, Bree—yes, Bree—at his mother's and that they were rekindling an old romance . . . she hadn't been hurt but relieved.

"Okay, then." Jerry shuffled his feet.

"Why do you ask?"

"Freya and Bree became friendly at the farm, and she suggested a double date, but I wouldnae if Hamish, or Bree, or you . . ."

Paislee went around the counter and hugged Jerry tight. She let him go and smiled with understanding. "Go on that double date. There are no hard feelings between Hamish and me. We didn't have what you and Freya have." Or Lydia and Corbin, or Mary Beth and Arran, Blaise and Shep . . . the list went on. She couldn't let it depress her, as it was her choice.

A knock sounded on the front door of her shop.

"See you later," Jerry said.

"Bye!" It would be Rhona, no doubt, early if she was dropped off by her mum on her mother's way to yoga class. If not, Rhona rode her bicycle. Grandpa would be in at noon.

Paislee peered through the frosted window—Rhona. No bike. She opened the door. "Good morning, Rhona! How are you doing?"

"All right," Rhona said. They went inside, and Paislee kept the door unlocked even though it was early. Not even half past nine. The young woman's eyes were red, at odds with her pretty pink sundress and summer sandals. Her long hair was up in a clip.

"How's Artie?" Paislee continued to remove the skeins from the box and then set the empty box in the back storage room, grabbing the label machine to price the yarn.

Rhona hung her handbag on a peg in the backroom, standing before the door. "He's not answering his phone."

"Oh!" The pair had been inseparable during the last few months. "Did you get intae an argument?"

"Nah. I hate my parents." Rhona rushed to the counter to grab Paislee's arm.

"What? I don't believe you! What happened?" Paislee had become accustomed to the teen's dramatic statements, but she usually loved her parents, Petra and McDermot, who were fine people.

"They willnae let me see Artie anymore. Mother forbade me. Can ye believe that?"

"Why?"

"They heard that he was cheating at the games. He wasnae, and when I tried tae call Artie tae get his side of the story, he didnae answer his phone. I begged Mum tae drive by so I could talk tae him, but she refused, and it's too far for me tae go on my bike."

"Where is it?"

"They live east, just over the river. Fifteen minutes by car, tops. Paislee would you please, please, please take me? I'm so worrit that it's making me sick. I cannae eat. I couldnae sleep. We had plans tae go on a hike, and it's not like him tae ghost me. What if something happened and his da kicked him oot like he threatened? We have time, it's early, before we open, and I promise, if we go over, I'll stay late tae make it up."

Paislee couldn't come up with a single reason against the angst in Rhona's face. The truth was she didn't believe that Artie had cheated during the competition either. His hands had been greasy instead of sticky with tree resin.

"We would need tae be very, very quick."

"You're the best!" Rhona raced up to the front door and locked it before running back to Paislee. She grabbed her handbag.

"If he's not there, then we are coming right back."

"Promise!" Rhona and Paislee left out the back, Paislee locking up and using her key fob to unlock the Juke.

Rhona slid in the passenger seat.

Paislee had a momentary twinge of going against what Rhona's mom wanted, but Rhona was nineteen and an adult.

Also, Paislee believed Artie was innocent and had heard Joseph threaten Artie about kicking him out of the house, whereas Petra hadn't.

"Has Artie been at work at the golf course?"

"He had off until tomorrow. We were going tae go hiking up near Nairn Falls together yesterday. We had plans, Paislee, that he wouldnae back oot on."

Unless he was being forced to for some reason. Well, Paislee thought they would know soon enough.

Paislee's phone dinged.

"I sent you Artie's address," Rhona said. "I told him that if he did get kicked oot, then mibbe we could get a flat together. I dinnae need tae shop. I could save money. That's when Mum freaked oot, thinking I might move in with Artie. She was looking for reasons that he's a bad person when he's not."

Paislee winced at this additional information from Rhona. She could see her mother's point of view, but it was too late to back out now.

They arrived in Artie's neighborhood within twelve minutes. "Okay. I'm going up tae the door with you just in case there's a problem with Joseph and his temper."

Rhona frowned with worry. "It's all I can think aboot."

The house was in a middle-class neighborhood with lots in varying sizes and full trees because of summer's lushness. They passed the field where Artie practiced the caber toss.

"His place is coming up on the right," Rhona said.

The GPS seconded that they had arrived.

Paislee slowed and drove down a gravel lane with a white picket fence about four feet high. A gate with a BEWARE OF DOG sign warned strangers away.

"They dinnae have a dog, really," Rhona said. "But Joseph doesnae want people on his property."

They were tucked back from the street. Rhona leaned forward, undid her seat buckle, and gasped. "That's Artie!"

Paislee held Rhona by the arm and took in the scene: front door open, a cement porch without a railing, and a young man covered in blood, eyes closed, on his back. She called emergency services.

Chapter 5

Rhona jumped out of the car and Paislee had no choice but to get out as well.

"Artie's hurt," Rhona shouted, opening the gate and racing through it. "I ken what tae do in an emergency."

Paislee also knew the basics of CPR, so she entered the gate on Rhona's heels.

Rhona dropped to her knees beside her boyfriend. Bright red blood was everywhere on Artie and Paislee scanned his body to locate an obvious injury, but there wasn't one. Head wounds were notorious for bleeding like a stuck pig, yet his sandy blond hair was clean. No marks on his temple or face, other than spatter. His T-shirt, once white, was crimson in color. To her relief, his chest moved.

Rhona patted Artie down, her hands coming away with wet blood. His feet were bare, his shorts khaki at one time, but now soaked to ruby.

"Don't move him," Paislee cautioned. "He's breathing."

"Where's all this blood coming from?" Rhona rested on the soles of her sandals in confusion. Her light pink sundress had red on her knees. "His back?"

Artie roused. "Da . . ."

"Did he hurt you?" Rhona demanded. She gently pushed his fringe from his forehead. "Hang on, Artie. An ambulance is coming."

"Da. Needs help," Artie managed between clenched teeth. He groaned and tried to get up but collapsed backward, out cold.

Paislee straightened, her intuition screaming in alarm. "Stay here. I'll check it out." She raised her mobile, prepared to use it for more than a phone call.

The front door was wide open; bloody handprints smeared the wall and doorknob. Paislee was very careful not to touch anything, as Zeffer's voice seemed to be in her mind. Walk in the center of the room, be observant, don't overreact. In the nearly three years since Detective Inspector Mack Zeffer had come to Nairn, delivering her grandfather to the door of Cashmere Crush, their adversarial relationship had grown into one of . . . dare she call it friendship?

"Joseph?"

No answer. Paislee inched forward with caution.

"Gemma?"

Still no answer. She tilted her head, listening intently. The home felt empty.

Paislee's skin dotted with goose bumps. She was very much on the verge of panicking. She didn't like the way Joseph had treated Artie with such disrespect. Had father and son argued? Gotten into a fist fight?

Or worse. Blood smeared the wall in the foyer. Paislee entered the kitchen and stopped in her tracks. Joseph was sprawled on his back, arm outstretched toward Paislee, eyes open and vacant. There was a center island separating the appliances from a square dining table. Blood was on the island and dripped to the tile. "Joseph?" He was clearly dead.

She scanned the room for any clues as to what had happened. The kitchen opened to the family room, where pictures of Cam competing hung on the walls. Cam and Artie. Cam and Joseph. Cam and Gemma and Artie. Cam was the center. And then, there were no more pictures of Cam or Artie.

He'd died two years ago in a car accident, his family emotionally dying with him.

Paislee didn't know the details, only that it was sad, and it had broken this family apart. She didn't understand how Joseph had died or the source of the blood. She took a deep breath and a closer peek.

His T-shirt was dark gray but black at his chest, the fabric punctured. Blood pooled beneath Joseph's body. Paislee didn't see a knife or a weapon. Blood had splattered on the stainless-steel appliances.

Dizzy, she couldn't look anymore and sucked in a breath that smelled like iron, stepping backward. "Gemma? It's Paislee! Are you here?"

What if Joseph had gone on a rampage? What if Artie had—*no, not Artie*—stabbed him to protect himself? Or his mother? Artie would go to jail. To prison—this violent response wasn't acceptable no matter how far Joseph had pushed his son.

"Gemma!" Paislee gripped her phone, grateful that Rhona hadn't seen Joseph in this bloodbath. Rhona was in for a world of pain when she discovered what had happened. But Artie was also covered in blood. What if he'd interrupted the killer? She wanted to believe that scenario more than Artie, *not Artie*, stabbing Joseph.

Paislee peeked into a room whose door was slightly ajar. Weights and fitness equipment. There were dumbbells in varying sizes, the stand holding them knocked over. "Gemma?"

She didn't have the courage to search the back of the house for Gemma.

Sirens sounded, coming closer. Paislee crossed her arms to her waist, not wanting to accidentally touch the walls or the door and went outside to the fresh air. She gulped in big breaths as the ambulance arrived with the police.

The ambulance parked, but Constable Monroe exited her vehicle first, taking in Artie on the porch, with Rhona at his side. "What's going on?" The officer was fifty and solid in her experience and temperament, despite her red hair. She was Constable Payne's opposite and rarely smiled. She read the sign and opened the gate, looking around the yard.

"There's not really a dog," Paislee said, her throat scratchy. She cleared it.

The medics unloaded the stretcher and entered the garden.

"Constable Monroe." With a hard swallow, Paislee gestured to Artie, who was out cold on the porch. Had he stabbed his dad and then hurt himself? Where was Gemma? It didn't track with the Artie she'd met.

"What happened?" Constable Monroe asked again in a harder tone.

"We came tae see why Artie wasn't answering Rhona's phone calls." Paislee stepped closer to the constable and lowered her voice. "Joseph Whittle is dead in the kitchen. I didn't touch anything, I didn't go farther, I called for Gemma but there was no answer."

The constable glanced at Rhona, who had backed up to let the medics care for Artie. "Does she ken?"

"No. She's under the impression—we both were—that Joseph would be the violent one."

"Stay here." Constable Monroe left Paislee on the lawn and passed by Rhona into the house. "Police!"

Rhona did her best to wipe the blood from her hands to the grass before joining Paislee, her body quivering in shock. "I hope Artie's okay. I couldnae see where he was hurt."

Paislee thought of dead Joseph in the kitchen, with wounds in his chest, surrounded by blood. Had Artie had enough, and killed his father? Would the handprints on the wall and doorknob belong to Artie?

Constable Monroe returned, her face set in a stony expression. "Tell me what happened. The detective and the medical examiner are on their way."

"What for?" Rhona peered toward the house. "Joseph?"

"I need you tae give me the exact last time you spoke with

Artie," the constable said as she took out her tablet. "Do you mind if I record this conversation? I'll transcribe it later."

"I dinnae ken anything," Rhona said, backing up from the constable.

Admittedly, it was scary to have your words being recorded.

"Fine." The constable brought out her stylus to tap in the words. "We'll do it this way. Why were you here this morning?"

Rhona brought trembling fingers to her throat. "Artie wasnae answering my phone calls or texts, so we came here tae check on him. We had plans yesterday tae go hiking at the falls, and it is oot of character for him tae avoid me." She blinked and continued, "Paislee and I both heard Joseph threaten Artie with being kicked oot of his house if he didnae improve his caber skills, after that awful caber toss. Artie believed someone set him up tae fail."

"You heard this too?" Monroe asked Paislee.

"Yes," Paislee confirmed.

"What was wrong with the caber toss?"

"Someone messed with his ointment, and with the log," Rhona said fast. "The timber cracked, and it shouldnae have, and Donnie— stupid Donnie!—accused him of cheating, and Joseph didnae do anything aboot it. He was more worried that Artie wouldnae perform well for the talent agent."

Paislee nodded. "And Lachlan said that he wouldn't sell the Whittles a caber from his construction site, remember?"

Constable Monroe tapped the info into her notes. "Donnie?"

"Donnie Weber," Paislee said. "And Lachlan Felling. They are both on the committee of the Highland Games, so I can get you their personal information if you need it."

"Noted. How did Artie seem after the competition?"

"He was upset," Rhona said. She stared at the medics as they placed Artie on the stretcher.

"Aboot what happened with the caber toss?" Constable Monroe asked, wanting Rhona's complete attention but not getting it.

"Not just that," Paislee said, after several seconds passed. "Joseph was flirting with another woman there, and Gemma asked Artie tae take her home early."

"That's right! It was so bad." Rhona blinked tears from her eyes. "I felt awful for Gemma and Artie both."

"Who was the other woman?"

"Dyana . . ." Paislee had to think back to the roster of volunteers for her last name. "Dyana Barclay. She was one of the women's events judges. You might know her—she's got a patented organic green juice she sells around town."

Constable Monroe continued writing. "Not a fan of veggies. So, Dyana and Joseph were flirting, and Artie saw this and got mad. Was he protective of his mother?"

"Of course! Since Cam died . . ." Rhona's voice trailed off as she watched the medics wheel Artie out of the yard to the ambulance.

"Cam?" Constable Monroe tapped her stylus to her tablet.

"Cam Whittle. He was in a car accident two years ago," Rhona explained. "Where is Gemma? Is she inside?"

"No," Constable Monroe said in a short tone.

"She'll need tae be contacted that Artie is in hospital." Rhona studied the dried blood on her fingernails. "I dinnae have her phone number, but I ken she works at a dental office."

The sound of tires crunched on the gravel as a familiar blue SUV arrived, following the medical examiner's vehicle.

DI Mack Zeffer parked and hopped out, in his typical stylish blue suit. He had thick russet hair cut fashionably and astute seafoam-green eyes. He scanned the lawn and followed the ME through the open gate of the white picket fence until he reached Paislee standing with Rhona and Constable Monroe.

Paislee had never seen something as gruesome as what had happened to Joseph Whittle. She couldn't imagine the killer to be his own son. They had to find proof to dispute this obvious path leading to Artie.

Rhona paled at the sight of the medical examiner.

"This family has suffered multiple tragedies." Constable Monroe made another note. "No excuse for murder."

"Murder?" Rhona asked.

"Joseph Whittle was stabbed multiple times," Constable Monroe said. "Artie was covered in blood."

"Artie did not kill anyone!" Rhona said. Her body quaked.

"Stay here, the both of you," Constable Monroe instructed as she met with DI Zeffer and had a quiet conversation.

"Paislee," Rhona hissed with fear and worry. "You ken my sweet Artie wouldnae hurt a fly." She started to cry.

"Hush, dear, hush now," Paislee soothed as she hugged Rhona. "Maybe it was self-defense? We both heard how awful Joseph was tae him."

After a hiccup or two, Rhona lifted her face to study Paislee. "He wouldnae. He let his da use him as a punching bag—literally."

"Maybe he had enough. Sweetheart, we will find answers. DI Zeffer has helped me many times." Her defense of his abilities had been well-earned through the years.

"I remember him." Rhona shivered and hugged her waist. "From when he was at Smythe Manor after Lydia and Corbin's wedding."

The DI went inside the Whittle home with Constable Monroe.

"I have tae call my mum." Rhona gestured from her ruined summer dress to the ambulance that was just leaving with sirens blaring. "She'll ken what tae do. Me mobile is in your car."

Paislee placed her hand on Rhona's wrist. "Let's wait until after we find out what the police expect from us, okay? They have protocol for these situations that might not include telling people what happened just yet."

"All right." Rhona looked doubtful. "I usually tell Mum everything."

"I'm not saying you can't, just tae wait."

DI Zeffer was out in less than five minutes, concern in his gaze. "You saw Joseph?"

"Aye." Paislee scuffed her shoe to the grass, calming the rise of nerves at the memory of his lifeless body. "It was awful."

"It never gets routine." Zeffer's tone was as serious as his expression. "I'm sairy you discovered him like that."

Paislee tilted her head, accepting his compassion. "What can we do?"

Zeffer rubbed his clean-shaven chin. "We've called Mrs. Whittle. The number for her work was written next tae the landline. She'll meet us at the hospital." He studied Rhona. "Artie is unconscious; however, we will post a constable ootside his room."

"Artie didnae do that terrible thing," Rhona said.

"We will search for answers," Zeffer said. He didn't give any hints of whether he believed Artie was innocent or not.

He was always one to hold the cards close to his chest.

Her mobile rang, and Paislee saw that it was Mary Beth, probably wondering if everything was all right, as it was quarter past ten and nobody was at Cashmere Crush.

Rhona realized the time. "I'm sairy, Paislee. I've made us late."

"That's the least of our worries, Rhona. It's okay—DI, what can we do tae help?"

"Nothing tae do," Zeffer said. "Artie will be at the hospital."

"I should be there!" Rhona said. "Just in case. I'll stay in the waiting room."

The DI seemed apprehensive but couldn't forbid Rhona from visiting a public place.

"I'll call Grandpa and have him come in early if he can. I'll drive you there but won't be able tae stay."

"Thank you, Paislee!"

DI Zeffer's mouth thinned as if he wished she wouldn't be so helpful, but it was in her nature. "Fine. I'm sure I'll have more questions—also, please dinnae talk tae people aboot what happened just yet, all right? Let us collect answers here first. It's heinous."

"What aboot my mum?" Rhona asked, her lip trembling. The poor girl was on the verge of a breakdown.

"Just the bare necessities, please," Zeffer said.

"All right. I'll be brief."

They got into the Juke, and Paislee drove them to the hospital, calling Grandpa via Bluetooth to ask him to come earlier to the shop, if possible.

"Of course!" Grandpa said. "What's going on?"

"I'll explain when I see you," Paislee hedged. "Thanks!" She gave Rhona some sanitizer wipes from the console, and the girl did her best to clean her hands. Rhona called her mum but had to leave a message.

Next, Paislee texted Mary Beth that she was having a late start and Grandpa would be there soon if Mary Beth had a yarn emergency.

"A yarn emergency?" Rhona asked.

"It happens," Paislee said, thinking back several years to when Mary Beth was working on a darling pink blanket and the dyeing machine broke. They'd pooled together to make sure Mary Beth's baby blanket was completed by the baby shower. "What did you tell your mum?"

"Just tae call me back," Rhona said as they arrived at the car park for the hospital. "Artie isnae violent."

Paislee was able to find a spot at the front, though it was packed. "I've never seen that either, but Rhona, people have different sides tae them. You've only known him a few months."

"Seven," Rhona said stubbornly. "We talk every day. He would for real give someone the shirt off his back. Once at the golf course when he was caddying, another caddy had spilled Irn-Bru down the front of his uniform right before his shift. It turned oot his co-worker also had a spare shirt in his car, so it was fine, but Artie offered just the same."

That was in line with the kindness Paislee had seen, but could you grow up in a house with a bully and not absorb violent tendencies?

They walked into the waiting room just as Gemma Whittle came in behind them.

"Rhona!" Gemma said. "What the hell happened?"

The woman appeared haggard compared to how she'd been two days before. There was no hint of pink lipstick though; her work attire was slacks and a blouse, her blond hair in clip.

"We found Artie on the porch," Rhona said. "When did you last see Artie? Was he arguing with his da?"

"I dinnae ken, love. I've been at a hotel since Sunday morning," Gemma declared tearfully.

A hotel?

Constable Payne arrived with Constable Monroe.

Gemma's knees buckled at the sight of the officers' solemn expressions. Paislee put her arm around the woman as she pleaded, "What is it?"

"Joseph Whittle is dead, and Artie is being evaluated for injuries," Constable Monroe said. "I'm verra sairy for your loss."

"Dead! Joseph?" Gemma straightened and shrugged away from Paislee. "How is Artie? Let me see him. You cannae stop me—I'm his mother."

"He's unconscious at the moment," Constable Monroe said.

"What happened tae him?" Gemma demanded.

"We dinnae ken," Constable Payne said. "We're trying tae find that oot ourselves. When did you see them last?"

"I was away Sunday and this morning," Gemma said.

"Away—where?" Constable Monroe asked.

"A hotel," Gemma said, her face flushing. "In Forres."

"The next town over, that Forres?" Constable Payne asked.

"Aye." Gemma hiked her chin defensively. "I had my reasons."

"I will need tae ken them," Monroe said, glancing at Rhona and Paislee as if wondering why they were at the hospital.

"We're waiting for an update on Artie," Rhona said. "He's my boyfriend."

"Ma'am, let's go over tae this side of the waiting room, and you can sit doon. Would you like some water?" Monroe asked.

"I dinnae want any damned water!" Gemma protested, her voice shaking. "You're sure he's dead?"

What an odd way to say that—as if Gemma Whittle had been afraid of Joseph.

"Mrs. Whittle, let's sit doon," Constable Payne said.

"I dinnae want tae sit doon!" Gemma shook off his gentle hand. "Did Artie kill Joseph? I should've taken Artie away and run for the hills!"

"We dinnae ken what happened," Constable Payne said soothingly. "We are collecting answers. Anything you can tell us will help us find the truth."

"I couldnae have left Joseph for guid; he'd have found me and dragged me back. For better or worse, we were married in the eyes of God." Gemma bowed her head and pinched the bridge of her nose.

"What can you tell me aboot Joseph?" Monroe asked.

"My husband was a bully!" Gemma stated. "He and Cam were two peas in a pod, but my Artie is more like me. We care." She patted her heart. "We are the ones who get hurt."

"Artie wouldnae kill anybody," Rhona said, as if she had to convince Gemma.

"How did Joseph die?" Gemma asked.

"Stabbed." Constable Payne watched Gemma closely. "Did Artie and your husband ever go hunting?"

"Joseph and Cam liked tae hunt. Not me or Artie." Gemma scowled. "Artie doesnae like blood. Passes oot at the sight of it." She turned to Rhona as the initial shock receded. "This doesnae make sense."

"It doesnae! Artie was supposed tae go hiking with me on Sunday, but he didnae answer any of my calls. I was verra worrit and asked Paislee tae drive me tae your house. We found Artie ootside on the porch covered in blood."

Gemma gasped. "What happened tae him?"

"We didn't see any injuries," Paislee said. "Joseph was inside, in the kitchen."

Rhona's mobile rang. "Mum!" She looked at everyone and then answered, "Hey. I'm at the hospital with Artie. He's injured. His da is dead." Giant tears poured down her cheeks. "Artie needs my help."

Rhona's eyes widened as she listened to whatever her mother was saying and then she ended the call.

"Mum doesnae understand what's going on."

"Your mum doesnae like us," Gemma said astutely.

Rhona blushed and nibbled her lower lip.

Gemma raised her palm. "It doesnae matter right now, does it? I want tae see my child. I failed both my sons, by being a guid wife tae Joseph, and look at where it's got me. Alone."

"We can contact the chaplain on staff here at the hospital," Monroe said, "tae help you, if you'd like."

"I dinnae ken. . . ." Gemma mumbled.

"Monroe, why dinnae you go back with Gemma and see how he's doing?" Payne suggested. He turned to Rhona and Paislee. "I'll follow up with some questions and join you."

Monroe nodded and then arched her brow at Gemma. "That's a guid idea."

The constable escorted the shocked wife and mother through the swinging doors and out of sight.

"What a tragic morning," Constable Payne said.

"It has been," Rhona agreed. "You must find oot what happened tae Joseph, Constable. Artie wouldnae do it. He faints at the sight of blood—his own mum said so!"

"Let's establish a timeline from when you last saw or heard from Artie," Constable Payne said.

Paislee smiled encouragingly at Rhona.

Rhona opened her mobile to the string of text messages. "I can tell you exactly. We texted late Saturday night, after Artie took

Gemma home. Joseph was being a pig and flirting with this lady at the ceilidh even though Gemma was obviously upset aboot it."

Payne tilted his head, listening.

"And then, once they were home, his mum got tae drinking, I guess, and decided that she was over Joseph's behavior. Artie calmed her doon and she went tae bed by midnight. Joseph wasnae back yet. Probably at Dyana's house. We were texting aboot getting away on Sunday for a nice nature hike at the falls."

"How late was that?"

"Three in the morning. We made arrangements for him tae come and pick me up at ten." Rhona showed Constable Payne the time. "Artie called me, and we talked aboot his moving oot. Where he might go. If we could mibbe live together. We talked for over an hour, and then"—she paused and sucked back tears—"then, that was the last I heard from him."

A woosh sounded as the door opened to the emergency room. In strode Rhona's mom. Petra Fuller had married McDermot Smythe, her family wealth almost as vast as his family's. Petra fumed.

"Rhona, go now." Petra jerked her thumb over her shoulder. "I told you I didnae want you tae see Artie, and I meant it. You—you go sit in my car and wait for me!"

"Mum, I need tae stay here with Artie."

And then Gemma raced out, seeing Rhona but not Petra. "I'm so glad you havenae left yet, Rhona, lass. They say Artie has a severe head injury, and they are worrit aboot a hemorrhage. His wrist is handcuffed tae his hospital bed. They believe he killed his own father." Gemma's eyes were wide with disbelief.

Petra moved around Constable Payne and shook her finger at Gemma. "I forbid you tae talk with my daughter again."

"Ma'am," Constable Payne said to Petra, "Let's take a moment here before we say things we might regret. It's true that Artie was found in suspicious circumstances, but we are gathering facts and dinnae ken what happened."

"Innocent until proven guilty," Gemma said, her chin trembling. "But that's not how you operate, is it? Better than everybody else."

"Ladies!" Constable Payne stood between the mothers and glanced at Paislee for assistance. She knew them both, he didn't.

Paislee stepped toward Gemma and gave the woman her Cashmere Crush business card and then a hug. "Please, please call me and update me with any news about Artie. I will keep him in my prayers. Let me know if you need anything."

"Thanks." Gemma shoved the information in her pocket, glared at Petra, but gave Rhona a wobbly smile before she ducked back into the emergency room and to her son.

"Well!" Petra crossed her arms. "Rhona, there is a reason we forbid you tae see Artie, and this is why. Killed his own father! We knew the Whittles were bad seeds."

"He's not either—Artie didnae cheat at the games, and he didnae kill anybody, Mum. I cannae believe you!" Rhona swiped her cheeks with her palm—in the other was her cell phone.

"Give me that." Petra pointed to the mobile. "And get in the car." She turned to Paislee. "Rhona will no longer be working for you. I apologize for the short notice."

Rhona's mouth gaped. Her mother was treating her like a child and not a young woman of nineteen. "You're embarrassing me, Mum."

"And how do you think I feel, being here with you, and you dating a murderer?" Petra tossed her ponytail. The fact that she was in workout clothes didn't make her any less regal. "Get in the car. Now."

Constable Payne didn't seem too keen on Petra's treatment of Rhona. Petra tried to grab Rhona's arm to pull her, but he cleared his throat. "I wouldnae do that if I were you, ma'am. She could press charges for assault. If your daughter wants tae get in the car with you, that is her decision."

Petra's eyes narrowed. Rhona snapped her mouth shut.

The constable turned to Rhona. "What would you like tae do?"

Paislee could see Rhona calculating her options, and in the end, she swallowed and pocketed her phone. "Thank you, Constable. I'll go home with my mother. Paislee, I like my job and would like tae keep it."

Paislee nodded. "Of course."

Petra glared at Paislee and gave the constable a wall of icy politeness as she left without another word, Rhona hurrying after her.

Paislee exhaled once the door closed. "Well, I'm glad tae not be in that car right now."

Payne read a notification on his phone. "I ran Rhona Smythe through the system. She's had some speeding tickets but nothing prior."

"She has. Her parents paid the fines, but she has tae pay them back, which is why she's working at Cashmere Crush. She's been riding with her mother to work or using her bicycle."

"Guid parenting. The lines get blurred when adult children still live at home. Like Artie too. If he'd moved oot on his own maybe he wouldnae have lost his temper."

"I don't think he did," Paislee said. She thought of the blood on the rim of the island counter and the doorknob. What if Artie had tried to help his father but fainted, and then made a mess as he left the house, still woozy?

"Really?" Payne had gotten to know Paislee in the last few years and commended her occasionally on her sound judgment. Perhaps this wouldn't be one of those times.

"Aye."

"Well . . . I'll make sure that we take extra care then, just in case something is overlooked. It seems pretty straightforward. But if he didnae hunt, and passed oot over blood, that adds more tae the story."

Paislee knew he would do all he could. "Thank you, Constable Payne. I've got tae get back tae the shop."

"Let's keep this under wraps until we hear from the DI. Give my regards tae your grandfather." The constable strode toward the door leading to the medical rooms, while Paislee left and went to her car.

The route she took meant that she passed the park and the fairgrounds—today was the last day for the carnival rides. She saw Kev on his hoverboard and waved, though he didn't see her, lost in his music. Headphones had to be dangerous, but then again, so was the hoverboard.

She was glad Brody hadn't wanted one, preferring to spend his extra money on games and comics with his best friend, Edwyn. Edwyn's father, Bennett Maclean, owned a comic book store with arcade games. He and his girlfriend, Alexa, were discussing marriage but in no rush. Would Brody and Edwyn want to go to the fair for the final day? Maybe she could suggest that Brody invite Edwyn. He'd been blue about missing his friend, who was hopefully back from London.

The line for the new ice cream shop, Scoops, at the corner of her street, was out to the sidewalk and around the building. The business was owned by a retired military man, and she couldn't be happier for his success. She parked behind Cashmere Crush at noon and went inside to see that Grandpa had several customers browsing. Paislee did an inventory of what would need to be replenished with a glad heart.

Empty shelves meant sales. Cinda from the Ramsey Castle gift shop had emailed her with a list needed there too.

She was afraid to say it, in case a giant shoe dropped, but her bank account was healthy and her credit cards paid off. She was able to put a wee bit aside for Brody's future so that if he didn't get a football scholarship, she'd have a backup for him.

Lots of teens these days ended up at home longer, because housing was expensive or they didn't have a plan. Brody had his plans, Paislee had hers, three times over. She couldn't imagine not having a plan.

Add in Grandpa's opinions too, and there was no shortage of ideas at the Shaw house. She felt bad for Rhona, at home, but also understood Petra's point of view.

There was a lull at two, and Paislee brought Grandpa up to speed about what happened at the Whittle house.

He was understandably shocked that Joseph Whittle was dead and that Artie, lanky, young, innocent Artie, was a suspect.

"I dinnae believe it, lass."

"Well, I don't either—but I think that Constable Payne will be very fair about it."

"He's a guid bloke."

"He sends his regards," Paislee said.

"And the DI?"

Paislee laughed. "Zeffer didn't say a word."

"He's on the case though."

"Aye."

"It will be solved then, hopefully sooner rather than later. Zeffer tends tae play the long game sometimes."

"True."

Her uncle Craigh had been the reason for Zeffer's move to Nairn years ago. He'd found Grandpa sleeping in the park after her uncle had disappeared. He'd worried Grandpa and Paislee might have connections to the Norwegian crime syndicate, which they hadn't.

Zeffer had bought Lydia's flat several months ago. Her bestie had thought about renting it out for added income, but when Zeffer hadn't been able to find anything suitable on the market, Lydia had showed him her place and he'd offered cash on the spot. It had been too good an offer to turn down.

Paislee didn't know why he'd decided to make Nairn his home. Would Zeffer have known about Cam Whittle's death? Probably not, if it had been deemed a reckless driving incident.

"I wonder . . ."

"Eh?" Grandpa asked. He straightened the skeins of wool along the wall.

The thought of Cam was cut off by the door opening and tourists shopping for the perfect bespoke item.

"It's nothing," Paislee said, smiling at the customer. "Welcome tae Cashmere Crush."

Chapter 6

Rhona arrived at Cashmere Crush at two thirty on her bicycle and stored it in the back room. "Hey! I am so sairy aboot what happened with my mum. I've never seen her act like that before. Well, except for yesterday when she forbade me tae have anything tae do with Artie."

"That's really tough—how was the car ride back?" Paislee asked.

"Baltic." Rhona shivered. She'd cleaned up and changed her clothes into capris, a tee, and sneakers.

"Does she know that you're here?"

"I left a note. She cannae just stop me from working." Rhona sighed. "I made a commitment tae you."

Grandpa squeezed Rhona's shoulder in commiseration. "I'm sairy aboot Artie, and Joseph. Did you ken him well?"

"Not really. When we hung oot at Artie's place, his parents were usually at work. Joseph was a freight driver and could be gone for weeks at a time. Gemma is a clerk at a dentist's office. Mum took my phone, so I need tae buy another one. So ridiculous!"

Paislee was very surprised at that extreme parental move. "For how long?"

"Mum didnae say, and since I went tae work rather than sit in my room waiting for the almighty Smythe judgment, it could be even longer." Rhona shrugged, not showing remorse for her decision. "Have you heard from Gemma?"

Paislee checked her phone, but there were no notifications or missed calls. "Why not use the landline tae call the hospital or Gemma?"

"I never had her phone number. I mean, Artie doesnae have my parents' either, right?"

"It shouldn't be too hard tae find," Paislee said. "Do you follow her on social media at all?"

"No, but that's a guid idea." Rhona sighed. "I have tae tell Aibreann what's going on. She doesnae ken and will totally freak oot. Mum was so mad when we got home that she demanded I give my phone tae her. I dinnae have a strategy on how tae live life withoot a mobile, and I def dinnae have any numbers memorized."

A customer came in and browsed the shelves of yarn. "Welcome," Rhona said, and joined the woman with a smile that hid her heartbreak.

"You ken who might help?" Grandpa suggested in a low voice. "Lydia."

"You're brilliant. Let me call her right now." Paislee stepped into the back room, bumping her knee on the aqua-colored bike, as she'd forgotten it was there.

It rang several times before her bestie answered, "Lydia here— I've got Petra on the other line, and I'm trying tae calm her down. She'd like tae blame you for what happened with Artie."

"Me?"

"But she has no grounds, so . . . Am I to assume that this call pertains tae the Rhona situation?"

"Aye—Rhona rode her bike here and is upset because her mother confiscated her phone."

"Oh no!"

"The lass is nineteen and a good girl, besides the speeding tickets. And even I would be tempted in that cute red roadster."

"Paislee, that's not helping. . . . Shoot. I'll call you after I calm Petra doon."

Lydia clicked back over to Petra.

"Paislee," Grandpa said. "Zeffer is here."

Paislee wasn't sure why she patted her hair or her stomach clenched, but she donned a smile as she left the back storage area and walked toward the counter with the register.

Zeffer stood confidently in the same suit he'd worn earlier. They had to be custom made as they fit his broad shoulders perfectly. He watched Rhona speak with the customer who had four rolls of pink yarn in her arms and was reading a pattern book to see how many were required for the project.

"I talked with Constable Payne," Zeffer said. "He mentioned that he might have ruffled Petra Smythe's feathers. She must have relented tae let Rhona work after all?"

"Rhona rode her bike and left a note for her mum. Petra confiscated her phone and Rhona's not pleased about it."

"Constable Payne seemed concerned that Petra might push things too far, but Rhona looks like she's all right."

"She is. More upset than hurt, I think. Rhona hasn't ever really been at odds with her parents before." Paislee walked around the counter, away from the alluring scent of Zeffer's aftershave.

"Angus. How have you been?" Zeffer asked.

"Fine, fine." Grandpa's throat was raspy from coughing, despite the honey lozenges that he consumed constantly.

"You had a cold?" Zeffer asked.

"Nothing contagious," Grandpa assured him. "Fell in the River Nairn, and it's landed in me chest. It's fine."

Zeffer raised a palm, hearing her grandfather's defensive tone loud and clear.

"I feel for Rhona," Grandpa said. "Everyone telling her what tae do when she's a bright lass and will figure it oot."

"If she's in trouble, it's good tae know help is around," Paislee said, trying to skew the conversation toward the doctor and an actual checkup for her grandfather.

"She's not in trouble at all," Zeffer said. "With the law, which is what I care aboot."

Paislee sighed, her plan not going how she wanted.

Gtandpa's exasperated exhale carried the scent of honey and lemon.

Rhona rang up the customer, with the addition of an extra skein and the pattern book. The young woman was a natural saleswoman. Paislee and Zeffer moved to a high-top table out of the way of foot traffic.

Lydia texted Paislee. **Petra is on her way. She had run home to talk with Rhona after our conversation and she isn't pleased.**

Paislee sent a thumbs-up. **Zeffer is here.**

Lydia gave that a heart emoji. Her friend was Team Zeffer since he'd had the cash to buy her flat outright. The symbol wasn't meant in a romantic way, just that she liked the DI and thought he made a good addition to their shire.

Rhona joined Zeffer and Paislee. "Hi, DI. Have you found oot what happened tae Joseph?"

"Not yet, but we are collecting answers. Talked tae Mr. Whittle's boss and the delivery company he drove for. One of his routes has him traveling tae Romania tae bring back glassware."

"Glassware?" Paislee asked.

"It's a three-million-pound import industry," Zeffer explained with a twitch of his lips. "I had tae look it up. Anyway, his boss doesnae think that Mr. Whittle was faithful in his marriage, and Constable Payne said you might ken more aboot that. We wondered if Artie had also been aware."

"Yes. Artie left the games early Saturday night tae take his mum home because Joseph was flirting with Dyana." Rhona's cheeks flushed. "When we talked later, he said his mum was verra upset but believed in their marriage vows even if his da didnae honor them."

"Was Artie angry?" Zeffer asked. "It would be understandable."

"No," Rhona countered. "He was hurt. Hurt for his mum."

Zeffer shifted toward Paislee. "What did you see the night of the games?"

"Joseph and Dyana were dancing provocatively." Paislee patted Rhona's shoulder. "They were . . . familiar."

"So, not a stretch of the imagination tae think he might have strayed while on the road." Zeffer sighed. "It means we'll need tae broaden the search for answers tae include his freight routes."

"How's Artie, DI Zeffer?" Rhona asked.

"He was still unconscious when I left the hospital." Zeffer placed his tablet on the table. "Does Artie have a skateboard?"

"No," Rhona said. "He only has a car. He doesnae even have a bike. Why do you ask?"

"We've canvassed the Whittle neighborhood. It seems the neighbor tae the right, closest tae the property, saw a figure on a skateboard Sunday evening. Also, Mrs. Whittle has reported some items missing. Possibly stolen."

"A robbery?" Grandpa asked.

"What if Joseph and Artie interrupted a robbery and that's why they were hurt," Rhona said. "Was Artie stabbed, like Joseph?"

"No. Most of the blood on Artie belonged tae his father. There was an injury tae the back of Artie's head that could have been inflicted by someone else, or perhaps when he fell backward and slipped on the blood in the kitchen. We will ken more if—when—Artie comes tae."

"*When,*" Rhona said, tears welling in her eyes. "And you'll see that he's innocent."

"How is Gemma?" Paislee asked. "Is she still at the hospital?"

"I followed her home, and we went through their house—that's when she discovered she was missing some jewelry. She was going back tae the hospital. Like you, Rhona, she strongly believes that Artie would not hurt anyone."

"He wouldnae!" Rhona exclaimed.

"So, I need a list of anybody Joseph Whittle might have had a bone of contention with. I'll add it tae the delivery route and drum up possible affairs." Zeffer withdrew his tablet and cleared his throat. "Dyana, you mentioned?" He observed Paislee.

"Dyana Barclay. Her personal information is at the town hall office for the Highland Games committee. Meri could get it for you—or we are having our meeting tomorrow night tae go over the event. All of the members will be in attendance tae discuss the games. You could drop by then."

Zeffer wrote down Dyana's name. "Anybody else?"

Paislee recalled the incident between Sandi and Joseph, sharing the details with Zeffer. "Sandi Peckett is a nurse and the volunteer coordinator."

"What was their disagreement aboot?"

"I don't know exactly, but it sure grew heated, and that was very unlike Sandi's normally calm demeanor. In fact, one of the other members of the committee suggested she not be allowed tae continue volunteering."

"Joseph had a way of needling people," Rhona said.

"It seems like it—but I saw what happened," Paislee said, "and it wasn't worth being fired over. Volunteers are hard tae come by as it is."

"All right." Zeffer made a note. "Anybody else?"

"Yes. Uh, Lachlan Felling. He owns Felling Construction and Lumberyard, the big construction company off the river road. He sells cabers for the caber toss event, but he wouldn't sell tae Joseph or any Whittle. He agreed with Drake, the convener for the games, that Sandi had gone too far." Paislee shrugged.

"It's a lot of drama," Zeffer said. "Why wouldnae Lachlan Felling sell tae the Whittles?"

"I don't know." Paislee thought back to how Lachlan had glanced toward Gemma on the sidelines before storming off. "It seemed personal, as if the men held a grudge over something."

"Did you see this too, Rhona?"

Rhona shook her head. "Not that, but dinnae forget that Donnie accused Artie of cheating when his caber broke. And somebody messed with Artie's tree resin cream for his hands. He was sabotaged, but Joseph blamed Artie and threatened tae kick Artie oot of the house if he didnae improve. Something tae do with the talent agent there tae sign him. Joseph was really mean tae Artie saying that he'd never be as guid as Cam."

"And Cam is?"

"Cam Whittle," Paislee said. "The older brother who was training tae be a champion strongman."

"Who died in a car accident two years ago," Zeffer said.

"So much grief," Grandpa said. "More than one family should have tae bear."

"Gemma had said she should have taken Artie and run, remember, Paislee?" Rhona said. "But she couldnae—her duties as a wife came before her duties as a mother, or something stupid like that."

"I don't understand that," Paislee said.

"Because you are a wonderful mother," Rhona said. "Mine normally is too, but she's being really strict right now."

"Speaking of, Petra is on her way," Paislee said.

"Here?"

"I don't know more."

Rhona stepped toward a customer heading to the register as Grandpa spoke about fishing with a man, the woman's husband, who was waiting for her.

"Bloke had a busy day." Zeffer read the list he'd written. "Did Joseph argue with anyone else?"

Paislee recalled the folks holding Lachlan back after Joseph had called Krissie's dancing slutty. "Kev and Leland stopped Lachlan from decking Joseph that night for insulting one of their friends."

"Kev and Leland?" Zeffer jotted that down. "Surnames?"

"I don't remember Kev's, but he works at the fairgrounds.

They pack up in the morning—he's got black hair and tattoos, and was hanging around with Fern McElroy, one of the Highland dancers. Constable Payne was there tae break up the altercation. It was right before eleven p.m. and the last dance of the games. I don't know Leland, but Rhona does."

"Okay. This gives me a guid place tae start," Zeffer said. He slid the tablet into his suit jacket pocket.

The front door to Cashmere Crush opened and Rhona turned pale as Petra Smythe stormed into the shop like a cold blustery wind. She'd changed from her yoga attire to designer jeans and a peasant blouse. Diamonds and gold adorned her ears, fingers, and wrists.

Petra acknowledged Zeffer, Grandpa, Paislee, and last, Rhona, with a cool gaze.

"Mum!" Rhona said on a squeak.

"We need tae have a conversation," Petra announced. "Lydia suggested ice cream. I dinnae like ice cream. Can we have a smoothie instead?"

"Uh, sure." Rhona sounded very confused.

"I forget that you're not a babe in need of boundaries. I dinnae approve of Artie—we've heard that he was cheating." Her blond hair was sleekly pulled back into a ponytail.

"He wasnae!"

"We should have listened tae you withoot punishing you." Petra's chin hiked as she pointedly ignored everyone else but her daughter. "Can we please go somewhere and discuss this like adults, in private?"

"Yes!" Rhona looked at Paislee. "Em, may I leave early?"

"Of course." Paislee smiled at Rhona. "You're welcome tae keep your bike in the back until tomorrow if your mum drops you off before yoga class."

Petra nodded stiffly. "Thank you."

"Thanks, Paislee. Bye, everyone!" Rhona shifted toward the detective. "DI Zeffer, thank you for listening aboot Artie."

"You're welcome." Zeffer smoothed the lapel on his blue suit as cool as you please.

The front door closed behind the Smythes.

"But if he is guilty, he will go tae jail," Zeffer promised Paislee. He scanned the shop. Grandpa talked with a browsing customer as the man and his wife had left.

"How is Amelia doing in her classes?"

"I dinnae ken. I imagine she'll do well—she studied and passed her physical requirements."

"It's remarkable tae me that she's going for it." Paislee remembered how Amelia had been afraid of the Henry family's nefarious past getting in the way of her dream career. "She'll be great at it."

"I think so too." Zeffer tilted his head. "How's Brody?"

"Moaning about school tomorrow." Paislee scrunched her brow.

He chuckled. "And Hamish?"

Her stomach whirled at the intensity of Zeffer's seafoam-green gaze. She swallowed, suddenly glad to clear the air. "Going out with someone he used tae date in university. His first love, Jerry said."

A smile flitted around Zeffer's firm lips. "I heard." He held her gaze as if to see what she really thought about that.

Paislee sighed, annoyed that she had to explain repeatedly. She'd made no promises to Hamish McCall, and he none to her. "We were just friends."

"I see." Zeffer's palm rested on the tabletop. "Friends are nice tae have."

Paislee's mouth dried, and she stepped back from Zeffer's gaze, her heart galloping and her pulse racing.

Zeffer had the nerve to smile wider. Did he know how he affected her?

He winked. Yep, he sure did.

Her traitorous face flushed red with heat. If Zeffer could flirt, it might go something like this. . . . He leaned closer, and she . . .

jumped back with relief when her mobile rang, and Brody's smiling face lit the screen.

"Hello!" Saved by the bell. Zeffer grinned and put one hand in his slacks pocket, leaving the shop as if nothing had happened at all.

"Hey—can I go tae Edwyn's? Bennett said he'd pick me up."

Paislee pulled her attention from the closed door to her son. "He's back from London?"

"Aye, and he has a new video game he wants tae show me. Can I?"

"Of course! Tell them hello from us, and let me know when you want me tae pick you up. I'll be at the shop until six-ish, but Grandpa can run by if you need tae be home earlier."

"Thanks—see ya," Brody said.

Paislee hoped that this would lift Brody's spirits regarding school tomorrow. Grandpa regarded her with a question in his brown eyes.

"Brody's going tae Edwyn's."

"That's great. Brody's missed his best mate."

Paislee hoped that Edwyn and Brody would remain friends no matter what direction their hobbies and studies took them, as she and Lydia had.

Cashmere Crush was busy, and it was just her and Grandpa handling sales, with Rhona hashing things out with her mum. His schedule was Monday and Thursday, and sometimes Saturday, with Amelia at police school. Brody loved puppy-sitting Snowball and making extra money for things that might catch his eye.

Snowball at the house helped with the puppy pang she'd suffered when Daisy, a sweet pup they'd rescued over Christmas, was homed to a family with children. Dr. McHenry's assistant had adopted Robbie. Puppy mills were awful things, and Paislee was glad to have played a part in shutting one down.

Grandpa suppressed a cough. Just when she thought he was on the mend, it would come from the bottom of his lungs, or so it sounded.

"Grandpa, it's not getting better."

"Dinnae nag me, Paislee."

"Let's make a deal—if you are still coughing next week, you will go tae the doctor. I care about you and don't want you tae be sick for so long."

He grumbled and made himself some hot tea with honey.

"What is it that you're afraid of?"

"Nothing!"

The response was quick, which meant he might be hiding something.

"When was the last time you've been tae the doctor?" He didn't answer, and Paislee pressed, "Do you have a primary care physician?"

"I dinnae need one!" Grandpa coughed and closed his eyes.

"Why don't you take a wee break in the back. I've got this." The shop only had two browsers.

She knew he didn't feel good when he went and sat down in the oversized armchair without argument.

She'd gotten Grandpa over two years ago, and it had never occurred to her to meddle in his health affairs. He had a small income. He didn't require much, so he said, and he didn't pay rent or for a car. He chipped in for the mobile bill and groceries. He was a braw cook.

Paislee peeked back at her grandfather and saw him dozing. Her heart warmed, and she decided to find a way to get him to the clinic. Sometimes you had to push those you loved.

It made her more empathetic to Petra and her dilemma with Rhona. What would Paislee do if Brody befriended someone who Paislee feared wasn't a good example? Talk, she supposed. Communicate. Be honest.

It was working for now.

Brody texted at five thirty that he'd be ready at six ten if she would please pick him up. She sent a thumbs-up and kept busy right until six. Grandpa had come out to tidy the shelves of yarn, moving slowly.

Paislee thought of calling Rhona to get an update and then remembered the teen didn't have her phone, as her mother had taken it. She phoned the hospital from the landline and was told that they couldn't give her any information on Artie Whittle.

Register prepped for the next day, Paislee turned off the lights. "Thanks for all of your help today."

"It's me job. What shall I make for dinner?" Grandpa asked.

"How does Chinese sound?" Paislee countered. It had been a while since they'd had takeout as Grandpa practiced his skills in their brilliant new kitchen.

"Splendid."

That night the Shaw family enjoyed Chinese food with extra fortune cookies. They played the game of creating better fortunes than the one that had come inside the cookie.

Grandpa was getting better and better with it. Brody went on about Edwyn and the new video game. He seemed less nervous about school since Edwyn was back and they'd spent time together.

Over tea on the back porch that night, sitting with Grandpa and watching Brody play with Wallace and Snowball, she acknowledged that her life was good, and full, and she knew she was very blessed. Poor Gemma was dealing with heartache, with her husband killed and Artie a suspect. But Paislee believed in their Nairn Police one hundred percent.

And that night, she dreamed of seafoam-green eyes, smoky aftershave, and blue suits.

Chapter 7

Tuesday morning, Brody surprised Paislee by being up and dressed before she had to wake him. He'd laid out his cereal bowl but was in the back garden with Snowball and Wallace, already dressed in his school uniform.

The blue sky on this glorious summer morning was one for the record books. Grandpa's door was closed, and Paislee hoped he'd sleep in. She'd heard him coughing in his sleep the night before, clearly getting worse.

He'd made a deal with her, and so she would be patient. She couldn't imagine life without her grandfather. She'd heard of people who were afraid of doctors but hadn't met one—until now.

In Scotland, medical care was free for citizens, and Grandpa had certainly paid into the system. Maybe if she suggested that he had a financial resource he hadn't tapped into, he might be more amenable.

Paislee heated the kettle for tea and Brody skipped up the steps, the dogs at his heels, and entered the kitchen.

"Beat you!" Brody grinned.

"That you did," Paislee said, laughing. "I admit I thought I'd have tae drag you from your cozy bed this morning."

"Naw—sairy aboot being crabbit. Grandpa's right, and some

days I dinnae ken which end is up." Brody patted the top of his head. Before making breakfast for himself, he added dry kibble to each of the dogs' bowls. They didn't share a dish but had their own. "Do ye think Wallace will be sad when Snowball goes home with Amelia?"

"I don't know. We could ask Dr. McHenry." The vet was very knowledgeable about many things when it came to their pups.

"She's cute. Maybe we need tae get Wallace a girlfriend."

Brody washed his hands and sat at the table, pouring cereal and then milk into his cereal bowl. Paislee brought out the orange juice and put four slices of bread in the toaster.

"Wallace is fine," Paislee said. "And if you think he's lonely you can take him tae the dog park." She wasn't going to be tricked into getting another dog before she was ready.

Brody shrugged and let the subject go. "Grandma Rosanna said she'd call tae see how my first day of school goes."

Paislee's instinct was to pad Brody from disappointment. Her mum had moved to America, leaving a hole in her life that felt like abandonment. Rosanna must have immediately remarried, as she had two children younger than Brody and no intention of returning to Scotland.

They were slowly building a relationship through letters and video calls that the kids thought was great. Paislee had a difficult time trusting Rosanna but was willing to try, for Brody's sake. It would be nice to keep the door open for her adorable half siblings.

Paislee brought the toast to the table, offering two to Brody and keeping two for herself. Orange marmalade for her son, butter for her. She selected a banana from the little fruit bowl in the center. The orange and apple had to be eaten today before they were past their prime.

"I'm sure she will call," Paislee said. And if she didn't, Paislee would send a text to remind her mother about it.

"I like Josh and Natalie. I want tae see America. We should sur- prise them with a trip."

"Brody, that's expensive, and we can't just hop on a plane." Paislee bit into her crunchy toast, studying her son to see how serious he was being about the idea.

"What aboot next year? We could go tae Arizona and visit them for the summer holiday."

"You will melt." Her mother had said it was 115 degrees, 46 Celsius.

"That's not a no," Brody said.

"You'd have tae get top grades at school tae earn it." Paislee wondered how far she could push the envelope before he'd stop badgering her about it. Arizona!

"All right," Brody agreed. "I'll try my best. Coach Harris says I need tae have decent grades in class, tae look guid for scouting football teams."

"Oh?" Paislee's expectations of the school year's grades rose the tiniest bit. Her son was an average student—didn't do the extra, but he didn't struggle. If he had two reasons to hit the books it might make a difference.

"I can do it," Brody said, giving himself a pep talk over his Weetabix.

"You can!" Then Paislee's mobile rang, and she answered it right away. "Hello?"

"It's Meri! Just wanted tae remind you aboot the committee meeting tonight," the chairman said.

"I've got it on my calendar," Paislee promised. "Have you heard anything from the constables? I mentioned that we'd have contact information for some of the people regarding Joseph's death."

Brody tilted his head in alarm. "Somebody died?"

Oops. How had that not come up over dinner last night? Oh, that's right—everything was about Edwyn and school.

"Constable Monroe left a message for me," Meri said. "I'll call her back. There was nothing in the paper this morning aboot it."

"I think they're trying tae keep things under wraps." Paislee could feel Brody's accusing scowl.

Meri continued, "How's Rhona holding up?"

"I hope okay—listen, let's chat later? I've got tae run Brody tae school."

They ended the call, and Brody glared at her.

"What?"

"Who died?" His voice cracked on the question. "How?"

"Joseph Whittle, Artie's dad." Paislee sipped her tea. She'd buried thoughts of how she'd found Joseph bleeding in the kitchen, but it would haunt her forever. She had to compartmentalize. "It's under investigation. Did you meet him?"

"No, I didnae. Rhona said he yelled at Artie for not doing guid enough, when he broke the caber during the toss."

"That's right." Paislee wiped her hands on her napkin.

"I was thinking that I was really glad he wasnae my dad."

Paislee studied Brody closely for signs that he meant just that. They didn't talk about his father. She wasn't sure how long that would last, but she knew there would come a day when he would have questions. "Joseph was very hard tae get along with and rubbed a lot of folks wrong," she said slowly. Was Brody anything like Calan Maxwell? She and Calan had been close that final year in secondary, bonding over their lack of fathers.

"I like Artie though," Brody said, bringing her back to the conversation. "He must be sad aboot it."

"Artie is in hospital." Paislee glanced at her phone, but there had been no new messages with updates. She hoped he would wake up and set the record straight regarding his innocence, or on the flip side, guilt.

"Why?" Brody gulped the last of his orange juice.

"They're wondering if there was a break-in at the Whittle house," Paislee hedged. "I don't know more. DI Zeffer and the constables are looking intae what happened."

Brody perused Paislee's last piece of toast with eager eyes. "I cannae wait for Amelia tae be a constable. She's going tae be awesome, and she'll tell us everything."

"I don't think that's allowed!" But Paislee would offer an ear, of course. She gave Brody half of her toast.

"Thanks. Amelia is amazing," Brody said. "Mibbe I should be a constable?"

"Instead of a star footballer?"

"Never mind!" Brody finished the toast in two bites, brought the empty cereal bowl to the sink, rinsed it, and loaded it into the dishwasher. The act had not grown old for any of them.

Paislee read the time on her phone. "Meet you at the door in fifteen?"

"'Kay." Brody walked—actually walked—up the stairs. Wallace followed his lad, while Snowball stayed with Paislee, wagging her tail as if to encourage a few morsels her direction.

Paislee made sure nobody was watching and tossed a corner to the pretty white pup. What would it be like to have a second dog?

She finished her breakfast and cleaned up, leaving a note for Grandpa with a wish to have a good day and a reminder that he'd paid into the system and health care was a benefit he was entitled to—if he felt like it.

Brody retained his cheerful mood as she dropped him off at school. She'd given him cash to buy his lunch in case there was something tastier than turkey and cheese from home. Last year, he'd had Jenni and Edwyn waiting for him—this year, nobody was there, but he seemed to take that in stride as he exited the car.

"I love you, Brody," Paislee said.

"Mum!" He closed the door with an eye roll and a wave.

Paislee would say it every day whether he responded or not. He was still good at verbalizing at night before bed, so she'd take that as a win.

She arrived at Cashmere Crush at the same time as Jerry McFadden, there to deliver her weekly order of yarn.

Jerry got out of his lorry, smoothing his mustache, eyes filled with concern. "Paislee. How are you doing?"

"I'm fine! Why?"

"I heard aboot Joseph—killed by his son, Artie, and you and wee Rhona were there tae find them. Surely, it's affected you," Jerry decreed. "We've helped solve some crimes, aye, but ye cannae be that jaded."

Paislee climbed up the stone steps and unlocked the back door. "Let's talk about it inside, and not blether for everybody tae hear."

Jerry scoffed but went around to the back of his delivery truck, selected two boxes, and entered the shop. Paislee moved Rhona's bike out of the way, or he might have knocked his knee on it as she had yesterday. Maybe she could install a bike rack? There was no room with all the shelves.

Plopping the boxes to the counter, Jerry crossed his arms expectantly. "Now. How are you really doing, Paislee Shaw?"

Paislee smiled at her friend, hearing his worry. "I'm truly fine, Jerry. It's been a shock is all, but I've learned tae separate my feelings so that I can do my job and be a mum and still care about Artie and Rhona."

"Why would you care aboot Artie, if he's a murderer?" Jerry asked, baffled.

"We don't know that Artie did such a brutal act—think, Jerry, the lad is kind tae everyone and doesn't possess the temper of his father."

Again, Jerry smoothed his mustache as if contemplating her words.

A knock sounded on the front door that Paislee hadn't unlocked yet—it wasn't even nine thirty.

"That's probably Rhona, if you want tae stay a minute, and we can find out the latest about Artie. As far as I know he's still in hospital."

"All right," Jerry agreed.

Paislee unlocked the door, and sure enough, Rhona stood there. Petra rolled her window down to call a greeting to Paislee before driving off with a honk of her horn.

"Morning, Rhona!" Paislee tugged the teenager inside and closed the door behind her. "Jerry's here and concerned. How are you holding up?"

Rhona blinked, her eyes red, but she held her tears at bay. "It was a brutal night, so I had Aibreann come over tae watch romantic comedies with me. I called the hospital first thing, but they willnae tell me anything because we arenae kin."

"Rumor has it that Artie is responsible for what happened tae Joseph," Jerry said carefully.

"He's not!" Rhona said. "He just needs tae wake up and tell everyone what happened and clear his name. Gemma is missing jewelry, and Artie wouldnae steal from his mum."

Jerry's expression conveyed that a lad willing to kill his da, probably wouldn't hesitate to steal getaway gold, but he didn't say the words aloud.

"Well," Jerry put his hand on Rhona's shoulder and gave it a light squeeze. "I hope Artie is all right then."

"Thanks, Jerry," Rhona said. "I finally convinced my parents tae give Artie a chance before they convict him, withoot proof. It wasnae easy. Aibreann reminded them of how kind he'd been tae her, and that helped a wee bit."

"They are trying tae protect you," Jerry said.

"Too much so! I dinnae need it," Rhona insisted.

"I remember saying the same when I was in school," Jerry said.

"I am oot of secondary," Rhona said. "No wean."

"On that note," Jerry backpedaled toward the exit. "Bye now."

Paislee called, "Don't you want your check?"

"I'll pick it up tomorrow," Jerry said.

"He wants tae know what is going on," Paislee deduced, "and this will give him a reason to stop by in the morning."

"You think so?" Rhona asked, her eyes wide.

"Yep." Paislee opened the box of cocoa brown and sage skeins, counting the correct amount.

Rhona got out the price labeler and applied a sticker to the yarn.

Paislee slit the top on the second box—ivory, yellow, and pink. All there. "These are ready tae price too. I'm glad tae have you, Rhona."

"I was worried Mum would fight me coming tae work this morning, but she apologized for being controlling. She just wants me tae be safe."

"That's understandable," Paislee said. "Any decent parent would."

"Artie didnae have a decent da." Rhona affixed prices to the skeins. "But he wouldnae have hurt him. Rumor, Jerry said. Who would gossip like that?"

"Nairn is a small shire, and people talk. Meri called this morning surprised that it wasn't in the paper."

"My da was too, actually," Rhona said. "He had breakfast with us this morning before heading tae the office."

McDermot Smythe worked in banking. "The constables do that on purpose sometimes if they're looking for answers and feel news might hinder the investigation. These days, with social media making information instant, it's harder tae do."

"You're right," Rhona said.

Her mobile rang, so Petra must have returned the phone, and Rhona pulled it from her back pocket. "What if it is Artie?"

"Answer!" Paislee said. They didn't open the doors until ten, and they had five minutes still.

"Hello?" Rhona tossed her long braid over her shoulder as she brought the mobile to her opposite ear.

Paislee stacked the empty boxes in the back room to give to Jerry to recycle.

"Oh, em, well, you can come tae Cashmere Crush if you want. I'm working here today," Rhona said. She paced before the counter. "Okay, see you soon."

"That didn't sound like it was Artie."

"Naw, Constable Monroe is on her way over for a quick chat since we both were at the Whittle house yesterday."

Paislee was happy to answer questions so long as it didn't interrupt the flow of customers. "I'll unlock the front door, then."

"How's Angus?" Rhona asked, patting her chest. "And his cough?"

"He's agreed tae go tae the doctor if he isn't feeling better in a week."

"A week?" Rhona's brows rose.

"I think he must have some hang-up about the medical profession." Paislee shrugged and unlocked the door.

Amelia had painted vibrant flower blossoms along the edge of the large window. It was very inviting for customers to peer in the frosted glass.

She stepped outside to the sidewalk and plucked a dying marigold from the window planter. Green ferns, marigolds, and purple begonias crowded the flower boxes on each of the businesses on Market Street.

Next to her place on the corner was a leather repair shop owned by James Young. Then Ned, who ran the dry cleaners where DI Zeffer had his blue suits cleaned; then the medical office managed by Margot, where Susan, Elspeth's blind sister, answered phones. Margot was dating their landlord, Shawn Marcus, the son of Lady Leery. Then was the office supply shop and the ice cream place. Scoops didn't open until eleven, but it would stay busy until it closed at nine.

She waved at Ritchie across the street who owned a florist shop and supplied their window boxes with plants. To her right, was the Lion's Mane pub.

They had the best fish and chips in the shire, and she'd tried plenty of other places to compare. It was dim inside, but that was part of the pub's charm. The food excelled. She might just treat herself and Rhona to a haddock special for lunch today.

Traffic on Market Street was steady, and happy tourists could be heard from the park and the Moray Firth to her left, which was also where the Nairn Police Station was located. Summer equaled joyful people, enjoying their lovely beach and rivers.

The Nairn Highland Games. Her smile slipped as the splashes of blood in the Whittle kitchen seeped into her thoughts.

With a sigh, Paislee returned inside. Joseph's brutal murder and Artie's questioned innocence ruined the peaceful vibe.

Knitting always calmed her, and she had a lot of inventory to replenish, so she chose a dusty pink yarn in a Shetland-Merino wool blend and got to work on a scarf that she'd do with a matching slouch hat in a simple stitch pattern.

Rhona took care of customers while Paislee knitted. Tomorrow, she'd start the blanket in the daisy yellow, from the online order.

At eleven, Constable Monroe arrived. The woman was more serious than Constable Payne, who had explained to Paislee once that he tried to focus on happy thoughts considering his job was often seeing others at their worst.

"Hey," Rhona said. She made sure the customer who was browsing didn't need anything and then stepped toward the register where Paislee knitted.

"Morning, Constable." Paislee put down the project with an inner sigh.

"Hello. Is now a guid time?" The constable looked around the shop with its lone customer.

"Yes," Rhona said. "You've caught us in a slow moment. How is Artie? We havenae heard a word from anyone. It's terrible, having tae wait like this. Can he have visitors?"

"No. He's still unconscious," Monroe said. "They are considering surgery."

"Surgery!" Rhona said.

"From what I understand, this procedure might alleviate the pressure on his brain," Constable Monroe shared.

"I didn't know it was that serious," Paislee said, putting her hand on Rhona's back.

"The injury is in line with falling backward in the kitchen and hitting his head on the counter behind him, more so than his being attacked by an intruder." Constable Monroe brought out her tablet.

Paislee recalled the scene in the Whittle's kitchen. "I can picture that—maybe he saw his dad and fainted, hitting his head, and then stumbled out tae the front porch tae get help. Artie told us that his da needed help—those words exactly."

"Not the actions of a killer. He didnae do it," Rhona said.

"What can you tell me aboot Kev Sloane?" Constable Monroe asked.

"Who?" Rhona asked.

"Kev Sloane worked at the fairgrounds, running the Twister ride," Paislee said. "He was dancing with Fern and was part of the crew tae grab Lachlan before he punched Joseph."

"Oh yeah! Black hair and scary tattoos." Rhona scrunched her nose. "Fern thought he was cute."

"Aye." Constable Monroe lifted her gaze from her tablet. "When did you see him last?"

"The games, Saturday, and the fair on Sunday," Paislee said, then shook her head. "Actually, yesterday coming home from the hospital. He was on that hoverboard thing. He had his headphones in so not very safe tae have on the road."

"It's why they are illegal tae operate unless on private property." Monroe read her notes. "You said that Mr. Sloane held Lachlan Felling back from fighting with Joseph Whittle?"

"Him and Leland," Rhona confirmed.

"Why do you ask? Kev's probably not even around anymore. The fair workers will be packing up this morning tae go back tae their home base."

"I'm telling you this because it will be common knowledge by this afternoon, but Kev Sloane was arrested early this morning at the caravan he lived in at the fairgrounds. We found a knife matching the wounds inflicted on Joseph, and Gemma's necklace. Fern McElroy was also missing a gold bracelet that was in Mr. Sloane's possession."

Rhona grabbed the counter to steady herself. "I told you Artie was innocent."

"We are gathering information—what if Artie and Kev were in on this crime together?" the constable queried.

Rhona shook her head. "No way."

"Just like we are checking every avenue, you must be prepared, Rhona, tae see the truth as well," Constable Monroe cautioned.

"Did Kev confess?" Paislee asked.

"No—that would be too easy. He says he didnae do it, but we can place him near the Whittle residence verra early Monday morning. Not the skateboard the neighbor thought, but the hoverboard." Monroe put her notes in her pocket.

"Then Artie is in the clear," Rhona said. "Why cannae they do the surgery now?"

"They're waiting for Gemma Whittle tae give the okay," Monroe said.

"Why would she wait?" Paislee asked. That didn't make sense to her.

"There is danger in the procedure, but there is danger either way," Constable Monroe explained. "It is no guarantee."

"She must be terrified," Paislee said. What an awful choice to have to make and when it is your only son, your only family . . .

"What time did you see Mr. Sloane yesterday?" Constable Monroe asked Paislee.

She thought back. Grandpa had been here, but he'd come early to help. "I can't say exactly, but around noon."

"I will add that tae the timeline for his whereaboots. Thank you." Monroe dipped her hat toward the customer holding an armful of cocoa brown yarn, listening to their conversation with avid interest.

"Is this aboot the dead guy killed by his son?" the woman asked.

"Where did you hear that?" Constable Monroe sounded concerned.

"I went for coffee this morning, and it was all anybody was talking aboot," the woman said. "Our shire used tae be much safer withoot all the tourists."

"The crime was not committed, that we ken of, by a tourist,"

Constable Monroe said, edging around the woman toward the door.

Killed by a local wasn't any better, Paislee thought with an inward cringe.

"It would be guid tae have more protection," the woman continued.

Constable Monroe reached the front door but didn't comment before quickly exiting.

"Can you believe what happened?" the woman said to Paislee, then Rhona. "Why was that officer questioning you?"

"The constables are canvassing the neighborhood," Paislee said, feeling bad for Police Scotland. The police, especially in Nairn, had made a huge effort with positive outreach and programs to be seen as approachable and friendly. Amelia would be great at that.

The woman put the skeins on the counter. Her eyes glittered as if she was bursting with information.

Paislee rang up her purchases, putting them in a nice bag with the customary keychain. "Did you know Joseph?"

"Not so much, but Gemma's the receptionist at my dentist's office. She always looks so bloody sad all the time. Honestly, they should find someone friendlier for the front desk."

"Her son died, so she has reason," Paislee said.

"I knew Cam Whittle—he was mates with my boys in secondary. He was always skirting trouble except for lifting weights. He lived tae compete and win." She accepted the bag. "Cam was so wild, I was glad when they grew apart. It used tae give me nightmares thinking aboot my kids in the car with Cam when it crashed. Bam, right intae a tree."

"I didn't know the Whittles," Paislee said. "And now poor Gemma is without her husband and her son. I'm sure she could use a friend. Did you need anything else today?"

"Naw. I learned tae knit when I was pregnant tae pass the time. You have the best selection of yarn."

"Thank you," Paislee said. She didn't mention the Knit and Sip, sensing the woman wouldn't be a seamless fit.

Rhona didn't either. She had good instincts.

The woman left the shop, and Rhona pulled her phone from her pocket. "Should I call the hospital again?"

"Rhona, lass, I think we need tae be patient. And we should get Gemma's mobile number, so we can talk tae her directly."

"That's a guid idea," Rhona said. "She must be oot of her mind with Artie in such a dire situation. Honestly, when I think aboot what she's had tae bear, it makes me sick. Artie has tae be okay, not just for me, or himself, but Gemma needs him."

The door opened and a trio of ladies with shopping bags entered. "This is the most adorable shop!"

"Welcome tae Cashmere Crush," Paislee said.

Chapter 8

They had no free time to call the hospital, as tourists and shoppers seemed to flood in along with Elspeth, who was working that afternoon. Being busy kept their minds off Artie and Gemma.

Paislee gave Rhona enough money to buy them lunch from the Lion's Mane, curry chicken—rather than fish, which would add an unwanted odor to the shop—on a roll, with crisps, for less than eight pounds each. A bargain!

Around three there was a lull in the foot traffic, and the ladies all took a moment to sit down and have a break. Paislee brought out three cans of lemon Perrier and offered them around, keeping one for herself.

"And how are you holding up, dear?" Elspeth asked, knowing that Artie was in hospital and that Joseph was dead but not much more. There hadn't been time to bring her into the loop.

"I'm glad tae be busy," Rhona said. "I'm so worrit aboot Artie. Constable Monroe told us that they arrested one of the fair workers, who had a knife that possibly matched the wounds on Joseph. Artie didnae have any stab wounds but had hit his head when he fell. He's not regained consciousness."

Elspeth cracked open her Perrier. "That sounds verra scary."

"I'm terrified." Rhona drank her fizzy water. "What if . . . I cannae say it."

Paislee opened hers, the scent of lemon wafting upward. The bubbles tickled, and she sneezed.

"Bless you," her workers said in unison.

"Thank you," Paislee said.

"My mum asked that I be cautious, but I ken Artie is innocent. The constables should too. Let me text Mum really quick tae let her ken aboot Kev being arrested. That will make her feel better aboot Artie." Placing her can on the polished cement floor, Rhona stood and walked toward the window, typing.

"What do you think, Paislee?" Elspeth asked quietly.

"I agree with Rhona's assessment of Artie's character. I feel like that's been corroborated with Kev's arrest." Paislee sipped her water. "I can't believe it. He seemed like a decent guy too—I mean, rough around the edges, which I attributed tae the carnival lifestyle but . . . murder?" She recalled Kev's genuine smile as he'd hung out with Fern, and she hoped that Fern was all right.

The shop door opened, and Paislee rose, gesturing for Elspeth to stay seated and enjoy her break for a while more. "I'll get it."

But it was Gemma Whittle barging in. She rolled to a stop seeing Paislee and Elspeth. "Where is Rhona?"

"On the phone," Paislee said, gesturing toward the right side of the shop. "How are you?"

Gemma didn't answer Paislee's question. "I need Rhona tae come with me tae the hospital, right now."

Rhona walked over from where she'd been standing, partially hidden by the table of bespoke knitted goods. "I'm here, Gemma. What's wrong?" The teen swayed. "Is Artie. . . ?"

"He's going tae have emergency surgery and cannae wait. I cannae be alone. I cannae lose my only son. My last bit of family." Gemma had crumbled Paislee's business card in her sweaty palm. "I knew tae come here." She was stick thin and seemed to have lost too much weight in mere days. "That Rhona worked with you. We need tae exchange mobile numbers, but I havenae been thinking clearly."

Gemma was in no shape to drive, and Rhona didn't have a car, just her bike. "Elspeth, did you drive?"

"No, I walked on this glorious day." Elspeth looked from Paislee to Gemma and understood the unspoken request. "Sairy!"

"Don't be. . . . I am going tae run them over tae the hospital and be right back." It was fifteen minutes there and back, barring any traffic stops or slow cars. "If it gets busy, just lock the door and the customers can wait."

A customer walked in with her two teenage daughters. "Hi!" the mother said.

"Hello," Paislee answered. "Please feel free tae browse."

She urged Rhona and Gemma out the back door, to where the Juke was parked and unlocked the doors. Gemma climbed in the front passenger side without complaint while Rhona hopped in the back, sliding on the bench seat.

"What can we do, Gemma?" Paislee asked.

"Artie needs surgery. I'm a bad wife and a bad mum."

"No!" Paislee said, trying to calm the woman down. "You're not."

"I was glad when Joseph was oot of town. *Glad.* He was so controlling." Gemma fisted her hands on her knees. "He had cameras everywhere all over the house."

"Cameras?" Rhona asked.

"Tae spy on me," Gemma said.

"That means they could see who broke intae your home! Who killed Joseph!" Paislee said. "This is good news."

"No," Gemma countered, her chin wobbling. "Artie knew aboot the cameras. They were all broken. Every single one."

"Why would your husband spy on you?" Rhona asked.

"Tae make sure I was being a guid wife. I should have been a bad wife and a better mum, and mibbe Artie wouldnae have done what he did."

"Artie is innocent," Rhona said. "The police have arrested Kev Sloane, one of the fairground workers. He had a knife and some stolen jewelry."

"Your necklace, I thought," Paislee said. "They must have contacted you. I believe Artie is innocent."

"Artie was verra angry with Joseph Saturday and Sunday, aboot how his da treated me," Gemma said. "Mibbe I encouraged him somehow? I dinnae ken aboot jewelry."

"What are you saying?" Rhona asked. She was leaning forward so that her face was between the front seats.

"I was drinking a lot, drowning my sorrows, but it didnae help, and mibbe, mibbe I said that he should protect me, if Joseph came home angry."

"Artie said you were verra upset, and he put you tae bed. He didnae say anything aboot that, so I dinnae ken, Gemma," Rhona said.

"What will I do if Artie dies?" Gemma cried mournfully. "Even if he goes tae jail, it would be better than dead. I'm a selfish person."

"He's not going tae jail!" Rhona said, annoyed. "Why would you think that?"

"I ken Artie and Joseph argued on Sunday—I heard it, from the bedroom where I was hiding. Artie told Joseph tae stop fooling around, and Joseph refused. Said my duty was tae put up with him. Artie and Joseph yelled all morning."

"But it wasnae physical, was it?" Rhona asked. "Artie didnae text me Sunday or meet with me, like he'd agreed."

"Joseph did whatever he wanted, and everyone else had tae fall in line." Gemma stared at her hands.

"Joseph had a temper," Paislee said. "That was common knowledge. Artie doesn't."

"Joseph dropped one of the curling stones they practiced with on Artie's phone and shattered it. The police have it, but I dinnae ken if it will be any use."

There had been an exercise room in the Whittle home but that made sense if Joseph, Cam, and Artie were all strongmen competitors. Joseph and Cam had been champions. Artie, according to Joseph, didn't measure up.

Paislee wanted to protect Artie from his childhood—which was a silly thought to have and far too late.

"That's why he didnae call me," Rhona said, understanding in her tone. "Did Joseph hit Artie?"

Perhaps Artie punched back in self-defense.

But that wouldn't explain the stab wounds—why had Kev been so violent? Were Kev and Artie friends, perhaps, and Kev decided that Artie'd had enough? Kev had realized Joseph was a bully from the dance at the games and maybe he'd befriended Artie.

Paislee glanced at Gemma. The traffic was so heavy that it would take an extra five minutes to reach the hospital.

She couldn't be in two places at once, so she stopped fretting, or tried to, about an overwhelmed Elspeth and focused on getting safely to the hospital.

"What is your number, Gemma?" Rhona asked.

Gemma gave it, and Rhona added it to her contacts, and then shared it with Paislee.

"Thanks," Paislee said. "Give Gemma mine too, please."

"Done. Gemma, did Artie and Joseph often argue?" Rhona asked in a quiet voice.

Gemma cleared her throat. "Not exactly argue—but they disagreed on a lot of things."

"Like?" Rhona pressed.

"Bodybuilding. Competing. Artie didnae have the drive like Joseph or Cam," Gemma said. "He's guid enough tae compete, but he was happy being a caddy at the golf course and didnae have big dreams of being a strongman."

"Can you think of why anybody might have sabotaged Artie on game day?" Paislee asked.

"No. Joseph was verra mad at Artie for that. Not only the ruined caber but embarrassing him in front of Ross. Joseph wants Artie tae care aboot the win, but he doesnae—that's just how he's made. He's like me."

"There's nothing wrong with that," Paislee said.

"Not according tae Joseph," Gemma said.

"Joseph isnae here anymore tae control you or Artie," Rhona said. Her words were filled with compassion.

Gemma peeked back at Rhona and then observed Paislee. "By the time Cam was in secondary, he'd shown a natural affinity for building bulky muscle, like Joseph."

"Was Joseph a bodybuilder when you met?" Paislee asked.

"No. He was a skinny lad who won my heart with poetry." Gemma gave a sad smile. "We were kids, it seems, and then he joined Forge Fitness and discovered another love."

"Joseph Whittle touted poetry?" Rhona exclaimed.

"He was verra romantic. Mibbe I wasnae romantic enough for him? I did everything he wanted. I dinnae ken why he broke his vows tae me." Gemma shrugged. "We married young. Nineteen. I wanted tae start a family more than anything else."

"People stray, and it isnae the faithful partner's fault," Rhona said. "It's the cheater's flaw, not yours."

Gemma turned toward the teenager. "And how do you ken that?"

"I had a verra serious boyfriend during my last year in secondary, and he did that tae me before our commencement ceremony. Mum taught me that, and then therapy helped too. He didnae want tae be so serious but didnae ken how tae tell me, so he acted like a prize eejit."

"My folks taught me tae be obedient. Our church teaches the same." Gemma faced forward and folded her right hand over her knee, staring at her wedding ring.

Paislee wouldn't do well in a marriage like that, so maybe it was better that she had remained single. She had way too many opinions to be obedient to another person.

Lydia and Corbin's marriage wasn't like that, or Blaise and Shep's, or Mary Beth and Arran's. Gemma had been conned into accepting bad behavior, and whose fault was that?

Paislee would lay the blame at Joseph's feet, though he was now dead. "Gemma, I hate tae pry, but could you tell me more about Cam? How were he and Joseph so alike?" Fern had told Paislee that Cam hadn't been faithful, and neither had Joseph. If Joseph couldn't be trusted, was that the same for Cam? Over what exactly? Artie couldn't be overlooked as a suspect despite his aversion to violence. Maybe he'd snapped. But then where did Kev fit in?

Gemma arched her brow. "Why?"

"Could Cam's and Joseph's deaths be connected somehow?"

Gemma exhaled; her lips pursed. "It's been two years. Cam died in a car accident, and Joseph was stabbed tae death. Not related at all."

"It's awful tae think aboot," Rhona said gently. "You said there were questions you had aboot Cam's death?"

"No mystery that he died in a car accident. He'd been at a party after a competition and slammed his car intae a tree. Joseph found him and called for emergency services."

"Was he with his mates?" Paislee asked.

Gemma pressed her hand over her stomach. "He'd had a fight with his girlfriend, Chantelle, so she didnae get in the car with him. The pair were inseparable, but that fight probably saved her life. Why didnae she take the keys from him, if he was oot of control? I ken it's not her fault. But why didnae she take the damned keys? If he'd been with Fern, that's what she would have done."

"I'm really sorry."

"Donnie was at the same party as Cam that night he died. He might remember more, but it really doesnae matter now. I've got tae save the son I have left."

Paislee arrived at the hospital, in the front rather than at the emergency room like a few days ago. "Here we are. Maybe take a rideshare or a cab when you're ready tae come get your car? I'll be there until six-ish. I have a committee meeting tonight for the Highland Games at six thirty." Her phone dinged a notification. Brody, wondering where she was at.

Paislee froze as she tried to center herself in day and time. Of course, it was the first day of school, and she'd not factored in picking him up. She wasn't winning mum of the year points.

On my way, she messaged back.

This day really couldn't get much more hectic.

Paislee smiled at Gemma and Rhona. "Please let me know what's going on. I will be at the meeting tonight until eight tae go over the event."

"And my husband's death," Gemma said.

"The constables have asked us not tae discuss the investigation," Paislee said.

"Please keep Artie in everyone's prayers," Rhona said. She exited the Juke and opened Gemma's passenger door for the distraught woman. "Let's go see Artie."

Gemma allowed herself to be tugged from the vehicle.

"What if he killed Joseph?" the woman muttered. "How can I handle that?"

"You're not thinking straight, Gemma. Stop even considering that your wonderful son would hurt a fly."

Rhona closed the door and peered over her shoulder at Paislee with angst clear to read in her expression. They were all afraid that Joseph might have pushed Artie too far.

Paislee arrived at Brody's school, expecting recriminations or an argument, but her son got in with a chuckle.

"Forgot?"

"I did. Sorry!"

"It's all right."

"Why are you in such a good mood?"

"Well, you being late gave me a chance tae talk with Lizbeth."

"Who is Lizbeth?"

"She's on the cheer team."

"Oh?"

"She's a fan of mine and has been watching me play football since last year."

Paislee headed out to the main road. "That's interesting." And stalker-y. Should she be worried?

Brody continued, "Her older sister has a car, and she's offered tae drive me home, so you dinnae have tae. Isnae that great?"

Paislee glanced at her son as she drove. "No. It's not great. How old is this Lizbeth?"

"Fifteen."

"Just no. You're thirteen."

"A teenager now," Brody continued blissfully. "Her sister, Toria, is seventeen and in her final year."

"No."

"Mum!"

"This is so not even up for discussion!"

Paislee dropped Brody off at home, and her son got out and slammed the door without a goodbye.

She wished Grandpa luck in dealing with Brody's attitude, but there was no way on God's green earth she would allow her son to ride home with a teen who'd just gotten her license.

How old did Lizbeth think Brody was, to flirt with him? To be a fan of his football team? Aye, her son was cute—but he was a child!

Steaming with indignation, Paislee parked behind Cashmere Crush, exited, and climbed the stone steps to her shop. At the back door, she took a deep breath and went in, stumbling over Rhona's bike. She dropped her handbag, swallowed a curse, and tried again—*retrieve the handbag, move the tire, and exhale.*

"Paislee?" Elspeth called from the register. "Is that you?"

Paislee forced a smile and strode inside. "It is! Tripped over the bike, but I'm fine." She scanned the shop—it was now five (where had the time gone?)—and ambled toward two potential customers by the bespoke scarves while Elspeth bagged up yarn for a tall woman with three small bairns.

"Hi. Welcome tae Cashmere Crush!"

The plump brunette caressed a scarf in the Shetland-Merino wool blend. "This is so soft. Is it cashmere?"

"No—did you know that cashmere comes from the underbelly of a goat?" Paislee loved to educate if a customer seemed open, and these two—possibly sisters, with similar eyes and chins—stepped toward Paislee with enthusiasm.

"No way. I thought all wool came from sheep!" the second woman, who was taller, said.

"It's quite interesting, actually. Wool is a natural fiber from sheep, of course, and there is a wide variety from the different breeds. Then there is the goat, and the camel." Paislee smiled at their raised brows.

"A camel?" The brunette popped her hand over her mouth in shock.

"In the camel family as well, like an alpaca or llama," Paislee said.

"I want a camel jumper!" the second lady said.

"Camel hair is a versatile product and very insulating, often used in coats, as it can be lightweight yet warm. I don't carry any of that here, though." Paislee gestured to the shelves full of colorful yarn. "Where are you from?"

"Edinburgh. Here on holiday with our family. I adore dolphins," the brunette said. "I even have a tattoo."

"Dolphins are pure magic," Paislee said. "And not something you'll find in the city."

"Exactly," the first woman said. "So how much is cashmere, if I wanted tae make a sweater?"

"I have a selection of cashmere skeins over here." Paislee led them to the wall of more expensive yarn, taking a skein of the Shetland-Merino blend with her. "You can feel the difference."

"Oh, sis, it's luxury." The first woman closed her eyes as she smiled and brought the skein to her cheek.

"It is," her sister agreed.

"Now feel this one," Paislee said. She'd requested from JoJo's farm a blend that could be comparable in softness to cashmere at a fraction of the price, and she felt as if this particular wool met the mark. "Here."

The sisters each took a turn to bring it to their cheeks for a comparison.

"It's verra close," the taller sister said.

"How much?" the brunette asked.

Paislee showed the labels where the prices were marked, and the brunette sister put the cashmere back on the shelf.

"I'd like the Shetland-Merino wool blend, please," the taller woman quipped.

"I think you'll be very happy with it." Paislee wanted customers to be pleased with their purchases. Sometimes cashmere was worth the extra cost, as the bespoke items at Ramsey Castle gift shop proved, but often the knitter simply wanted an affordable soft option.

Paislee rang them up for enough skeins to knit an open cardigan, and a knitted slouchy hat for the sister with the dolphin tattoo. She gave them two keychains.

"And if you ever want a bespoke gift item, my website is on the receipt."

"Cheers!" the sisters said.

It was six on the dot when Elspeth helped the last customer of the day and locked the door behind them.

"It's been so nice and busy," Elspeth said. "I've put puir Artie from my mind. Any news from Rhona?"

Paislee had silenced her notifications, knowing that Brody and Grandpa would be fine together, and needing to focus on the store. She read the messages on her mobile.

"Rhona texted that Artie's surgery will be scheduled for first thing in the morning—if he can be stabilized." Paislee looked up and sighed toward Elspeth.

"That's so scary." Elspeth straightened stools beneath the high-top tables.

Paislee continued reading. Nothing from Brody—like an apology, her crabbit laddie—but Meri reminding her about the meeting and saying she'd brought meat and cheese, so not to worry about dinner. That was a relief.

Rhona arrived, coming in through the back entrance as Paislee sorted the money in the register.

"Hey!" Paislee said. "Glad you got here in time. Did you take a cab?"

"No. Me and Gemma were brought here by Ross, the talent agent. He's been a big support tae Gemma. She's going tae the hotel tae rest, since they arenae doing the surgery until tomorrow."

Poor Rhona's eyes were red-rimmed from tears. Young love was still love.

Paislee checked the time. Ten after. "I have tae be at the committee meeting at six thirty, but I can just make it if you'd like me tae drop you off with your bike, so you don't have tae ride."

"That's verra sweet but I need the exercise." Rhona rolled her shoulders. "I havenae danced in days, so it will be guid tae stretch my muscles."

"All right." Paislee relaxed a wee bit and finished counting the money, putting it in the safe as she prepped the drawer for the following day.

"I'm going tae the hospital with Gemma at seven in the morning," Rhona said. "I really wish I had my car. I asked Mum for it early, and she willnae budge on the punishment."

Elspeth gave Rhona a side hug.

"I'll take a rideshare, so it will be fine. Paislee, I'll keep you in the loop for what happens. What if Artie dies?" Rhona sucked in a sob.

"Oh, Rhona. Let me know what you need. Don't worry about being here unless you want tae be," Paislee said.

Sometimes it was good to be busy, but other times, it was best to be in the moment for whatever might happen.

Elspeth nodded. "Should I come in early?"

"Let me ask Grandpa how he's feeling first," Paislee said. If things were really hopping, she might tap Mary Beth to run the register. Her girls were back in school, like Brody. She'd offered to help when Amelia went to police training school to cover for Saturdays. Busy was a good problem to have.

Paislee finished closing chores as Elspeth and Rhona chatted, Elspeth offering to add Artie to her prayer chain at the church.

"Thank you! I dinnae ken what religion Artie is, if any," Rhona said.

"That doesnae matter tae God," Elspeth assured the teen. She left to pick up her blind sister, Susan, who answered phones four days a week at the clinic three doors down. The sisters would walk home with Susan's guide dog, a labradoodle named Rosie.

Rhona and Paislee exited together. "You're sure you are okay tae ride your bike home?" Paislee asked.

"I want tae!" Rhona put on her pink bike helmet with white daisies. Her long braid was an arrow down her back.

"Be careful, and let me know what you need, okay?"

"Bye, Paislee," Rhona said, and rode off.

Sighing heavily, Paislee got in the Juke and drove toward the town hall. She called home via Bluetooth, and Grandpa answered. "Hello!"

"Hey, it's me. How are things going over there?" She felt a tiny bit bad about sending Brody to her grandfather without a warning or explanation for his foul mood.

"Well, your son believes you are tryin' tae ruin his life and embarrassing him in front of the lovely lass Lizbeth, an older girl."

"That's what I was afraid of," Paislee said. "His life will have tae be ruined."

"I understand," Grandpa chuckled. "Brody, not so much."

"Where is he now?"

"Oot back, practicing his football drills for practice. He has tae impress Lizbeth at the next game." Grandpa's laughing brought on a cough.

"Did you see my note?" Paislee tensed until he stopped coughing.

"Aboot my unused assets for medical care? Aye, I did. I'm fine."

Paislee bit back a retort. "Next week. You promised."

"And should I save any dinner for you? I made a pork roast with tatties."

"Sounds good, but Meri brought food for the meeting."

"Guid luck," Grandpa said.

"What for?"

"Everyone will want tae talk aboot Joseph and Artie—I doot the Nairn Highland Games agenda will be adhered tae."

"You might be right. I'd better go." How to handle the meeting and the questions in a way that Zeffer might approve? Then again, what did she care about his approval?

"See you later, lass," Grandpa said as he ended the call.

Paislee blushed as she thought of Zeffer's sassy wink and his knowing saunter out her front door.

She cared, perhaps a bit too much.

Chapter 9

Paislee drove past the fairgrounds where the rides and games had been. Everything was packed up except for a single caravan, where Kev must've stayed, that buzzed with police activity—including a forensics van.

She slowed, recognizing DI Zeffer's blue SUV. Her stomach whirled with nerves, and she attributed them to her vested interest in this case. She hoped they'd find proof of Kev's crime and set Artie free—if Artie survived his surgery in the morning.

Constables Monroe and Payne were also there. Neither officer caused butterflies.

Paislee passed the car park and turned onto the street leading to the town hall, nabbing a space before the building, behind Meri's SUV.

She hurried into the building and down the hall to the office where they had the committee meetings. Voices could be heard through the slightly open door.

"Hey," Paislee said, entering the fray as people talked over each other to catch up. She heard Joseph and Artie's names a lot. Grandpa had been right.

She located Meri by the long counter with a selection of rolls, meat, cheese, and condiments.

"I'm here. It sounds like World War Three."

Meri turned to smile at Paislee. "Fortify yourself, my friend. It's going tae be a long night. Did you see the forensics team at the caravan?"

"Aye." Paislee chose a paper plate and put a roll on it, splitting it open with a metal table knife. Nairn town hall didn't use plastic if they could help it, unless it was the recycled variety, such as garbage bags.

"What's up with that?" Meri murmured. "Could one of the fairground workers have killed Joseph?"

Paislee knew Meri could be trusted and put her finger to her lips before whispering, "Kev Sloane, the young man who intervened in the fight between Lachlan and Joseph on Saturday?"

Meri nodded. She piled turkey and Swiss on an open roll. "Black hair, tattoos, guid dancer."

"Yep." Paislee chose ham and cheddar, with a slice of pickle and shredded lettuce. "Kev was found with Gemma's stolen necklace and a knife that could have been used on Joseph. Fern's gold bracelet too."

Meri snapped her gaping mouth together. "Holy crow."

"Kev is in jail," Paislee said. "That's all I know. I told the constables about the meeting tonight, so I wouldn't be surprised if they show up—but maybe they won't, if Kev is their man."

"Why wouldnae he be?" Meri asked.

"I don't know." Paislee added mayo and flipped the top of her roll on the rest. Yes, it was a sad subject, but she was starving. She leaned against the counter. "Artie's having surgery in the morning. Of course, Rhona will want tae be at the hospital with Gemma."

"Does that leave you shorthanded?" Meri chose a bag of plain crisps.

"I think I'll be fine. Elspeth comes in at noon."

"Call me if you need any help," Meri said. "I'm actually free tomorrow."

"That is very sweet of you—I was thinking I might ask Mary Beth, but if you have the time, that would be great. Rhona will let me know in the morning—poor darling is rightfully scared that Artie might die. It's a very dangerous surgery."

"And then Kev would be in for two murders, which explains the activity at the caravan." Meri bit into her turkey and Swiss.

"What are you two whispering aboot?" Sandi asked. "Or is it a secret?"

"No secret," Paislee said. "I'm shorthanded at the shop and Meri has offered tae fill in."

Sandi's cheeks pinkened. "Sairy. It's none of my business, but Lachlan is giving me the cold shoulder, and I dinnae like it. Neither he nor Drake will talk tae me aboot the accusation that I shouldnae be on the committee anymore." She put two rolls on a paper plate and proceeded to make two sandwiches with ham, turkey, and provolone.

"Lachlan is obnoxious," Meri said. "Ignore him if you can. Drake is usually reasonable, but he did see what happened."

"He willnae let me explain. Dinnae forget what I told you aboot Lachlan and Dyana." Sandi chose a packet of sour cream and onion crisps. "They want tae oust you, as well as me, because of the duck-herding fiasco—which is really aboot Lachlan wanting tae charge for seating at the games."

Paislee sighed. Why couldn't people just get along?

"I appreciate the warning." Meri moved toward the rectangular table. Paislee followed her, and the pair sat down.

Any other private conversation would have to wait.

Paislee studied the others in the room. Donnie and Krissie both had food at the other end of the oval table. Donnie treated Krissie like he was too good for her, and Krissie acted like she didn't care, and yet, Paislee wondered if Krissie protested too much.

Lachlan and Dyana were talking as they each held a plate with sandwiches in their hands. The Lord of Cawdor was a nominal member and didn't come to the meetings, but Simon was his right-hand man, and had earned the teasing title of chief duck catcher.

Meri glanced at the clock on the wall. It was quarter till seven, so she had some time before she would call the meeting to order.

Paislee smiled at Drake, who happened to look up from his phone at that moment, and he smiled back. The convener had his own agenda. What might that be? Did he want the games to remain free or did he want to charge?

Simon, being such good friends with Lord Cawdor, would want to keep them free, for sure. There were nine people in attendance, assuring that there would not be a tie vote if it came to that.

Paislee would vote to keep the event free. It was nice to offer something in a world that seemed to grow more expensive all the time. She didn't have a personal stake in what Lachlan thought of her, and if pressed would go with Simon as the kinder man.

Drake had overheard Sandi and Joseph argue and wanted Sandi ejected from the committee, as did Lachlan. Paislee would vote to keep the woman, and there was no wiggle room in her decision.

Satisfied, she bit into her sandwich. She would vote as her conscience bade her and didn't care about the politics.

At seven, Meri stood and clapped her hands. "I'd like tae call the meeting tae order. Everyone, please take a seat. We have several topics tae discuss but most importantly is a recap of the Nairn Highland Games."

Dyana and Lachlan sat down, and so did Simon.

Meri remained standing as she greeted everyone around the table and stopped at Simon, who was this year's accountant. "Simon. I'm afraid tae ask, but how did we end up with sales?"

"They exceeded expectations." Simon gave a number that was an improvement by ten percent. "As you ken, this year the profit will fund the miniature golf course, something near and dear tae Lord Cawdor's heart."

Lachlan cleared his throat. "That is a drop in the bucket tae what the profits could be if we charged for seating outside the arena and upped the charge for permanent seats inside on the field. We could host tents where the individual clans could sell clan items and give a percentage of sales tae charity—I'd like it tae be split between the food bank and programs for struggling families."

Simon's gaze clouded with anger. "Lachlan, the answer was clearly told tae you, no, and I willnae budge. We are not charging."

"We should have a discussion," Dyana said. "A show of hands perhaps tae see if it's worthwhile tae bring it tae a proper vote."

Drake leaned back and rested his arm on the chair, eyes narrowed at Dyana.

Paislee wasn't surprised to see Dyana's hand raised with Lachlan's. Simon's mouth dropped.

Donnie's hand went up.

Meri, Sandi, Paislee, Drake, and Simon's hands stayed down.

Slowly Krissie raised her hand too. "I would be interested in finding oot more information regarding the pros and cons."

Meri gasped.

"Five tae four," Sandi said to Simon. "Not enough tae win."

"Why did you change your mind, Donnie?" Meri asked. "We are making a profit."

"It could be better, bigger," Lachlan said, overriding whatever Donnie might say. "Bigger and better helps the hotels and local businesses with tourism dollars. Nothin' wrong with that."

"Lachlan," Drake said in a very slow manner, quieting the chitter-chatter. "You are a member of the Highland Council, and it is your duty tae think of the common guid for all of Nairn, not just your pocket."

Lachlan's eyes narrowed. "I have Nairn's best interests in mind, always."

"And where would the lumber come from if we were tae build permanent seating, as you suggest?" Drake asked. "Your construction company?"

Paislee's stomach tightened. She was proud that Nairn had once been a royal burgh and had been since the twelfth century. The Highland Council oversaw certain assets and sales, but the folks of Nairn had rights concerning spaces that were deemed for the Common Good. She wasn't interested in being part of the council, but she kept abreast of the news—this was for Brody and his descendants moving forward.

She wasn't a fan of sneaky politicians, and Grandpa shared her views. The Highland Council, after being called out for trying to sell land for development that wasn't theirs to sell, had invited four volunteers from Nairn to be part of future meetings and to have a say.

"I would offer a discount," Lachlan said.

"It should be offered at cost, if it were tae happen," Sandi said.

"Cost?" Lachlan rolled his eyes. "And then my business would fold, because I couldnae afford tae pay my employees. Dinnae be an eejit."

"There will be no name calling, Lachlan," Meri said.

Simon leaned across the table from behind his accounting ledger. "Donnie, what did Lachlan promise you tae change your vote?"

Donnie jutted his chin. "Nothing," the bartender stammered.

"If he offered you anything at all, that is bribery," Simon said, his palm smacking the table.

"He didnae!" Donnie said again. "He painted a rosy picture of the future, but no promises were made. How could they be?"

"Exactly," Lachlan said.

"Krissie?" Simon asked. "Why did you profess an interest? You have a nice job at the Delphin Hotel."

"Information is never wrong," Krissie said. She glared at Lachlan and then sniffed, tilting her nose.

"I want tae put together a proposal for the Highland Council," Lachlan went on. "I'll go door tae door tae every person in Nairn and talk it up. We could be *the* Highland Games in Scotland—bigger than Inverness."

"At what cost?" Drake asked. His tone wasn't accusatory but thoughtful. "The beauty of our games is that we offer a small shire feel."

"I was talking tae Ross," Lachlan continued, "and he wondered what it would take tae make our amateur games a professional venue? Imagine the fees we could charge."

"The talent agent?" Donnie queried. He shook his head. "We caught Artie Whittle trying tae cheat for an amateur competition. Can you imagine the chaos of trying tae control the pros?"

"Artie Whittle says he didn't cheat," Paislee said. "He claims he was sabotaged."

"Why?" Krissie murmured. "He's no Cam. There's no chance he'd win, say, over Donnie."

Donnie shifted toward Krissie. "True. But Cam might've been using. I wouldnae put it past Joseph either. That man is cut. You dinnae get definition like that at forty-three from only hard work."

"We had a tip that there might be athletes doping," Sandi said to those who hadn't known.

"When?" Dyana asked.

"Before the competition." Sandi tapped her fingers to the table.

"Who?" Drake asked, legitimately mad.

"It was an anonymous tip, and they didnae say." Sandi shrugged. "It's a pet peeve of mine, and I have tae agree with Donnie. Joseph had tae be using steroids for a physique like that."

Meri stared at Sandi. "That is a verra serious accusation."

Sandi's cheeks turned bright red. "It is my professional opinion."

"Is that what you were arguing aboot the day of the games?" Drake asked the question that had been on the tip of Paislee's tongue.

"I'd warned him tae be careful, that we dinnae condone doping. Not accusing, but that's who I thought of after that tip the morning of the games." Sandi sipped from a glass of water she'd poured for herself. "He told me what he thought of me, and things escalated."

"Why would he have a bad opinion of you?" Paislee asked.

Sandi put the glass down. "I was the nurse on duty in the emergency room when his son Cam was brought in. I'd suggested they look intae the accident, but Joseph said he'd been drinking, and all accounts from his girlfriend at the time say he was pished."

"Why did you question that?" Meri asked.

"I wondered if he'd been using steroids. An abuse of the substance can cause rage and loss of control. He'd been winning big that summer, thinking aboot going pro. He was twenty. Remember, Donnie?"

"Aye, that I do," Donnie agreed. "He was verra well developed."

"He was training hard," Drake said. "Noticed myself when he was at Forge Fitness."

"Hard work pays off, but it's dedication and sacrifice," Sandi said. "I agree. Cam was that wee bit extra, as is Joseph."

"You wanted tae have tests done tae see if Cam had steroids in his system the night he died?" Drake asked, his brow arched in disbelief.

"Aye." Sandi shrugged, her tone bitter. "I was overruled. Joseph had Cam cremated within days."

"That's his right," Lachlan said. "I dinnae like the man, and now that he's dead, I willnae change my opinion. His son was dead, and knowing aboot the steroids wouldnae change that harsh fact."

"Can you overdose?" Meri asked. Her expertise was in the bagpipes.

"You cannae overdose *per se* on them," Sandi said. "But you might have a cardiac arrest or stroke. Liver damage. Rage. It's not right, and Joseph had tae ken. I wanted him accountable for his child."

Paislee found herself agreeing.

"Cam was an adult," Dyana said.

Lachlan blew out a breath. "Joseph might have pushed the rules regarding the competitions, which I dinnae condone at all. Like Sandi and Drake, I am antisteroids."

"Me too!" Donnie said.

"I agree," Krissie chimed in.

Dyana gave a nod. She and Joseph had been close—would she know if Joseph had been using steroids? Would she care?

Her morals meter didn't seem as high as the others in the room.

"I am all aboot healthy, organic living," Dyana said when the committee members looked her way. "It's my brand."

Paislee made a note on her mobile to ask Zeffer, no, Payne or Monroe, if they could tell whether or not Joseph was using steroids. He certainly had the rage and ill-temper down. Poor Gemma practically shook in her camp chair next to him.

"Let's keep focused on the agenda," Meri said.

"I want Sandi released from her duties," Drake said in a calm voice.

"What?" Krissie sputtered.

"She was overheard arguing with Joseph and using foul language. We have strict codes of behavior at a family event." Drake wasn't afraid to meet Sandi's gaze. "I ken you've been part of the games since you were a wean, but that is no excuse." His gaze landed on Paislee. "You heard this altercation."

"I did, and I disagree that it was cause for dismissal. Everybody has a bad day, and Joseph was at the root of most of these disturbances," Paislee said.

Drake seemed taken aback that she, a newcomer, would disagree with his pronouncement.

"I know the O'Connors very well, and they were not put off in any way. They were happy tae help with the toddler race, right, Sandi?"

"Right." Sandi nodded stiffly at Paislee. "I was so upset by the idea of someone cheating with steroids that I did lose my patience." She peered around the table, her gaze reaching each person. "I apologize sincerely."

"That works for me," Meri said. "Drake?"

Sensing that he wouldn't get a resounding agreement to boot Sandi aside, he shrugged. "Aye. Guess so."

Sandi didn't push. Donnie snickered.

"Do you have something you'd like tae add, Donnie?" Meri said. It was clear she wouldn't tolerate a bully. "You also had an altercation with Joseph."

The bodybuilder bartender paled. "I didnae do anything tae that man."

"What about tae Artie?" Paislee asked. "Somebody messed with his caber and the resin he used on his hands tae grip the log."

Krissie studied her phone as if very interested in anything but the conversation.

"Krissie?" Meri asked, noting where Paislee's attention had gone. "Do you ken anything aboot Artie's equipment?"

Everyone around the table burst out laughing at the inadvertent salty question that had many possible answers.

Meri cracked a smile. "You ken what I mean." But the laughter had lightened the air in the room.

Krissie glanced at Lachlan. Lachlan's mouth firmed, and he gave a single head shake.

"The police will be involved," Paislee said in a casual tone. "I mentioned that we were all here tonight if they wanted tae question anyone regarding the games."

"I saw Lachlan switch oot Joseph's hand cream that he had Artie use," Krissie squealed. "I'm not going tae cover for you—I dinnae owe you anything and I cannae be 'bought' like you've insinuated. I do not have a price."

"Everyone has a price," Lachlan said.

"Why would you switch creams?" Meri asked. "Artie is a young man who never did a thing tae you, Lachlan Felling."

He was the color of the begonias in Paislee's window box. "It wasnae personal tae Artie but as a payback tae Joseph."

Meri leaned over the table to look at Drake. "That is a legitimate reason tae fire someone from a volunteer position. Artie was sabotaged. That caber could have landed on someone and hurt them."

A chorus of agreements rounded the table.

"You cannae fire me," Lachlan said.

"I'll check the protocol," Meri said. "I'll be resigning as chairman once the year is up. This is a lot of work when you cannae rely on your teammates."

Shocked replies ping-ponged around the room.

"I'd rather have Meri stay on the committee than Lachlan," Krissie said. "Would you reconsider, Meri, if Lachlan goes?"

"I'm not going!" Lachlan said. "*Sairy*. Okay? It worked for Sandi. Let's move on."

"Sandi was sincere," Paislee said, before she could think twice about it.

Krissie applauded.

Drake's jaw clenched. "Can we discuss that later, Meri? As you say, we should get through the games and decide what tae do for next year. Sandi was up, right?"

"Being in charge of the volunteers means everything tae me. I love the Nairn Highland Games because of the community. I see folks pitching in where needed tae help." Sandi regarded Paislee. "The O'Connors were verra lovely, and Suz is going tae learn tae Highland Fling. For next year, I suggest getting volunteer T-shirts in smaller sizes as Suz swam in the adult small."

Dyana, secretary, made the notes. "Guid idea." She sipped from her tumbler of her healthy greens. "Paislee, what did you think of my juice? I can give you a discount if you order by the case."

"It's not for me," Paislee quickly said. "But it did give me energy, I'll admit."

"Before we get too far doon on Lachlan Felling's misbehavior," Lachlan said, "how aboot the fiasco that the duck-herding turned oot tae be? Ridiculous! That duck was gunning for Lord Cawdor."

Simon raised his hand in protest. "Hold up right there. Lord Cawdor was verra amused by it and not at all offended. If we vote tae keep the event, we should clarify sheep only, that's all. Meri, you did a guid job thinking of ways tae bring in more people, which equals more money for Nairn."

Meri's cheeks went rosy at the compliment. "My thanks. It takes a team." While Meri had overseen things, she'd delegated to make sure the event went smoothly. Drake, convener of the games, was in charge of the events and the speakers. Lachlan had handled setup as well as clean up, while Donnie had managed concessions. Krissie, water stations. Paislee trophies and ribbons. Sandi, volunteers.

It was after eight o'clock by the time they'd all shared their news. The atmosphere had calmed as the evening progressed. Meri did a brilliant job of keeping the topic away from Joseph's death.

Paislee had started to rise and leave for home when a knock sounded on the door.

Lachlan, closest to it, got up and opened it. "We're heading oot," he said. They had the office until eight and normally being a few minutes over wasn't a problem, as the cleaning crew came in after hours.

"Hi. I am Constable Monroe, and this is DI Zeffer. We had a few questions regarding the murder of Joseph Whittle."

Krissie sucked in her breath. "For real."

Paislee hadn't been sure but thought it worth the gamble to get Krissie to tell the truth, and it had worked. Lachlan had set Artie up.

Meri gave her a slight nod. She knew what they might say but would keep the information close to her chest.

Lachlan gestured to the interior. "Come in—would you like some water, or tea? Coffee? Dyana's organic juice?"

"No thank you," Monroe said. The constable was taking the lead and DI Zeffer stood behind her, observing with those intense eyes.

"Nothing for me either, thanks," Zeffer said.

"Sit doon," Monroe instructed Lachlan.

Lachlan returned to his seat with a speculative gaze. He was on the Highland Council and a businessman willing to risk innocent people to get back at Joseph. He had said he would never sell his cabers to a Whittle.

Why not?

Paislee understood Sandi's aggravation because of the possible steroid use. She was a nurse and had wanted to prove Cam's abuse of the drugs but had been vetoed by the doctor in charge. Joseph had said Cam had been drinking and driving. That was that.

"How can we help, Constable?" Drake asked.

"I have several reports that many of you had an argument with Joseph Whittle the day of the Highland Games," Monroe said. "Raise your hands if you had an altercation."

Sandi, Donnie, Lachlan raised their hands.

Dyana pointed at Krissie. "You did too."

"Joseph insulted me on the dance floor, Dyana." Krissie batted those fake lashes. "His problem, not mine."

"Lachlan defended you. Leland and Kev, the carnival worker, held Lachlan back," Dyana said. "Joseph wasnae worried." She glared at Lachlan. "Mibbe he should have been."

"I didnae hurt Joseph, your boyfriend. If anybody should have been called disparaging names, Dyana, it was you," Lachlan said. "Puir Gemma had tae leave early."

"Puir Gemma, is it?" Dyana asked.

Monroe cleared her throat. "Did any of you see Kev Sloane argue with Joseph one on one?"

"No. We were dancing, last dance," Krissie said. "He was that cute guy with long hair and tattoos, hanging oot with Fern, right?"

"Right," Dyana said. "Fern dated Cam back in the day." She leaned to Sandi. "I hear you, you ken, wondering aboot what might have been happening behind the scenes, but Cam was drinking verra heavy. It was no shocker that he'd gone off the road."

"What do you mean, behind the scenes?" Monroe asked Dyana. She squirmed under the spotlight. "It's nothing," Dyana said.

"Steroids," Sandi said, not hiding her accusations. "I was wondering if Cam Whittle or Joseph Whittle had been doping, even though it is against the rules of the competition."

Zeffer's eye twitched.

Paislee had learned that was never a good sign.

Chapter 10

Constable Monroe hummed and scanned her notebook. "You are Sandi . . ."

"Sandi Peckett. Retired strongwoman, emergency room nurse at Nairn Hospital. Volunteer coordinator for the Nairn Highland Games."

She didn't shrink away from the police officer's gazes.

"You confronted Joseph Whittle, verra loudly, aboot whether or not he was cheating, correct?" Monroe said.

"Correct. I have apologized tae the committee for losing my temper. I did not kill Joseph. I am a *healer*."

"Kev argued, Sandi too . . ." Constable Monroe looked up from her list at Lachlan. "Mr. Felling. You refused tae sell your timber tae *any* Whittle. Why is that?"

"They dinnae deserve the best," Lachlan murmured. "I . . . I played a prank on Artie Whittle and switched his tree grip resin with linseed oil."

"Why would you do that?" Monroe asked.

Lachlan squirmed. "Joseph and I have never gotten along," he said.

Dyana snickered. "Not since Joseph stole Gemma right oot from under your nose. A sweet church girl swept off her feet by hunky Joseph."

That made sense, Paislee thought. Poor Gemma. She probably regretted that choice every day.

"We had an understanding," Lachlan said softly. "Joseph had no regard for the Luckenbooth brooch she wore."

"Gemma gave it back, didnae she?" Dyana said snidely.

Paislee saw Zeffer take interest in this information. Dyana sounded jealous, and Lachlan had been jilted. Constable Monroe didn't mention Kev being in jail or how Joseph had been killed. Stabbed. Nor that Artie was in hospital and might die, needing emergency surgery. He couldn't tell his side of the story and might not ever be able to clear his name.

"There will be consequences for Lachlan's actions," Meri said with assurance to the police.

"Jail?" Donnie quipped. "The slippery caber almost hit Artie's mum. It broke and he said it hadnae been cracked. Guess I owe Artie an apology." The strongman flexed his biceps as he glared at Lachlan. "What else are ye up tae, ye doaty dobber?"

"I didnae kill Joseph," Lachlan said. "This is a volunteer position—you cannae fire me, and I'm not quitting."

"That's your stance?" Sandi was justifiably angry. "Different rules for you than me. So typical."

"Lachlan, you disregarded the spirit of sportsmanship," Donnie said.

"It willnae be tolerated." Drake smacked his hand to the table. "You certainly willnae be allowed tae profit from the games, Lachlan."

"I agree with that," Simon said. "Mibbe we should take a *vote*?"

His suggestion held heavy sarcasm that Paislee understood but Zeffer and Monroe wouldn't, so she'd explain later how Simon had been blindsided by Donnie and Dyana supporting Lachlan's idea to charge. Dyana and Lachlan had each been romantically linked to different Whittles, but now that Lachlan was under scrutiny for his actions, where did that put Dyana's loyalty?

"Let's stay on track." Monroe zeroed in on Dyana, next to Simon. "You didnae argue with Joseph but had a different relationship with him."

"I'm not married," Dyana said, hefting her chin.

"But Joseph is," Lachlan said. "Was, I mean."

"Now Gemma will be a free agent," Dyana said. "Still have that Luckenbooth brooch of your grandmother's?"

"That's verra cold, Dyana," Meri interjected.

Dyana reached for her tumbler of green juice, but it was empty, and her mouth thinned.

"Please answer the question," Monroe continued. "Were you having an affair with Joseph?"

"I wasnae the only one," Dyana said. She shook her empty tumbler. The woman loved her green juice.

"Answer the question—yes or no," Constable Monroe said. "Were you sleeping with Joseph Whittle?"

"Aye." Dyana's nose flared. "The man was a tomcat."

"Was he taking steroids?" Constable Monroe asked.

"Uh, Dyana, dear, should you be answering these questions so freely?" Krissie suggested. "Mibbe you want a solicitor or something. I see that on the telly."

"All the time!" Sandi seconded. "You sound verra jealous of Gemma. Did you kill Joseph, Dyana?"

"No! I dinnae have anything tae hide," Dyana said. Her eyes narrowed.

The idea of a solicitor made everyone squirm.

Constable Monroe glanced at the detective inspector with a practiced nod.

"We are in the middle of an investigation," DI Zeffer said calmly. "You can choose tae answer or not—we can always bring you intae the station, one at a time."

"Thanks, Krissie," Donnie said, shaking his head with disapproval toward her.

"What? I saw it on television. Never claimed tae be a solicitor myself," Krissie pouted.

"I'd like tae go," Donnie said. "I have a shift at nine tonight at the bar." He pushed back from the table.

"Mr. Weber, I have specific questions for you regarding your antagonism toward Joseph Whittle," Constable Monroe said.

"Fine, but I'll come tae the station. I dinnae need tae air any dirty laundry in front of these jokers. Tae be clear? I hated Joseph." Donnie jammed his thick pointer finger to the table. He didn't wear rings. "I'm not the only one and not just in this room. I heard the members at Forge Fitness cheered the loudest when they heard someone had finally done him in."

"Thank you everyone for your time." Constable Monroe wrapped things up. "Give me your contact information and then you're free tae go. What time tomorrow works for you, Mr. Weber?"

"I bartend so early morning isnae guid." Donnie scrubbed his bristly jaw. "Noon? I need tae be at the gym by two."

"Great." Constable Monroe smiled like a cat about to catch her prey.

Paislee gathered her bag and phone. Zeffer nodded at her but didn't make conversation or look like he wanted to talk to her, so she said goodbye to Meri.

"Let me ken aboot tomorrow morning at the shop," Meri said.

"I will."

"Can I get the door for you?" Zeffer asked. He passed her a note asking her to call him from her car.

A note, really?

And why did that make her insides flutter?

Silly, silly.

Paislee climbed into the Juke and noticed two calls from Grandpa. Thoughts of Zeffer and his note went out the window.

Grandpa answered on the first ring.

"What's wrong?"

"Och, Paislee, lass, didnae mean tae worry you—I was hoping

you'd pick up some honey on the way home. We're oot. It soothes my cough."

"Of course!" Paislee exhaled. "I'm so used tae texting these days that a phone call worried me. How are things at home?"

For the second year of secondary school, Brody would be allowed to stay up until nine thirty instead of nine, with TV for thirty minutes in his room, then all electronics off. Up at seven thirty, with school at nine. She liked a routine.

"We're watching a movie which will be done by nine," Grandpa said. "How'd the meeting go?"

"I'll tell you about it when I get home. I could use your logic regarding what happened tae Joseph Whittle."

He chuckled. "This old mind is happy tae help."

"Sharp mind," Paislee corrected. "See you!"

Zeffer tapped on her driver's side window, and she gasped in surprise, then rolled it down. "Everything okay?" he asked. "You seem worrit."

"Aye—Grandpa needs some honey for a cough—what's up?" Paislee found herself noting the details of his handsome face. No freckles for Zeffer but smooth skin. Brows arched over intense eyes . . .

Zeffer asked, "What did you think of the committee meeting tonight?"

"It was a lot of drama. I'm glad you and Constable Monroe were there. You have quite a few people of interest. For myself, I'm curious about whether or not Joseph had steroids in his system."

A smile flitted across Zeffer's mouth but didn't stick around. "Of course you are. And, yes, there were steroids in his system."

"What about Artie's?"

"Clean as a whistle."

Paislee's shoulders relaxed. "Artie is innocent." She glanced at him. "He's having surgery in the morning."

"I ken. We still have an officer on guard duty at the hospital."

Zeffer stuck his hand in his pocket. "Just hope Artie doesnae die before he can give his version of what happened."

"Hey! I will keep him in my prayers," Paislee countered.

"If that makes you feel better, then there is no harm in it." Zeffer's eyes glittered, and she sensed he was teasing her. "Angus still has that cough?"

"Aye. He refuses tae go to the doctor. Well, we made a deal that if he is still coughing next week, he'll go."

"He's a stubborn one," Zeffer said. "How did Brody survive his first day of school?"

"A cheeky fifteen-year-old has been watching him play football, and her sister, seventeen, offered tae drive Brody home. I said no. He hates me." Paislee tapped the steering wheel. "He's taller than me now."

Zeffer chuckled. "That's a tough age. I'm sure you'll handle it just fine though."

"I pray every day that I don't mess it up," Paislee confessed. "Did you hate being thirteen?"

"It was different for me. I had a tutor, because I worked."

"What?"

Paislee's phone rang—Grandpa.

"I have tae go," she said, her curiosity on fire. What kind of work did Zeffer do at thirteen? She'd probably misunderstood.

"Drive safe, Paislee." Zeffer patted the top of the Juke and stepped away.

"I will," she told Zeffer and answered the phone. "Grandpa?"

"Paislee—could you pick up some lemon too? A fresh one would be guid, but the container will work." Grandpa coughed and tears welled in Paislee's eyes.

"Not a problem." She hung up and tossed her phone in the cupholder. When she checked her windows, Zeffer was gone, but Dyana and Lachlan were conversing. Was Dyana hoping to find another lover now that Joseph was dead? Not her problem.

Paislee stopped at the market and lucked out with a lemon that had wrinkled skin, but she hoped it would be okay.

Zeffer had a tutor? He'd worked as a teenager? She knew his father had been in the fishing industry but had died young. Determined young Mack Zeffer had become a detective because of the mystery surrounding what had happened. She had a lot of respect for him and so many questions.

Paislee texted Lydia about Zeffer before driving home. Her bestie might know more details, as she'd sold him her flat. Once in the Shaw house, it was chaos, as Wallace and Snowball greeted her so rambunctiously that she tripped and banged into the wall.

"Just call me Grace," she chided herself.

Brody came out from the living room area. "You okay, Mum?"

"Aye. Klutzy here too."

"Mibbe it runs in the family," Brody said.

"Sorry about that," Paislee teased back. It seemed he'd decided to let the teenager driving him home go, thank goodness. "Where's Grandpa?" She brought the honey and wrinkled lemon to the kitchen.

"He just took a shower. The steam helps his cough," Brody said. "We checked it oot online. Who needs a doctor these days?"

"Brody, don't even think that solution is okay. Doctors provide important health checkups and medicine when we are sick."

"Lay off, Mum." Brody slung his arm around her. "I was just kidding."

"Sorry." Paislee side hugged him back. "It's been a long day. How was school?"

"Lame. Me and Edwyn have different lunches, but the worst is Mr. Buckle."

Paislee ran through the names of his teachers for this year. Brody would have math, English, Spanish, science, and social studies, technology, and several electives. School was only mandatory until the age of sixteen though she would push for a higher education. "The science teacher?"

"Aye. He wants us tae keep a science diary." Brody appeared horrified as he slipped from her hug. "Diaries are for girls."

"Who told you that?" Paislee shook her head. Where on earth did Brody get these notions?

"Everybody knows that."

"Well, everybody would be wrong. Besides, I don't have a diary. What is the purpose of this science diary?" Paislee went to the washer-dryer combo and took out a load of towels to fold at the kitchen table.

"We have tae study how we use energy every day." Brody wrinkled his nose. "I'm not going tae worry aboot it until tomorrow."

"Is that what Mr. Buckle instructed?"

"We dinnae have tae start until the morning, but we would get extra credit if we did it tonight."

Paislee searched for Brody's backpack by the table or in the lounge but didn't see it. "Doesn't your coach want you tae excel in your grades this year? That means doing the extra credit."

Brody scowled but then exhaled loudly. "Fine." He'd hung his backpack on the special peg Lydia had created in the foyer for their things and went to get it, dragging it back to the kitchen table as if it held rocks.

Grandpa emerged from his bedroom, his damp hair combed back, glasses on, in jeans and a sweatshirt. "What's that racket?"

Paislee chose another soft towel, folded it, and added it to the stack on the chair. "Brody is doing extra credit for science class."

"Arenae diaries for girls, Grandpa?" Brody asked.

"Not that I've heard," Grandpa hedged. He noticed the honey and the lemon. "Thank you, lass." He walked to the electric kettle.

"We have tae do a science diary for how we use energy every day for a whole week."

"This is using energy," Grandpa said as he flicked on the switch for the kettle.

Brody pulled out a notebook and sat at the table. A piece of paper dropped to the floor. He wrote down electric kettle for tea before picking the page up. "Thanks, Grandpa."

"And turning on the telly," Grandpa continued.

"Folding towels is energy," Paislee said. She folded the last one and put it on the top of the stack.

"We use energy in all of our actions," Grandpa said.

"Cool! Mr. Buckle said that if we're guid in class we can use the science lab."

"That sounds fun!" Paislee said. "Don't you think?"

"I guess." Brody put down his pen. "I just like football."

"What else do you like?" Grandpa asked. He washed and sliced the lemon, and put a teaspoon of honey into an empty mug.

Paislee got out a Raspberry Zinger herbal tea bag and a giant cup. "Just in case the football thing doesn't work—what would interest you for a career?"

He shrugged. "Edwyn will get tae have the comic book store. He likes tae draw and design video games. That's not really for me."

It surprised Paislee that he'd given this some thought. The electric kettle clicked off and Grandpa filled their mugs. They sat at the table with Brody.

Snowball jumped into Paislee's lap for a pet. Wallace whined, because he wanted up too, so Grandpa scooted his chair back enough to pick up the terrier.

"Can I write that everything takes energy and be done with it?" Brody asked.

"That might save your hand from getting a cramp," Grandpa teased.

"What do you like besides football?" Paislee persisted.

"I dinnae like tae play music, but drama might be fun. I am not dancing either. Computer programming is all right. It's like a secret language. Me and Sam are both guid at that."

Computer programming was a versatile skill that was very marketable. "Maybe we can get you a new laptop if you do well in school."

Brody's eyes lit up. "A gaming laptop?"

"One for programming," Paislee said.

Brody jumped up and gave her a hug. "Brilliant!" He sat back down, still smiling and confident that he'd succeed.

"What is that piece of paper?" Paislee asked.

Her son opened it and his smile widened. "Sam invited me tae laser tag on Sunday, for his birthday."

"Where?"

Brody passed her the invite. "In Inverness. They've got the outdoor games. We'd talked aboot it before but didnae go. Cool that he gets tae for his birthday! Can I go?"

"Sure." Paislee scanned the page for the pertinent details: name, location, and time. "Think of what you want tae get Sam for a gift, and we can pick it up on the way. Also, I'm going tae invite Aunt Lydia and Uncle Corbin over for dinner on Monday night. I miss them." Party from two to four thirty, with burgers and cake.

"All right. We just saw them on Saturday though." Brody grinned. "Uncle Corbin played football when he was my age too, did you ken that?"

"I didn't!"

"We had a chance tae catch up the day of the games, since I'd hurt my knee. He's awesome."

"Aunt Lydia and Uncle Corbin think you're pretty great too." Paislee was thrilled to have Brody's extra credit sorted. It was no easy job to be a mum, but it was worth it to see Brody's smile.

The next morning Grandpa was sleeping when they left. After dropping Brody off at school, Paislee arrived at Cashmere Crush, with a text from Rhona that Artie was still in surgery; the night had been touch and go over whether the doctor felt confident that Artie was stable enough.

Paislee opened the shop and then texted Rhona to take the day off if she wanted.

Her phone rang. Rhona.

"Hey, hon, how are you doing?"

"I am a wreck. Gemma is a mess and praying with the chaplain at the hospital right now. Ross has been with us this whole time, making sure we have food and tea. He's broken up aboot the whole family. Aibreann is here too. We need our best friends but Gemma doesnae have one. Isnae that rotten? I'll let you ken once he's oot of surgery." Rhona paused to take a breath. "I think it's best if I'm here, if you dinnae mind."

"Not at all!" Paislee looked around the shop, which was in good shape, in case it got busy, as it would be just her until Elspeth arrived at noon. She had the blanket to work on and smaller projects that were simple to set aside.

"Thanks, Paislee." Rhona sounded tense. "You're sure it's okay?"

The shop was swept every day at least once and the shelves dusted. Paislee would handle whatever came next.

"Don't worry about a thing—I will add my prayers tae yours." Maybe Gran could be a guardian angel during Artie's surgery. Paislee sent up a plea heavenward.

"Thank you. I'll call you back—the doctor is here."

Not five minutes later, Paislee received an all-caps text.

ARTIE SURVIVED THE SURGERY!

Chapter 11

Paislee sent a prayer of thanks and then put her fingers to work. Meri stopped in, which was a good thing, as Paislee had been slammed since the doors opened at ten. Meri was familiar with the store and handled the register just fine.

There was a joyous atmosphere in the shop thanks to Artie's survival.

"Thank you for coming," Paislee said, as she walked a customer to the door. She straightened a shelf of scarves and tams, noting that she'd need to replace a lightweight cardigan as soon as possible. Possibly a project she could work on while the boys played laser tag in Inverness—no, she had the yellow afghan to finish.

She'd set a reminder on her phone for three thirty so that she'd pick up Brody at four, needing to adjust to the not-summer-any-more schedule.

Rhona and Aibreann arrived at eleven in high spirits, coming in through the back door.

"I borrowed Mum's car," Aibreann said. "Tae help Rhona today. I just need tae pick her up at three."

"What does your mother do?" Paislee asked.

"She's a primary school teacher," Aibreann said. "She loves teaching the little ones, and it gives her time tae teach dancing lessons, her other love. Mum and Letti Cornwall are mates from their neighborhood and totally support each other. Letti prefers the older kids, and for Mum, it's always been the weans."

Paislee had met Letti at the Nairn Highland Games, where she'd been a judge. The woman was fortyish and knew the dances inside and out. Her cheery personality was a natural match for teaching dance.

"I'm trying tae convince Letti tae hire me," Rhona said, "so I can pay off my mum faster. She willnae budge aboot the car and doesnae understand how serious things are with Artie. Or worse— she doesnae care."

"Petra loves you!" Paislee said. Rhona, while sweet, tended to be dramatic. "If you *do* get a position with Letti, just let me know and we can move the schedule around. Amelia will be finished with school in another few weeks, but she might not want her Saturdays back." She sighed and patted Rhona's shoulder. "I need two of you."

Aibreann slowly raised her hand. "I would love tae work here a few days a week—I could only do part-time though, because I'm helping Mum at her studio, and I waitress at the Lion's Mane."

Paislee immediately nodded. "I think that might be just what we need. Rhona gets her forty hours first, and then Elspeth has eighteen, and Grandpa has eighteen—we will keep our options open. I think being a teacher is a wonderful idea, especially if dancing is what you want tae do with your career."

"I wasnae sure before, but things are clearing up for me, because of Artie and my parents," Rhona said. "I need tae be independent, and that takes money."

"My granny taught me that and encouraged me tae open Cashmere Crush. Knitting was my skill, rather than dance, and I took business classes. I sold online at first and then moved tae this building. I lucked out with the location becoming available. Gran signed on with me for the first year and I've carried the lease on my own ever since."

"Your gran sounds amazing," Aibreann said.

Paislee swallowed over the lump in her throat. "She was."

Meri rang up a customer with yarn and a pattern book. After the customer left, there were two ladies browsing, so Meri gave Rhona a quick hug. "How are you?"

"Terrible," Rhona admitted. "Thanks for covering for me this morning. I would have stayed at the hospital, but Gemma suggested that I go. She promised tae call if anything changes with Artie."

"Not a problem," Meri said. "Did I overhear that you teach dance, Aibreann?"

"Tae little kids, so it's more like making sure they dinnae hurt themselves in their ballet slippers," Aibreann joked.

Elspeth arrived at noon with her customary friendly greetings to everyone.

"It's busy," Meri said. "I can stay until two, Paislee."

Paislee nodded her thanks.

"I'm on until six," Elspeth said. "How's Artie?"

They caught her up as Paislee calculated the hours Meri had been working to give her cash under the table.

Rhona's phone dinged with multiple notifications. She scanned them quickly.

"I never learned how tae knit," Aibreann said. "Is it hard?"

"No," Meri said. "This is the perfect place tae learn. I find it soothing and something tae do with my hands."

"I like tae read tae relax," Aibreann said. "But sometimes I dinnae have the mental energy tae concentrate, so knitting seems like it might be a fun alternative."

"I'll show you," Meri said.

"Please do!" Paislee said.

"Fern is coming here, her and Delilah," Rhona said. "Is that okay? They want tae see how Artie is doing, but he isnae allowed visitors. She was at the police station."

"It's fine." Paislee gestured to a high-top table off to the side.

"Why don't you get comfortable there?" It was out of the way as much as it was possible to be so.

"You're the grandest!" Rhona smiled at Paislee.

"These are extenuating circumstances," Paislee said. "It's really all right." She was curious as to why Fern had been at the station herself. Had the police wanted to question her about Joseph?

Paislee didn't have long to wait, as Fern, followed by Delilah, entered the shop. Her second question was wondering what they all did for work that left them free to roam Nairn.

"Rhona! Aibreann!" Fern said.

The young women all exchanged tearful hugs.

"How's Artie?" Fern asked. Her eyeliner was expertly swooped.

"Alive, and that's all I ken," Rhona said with a sniff.

"Why were you at the police station?" Aibreann asked.

"Tae identify my bracelet that Kev stole. Can you believe it?" Fern sounded shocked. "He is in jail. They think he killed Joseph Whittle."

"We heard that too," Rhona said. "It's better than believing Artie could have done it!"

"I have a hard time imagining Artie standing up tae Joseph," Fern said. "Kev wanted me tae give him an alibi for Sunday night, but the last I saw him was Sunday around five. We grabbed a burger—he gets tae eat for free at the fair—and then me and Delilah left tae hang oot with Leland and Jason."

"Can I offer you anything tae drink?" Paislee asked. "I have Perrier or tea."

"No thanks, Paislee," Fern said. "Is it all right that we're here?" She perused the shop, but Meri and Elspeth were handling the customers. "We willnae stay long."

"Not a problem," Paislee assured the young lady. "Did you see Kev?"

"Nah—he's in custody," Fern said. "But you ken who was at the station? Donnie. Him and Krissie."

Donnie had had an interview at noon, Paislee recalled. Maybe

Krissie had gone for moral support. She'd seemed a little squirrely, so maybe it was more.

"Separate interview rooms," Delilah noted. "Mibbe they are-nae so sure that your boyfriend did it," she teased Fern. "If they are still asking questions."

"Kev isnae my boyfriend," Fern said, not amused. "We had some laughs—and then he stole my bracelet, so it's not like I care if he languishes in jail. He totally used me."

"He had Gemma's necklace too," Rhona said. "He was inside the Whittle's house."

"A thief!" Fern tilted her chin. "And a killer."

"Yep. You ken how tae pick 'em," Delilah said, elbowing her friend.

"Back off, Del. Your guys are no better."

"You dated Cam," Paislee said, bringing the subject back around to the young man who'd been on her mind.

"That's right," Fern said. "Why?"

"Gemma brought up his girlfriend Chantelle," Paislee said. "She said how you would never have let Cam drive if he'd been wasted. You would have taken the keys."

"Gemma never liked me when I was with Cam, but she's right, I would have swiped them and hidden them." Fern dabbed her lashes to stop the tears from falling and ruining her makeup.

"She knows that now," Paislee said.

Fern blinked quickly and fanned her eyes.

"Better late than never, eh?" Delilah clapped her hand on Fern's shoulder with commiseration.

"I realize Cam had a wild reputation, but he loved Artie," Fern told Rhona. "He'd be sick aboot what's going on."

Rhona squeezed Fern's hand. "Artie knows his brother was no saint, but that was still his big brother, no matter what."

"I remember Artie when he was just a wee bairn—it took a while before he grew, and other kids would tease him. Cam would-nae have it," Fern said. "He protected him, in his own way."

"I was an only child," Paislee said. "I used tae wish I had a brother or sister."

Aibreann laughed. "I'll loan you one of mine! There's six of us in our family."

"I'm an only," Rhona said. "But there are a lot of Smythe cousins, so I've never really felt lonely."

"I have an older sister. She's great now, but when we were in secondary, it was awful. We would have literal hairpulling fights over clothes and makeup." Delilah shuddered.

"I had Lydia, who was like a sister. The best of both worlds, I am realizing," Paislee said.

Fern's phone vibrated and she read the message. "What should I do aboot Kev? He wants me tae loan him money."

"No!" they all chorused.

Fern rolled her eyes. "Got it!"

"He is guilty of murder," Rhona stated. "I ken it wasnae Artie."

"They have a guid case—Kev was in the house, he had Gemma's jewelry, and he was seen in the neighborhood by a nosy neighbor." Delilah patted Fern. "Not tae mention your bracelet. It's best tae walk away. You have the biggest heart, Fern. Too big! You cannae save everyone."

"You're right." Fern brushed her hands together. "I wonder if we should just wait at the hospital for news?"

Rhona showed Fern her phone, which was not leaving her side. "I'll let you ken as soon as I hear anything. I promise!"

"Patience is a hard quality tae endorse," Paislee said. "I'm concerned too, but let's just keep the Whittles in our prayers as we move on with our day."

"I have tae work anyway," Delilah said. "My shift at Tesco starts at four." She told Paislee, "I manage the produce section."

"I'm at the register," Fern said. "It's not glamorous, but we get tae pick our hours, which matters for dance competitions. I'm off until tomorrow."

"Hey, do you know how tae get in touch with Chantelle?" Paislee asked. "I'm curious if she'd tell us about that night when Cam died."

"It was a long time ago." Fern brought out her phone and scrolled social media. "Cam's page is still up. I loved him, so yeah, I check it oot every once in a while." She glanced at Delilah. "Dinnae judge!" She showed Paislee a picture of a very built Cam Whittle and a tiny doll of a woman with bleached blond hair and big green eyes.

"She's so little!" Paislee said.

Rhona looked, then Aibreann. "Oh—I saw her on games day. I only remember because she was so petite but with that great hair. She was talking with Donnie."

Donnie knew Chantelle? And hadn't he also been at the party that fateful night?

Delilah nodded. "Chantelle hangs oot with Krissie sometimes at Forge Fitness. She's a gym rat. She likes that green juice garbage Dyana makes. Lives on it probably."

"I tried it," Paislee said. "It tastes . . . like herbs."

"Seaweed!" Meri said, as she heard the direction of the conversation.

"Nailed it!" Delilah gave Meri a high five.

"Well, we're oot of here," Fern said. "Please let us ken right away, Rhona, if you hear anything. I will too, for you."

Delilah and Fern left the shop. Aibreann continued with her knitting lesson. "I'm buying an easy pattern," Aibreann announced. "I can make scarves for Christmas gifts and that will save a bundle. I have a holiday budget that I always blow, but not this year—thank you Paislee and Meri."

"You're welcome!" Meri said.

Paislee grinned.

"Budget?" Rhona said. "I dinnae ken anything aboot a budget. I get an allowance. Well, I did, but now . . . I feel kinda foolish."

"You aren't," Paislee said.

"Nope!" Aibreann agreed. "You were raised with money, and I wasnae. I learned quickly that if I wanted something, I had tae work for it, that's all. We had no extras with six kids. Mum was verra glad tae go back tae work when Maisie went tae school. As a teacher, she has summers free, like we did, so it was wonderful."

"Your mum is great," Rhona said.

"Yours is too, just . . . different, right now. You were always so guid that they didnae have tae discipline you." Aibreann nudged her. "It's their fault for buying you a fun car."

"I've promised Mum that I willnae ever speed again." Rhona's mobile rang. "It's Gemma!" Her face paled as she answered, "Hello?"

Aibreann, Paislee, and Meri drew closer to the phone, letting the customers fend for themselves.

"Okay," Rhona said.

"What?" Aibreann asked.

Rhona put the mobile on speaker.

"Artie is still resting, but he's doing much better," Gemma said. "No visitors, of course. I see that Fern has tried tae call. She's a dear."

"She stopped in at Cashmere Crush—she sends her best wishes tae you and tae Artie," Rhona said.

"Sweet lass, so much kinder than Chantelle." Gemma inhaled loudly, as if sipping air through clenched teeth. "No matter. I just wanted tae let you ken that I'm going tae the hotel tae rest for a few hours. The police have a guard here. Not sure tae protect him from harm or if they really think he's going tae rally from the hospital bed and escape."

"Not likely," Rhona agreed.

The handcuffs had only been on the first night.

"I've got tae run—talk tae you later, lass." Gemma ended the call.

Paislee rubbed Rhona's back as the teen blinked away tears and focused on Aibreann with the knitting needles and a simple pattern.

"I'm going tae learn tae knit too," Rhona declared.

"It's been a life-saver for me," Paislee said. "How lucky for me that my staff all knits!"

"Except for me," Elspeth said. "I can, but I prefer my needle-point."

"What's that?" Aibreann asked.

Elspeth showed her.

"Also giftable." Aibreann winked. "I'm thinking holiday."

"Guid tae plan ahead," Elspeth said.

Paislee loved that knitting and crafting crossed age groups and economic circumstances so easily.

At two, Paislee gave Meri an envelope of cash and her immense gratitude. "Thank you!"

"It was fun tae do, so anytime—I mean it," Meri said. "I might put my hat in the ring for the occasional Saturday."

"You could be sorry you offered," Paislee warned.

"Never!" Meri gestured for Paislee to walk out the back door where her black SUV was parked next to Paislee's and Aibreann's mother's Fiat.

"Thanks again," Paislee said, standing on the back stoop.

"Any word from Zeffer or the constables?" Meri murmured.

"No. It was interesting that Donnie and Krissie were both being interviewed, in separate rooms, at the station. I wonder what they told the police?"

"They didnae seem tae ken anything last night, did they? I thought for sure Donnie had messed with Artie's caber and the resin, but it was Lachlan." Meri palmed her keys and skipped down the last step. "That was a shock."

"It was. I saw Dyana and Lachlan talking for a while in the car park after the meeting, and it made me very curious. I didn't get at-traction vibes. Did you?"

"No," Meri said.

"Could be they're talking about a side business of some sort. They are both entrepreneurial, so that would make sense."

Paislee heard Zeffer in her mind saying, with a tsk, *speculation*.

Meri waited by the door of her SUV. "Hopefully, this will be wrapped up by next Tuesday, and our committee meeting can put who murdered Joseph—not at the games, thank God—off the agenda." She sighed.

"You did a wonderful job, you know. Lord Cawdor told Simon he was impressed."

Meri smiled. "He was being kind, but it felt guid, I willnae lie especially since Lachlan hoped I'd fail. The walloper."

"But you didn't. Are you sure you won't run next year for chairman?"

"I dinnae want it, Paislee. It's too stressful. I'd rather expand my commitments with the Piping Association."

The cheating during the last bagpipe competition had been over the top with bets and side bets galore. "That's saying something."

"I love Nairn, and so I will always serve in one capacity or another." Meri put her hand on her heart.

"Hey, I know!" Paislee said. "You could run against Lachlan for the Highland Council position."

Rather than laugh it off, Meri's eyes narrowed. "That's not a terrible idea. I could help change what's wrong at the foundation."

A knock sounded on the metal threshold behind them. "Paislee? It's Constable Monroe," Rhona said.

"Phone?" Paislee asked, turning toward her employee.

"No, here." Rhona lowered her voice. "She's not so chatty. Constable Payne is with her."

Paislee nodded and shifted back to Meri with a wave of her fingers. "Bye!"

"Guid luck," Meri said. She climbed into her vehicle and started the engine.

Paislee stepped inside, keeping the back door open for the fresh cooling breezes. The constables were shoulder to shoulder by the register. She stifled disappointment not to see russet hair and a fitted blue suit.

"Hi! How can I help you?"

Monroe gestured to the back room and away from the front of the shop. "Can we talk in private?"

"Sure—sorry it's so crowded." There was a restroom to the right, as well as an oversized armchair that she and Brody used to both fit on, and a small refrigerator for cold drinks. A wee telly perched on top. A tea station with an electric kettle was on a skinny shelf that barely fit. The left side stored bins of yarn and shelves stocked with cleaning supplies. It might appear cluttered, but she knew where everything was at.

"Not a problem," Constable Payne said. He'd trimmed down since she'd first met him but was still a solidly built man. He stepped back to let Constable Monroe take the lead.

"You might recall from last night's committee meeting that we wanted tae interview Donnie Weber," Monroe said.

"Yes."

"What a piece of work—but we learned that he'd suspected Joseph Whittle of doping. DI Zeffer said you were aware of the situation." Monroe tapped her stylus to her tablet.

"I am. I also know that Artie tested clean."

"True," Payne said.

"We've asked Gemma aboot Joseph's usage of steroids, but she claims tae ken nothing, which I find hard tae believe." Monroe shrugged.

Paislee hated to condemn the woman who had been through so much. "It's *possible* that Joseph only did it while he was away, on his delivery route tae and from Romania."

Constable Monroe thinned her lips. "We have a field agent interviewing folks along Mr. Whittle's route."

"We havenae found a doping kit," Payne said. "Though his body had marks from recent applications of the needle. It could be he abused them only while away from home, though not likely."

"Do they make you"—Paislee paused until she found the right word—"high?"

"Not exactly. They can affect mood over time. A common side effect is lack of libido, but that doesnae seem tae be the case for Joseph. The amount of steroid in his system suggests he took a large dose before he was stabbed." Monroe watched Paislee's face. "Did you see any equipment in the kitchen? Like a needle or syringe?"

"No. No knife either."

"Okay," Payne said. He seemed disappointed. "We had tae let Kev go. The knife in his possession belonged tae the Whittles, but it wasnae the knife that stabbed Joseph."

"Can you OD on steroids?" Paislee asked, trying to understand.

"It is possible tae OD on steroids, but it is verra unusual. Too many steroids might lead tae a heart attack or a stroke. We talked tae Sandi Peckett at length. If she wasnae so helpful, she might be a suspect." Constable Monroe's dry tone suggested a hint of gallows humor.

Payne cleared his throat. "Gemma Whittle has had a lot tae bear. Sometimes *the spouse* has reached the point of enough."

"Gemma?"

"We are crossing everyone off one at a time," Monroe said.

Payne was more conversational, probably because they'd known each other longer. "We cannae prove that Kev Sloane killed Joseph Whittle. It's possible, but we dinnae have actual footage of him inside the home. The timing of the neighbor seeing the skateboard— in this instance, hoverboard—is off slightly. A solicitor would toss the case aside. We must look at the spouse and the family, Gemma and Artie. What if they hatched a plan together tae take the 'bully' oot?"

"I am so-o-o sairy," Aibreann said, leaning against the threshold of the break room and shop. Her expression conveyed her discomfort at interrupting. "But I have tae return my mum's car that she let me borrow."

Paislee kept her arm folded to her stomach as she digested this information. The constables made room for Aibreann to pass between them.

"Thanks, Paislee," Aibreann said. She gave Paislee a hug, glaring at the police officers. "You arenae in trouble, are you?"

"No!" Paislee laughed. "Not this time, anyway. Drive safe and let me know if you need any help with your knitting project."

Aibreann hefted her chin with narrowed eyes and then hurried down the stairs to her mum's car, driving away perfectly, as the police were watching.

"Aibreann would have been verra upset with us if you were in trouble," Payne chuckled. "You've gained another admirer."

"She's a sweetheart and learning tae knit. She might fill in sometimes if I need her tae be here." Paislee blushed. "The offer stands for you both as well. I'm happy tae teach you tae knit—it's very relaxing."

"No thank you," Payne said.

"You sound like Grandpa!"

"Mibbe," Monroe said. "After the case is over."

"All right," Paislee said. "I don't know if this matters or not, but we found out that Gemma blames Cam's ex-girlfriend, Chantelle something, for not taking Cam's keys that night at the party."

"It would've been guid if someone had, but it's not her fault—it was Cam's," Monroe said gently. "For getting behind the wheel."

"I know that. Gemma does too, but she's trying tae find reason in this awful situation. Did Donnie mention being friends with Cam?"

"No," Payne said. "Why?"

"They were at the same party that night, is all," Paislee said. "Were you aware of the incident when it happened? I don't recall hearing about it."

"Inspector McCleod mentioned the car accident tae us when he heard the Whittle name. He said it had seemed a verra open-and-shut case—driving while intoxicated and crashing intae a tree. Joseph Whittle didnae press and seemed content tae leave it," Payne said.

"There was a note in the file from the old inspector, who is now retired, aboot the vehicle being on a straightaway rather than a curve, as Joseph had reported. Cam must have passed oot and gone off the road at full speed. The story obviously struck a chord for him tae have mentioned it."

"Why would Joseph lie about that?" Paislee asked.

"Perhaps there was more tae the night Cam died than meets the eye," Constable Payne suggested. "Secrets that died with Cam."

Chapter 12

"I wonder what Gemma and Artie remember of that night?" Paislee rubbed the back of her neck, which tingled with apprehension.

"We cannae ask Joseph Whittle, he's deceased. Gemma 'doesnae remember' and is concentrating on her only son's survival. Artie is unconscious. Touching base with Chantelle might be a guid direction," Monroe said.

"Fern could help you too." Paislee's phone alarm went off with the sound of a blow horn. "Brody!"

Payne noted the time. "School's not oot for another twenty minutes."

"Yesterday, I forgot him," Paislee admitted. "My head was in summer hours."

Monroe made an "oops" expression. "Makes me like you more, Paislee, tae think that you are human like the rest of us."

"What do you mean?" Paislee asked. To her mind, she was constantly juggling and falling short of the mark.

"You just seem tae have your act together more so than most," Payne said in a diplomatic tone.

Paislee's face flamed with heat, which equaled cherry red. "Has this been a topic of discussion?"

"Amelia brags aboot you," Monroe explained. "And your skills as a mum."

Paislee's shoulders relaxed at the innocent explanation. "That's sweet. Hers wasn't the best example." In fact, Letitia Henry made Paislee's mum Rosanna seem like an angel.

"Also, a fair point," Payne said.

"She's almost done with police training," Paislee said.

"Two weeks tae go. She's working verra hard," Monroe said. "I'm proud of her. She has the grit tae overcome obstacles, which will make her an asset tae our team."

"I could not agree more," Payne said. "I realize you're in a time crunch. What do you think of Donnie?"

"He's arrogant and thinks highly of himself. He's intae body-building as much as the others at the games. He knew Cam. I wonder if kicking up information about the night Cam died would bring clues tae light for what happened tae Joseph?"

"We've discovered a gym culture here in Nairn," Constable Monroe said. "I was unaware of it."

"Donnie is dedicated tae his physical prowess when it comes tae strength and diet," Paislee said. "All-natural. He didn't like Joseph and didn't care who knew it, so probably not devious enough tae have killed him. I think it had tae do with the doping aspect of the sport. He works hard for his physique, and his admiration of Joseph was tainted by it. He mentioned Cam too, as not being trustworthy."

Monroe nodded. "That's our conclusion also. Krissie and Donnie were both at Forge Fitness, a twenty-four-hour gym, on Sunday, early Monday, and then they went tae Donnie's flat together. Validated on CCTV."

They were each other's alibi. Paislee had seen them flirty the night of the games, but other than that, they had been like two cats in a bag. Obviously, that was just for show.

"I didn't get tae know Krissie as well as the others, but she's strict with her diet and health. She even drinks that organic green juice of Dyana's." Paislee's nose wrinkled at the memory of the awful taste.

"Not a fan?" Payne chuckled.

"It's reminiscent of seaweed, as Meri pointed out." Paislee shivered. "For all I know, it might be one of the ingredients."

"Krissie is going tae be the spokesperson for Dyana's juices," Payne said. "As a side job, in addition tae her clerking at the hotel, until she reaches the ancient age of thirty and will turn tae coaching rather than competing."

Thirty felt ancient, so Paislee could commiserate. "Doesn't Krissie care about Dyana and Joseph messing around?" Paislee asked.

"Krissie said, and I quote, 'It's none of my business who she hooks up with,'" Monroe murmured softly.

"Makes me feel even worse for Gemma." Paislee noted the time. "I really do have tae run."

"All right—thanks for your insight," Payne said. "I think we can move Donnie and Krissie, and Kev, doon the list of who killed Joseph."

Which meant Artie stayed at the top. Monroe moved through customers toward the front of the shop, Payne at her heels. It wasn't right.

"Bye, now," Monroe said to Paislee, including a wave at Rhona and Elspeth. Constable Monroe was thawing.

The officers left and Paislee said, "I'll be back after dropping Brody at home. Call me if you need anything."

Rhona was helping a customer at the register, but Elspeth called out, "See you!"

Paislee phoned Lydia while she drove to pick up Brody to invite her and Corbin for Monday night pizza.

"Hey, Paislee," Lydia said in a cheerful tone. "And what can I do for my favorite yarn artiste?"

Paislee chuckled. "I'm hoping you'll be free on Monday night, for pizza. You've been gone so much this summer that I miss you."

"Yes! I've been meaning tae talk with you aboot something anyway. Also, I've been thinking aboot Rhona's lack of direction, and I wish I could help her more. Corbin suggested that I butt oot—in a nice way, of course."

"You're so thoughtful, Lydia."

"So, my idea is tae help Brody, my godson, be the best he can be," Lydia continued.

"A star footballer? Do you have connections in the club?" Paislee made the turn into the school car park. "He's also considering a backup intae computer programming if his kick doesn't make him famous."

"That's brilliant," Lydia said. "Should I buy him a new computer?"

"No, you should not—he's thirteen and could change his mind a million times between now and graduation." Paislee arched her brow at the dashboard, not that Lydia could see her.

"You're no fun," Lydia said. "I saw a sale on laptops. Mibbe for Christmas?"

"How much?"

"Seven hundred pounds."

"It's a good thing I've been so busy at the shop, and Ramsey Castle. I can swing that without putting it on the credit card. If that's a good direction, Lydia. I don't want you tae spend that much. I will do it."

"It's just money. I'm really proud of you, Paislee," Lydia said. "You deserve a vacation."

"Vacation?" She hadn't been on a vacation, other than weekend trips—well, ever.

"What do you think aboot joining us in Germany for a week?"

"Em, er, no?" Panic filled her at the thought of leaving Nairn at the drop of a hat. She had responsibilities.

"Why not?"

"I have the shop tae run, a child in school, and . . . and if we go anywhere, it's probably going tae be Arizona next summer."

Lydia burst out laughing. "You have got tae take care of yourself. Brody is thirteen now, and it's time for some self-care."

"I will put it on the list," Paislee said, for when Brody was eighteen.

"I ken that tone. You're going tae ignore me and my excellent advice."

"Possibly." Paislee smiled at how well her friend knew her.

"Well, how aboot a new bike for Brody? One of the electric ones that can go really fast. He could take himself tae school and back. That would give you more time and freedom."

"Lydia! I like picking him up from school. We have a routine."

"Forget I said anything. Oh, as for Zeffer's wealth? I dinnae ken it's origin, but I think he's made savvy decisions in the real estate market."

Paislee could see that. He was very smart, and the tragic death of his father had made him an incredible detective. "I'm here at the school. Let's talk later, okay?"

"Love you!" Lydia said and ended the call.

Brody hopped in, his backpack at his feet. "Hey." He closed the door and buckled up.

"Hi! How was your day?" Paislee smiled at him before joining the queue leaving the school.

"Long. I dinnae like Spanish. My tongue doesnae do the trilling thing that makes it sound so cool. Mibbe I should take French."

"Well, you chose Spanish because so many great football clubs are there, so it would be a useful skill. Maybe you can learn tae roll your *rs*? We can practice."

"All right." Brody proceeded to make a raspberry sound that cracked them both up.

"How was Mr. Buckle?"

"It was guid that I'd done the extra credit—people who had it done, didnae have tae take a quiz." Brody's hair had been styled for school like one of his football heroes, Stuart Armstrong. Paislee had just been happy he'd been willing to get it cut.

"Awesome!"

"Mr. Buckle clapped his hands when I told him that 'everything' we do is energy, like folding the clothes." Brody smirked.

"Then he wanted tae ken the different kinds of energy—as if I was that smart."

"You are smart!"

"Not Einstein smart," Brody assured her. "When I said that, Emma laughed. She's really cute and sits next tae me in class."

"Emma, huh?"

"She's new this year and doesnae really ken anybody, so I told her I'd sit with her at lunch tomorrow."

Paislee glanced at her son. "That's really nice of you, honey."

By the time they reached the house, Brody was still chatting. Paislee would hate to miss these conversations, which wouldn't happen if he had a bike to ride.

"I'll see you guys for dinner," Paislee said, as Brody exited. He raced inside the house and out of sight. They had a routine that worked.

"And back tae the shop," she muttered aloud, patting the dashboard of the Juke. Eddie had given the SUV new brakes and a tune-up two months ago, and the car rode like a dream. It would be a good car for Brody when he got his license at seventeen, if he was interested.

She'd wanted freedom too. Her dad was gone by then and her mum distracted. Her first car had been a junker, but it got her around.

Parking in the back of Cashmere Crush, Paislee went inside the shop. Elspeth was taking a tea break as Rhona swept the front. The single customer was paging through a pattern book and didn't seem to be in a hurry.

"Hey!" Paislee said, putting her handbag on the shelf below the register.

Rhona smiled and finished sweeping, walking to the back room to put the dirt in the bin. "Hi!"

Elspeth lifted her tea mug. "And how is Brody?"

"In a good mood—a different boy than yesterday," Paislee said.

"I'll take it." She put her hand on Rhona's shoulder. "Any word?"

"I talked tae Gemma, and Artie is resting, which is the best thing for him after the surgery." Rhona sighed and touched her scalp. "They had tae drill intae his head tae alleviate the pressure."

"When do they think he'll wake up?"

"It's different for everyone, so it's just a wait-and-see kind of thing. On another note, Aibreann offered tae train me with the little girls tonight so that I can gain experience until Letti decides on my application," Rhona said. "I'm nervous. What if they dinnae like me?"

"How old are they?" Elspeth asked.

"Five." Rhona put the broom away.

"That's such a precious age," Paislee said.

"I remember when Mary Beth's girls were five—I cannae believe how much they've grown this past year." Elspeth sipped from her tea.

"Anna and Iona were very sweet, so I think you'll be okay." Paislee sat down and took a breath. "Suz was a cutie too."

"What did the constables say?" Rhona asked. "It must have been important for them tae come here."

Paislee considered what she could share with her crew. "They aren't sure that Kev's stolen knife was the one used in the . . ." *Stabbing.* "Crime."

"Which means they're back tae suspecting Artie?" Rhona shook her head. "That's as messed up as thinking Gemma might have something tae do with it. They asked me aboot where she was and the last time I'd seen her. Gemma said they'd called the hotel tae check that she was there on Sunday. She's still staying there and doesnae want tae sleep at home."

"Due diligence," Paislee said.

The door opened and two ladies walked in.

"Welcome tae Cashmere Crush," Rhona said.

"I have a question aboot this pattern," the reader said.

"I'd be happy tae help you," Paislee replied, walking to the woman with the pattern book as Rhona assisted the others. Elspeth, break over, went to the register. It was nonstop until closing time.

Paislee was able to catch her breath Thursday evening for her Knit and Sip night. Lydia had made a smoked salmon and avocado fromage to spread on whole wheat crackers and to be paired with a German chardonnay.

"Amazing," Mary Beth declared as she swallowed a dainty bite. Instead of wine, she had lemon Perrier. "I'll want this recipe, Lydia. I ken Arran will love it too."

"Sure," Lydia said. "Found it in my magazine, and the picture sold me."

"What a treat!" Meri said.

"I'd also like the recipe," Elspeth seconded. "It's so light and refreshing."

"I'll bring it next Thursday," Lydia promised. "Meri, what is the latest for the Nairn Highland Games?"

"Simon said it was the biggest yet. We made enough of a profit tae pay for the miniature golf course Lord Cawdor wants tae build." Meri sipped her whisky and then put it back on the floor by her feet, picking up her cardigan project she was knitting in a vibrant aqua blue. "We will vote on Tuesday whether or not tae keep the dog-herding event."

"Meri got special praise from Lord Cawdor, through Simon, for her efforts," Paislee said, outing her friend.

"It's nothing," Meri said, her face turning red.

"It's a big deal!" Paislee insisted.

"Will you stay on the committee then?" Mary Beth asked.

"I dinnae think so." Meri shrugged. "It's a lot of drama that I just dinnae have the energy for. And even though Joseph didnae die during the games, I feel like it's connected tae them." Her tone was sad. "Joseph wasnae a nice man, but he's still dead. His son Cam is dead, and Artie might be guilty of snapping—for a guid reason? Artie was physically and verbally abused by his father, yet he should've left rather than kill him. Murder isnae okay."

"I don't think Artie is guilty. I wish he'd wake up and clear his name," Paislee said. "Elspeth, Mary Beth, do you remember anything about the car accident Cam died in two years ago? I don't."

"Not a peep," Elspeth replied.

"Me either," Mary Beth said.

"Sandi said that Joseph had Cam cremated right away. There was no chance tae do any tests on him, tae see what was in his bloodstream. Joseph's body was loaded with steroids." Paislee knitted on the blanket of cheery yellow, but for once, the color wasn't working to raise her mood. She was worried about the Whittles, and Rhona.

They ended the night with Lydia promising to bring the recipe the next Thursday, and Meri offering to help out on Saturday, with Elspeth. Everyone agreed to keep Artie in their prayers.

Another Sunday Funday had arrived. Paislee had been up all night listening to Grandpa cough. It hurt her to hear him, and it had been so bad that she'd gone down and knocked on his door to wake him up. After a hot steamy shower, Grandpa had been able to breathe and went back to sleep.

Brody's laser tag wasn't until two, so Paislee also grabbed another few hours of rest. She was up at eight, as was her grandfather.

He had large bags under his eyes, visible behind his glasses. "I dinnae think I'm up for going tae Inverness with you today."

"That's fine. I will work on my blanket project while the lads have fun shooting each other." She chose the last banana which was on the edge of too ripe. "After breakfast, let's go for a ride."

"Where tae?" Grandpa asked suspiciously.

"The clinic."

"No, I'm—"

"Don't you tell me that you're fine! We've done this your way, and it's not getting better. You can't sleep, which means that I can't sleep." Paislee hated to pull the guilt card when she really just wanted him to get well, but he'd left her no other options.

His chin jutted in a manner she normally saw from her son, the beard thick and full though silvery white.

"Please, Grandpa. For me."

His shoulders braced and then eased. "Fine."

"Thank you." Using her mobile, she looked online for the clinic's hours while she finished her tea. "We can go at nine which will give me time tae come back and get Brody ready for Sam's birthday party."

"What can the doctors do?" Grandpa asked. "You think they can perform miracles when that isnae how it works."

"They are physicians and will make you better." Paislee bit her tongue about miracles, but medication had been just that for many people.

Grandpa finished his breakfast and went to his room, perhaps pouting a wee bit.

Paislee passed his closed door on her way to the stairs and called, "Fifteen minutes!"

He didn't answer, but Paislee wasn't giving up. She brushed her teeth and twisted her hair in a clip, washed her face, skipping make-up, as she hoped she wouldn't run into anyone she knew. It was early on a Sunday, so chances were good she'd be in the clear.

Grandpa was in the foyer waiting for her, exuding unhappiness from his pores. He didn't speak.

That was fine. He could talk to her when he could draw a breath without coughing.

They arrived at the clinic at nine. He didn't get out.

Paislee reached across the console to touch his arm. "Grandpa, what is it you have against doctors? This is more than being stub-born."

Grandpa glanced at her, then down at her hand, which she hadn't moved. "We never went tae the doctor, that's all. You went tae the doctor when you were dying. I'm not dying," he said in a low whisper. "I have things tae do yet."

Her heart broke, and she patted his forearm matter-of-factly, so she didn't start to cry. "You have something in your chest is all. Let's go find out."

"My da had lung cancer," Grandpa said.

Paislee slid her hand to his and squeezed. *That* was the root of his fears. "I'm very sorry."

"What if that's what's wrong with me?" Grandpa finally met her gaze.

It could be a legitimate reason, but she prayed it was just an infection from his slip in the river. "Let's go in together," Paislee suggested. "We can be each other's support."

"All right."

Cancer had stolen Gran, and she couldn't let it take Grandpa too. She thought of Dyana's organic juice and wondered what they could add to it to make it taste better—it was so mossy green that it had to be healthy.

They walked into the clinic and Paislee checked Grandpa in. He had to fill out paperwork, but they were seen right away by a female doctor of about sixty years old.

"Mr. Shaw! And what brings you in today?" Dr. Lewis had dyed red hair, copper-colored glasses, and a welcoming manner.

"My granddaughter," he said gruffly. "Thinks I need tae have you poke around."

"He was fishing and slipped, tumbled intae the river," Paislee explained. "He has a cough that won't go away."

"When was this?" Dr. Lewis brought her stethoscope from the pocket of her white medical jacket.

"Four weeks now," Paislee said.

"All right." The doctor listened to Grandpa's chest. "I can hear the congestion."

Grandpa did his best not to cough, but he couldn't help it. He looked worn out, and Paislee wanted to cocoon him in her finest cashmere until he was healed.

"Let's get some bluidwork tae be sure, but I bet you have bacterial pneumonia, which can be treated with an antibiotic," Dr. Lewis said. "You should feel better within three days. We can also try a nebulizer tae help with those painful lung spasms."

"I dinnae have tae go intae the hospital?" Grandpa asked.

"No. Well, not unless it gets worse." Dr. Lewis shook her finger at Grandpa. "Please dinnae wait so long if you're not feeling right—there is no need tae suffer," she chided.

Paislee didn't say, *See, I told you so*, though she sure thought it. They made an appointment for a follow-up and picked up the prescription for an antibiotic and a cough syrup that soothed much better than tea and honey.

They were home by ten thirty, just as Brody was waking up. Snowball and Wallace raced down the stairs first, and Paislee let them out the back into the garden.

Her son came down next, his hair was all mussed from sleeping on it after a shower.

"Morning!" Paislee rummaged through the pantry for a muffin mix that she only had to add egg to and it would be ready in minutes. "Hungry?"

"Starving." Brody noticed the medicine on the table and then looked at his great grandfather, reading the paper. "You caved, Grandpa."

Grandpa handed over the comics, focused on the business section. "It was important tae your mum, so I went along with it."

"Hey!" Paislee said. Grandpa placed the sales section at the spot she liked to sit for her to read later.

"What's wrong with you?" Brody asked.

"Pneumonia," Grandpa replied. "No big deal."

Paislee rolled her eyes. "It was a big deal."

"I'm glad that you went." Brody sat down and read the comics.

"Ta, lad." Grandpa kept reading the paper, but she heard the love in those two simple words.

Paislee quickly whisked the mix together and poured it into a muffin tin, just as the stove beeped to let her know it was at baking temperature. She put it in and set the timer, then topped off Grandpa's tea as she made herself a cup. Brody had juice.

She noticed an advert for a laptop and wondered if the price was as good as what Lydia had sent her yesterday. She could save for it if Brody had an affinity for computer programming. There'd been no updates in the paper about Joseph Whittle's death.

It didn't make sense to drive home twenty minutes after dropping Brody off for the party, so she'd bring the blanket and yellow yarn to work on while she waited for him. She could run into Tesco and get a few things for school lunches, as her Brody didn't always care for what was being served in the cafeteria. The muffins smelled tempting, and she quickly got them out when the timer went off, setting them to cool.

Brody glanced up from the comics and pulled his mobile from his shorts pocket. He read the message. "Edwyn texted—can he get a ride tae Sam's party with us?"

Paislee brought the muffins and plates to the table. "Of course! We should probably get Sam's gift before we pick up Edwyn. Do you know what you want tae buy for him?"

She was friends with Bennett Maclean, Edwyn's da, but not as close with Ryan's folks, or Sam's, though they were friendly from the football practices.

"He wants a new football," Brody said. "Edwyn's giving him a video game, which is way better."

"If you're getting him something he wants, that's cool too," Paislee said. She went through the ads and enjoyed the berry muffin. Grandpa had one. Brody ate three.

"I'm still hungry," Brody said.

"Eat some cereal," Paislee said.

"I hate cereal."

"Porridge?" Paislee queried.

"Fine." Brody went to the pantry and got out the box of Weetabix.

"You could have a piece and jam," Grandpa said.

"I had the last of the orange marmalade for a midnight snack. Oh, I ken—I'll make a crisp sandwich," Brody said, eyes bright.

"We don't have crisps." Paislee cringed at the idea of sour cream and cheddar crisps stuffed between two pieces of buttered white bread. She didn't understand the popularity of potato between bread.

Brody exhaled like it was Armageddon and proceeded to pour cereal into a bowl. "It's not fair. Can we get some crisps for lunch this week?"

Paislee mentally added it to the list of items to buy at Tesco. "Ham or turkey for lunches, but I'll buy some for at home."

"Thanks, Mum."

"Grandpa? Can I get you anything?"

"I'm fine, lass," her grandfather rumbled.

And this time, Paislee believed him.

Chapter 13

Paislee got up early that Monday morning to make her son's lunch. He planned to sit with Emma, who brought her midday meal from home. He'd asked her to make him ham, cheese, and tomato. She'd also bought his favorite sour cream and cheddar crisps as a treat. Two chocolate biscuits, and an apple.

Brody came down for breakfast and let the dogs out back before sitting at the table, pouring cereal into a bowl. His polo shirt and black trousers for school were brand new, as he'd grown so much over the summer.

Her examination paused at his bruised face. Brody had a legit black eye this morning from yesterday's adventure. She'd hoped it wouldn't leave a mark.

"You look like you've been in a fight," Paislee said.

"It's so cool!" Brody added milk and fresh berries.

The boys had had so much fun playing laser tag in the outdoors that he hadn't complained, and Paislee didn't notice anything wrong until he'd showered the dirt off and was ready for bed. It was not an intentional hit, but he'd tripped and fallen over a log. The tag game with lasers should have been safe but his feet were awkward, as was his balance, unless he was on the football field.

"Makes me look tough," Brody said with a grin.

Paislee had worried he'd be upset—thinking like a lass, according to Grandpa—but Brody didn't mind the least. He'd evaded being laser tagged to survive and win the game, which was worth the epic bruise.

What a story!

The door to Grandpa's bedroom was closed and the paper not brought in yet. Paislee hadn't heard him cough last night, so hoped he was mending. She left the paper on the kitchen table as Brody fed the dogs, and then they got into the Juke for school.

When she dropped Brody off, a cute girl with brown hair and eyes was waiting for Brody, with Ryan and Sam. Was that Emma?

The car behind her in the queue honked, so she had to stop gawking and go.

Arriving at Cashmere Crush, Paislee quickly readied the store for customers, hoping for another busy week. August was traditionally a splendidly busy time for tourists, and Paislee had been getting more word-of-mouth customers every year.

There were just two more rows of her blanket to finish, and she could ship it off. Unlocking the front door and stepping out to check the flower boxes, full of blooms, she greeted James Young, the older man who owned the leather repair and gifts shop. She'd bought Grandpa a belt and a wallet for his birthday in May and had her eye on a handbag in the window.

"And a fine morning tae you, Paislee," James replied. "I read in the paper aboot Joseph Whittle's death and Artie Whittle in the hospital. How is Rhona holding up? He'd seemed like a nice young man."

"Artie is, James. What's happened is tragic." Served her right for not reading the paper this morning.

"Isnae he a suspect, then?" James asked. "Though I had tae admit that the lad I'd met didnae seem like the kind tae stab his da."

"They are investigating." Paislee heard the shop phone ring and waved goodbye to James. "I'll keep you apprised of news, but maybe don't mention anything tae Rhona? She should be here any minute now."

"I willnae," James assured her.

Paislee hurried inside and leaped for the landline on the counter by the register. "Cashmere Crush!"

"Is Paislee there? It's Gemma Whittle. I've been trying tae call Rhona, but she's not answering her mobile." Gemma's voice was strident.

"She should be here by ten," Paislee said. "Is everything all right?"

"No. It's not going verra well. The article in the paper this morning practically accused Artie of killing Joseph. It's not true!"

"I haven't read the paper." Normally that was how they started the morning, but Grandpa had slept in, and the paper remained rolled up.

"I'm quite disappointed in the Nairn Police. I've called that Constable Monroe tae let her ken how I feel aboot their disrespect tae our family."

"I'm so sorry," Paislee said.

"I am too. I've given the guard on Artie's door a lecture as well, but he's simply following orders. Artie's hardly even been awake for long, and he's not likely tae bolt," Gemma continued.

"Is there anything I can do?"

"Well, I hate tae ask it of you, but Ross has offered tae pick Rhona up from your place, so I have company. He's been staying with me here at the hospital, but he's got work tae do. He's spent all weekend here and been a real rock. I ken it's an imposition, but I am afraid for Artie if I'm not here every second—and what I might say tae the police if left on my own."

"I will let her know that you've called and have her call you. It's fine with me."

"I dinnae have my mobile. The battery is dead. I'll call back at ten. I'm a mess, Paislee. A pure awful mess."

"Do you knit or crochet?"

"What?" Gemma's tone suggested Paislee was speaking another language.

"It's just that I find it relaxing tae have something tae do with my hands when I'm stressed. I can send yarn and needles with Rhona."

"Oh, no—no, that's sweet. I never picked up the skill."

Paislee didn't push and say it was never too late, when it was obvious that Gemma was on her last bit of patience.

"I'll call back at ten," Gemma said.

"Okay, then." Paislee was speaking to a dial tone. It was only nine thirty, so she pulled her blanket project from her bag and concentrated on another row, getting halfway by the time Rhona arrived.

Rhona wore a stormy expression as she entered the shop.

"Good morning," Paislee sang.

"My mum is the worst," Rhona said. "On my break, I'm going doon tae the police station and give them a piece of my mind. The paper practically blames Artie for Joseph's death."

"I haven't read it yet," Paislee admitted.

Rhona raised her hands and exhaled. "Let me start over. Guid morning, Paislee. It's not your fault that I've been arguing with my parents since breakfast. Because it's in the paper, it must be *true*."

"I'm sorry, sweetie. Gemma called looking for you—she asked if she could send her friend tae pick you up and sit with her at the hospital. She read the paper too, and she's very angry."

"Is that all right for you? This is your busiest time of year, you said." Rhona placed her handbag on one of the shelves in the back room.

"It is, but I can manage." Paislee wondered if Meri would be available just in case she got slammed. "It sounds like Gemma could use some emotional support."

"You are so kind," Rhona said. "Who is coming?"

"Ross—he has tae work, so can't take any more time off tae be there. It's too bad she doesn't have any other friends." Paislee thought of the rude woman who'd said Gemma shouldn't be allowed to work at the front desk for being too sad.

"Gemma says it's her own fault for not making more of an effort, but she is just so tired all the time. I bet she's depressed. I feel terrible aboot leaving you again Paislee, but Gemma must be in an awful jam if she's asking for help."

"I agree."

"Oh!" Rhona shrugged off her cute backpack and unzipped it, pulling out a small bag that had Paislee's name on it. "For you, as a thank-you."

"Now, who is being thoughtful?" Paislee peeked inside the bag and pulled out a silver bracelet with a ball of yarn charm.

"Do you like it?"

"I love it." Paislee put it on. "Thank you. Hey, how did dance class go, with Aibreann's weans?"

"It was great. I really, really hope that Letti hires me," Rhona said. "I can make a decent living as a teacher. Not that Mum seemed impressed when I told her the salary, but I could pay my own bills doing what I enjoy."

"You are a bright young woman and will figure it out. You've grown so much since I've known you." Paislee's gaze dropped to the cup of pens and crochet hooks by the register, and the business card for Constable Monroe. "You could always call."

Rhona pocketed the card. "I just might! Let me cool off first." She got a can of Perrier from the fridge.

The front door opened at five till ten, and Meri walked in. "Hello, my friends. I thought I'd stop in tae see how things are going."

"Did you read the paper?" Rhona said with a sniff.

"Aye," Meri admitted.

"Terrible, but Gemma called and asked Paislee if I could hang oot at the hospital with her, so I'll get tae lay eyes on Artie for myself. I havenae seen him since the surgery."

"Why not?"

"No visitors," Rhona said.

"I'll stay and help, Paislee, if you'd like?" Meri offered.

"I would, actually. You were quite good."

Rhona sighed. "I feel so much better tae not leave you in a lurch. Thanks, Meri."

The shop phone rang, and it was Gemma.

"It's all arranged," Rhona told Gemma. "I'll wait ootside for Ross."

"Give Gemma and Artie my best wishes," Paislee said. "Just text me tae let me know what is going on, and if you'll be out for the whole day."

"Okay!"

The teen left, and it was nonstop customers. Grandpa arrived at noon, his color much better after just one day of medicine.

"You look guid, Angus," Meri told him.

"I slept all night," Grandpa said. "Amazing what medicine can do."

Rhona returned at two with a huge grin. "Artie woke up, and we got tae visit for a few minutes—he doesnae really remember anything, but the doctor says that's normal, and his memory should return shortly."

"When will he be oot of hospital?" Meri asked.

"Not for a while yet. Gemma went back tae the hotel tae sleep and rest now that Artie is oot of the woods."

"What a scary time," Paislee said. "Doctors can be miracle workers, right, Grandpa?"

"I suppose so," he conceded. "Dr. Lewis knew her stuff."

Meri left at two thirty, with another envelope and Paislee's thanks. "Dinnae forget the committee meeting tomorrow night. We should be wrapping up the season."

"I'm ready for my Tuesdays back," Paislee said, though she hadn't minded too much. Somehow, she was able to finish the blanket and prepped it in a box to send to the customer.

Two online orders came in for cashmere jumpers, customers from Ramsey Castle. The influx of money was welcome.

"Should I come back after dropping Brody off?" Grandpa asked.

"Nah—you can stay home too, if you'd like. Maybe tidy the kitchen? Lydia and Corbin are joining us at six thirty for pizza. I ordered watermelon ice cream cake from Scoops that I'll bring home."

"I'm looking forward tae seeing them," Grandpa said. "Now that I'm feeling better. They were away for a lot of the summer."

"I know. Lydia says she wants tae talk with us about something, and it seemed serious. I hope I'm reading it wrong."

Grandpa left and it was just her and Rhona until six. Rhona picked up the ice cream cake from Scoops on the corner and ran it back to Cashmere Crush to save Paislee a trip. It had been a summer special that she couldn't wait to try.

"Thank you, Rhona," Paislee said. "You need a ride home?"

"Nah, Aibreann is picking me up and taking me tae the dance studio. I had so much fun with the weans that I'm doing it again this week. I have an interview with Letti next month."

"Really great."

"They are so cute, but a lot of work. I cannae imagine having kids of my own."

"It's a choice tae make when and if you're ready. You don't have tae—Lydia and Corbin don't want bairns of their own, which is lucky for Brody. He gets extra spoiled."

Rhona's phone dinged. "Aibreann is five minutes oot. I'll meet her in the front."

"How was Gemma? We haven't had a chance tae talk."

"Exhausted. I think she's not sure if her own son actually killed her husband. I ken Artie is innocent. It's like Gemma is afraid tae believe all the way."

"She's had so many disappointments."

"Still," Rhona shrugged. "I asked her aboot Cam too. You're right aboot the disappointments. He wasnae verra nice tae her at times, and neither was Joseph. Her and Artie were close. *Are* close!"

"I imagine it would be too much tae bear if Artie turned out tae be a killer," Paislee said, putting herself in Gemma's shoes.

"He's not." Rhona hugged Paislee. "See you tomorrow." The teen went out the front.

"Thanks again for the bracelet!" Paislee locked the front door and went out back to the Juke, which wasn't there. Grandpa had the car.

Well, that plan had gone awry.

Paislee went back inside and called Grandpa. The pizzas would be delivered to the house, so she was the only one to need a ride, with the watermelon cake, before it melted.

No answer.

She called Lydia, who did. "Paislee! What's up?"

"I'm at the shop and would like a ride tae my house. Can you swing by?"

"Yes, of course. Mibbe it's time for a second car?"

"We don't need a second car—I need a working brain," Paislee said with a self-deprecating laugh. "It's been so busy that I literally forgot. It sucks tae be over thirty."

"We are not old," Lydia replied. "Corbin is driving separate from me, so I'll be there in five!"

"Why?"

But she was talking to silence. Better than a dial tone.

Lydia was there in five minutes as promised, and Paislee hurried down the back steps to climb into her little sports car, balancing her handbag and the ice cream cake.

"Hey, bestie!" Lydia said with a grin.

"Thanks for rescuing me," Paislee said. "Again. Where were you?"

"I'd just left the estate office. I had tae sign papers with Zeffer. Ooh, is that shaped like a watermelon?"

"It tastes like it too. Zeffer?"

"Yum! He's a client. I just sold him a piece of property that he's thinking he'd like tae build on someday. I would love tae ken how he's made his money, but he's verra tight-lipped."

"Wouldn't you have his banking information?"

"He pays via money transfer." Lydia gave a happy sigh. "So, dinnae be mad, but we may have a gift for Brody."

"Something from Germany? You guys spoil him, and all of us."

"It's not that, but I cannae wait tae see Brody's face! I'm not going tae give you any hints, since you shot doon the idea of a bicycle so quickly. I'd rather apologize later," Lydia said. "Giving gifts is the best."

What did Lydia have up her sleeve that she would need an apology? "You are an amazing gift giver."

"It's my love language. It doesnae have tae be expensive, but I have nothing against it. Money is wonderful."

"Yes, it is!" Paislee agreed, grateful that she had more this year than ever before. She worked hard for it and was glad to be able to provide for Brody.

"How's your mum?" Lydia asked.

"We are taking things slow and steady, but she's been good about following through with Brody. He really does want tae go tae Arizona over the summer."

"Would it be so awful? I wasnae kidding aboot you needing a vacation, my friend."

They arrived at Paislee's house. Corbin's giant SUV was there, the back hatch open with gift-wrapped poles.

"What on earth?" Paislee said.

"Just wait! You'll be so surprised. Trust me!"

Paislee exited Lydia's car, grabbing her handbag and the cake. It was now six twenty, and the pizzas would arrive in ten minutes.

"I do, Lydia. I do."

Lydia shouldered her handbag with a loving smile. They entered the house and went straight to the kitchen. Corbin, Grandpa, and Brody were all talking, the mood festive. Wallace and Snowball were outside on the back porch.

"Hey!" Paislee said. She put the cake in the freezer.

Lydia tilted Brody's chin. "How did ye get that incredible shiner?"

Paislee studied the bruise which was a dark plum color. "How does it feel?"

"It doesnae hurt." Brody shrugged and stuck his hand in his shorts pocket. He'd changed from his school clothes to summer attire. "Emma kissed it tae make it better."

Paislee gasped. "She did?"

Lydia chuckled. "Who is Emma?"

"New girl at school." Brody blushed.

"Is she cute?" Lydia persisted.

"Verra!"

And forward, Paislee thought, but kept to herself. "She's the girl with brown hair that was waiting for you this morning?"

"Yep. Were you spying, Mum?"

Lydia and Corbin both burst out laughing.

"Busted!" Lydia said.

At six thirty, the doorbell rang, and Paislee went to answer it, expecting pizzas.

Zeffer stood on the stoop, holding a gift bag from a video game store with Brody's name on it.

"Oh!" Paislee's emotions ran the gamut from surprise at seeing Zeffer in jeans and a polo the same seafoam-green as his eyes to an unfamiliar hunger at how well he filled out those jeans and the polo, followed by curiosity as to why he was there—sure it had to be a mistake, but she didn't want him to leave.

Zeffer studied her closely. "Is it okay that I'm here? Mibbe I should've called."

"It's fine," Paislee said, hating that her cheeks had to be twin crimson flames.

Brody had run behind her. "Is the pizza here?" He saw Zeffer and maintained his smile. "Hey!"

"Happy birthday," Zeffer said, offering Brody the gift.

Brody didn't take it. "Uh, it's not my birthday, but you can stay for pizza anyway. We ordered four larges."

Lydia walked down the corridor to where Paislee and Zeffer waited on the porch. Zeffer scuffed his heel uncomfortably.

"Hey!" Lydia said. "Glad you made it."

"The gifts?" Zeffer pointed to what was in the back of Corbin's SUV.

"That's a surprise for my godson." Lydia's mouth twitched as if she was holding back a smile. "Paislee, Brody, I hope you dinnae mind that I invited a dinner guest?"

What was her bestie up to? Was this what she'd wanted to talk about?

"If you dinnae mind?" Zeffer asked. He glanced at Paislee and then Brody.

"Nope. There's a ton of food and watermelon ice cream cake." Brody looked toward the street. "There's the pizza guy." He raced down the steps.

Zeffer's gaze glittered with humor. "Cake, pizza, and gifts, but not a birthday?"

"Yeah." Paislee stepped back, bumping into Lydia behind her. "That's how we roll."

Brody had all four of the pizzas and rushed them inside, while Lydia followed him. Zeffer wore a very confused expression and stayed with Paislee on the stoop.

The driver honked and drove away, leaving Paislee and Zeffer on the stoop. She'd already paid and tipped.

"So much for my powers of deduction. I thought it was Brody's birthday party," Zeffer drawled. "Brody can keep the gift card—I didnae ken what he liked."

Her stomach fluttered as they went down the hall to the kitchen. The way her insides were jumping around felt like a party all right.

"He doesn't need a present. Lydia and Corbin spoil us all. What would you like tae drink?" Paislee asked. "We have everything from Irn-Bru to whisky."

"I'll take a whisky," Zeffer said.

This also was a shocker. "Not on duty?"

"No, Paislee." Zeffer narrowed his eyes as he studied her. "Is that all right?"

"Oh, yes." Paislee nibbled her lower lip, her skin flushed. "I think so."

Zeffer responded with a low, husky laugh. "I hope it is. I've been waiting a long time."

"Mack!" Corbin said, stepping from the lounge to the kitchen. "Glad you could make it. Between the three of us we should be able tae put Brody's gift together fast."

"I'm intrigued." Zeffer scanned the Shaw family and Lydia around the table. He and Corbin had their backs to the sink. "I hope I'm not intruding. When Lydia mentioned pizza and cake, and gifts, I wrongly assumed it was Brody's birthday."

Brody laughed. "You crashed our pizza party, DI, but that's cool."

Zeffer placed the gift bag on the counter. "Call me Mack, Brody."

Brow arched, her son nodded. "Awright."

"You're welcome tae stay," Paislee said. She turned to Lydia. "What needs tae be put together?"

Grandpa poured Zeffer a whisky from his good stash and then handed it to him. Everyone had drinks of some sort. "Sláinte."

"Sláinte," Zeffer said.

"Later, my friend, later," Lydia said to Paislee. "We need sustenance first. I have my eye on the chicken alfredo pizza."

"Pepperoni is classic, Aunt Lydia," Brody said. "Chicken doesnae belong on a pizza." Her son turned to Zeffer. Mack. "Where do you stand on pepperoni?"

Mack picked up a paper plate and perused the choices. Two pepperonis, one chicken alfredo, and one veggie. Paislee loved the veggie pizza for breakfast, cold from the box.

"I'll leave the chicken alfredo for those who love it," Mack said, choosing a slice of pepperoni and a slice of veggie.

Brody stacked his plate with three slices of pepperoni, adding red chili flakes and parmesan. They took their food to the living room. Mack ended up cross-legged on the floor, by Paislee, on the sofa.

"Do you want a chair?" Paislee asked.

"I like tae sit this way," Mack said. He bit into the pepperoni and gave Brody a thumbs-up. "This is brilliant."

"Right?" Brody laughed, and shook his head at Lydia and Corbin. "Classic choices, family, bring no regrets!"

"Mine is great too, ya wee dafty," Lydia said. Corbin bobbed his head and kept chewing.

"I like my pizza for breakfast the next day," Mack said. "Sometimes I order extra just tae have it."

"Cold?" Lydia asked intently.

"Aye." Mack finished the veggie slice next.

"Mum likes hers that way too," Brody said. "It's okay cold if you're in a hurry, but it's way better with the pepperoni slices hot and the cheese melty."

Wallace and Snowball whined at the back door, no doubt thinking they'd been forgotten and wanting a taste.

"Paislee, how are you feeling?" Lydia asked—her bestie was in the middle with Corbin to her other side. Grandpa had the armchair, and Brody also sat on the floor, his plate on the low table.

"Why?"

"Well, we have news tae tell you, and I want tae make sure you're in a guid mood before we share it," Lydia said. "It's not for sure yet."

Paislee's stomach clenched.

Corbin cleared his throat. "What a buildup, Lyd!" He leaned over his wife's lap. "We are thinking of moving tae Germany for a year or two, tae study wine for a possible investment."

Paislee couldn't think for a minute. Was this why Lydia and

Corbin had brought gifts to Brody? But, no, Lydia wasn't like that. She loved to give gifts just because.

"Awesome!" Brody shot to his feet. "Anybody want more pizza?"

None of the adults had wolfed theirs down, so they were still eating.

Lydia bumped her elbow to Paislee's. "Would you come and visit if we did?"

"Is this why you said I needed a vacation that wasn't Arizona?" Paislee felt a tiny ache begin behind her eyes. Lydia couldn't leave the country. Panic started.

"You work verra hard, Paislee," Mack said. "Germany is gorgeous, especially the vineyards."

Paislee turned to the wealthy detective. Of course, he'd know about beautiful Germany. He'd probably traveled the world. What did she know? It was none of her business to know. She shifted back to Lydia. Her best friend was staring at her with concern. "We dinnae ken for sure."

"I will support whatever you want tae do, you know that." Paislee's throat was thick with emotion. She thought of their weekly Knit and Sip meetings, the daily phone calls, the impromptu drop-in lunches, and stress baking. Just being fifteen minutes away. That would *change*. She'd never thought Lydia would leave Nairn—it was incomprehensible. They'd promised one another to always be there.

"It's not a sure thing." Lydia's gray eyes welled. "It would be a brilliant investment. My job would allow me tae scale doon and work remotely. I'd return quarterly. I was really hoping tae train Rhona. She'd be splendid at the estate office."

Corbin finished his pizza and put the empty paper plate on the table. "I agree with Lydia, but Rhona has her own mind, which is why we want tae support Brody in his dream tae be a career foot-baller."

Paislee swallowed the pizza, though it didn't sit well. If Lydia and Corbin moved, things would change, but wasn't that life?

"What did you bring?" Brody said, coming back with two more pieces. He dropped effortlessly down to the floor, knees akimbo.

Paislee could feel Mack's eyes on her, and Grandpa's too, with concern. She raised her chin. "You have tae wait, son. Lydia, Corbin, if it is as wonderful an opportunity as you think, you've got tae go for it."

"You mean it, Paislee?" Lydia asked.

Corbin's smile widened.

"I do." Paislee forced a laugh that came out smoother than she'd anticipated, considering how many jagged lumps were in her throat.

"You'll have tae come and visit," Corbin said. "We should ken next week. The Smythe family board wants tae make sure it's a sound investment before parting with cash." He took Lydia's hand. "Which means my reputation is on the line if it fails. I believe in the vineyard, but I also need tae have boots on the ground if there is a problem. Lydia took some convincing."

"It's only a two-hour flight, nonstop," Lydia said to Paislee. "That's less than it takes tae get tae Edinburgh and my parents."

"What do they think?"

Lydia shrugged. "I havenae mentioned it tae them—you guys are my family here."

Brody finished his second round of pizza. "It'll be verra cool tae go tae Germany and Arizona. Mum, we need tae get passports."

Paislee put her pizza plate on the low table, passing close to Mack, and not understanding why she had the urge to cry—she swallowed it down along with the pizza. *Change.* "Passports it is. Lyd, you've been my best friend since we were bairns. If you need my support on this, you have it. I was selfishly thinking of the baked goods we'll be missing out on every Thursday, but this could be my chance tae lose that extra around my middle."

She felt Mack's approval at her reaction to the worst surprise ever, but Lydia and Corbin were married, and that relationship had to be honored.

"You're not chubby, Mum," Brody said loyally. "I love your hugs."

Grandpa laughed so hard it turned into a coughing fit, and Zeffer jumped up to pat his back.

She could pout later, and as Lydia said, the move might not even happen.

"Can we please, please, please see what Aunt Lydia and Uncle Corbin brought over for me?" Brody pleaded, laying on the charm. "We can have ice cream cake afterward."

Paislee kept that smile on her face. "It's up tae Aunt Lydia and Uncle Corbin." She cleared the plates and tossed them in the bin, loading silverware into the dishwasher.

"Mack, and Angus, can I get your help? Brody, do you mind taking the dogs upstairs?" Corbin asked.

When everyone had gone to their posts, Lydia faced Paislee at last. "Are you really okay with the move?"

"Of course I am, but why didn't you tell me in private?" Paislee asked.

"Corbin wanted tae surprise you too. He doesnae realize how close we are, no matter how many times I say it. He loves you, and he loves Brody. I promised I would always be there for you and Brody, after my divorce. I feel like I'm leaving you." Lydia sighed. "I feel guilty."

"You shouldn't! We will always be best friends, no matter where you move. We can share tea and bad days over video chat." Paislee saw how miserable Lydia appeared and hugged her close before releasing her.

"It's important tae Corbin tae succeed in this Smythe Winery business. He sounds like you did when you were starting Cashmere Crush. I am so proud of you, Paislee. You are a successful entrepreneur."

"It's nothing." Paislee straightened the kitchen towel by the stove.

"It's not nothing. I've had tae listen tae Cobin come home from those family meetings, and I ken the statistics—sixty-five percent of businesses fail in the first ten years."

Paislee shrugged. "We had tae eat, and that was a big motivator. We had Gran's support and yours."

"You took risks." Lydia nudged her arm as they looked out the window to the backyard, where the guys were bringing in poles. And a net?

"What is that?"

"A regulation goalie net," Lydia said firmly. "I want Brody tae achieve his dreams and I will encourage him however I can—Corbin too. He and Brody had a wonderful conversation that day at the Highland Games. I am going tae miss the next year of watching his football games. He's really guid, you ken? I believe he has a braw talent."

Paislee had seen a hint of that herself. "His coach wants Brody tae play Edwyn's position. He's nervous that he'll fail."

"He willnae," Lydia said immediately. "Brody let Edwyn take the spotlight. He's a guid person."

Mack, Corbin, and Grandpa were putting the goalie net in place.

"Can I come doon yet?" Brody called.

"No!" Paislee and Lydia shouted in unison.

"Are you mad that I invited Mack?" Lydia asked. "He's handsome, and single, and rich—and intae you, my feisty friend."

Paislee felt the butterflies in her stomach flutter to life. "I'm not mad. Just don't push, Lyd."

"I willnae. At the rate you move in your relationships, you should just aboot be on your second date by the time we come back from Germany." Lydia jumped out of the way as Paislee tried to shove her.

At last, the net was up, and Corbin waved to Paislee and Lydia waiting by the kitchen window. "Have Brody come on doon!"

Her son must have been listening from the top of the stairs, as Brody and the dogs raced down the steps and hurried past Lydia and Paislee, out the back door, to the garden. The net took up the width of the lawn, covering the front of the shed, which had always been an eyesore.

"Awesome!" Brody shouted, hugging Corbin, Grandpa, and even Mack.

Paislee and Lydia joined them on the lawn.

"What is the occasion again?" Mack asked.

"Just because," Lydia said. "We love our family and want tae support our pro footballer."

"Well," Zeffer said. "I played goalie. Corbin? Angus?"

"I'll sit this one oot," Grandpa said. "Two left feet."

"I can play a little," Corbin said.

Before Paislee realized it, the guys had a game. She sipped her hard cider and took a seat on the back stairs next to Lydia and Grandpa, content. Her stomach was full, and so was her heart. The detective fit in perfectly, patting Wallace, holding Snowball without getting fur on his polo shirt. He didn't complain about his designer loafers getting muddy and was good in the goal.

"Who knew?" Lydia said to Grandpa as Zeffer blocked a goal.

"Not me." Grandpa nodded at Paislee. "What do you think of this?"

"It's strange," Paislee admitted. She couldn't pull her gaze from Mack.

"But nice," Lydia said. "I can tell."

"I don't want tae be rushed," Paislee said again.

"Mack knows that too," Lydia said. "It's been years since he brought Angus home tae you."

It had been years. He knew her. She didn't know him at all. But that wasn't true. She knew he had integrity and kindness. And those seafoam-green eyes. . . .

Lydia tugged Paislee's hair and burst out laughing. "You are smitten."

Paislee was saved from answering by the ring of her landline. She lifted the receiver and was tempted to let it go to voicemail, but if her mum was following through, she could do her part.

"Brody, Grandma Rosanna wants tae talk tae you about school."

Family.

Chapter 14

Though it had been a late night for everyone, Paislee and Brody were still out the door by half past eight so that Brody could meet with Emma before school. The lass was a cutie and waved to Paislee before the two went inside.

She arrived at Cashmere Crush by nine and was surprised to hear a knock on the open back door. She turned, expecting Jerry with her Tuesday morning yarn order, but it was Zeffer.

Her insides did a little dance of excitement to see him. He carried a to-go box with hot cups and a napkin around two scones.

"Hi," she said, feeling shy. Last night had been so pleasant that she'd been silly this morning, thinking of Mack and breaking into laughter for no reason.

"Hey," he said. "I brought you tea and a blueberry scone."

"Come on in." Could he tell that he'd been in her dreams?

"I saw your Juke go by the station," Zeffer admitted. His cheeks turned pink. "Not stalking you. I was hoping we could be . . . friends. And spend some time together. It occurred tae me that I dinnae ken your favorite color."

He stepped by her to the counter with the cash register. His honesty compelled her to be as honest, that she'd really like that, but her tongue was tied. She accepted a cup of tea and a scone, managing a smile. "It's sage." Close to the color of his eyes, but she didn't say that either. "Yours must be blue, if your suits are anything tae go by."

"It is blue," he admitted. "Jerry should be here at nine thirty, eh, and Rhona at ten?"

"Now that could definitely be described as stalking," Paislee teased.

Mack exhaled and sat on the stool. "It was verra nice tae be with your family last night," he said. "I hope it wasnae an imposition?"

"It wasn't! Even Brody said that it was wonderful tae see another side of you. You can play football, and as goalie, which won him over."

"Lydia suggested that Corbin might need a wee bit of help putting up the goal posts. I admit I took that as a verra loose invitation."

"And what would you have done if you'd not been welcome?"

"I would have left, brokenhearted." Though his tone was light, the words were serious. Hadn't Paislee always suspected that Zeffer had a heart beneath his stylish blue suits? She was beginning to think he might have feelings for her that went beyond friendship.

A relationship with her meant kids. Family. Chaos.

Remembering a prior conversation they'd had last year, Paislee said, "You mentioned that you didn't want children. . . ."

"I have a lot of siblings," Zeffer said carefully.

She knew about a sister in Stonehaven. "Corbin doesn't feel the need tae reproduce because of all of his cousins, and nieces and nephews."

"The Smythe line is strong," Zeffer joked. "The Zeffer ancestry is not as vast, but I am not one of those tae feel like I have tae generate more little Zeffers. The world is a strange place right now."

"That it is." Paislee broke off a piece of the scone and ate it, peering at Zeffer behind a fall of hair. Who was this introspective man?

"I ken the subject is off limits, but we are alone. I want tae be involved in your life, and so, I am going tae risk offending you, for what I consider the greater guid."

Paislee's stomach clenched with apprehension.

There was only one subject that was off limits. Zeffer didn't dare.

His gaze held hers, unwavering. "Does Brody ever question you aboot his father?"

Her mouth dried. "No."

"These days, DNA and ancestry is all around. In secondary, Brody will have the opportunity tae test his DNA—I dinnae ken if you realized that?"

"How do *you* know?"

"One of my nieces was raving on aboot it," Zeffer said. "Saying it should stop infidelity in relationships."

"Not in Nairn," Paislee said, as incoherent thoughts overran her brain.

"Aye. It's an option in the sciences is what I'm trying tae warn you aboot." Zeffer reached for her hand, but Paislee wrapped it around the cup of tea. His tone was caring and warm, and dangerous.

"No." She raised her shields against the DI; she should have known better than to lower her guard.

"Paislee," Zeffer said. "I'm just suggesting that this might not be a secret you can keep. DNA kits are everywhere, and if Brody wants tae ken, he can find oot withoot your knowledge."

Paislee and Brody had a relationship built on trust. He trusted her. . . . Was she letting him down somehow?

"It was a one-night stand, over graduation," Paislee whispered. "Not my proudest moment." Her stomach roiled, and the blueberry scone rose up her throat.

She couldn't even look at Zeffer.

"Paislee, lass, I can see your emotions all over your face. You have nothing tae be ashamed of—you are an incredible mother. The love in your house is obvious tae anyone. I cannae imagine being eighteen, making that decision, and following through so brilliantly."

The secret she'd thought to keep was suddenly not secure or buttoned down. "You have tae go. I don't want tae see you again."

"Paislee!"

"I mean it. Go." She couldn't look at him.

Zeffer stood, and the stool scooted backward. He tilted her chin, anguish on his expression. "I dinnae mean tae hurt you—I am trying tae help you. Just consider talking tae Brody and see what he says aboot it. If you want me tae do a search on the father, I have resources you dinnae. Let me help you."

"Get out." Vulnerable and afraid, Paislee shook so hard her teeth rattled. She was embarrassed. Worried she'd made the wrong choice by trying to keep Brody's father away from him. The ceiling landing on her and Hamish that day in the kitchen was nothing compared to the shock of cold engulfing her right now.

She'd tried so hard to do the right thing by Calan Maxwell. He was seventeen and wanted to be an officer. Raised by his grandfather, he and Paislee had hit it off, but she'd known it wouldn't be serious as he was leaving within the week. Bonding over dead fathers might seem a little dark, but it was secondary, and they were teenagers. He'd never even written to her. He hadn't been on social media and then, after the fiasco with her mum, she'd decided to do it alone. Well, alone but with Gran and Lydia's help.

The sound of Jerry's lorry arriving was the worst timing and yet allowed her, forced her, to take a breath.

"Paislee," Zeffer said, glancing toward the back door.

"Out, Zeffer. I mean it. Don't come back."

She had to figure out a solution, but now was not the time. Oh, how could he be so cruel? Was it possible to find out about Calan?

Did Brody want to know?

She hated Zeffer for forcing her to look at this after all this time, to uncover her secret and lay it bare. Worse: he was giving her the awful choice to reveal the secret before Brody had even asked.

"Hey, Paislee—what a pure barry day!" Jerry said, as he brought in a box of yarn.

"Morning." Paislee's voice sounded strangled and she cleared her throat. "Zeffer was just leaving."

"DI." Jerry placed the box on the counter. "This have tae do with the Whittle investigation?"

"No," Zeffer said, as Paislee sucked in her lips.

She couldn't tell Jerry that Zeffer had upset her terribly. A knock came at the front door. "Please go," Paislee told Zeffer. She crossed the floor, head high, her spine ramrod straight—mind a stormy mess.

Though she didn't turn around, Paislee knew when Zeffer was gone. Unlocking the door, she smiled at Rhona.

"Hey," Rhona said. "You okay?"

"Of course! Too much ice cream cake last night is all—I didn't sleep well." Paislee kept her head down so that she could avoid eye contact with Rhona. "How was the dance class?"

"It was fun. It's guid tae be busy," Rhona said.

"How's Artie?" Jerry asked, as Paislee and Rhona walked closer to the register.

"He's awake but not lucid. Still doesnae remember what happened. Aibreann will take me tae visit at lunchtime."

"Do you need more time off?" Paislee asked.

"No, I need tae work, so I can pay my folks off and get my car back. Not having wheels is starting tae cramp my style." Rhona hugged her middle.

"Send my regards tae the lad," Jerry said. "Any word on what happened tae Joseph?"

"Jerry!" Rhona exclaimed. "He is innocent. Gemma said they still have a guard ootside his room. She's verra mad aboot it."

"I've got tae run," Jerry said. "I have an extra stop today, and the construction on the roads slows me doon."

"Be safe, Jerry," Paislee said with a wave. Growing pains, Lydia called the new roads, and was surprisingly tolerant of them.

The day passed in a blur of customers, denial, projects, and Rhona's low spirits when Aibreann brought her back from the hospital visit.

They'd had to shave part of Artie's head to drill into his skull, but it had made a big difference. The doctors said it was normal that Artie still didn't recall what had happened and had been shocked to find out that Joseph was dead—and worse, that he was a suspect.

"Artie kept saying that he didnae do it," Rhona said tearfully. "He wants tae go home."

"How soon before they release him?" Elspeth asked.

"Three nights at least," Aibreann said. "A lot depends on Artie's ability tae walk and move around."

"That seems so soon," Paislee said.

"If there are any complications, it will set him back, and he might need tae go tae a rehab facility." Rhona knocked on the wooden high-top table. "Something has tae go our way."

"What does Gemma think? She will have tae care for him," Paislee said.

"She wants him home," Rhona said. "She had a cleaner come in and disinfect the house tae make it livable. She's checking oot of the hotel today."

"Gemma wants Artie away from the constables," Aibreann added wisely.

"I dinnae blame her!" Rhona said.

"Can she lift him if he needs assistance?" Elspeth asked.

"I doot it." Rhona frowned. "She's lost a lot of weight since the incident. She should ask Ross tae stay with them for a few nights, just in case Artie needs more help. I could offer tae do it, but that might seem awkward."

"You think?" Aibreann shook her head.

"I am strong!" Rhona protested.

"You are Artie's girlfriend," Aibreann said slowly. "Where would you sleep? Does she ken how close you are?"

Rhona's cheeks flushed. "Oh, that." She fluttered her fingers. "I could sleep on the couch. It's not romantic, it's an offer of extra hands."

"Joseph was murdered there. You shouldnae stay over," Aibreann said. "What if Joseph's ghost is haunting the place? Or Cam's?"

"Cam didnae die there." Rhona appeared concerned. "We should buy some sage and cleanse the house, you ken, tae make sure that Joseph isnae hanging around."

"Girls," Elspeth said firmly. "There arenae ghosts, and if there were, they cannnae harm you. I'll say a prayer for Joseph's soul so that he finds peace."

"Joseph was stabbed," Aibreann said, wide eyed. "He has a reason tae be mad aboot his death. He might decide tae say forget heaven tae bully Gemma. We need tae find oot what happened tae Joseph so that he can be at peace. That's more important than sage."

Rhona nodded. "Gemma said that Constable Monroe was asking aboot the night Cam died."

"What does Gemma remember?" Paislee asked. Despite two years going by, the constables were making sure there was no connection. How could there be?

"Joseph told her that Cam had been in a car accident. DUI. She never questioned what happened." Rhona shrugged. "There was an after party for a competition that Cam hadnae done well in, and he was probably blowing off steam."

"She had every reason tae believe her husband," Paislee said.

"You're right. She said that Joseph heard the crash and called nine-nine-nine. Cam was taken tae the hospital but was already gone. It had tae be around midnight, as Gemma had already gone tae bed and Joseph woke her up. Artie was oot with mates and hadnae come back yet."

"It happened close tae their house then?" Paislee imagined the drive she'd taken to the Whittles. The side street had two lanes each with houses on one end and the field and pine trees on the other.

"It must have. We can ask Artie, he might ken for sure," Rhona said. "It cannae be a pleasant memory."

"Was Cam alone?" Aibreann asked.

"Gemma didnae say. Just that Chantelle didnae ride home with him." Rhona jotted down a note to ask Gemma or Artie later. "It might not be related, but I think we should leave no stone unturned tae prove Artie's innocence."

"I feel bad for Gemma," Aibreann said. "What other secrets might Joseph have had? Besides his infidelity. Or doping."

"Doping?" Elspeth asked.

"Aye, he was using steroids tae build muscle and had them in his system when he died." Paislee glanced toward the door as a customer entered. "We should shelve this conversation for now."

Elspeth frowned with concern. "I have so many questions!"

Rhona sighed. "So do we." She turned and smiled at the woman with her toddler daughter. "Welcome tae Cashmere Crush!"

"Hi," the woman said. "We moved tae Nairn a few months ago, and this is the first time we've been in. I've always wanted tae learn tae knit."

"I'm Paislee." She stepped forward. "It's nice tae meet you. We have a group of knitters who get together for a social evening on Thursdays, if you're interested."

"I'm just learning," the woman protested.

Elspeth joined Paislee. "I dinnae even knit but do needlepoint. Another of our members brings the tastiest appetizers, and she doesnae craft at all."

The woman chuckled. "Tell me more!"

Paislee sold the woman a pattern book for a scarf in pink for her daughter and included the store information with a reminder about the Knit and Sip.

"Aibreann had tae go," Rhona said. "Her mum needs the car."

"It's nice that they can share," Paislee said.

"And yet mine is being so selfish and not at all understanding," Rhona complained.

Elspeth assisted the next customer, and Paislee raced out to pick up Brody and take him home. It was time in her day that she didn't begrudge her son, and it allowed her to catch up with Lydia, or Meri, or Grandpa. Did he look at all like Calan? Did he want to know about his da?

"I have the Highland Games committee meeting tonight," Paislee told Brody when she dropped him off. "Grandpa suggested leftovers for dinner since we have an entire pizza."

"Pepperoni is my favorite," Brody said. "I could eat it every day."

"You might have tae—I didn't expect for there tae be a whole one left from yesterday," Paislee said.

"I did my best to eat it all."

Grandpa opened the door to wave at Paislee. "Mail came. Something from Rosanna."

"Grandma said she sent me something for school!" Brody dashed out of the Juke and Paislee, curious, followed. Now that they were communicating, which was admittedly nice, this was the first time her mother had sent a gift just because.

What if Brody had family other than her mother out in the world? Calan's grandfather had moved once Calan had joined the military. She'd had no need to contact him. Then again, her grandpa was a huge important piece of her life.

They went inside and Paislee greeted the pups. Wallace and Snowball were working in tandem it seemed to trip her.

Paislee, laughing nervously, managed to reach the table alive. An envelope stamped from America sat in the center.

Brody ripped it open to find a map of Arizona, with where they lived circled and starred to signify the importance. There was a list of all the fun things to do, including hiking in the red desert mountains. There was also a journal with his name on it separated into subjects. There was a note signed from her mom, her mother's husband, and Natalie and Josh, her half siblings, younger than Brody.

"That was verra kind." Grandpa met Paislee's eyes across Brody's bent head.

"It was," Paislee conceded.

"This is brilliant," Brody said. "I'm going tae hang the map on the wall in my bedroom. I cannae wait tae meet them. That's what I want for my birthday next year, Mum. A trip tae Grandma's house."

Paislee inwardly counted to ten. This seemed to be her week for tough options without simple solutions. Mack, Lydia, her mother. She smiled. "Let's do some research on the best times tae travel tae the States. I'm off tae work."

Chapter 15

Paislee locked up Cashmere Crush and left for the committee meeting at the town hall. The absence of the fairground rides left room for tourists to park and shop at the nearby stores.

One of her favorite places was a café, called Basil Harbour, that had scrumptious homemade treats, from savory to sweet. She'd planned to order something for takeaway before the meeting, but Meri had texted her that she'd brought Chinese lo mein for everyone as a thank-you for being on the committee.

Paislee offered to bring dessert, but Dyana had already said she'd bring chocolate chip cookies made from scratch with almond flour and coconut sugar. One of the things her mum had found amusing and had cracked Brody up was that in America a cookie is a "cookie" and not a "biscuit," which is how the plain sweet variety is referred to in Scotland.

Would he really want to go for his birthday? She'd have to search for travel deals and stash money away. It could be educational to include him in the planning. Mack's compassionate gaze as he warned her that Brody could find out about his father without talking to Paislee about it stung, so she stomped it down to be examined later.

Parking next to Meri's SUV, Paislee climbed out and grabbed

her handbag and mobile. She couldn't help but keep her eye out for Kev Sloane's slight figure and long black hair, though the caravan was gone.

It didn't make her feel safer to know Kev was out of jail and wandering the shire—or wherever he'd holed up after being released.

She'd rather believe that Kev was guilty than Artie, despite the evidence to the contrary. What if he'd ditched the actual knife in the Moray Firth?

Entering the town hall, Paislee nodded toward Krissie and Donnie, attached at the lips. Each wore a tight Forge Fitness T-shirt, and they broke apart when she passed them. Neither had a significant other, so Paislee didn't understand their guilty expressions.

Honestly, she had so much other drama in her life that she wouldn't even give it a second thought—unless their guilt had to do with Joseph Whittle, or Artie?

Paislee stopped and turned, to find them directly behind her.

They widened their eyes and stumbled backward.

"Sorry!" Paislee said. "What's going on?"

Donnie shook his head. "Nothing."

"Not true, obviously," Paislee said. "I don't care if you're kissing."

"Delilah likes Donnie, and they went on a date," Krissie said. She blinked her long fake lashes quickly.

Donnie sighed. "We arenae married, Krissie. I am never getting married because I want tae put myself first, which means I can kiss who I want. I'm a verra guid kisser."

Paislee adjusted her handbag strap over her shoulder that had slipped when she'd stopped so abruptly. Donnie was at least self-aware, if arrogant.

"It's true." Krissie sounded disappointed in herself. "I wish you werenae. I have too much self-respect tae hook up with you."

Donnie smirked. "Again. Face it—you crave me like a chubby kid craves a donut."

"Keep talking like that, and I will be over you by the end of the meeting," Krissie assured him.

"It's difficult," Donnie rubbed his knuckles over his muscled chest as if polishing his fingernails, "but I will take responsibility for my sex appeal. You want some, Paislee?"

"That would be a big no." Paislee turned and hurried down the hall, reaching the partially open door of the meeting room.

Krissie laughed and laughed. "That was a guid one," she said as she passed Paislee and went inside the room.

The scent of Chinese food lured Paislee right on Krissie's heels.

Donnie was behind her, wearing way too much cologne, which was another thing she didn't find appealing about him.

"Welcome, everyone," Meri said. "Help yourself tae noodles. Dyana made dessert that I thought we'd save for a wee break after our first half of the meeting. We must get new members on the ballot, as I will be stepping doon."

"Are you sure we cannae change your mind?" Simon kept his back to Lachlan, who wanted to be chairman. "I will feel the loss of your support for Nairn."

Oh, that was a good angle to take to appeal to Meri's community-mindedness.

"I'm sairy," Meri said, with a polite smile. "My mind is made up. I willnae have time, as I've been offered a new position on the Piping Committee that is more in line with my personal interests. I love playing the pipes, but I am not a happy politician."

"Got it," Simon said forlornly.

"I love politics!" Lachlan declared. "We have tae make sure our voices are heard, and I am happy tae be our representative."

"I bet," Sandi said snidely. "You get a kickback?"

"I dinnae take bribes, Sandi," Lachlan said. "What are you doing here, anyway? I'd hoped you'd realize that it was time tae step doon from your volunteer position."

"You were the one found with unsportsmanlike behavior," Sandi countered. "Setting up puir Artie Whittle tae get back at Joseph. Say, how did your meeting with the police go?"

It was hard to believe a week had passed since the attack on Joseph. Since Artie was in hospital.

"How do you ken I had one?" Lachlan asked in surprise.

"I didnae, until now." Sandi twirled long noodles around the tines of her fork and slurped them into her mouth.

Lachlan's face turned beet red with anger.

"Five minutes, and then we can call the meeting tae order, all right?" Meri said. "Paislee, have a plate of noodles. We have chicken or vegetarian."

"Thanks for that consideration, Meri," Dyana said.

"Chicken for me." Paislee scooped noodles and chicken onto a paper plate. "I admire your dedication tae living cleanly."

"I am doing my part for the planet and my health." Dyana sipped her green juice after a bite of the veggie noodles. "My body is a temple."

Drake nodded at her figure. "That it is—mine too, come tae think of it, but I still want the chicken, and I'll have a whisky."

"Afterward," Meri said. "We need clear heads tae discuss the new direction of the Nairn Highland Games. Dog-herding, yay or nay, charging, yay or nay?"

Somehow Meri was able to continue in a calm manner through the meeting's pitfalls. At the halfway point, Simon had suggested Paislee as a possible chair, but Paislee quickly declined. The only reason she'd participated was because of Meri.

"I'm afraid my time commitments won't allow it," Paislee said. "Brody doesn't want tae take part next year either, as he will be playing more football."

Nice and vague and true.

In the end, Drake nominated Simon to be chairman. Dyana said she would continue to be secretary, and Sandi would stay in the volunteer coordinator position. Lachlan was not allowed to be on the board as a chairperson because of his behavior toward Artie Whittle. He was lucky, Drake said, not to be banned from the Nairn Highland Games permanently.

Dyana's cookies were divine. "May I take a couple home for my guys?" Paislee asked. "They both have a sweet tooth."

"I'd love the recipe," Meri said, after her first bite.

"A baker never tells," Dyana simpered. "Of course, Paislee. If there are any left." The woman turned to Lachlan. "Mibbe I could sell the green juice and the cookies at a kiosk throughoot the year."

"That would require special licensing," Simon said.

"Lachlan and I will talk aboot it later, then," Dyana said.

"That seems shady tae me," Donnie said.

"Yeah, it does," Drake seconded.

"It's not!" Lachlan assured the group. "We have collaborated on several projects because we're likeminded in our business affairs. I resent the inference otherwise."

His protest was loud—perhaps too loud, Paislee thought. She and Meri exchanged a look.

It was good that Meri was doing something else next year. They voted to keep the dog-herding event, so long as it was just sheep. The meeting was winding down. Meri brought out the whisky, which mellowed the mood.

"Can any of the day's activities be linked tae Joseph's death?" Simon asked. "I hate for the stain of murder tae be on the record."

"I dinnae see how," Lachlan said. "Trust me, if there was a way tae bust him for his usage of steroids, I'd want tae bring him doon."

Dyana smirked. "What would Gemma think of you then?"

Lachlan ignored her statement.

"Was Artie using?" Krissie asked.

"No," Sandi said. "I talked tae his girlfriend, Rhona, aboot it. Artie was antisteroids."

"Did Artie ken his dad was doping?" Drake looked at Paislee. "Isnae Rhona working for you?"

"She is," Paislee said. "Artie is in hospital right now recovering from a head trauma that required surgery, and I don't know what he knows."

"I heard that, puir guy," Simon said. "Also, that he may be the killer. Nobody would blame him for getting fed up with Joseph's verbal abuse."

"I don't think he is the guilty party," Paislee said.

"There's no excuse for murder," Meri said sternly.

"Sometimes there are extenuating circumstances." Sandi tapped the table. "I've seen it all in my job at the hospital. How I wish we could bring Joseph tae justice."

Paislee studied the strongwoman who had professed dislike for Joseph and Cam. Could she have killed Joseph? She had the physical strength, and the motivation.

"Sandi, do you know what happened tae Cam the night he died?" Paislee asked.

"He arrived by ambulance, DOA. I have a friend who is an EMT. Joseph supposedly heard the accident from his house." Sandi pursed her lips. "Never made sense tae me, but the inspector had pulled Cam over before for drinking and driving. Joseph made a point of saying Cam had been drinking heavily, but I didnae smell anything and neither did my medic mate. The doctor overrode my questions because Joseph had signed a statement saying Cam had downed a bunch of whisky."

"Cam was a loudmouth blowhard especially when he was drunk," Donnie said. "Nobody could stand him like that, not even his girlfriend, Chantelle."

That was the pot calling the kettle black, Paislee thought. "Fern and Delilah saw you talking with Chantelle at the games."

"Yeah. She's all aboot guys with muscles." Donnie flexed his biceps. "She's always been a fan of mine."

Paislee didn't see the appeal.

Donnie continued, "The constables asked aboot Cam too. The truth is he'd lost big at the competition and was oot of control. Going on aboot his special roids concoction that would make him stronger for the next one. Didnae try tae hide that he was using. It's why I was watching Artie so closely."

"Artie wasnae using," Sandi said.

Paislee thought of Fern and jotted a note on her mobile to call her and find out if she knew more about what happened the night Cam had died. Did she also know about the steroid use?

"Let's leave Joseph's murder tae the professionals," Meri said. "Do we have any other loose ends tae tie up as I adjourn this meeting?"

"You will be missed." Simon handed Meri a framed certificate for her excellence on the board. "If you ever need a friend, Meri, let me ken, and I will see what I can do."

"Thank you," Meri said. She raised her mug. "Tae Nairn, the best shire in Scotland."

"Sláinte!" Paislee seconded, with feeling. She loved Nairn as well.

After the toast, Paislee stayed to chat with Meri for a bit and congratulate her on the award as well as thank her for her dedication and hard work.

"My pleasure," Meri said.

"Oh, no leftover cookies. Darn it. They were amazing," Paislee said.

Dyana was gone, as was Lachlan. Were they conferring in secret? Again, neither were in a relationship, so there was no reason to hide that Paislee could imagine.

Simon waited to chat with Meri as well, and they probably had things to discuss as one chairman to another, so Paislee left the meeting.

"Bye, guys!" Paislee said.

She walked down the hall, scanning her mobile and seeing a message from Brody about a special deal to Arizona. He even offered to help her pay for the excursion. Grandpa had offered to watch Wallace while they were away.

Well, Brody wasn't kidding.

Paislee went out of the town hall, having walked slow enough that nobody else was around. She clicked the fob to unlock the Juke. At almost nine the sun was still out, though softer as evening drew to a close.

Her mother. Her siblings. Brody's cousins. Brody's da.

She climbed into the vehicle.

"Paislee?"

She squealed and laid her palm on the horn in alarm.

"Hey!" Zeffer said.

"Oh—it's you," Paislee said, lifting her hand to block his handsome face from view.

"I just wanted tae apologize for earlier today."

"I am still mad," Paislee said. "I really don't want tae be your friend."

Zeffer winced. "You ken what I mean when I say I want you tae be in my life, and that I want tae be in yours?"

His pleading gaze hardly touched her hardened heart. He shouldn't have gone there, not when it was her one rule.

"I can't trust you," Paislee said.

"That's not true!" Zeffer leaned against the open door of her driver's side on the Juke. "I told you so you would be prepared."

"I don't need your interference."

"Paislee . . ." His tone suggested otherwise.

"I will give it some thought. Right now, I have tae deal with my mum, who Brody wants tae meet, in America."

Zeffer didn't relax his intense stance. "He's curious aboot his family, which proves my point."

She started the SUV. "I wish you'd go find who killed Joseph instead of badgering me about things that aren't your business."

"What will you do?" Zeffer asked.

"Zeffer, I mean it. You are not a friend, and I can't see a future between us. I had one rule, and you broke it."

"Tae protect you," Zeffer whispered.

"Justifications." Paislee gritted her teeth.

"I'm sairy if I crossed a line." With that Zeffer left.

Paislee drove to the beach and stared out at the waves, tears streaming down her cheeks. She'd wanted Zeffer to kiss her, to hold her, to love her. Why had he done the one thing that she couldn't forgive?

Chapter 16

Wednesday morning was the absolute worst for Paislee, as she couldn't get out of her own way. She'd dreamed of Calan Maxwell all night—his youthful face morphing into his grandfather's, and they all blamed her for keeping Brody a secret.

Had her pride kept her from reaching out to Calan? She didn't think so, and she'd dissected her decisions from every angle. It had been her choice. Her granny had supported her decision by teaching Paislee to hold her head up, how to knit, how to think of community, and to take business courses. To move her online knitting business to an actual shop. She had a way to support her and Brody, and then Grandpa, when he joined their family.

After her shower, she slipped and stubbed her toe on the wooden threshold. "Ouch! Son of a . . ." She limped across the hall to her room, muttering curses.

"You okay, Mum?" Brody asked from his bedroom, the door open. He was halfway dressed, and Snowball and Wallace were on his bed.

"I'm fine!" She studied his features. The bruise from his day playing laser tag was fading. Did he resemble Calan at all? No, he looked like Da, and Grandpa, and her. Maybe the cheekbones, but it would be a stretch to say so.

Brody belonged to her.

"How's the science project coming along?" He'd been done with homework and watching TV in his room when she'd gotten home last night, close to ten.

"It's fine. It's Spanish that's so lame. Even Emma doesnae like it."

"She's cute," Paislee said, her toe throbbing. "See you downstairs in a few."

"Mum?"

"Yes?"

"You would've had tae put money in the swear jar," he teased. "How come that never got replaced when Aunt Lydia did the kitchen?"

"We could ask her, but I'd rather save my cash."

"What did you think aboot my idea for America?"

"It's a good one."

"Really?" Brody pumped his fist in the air.

Chuckling, Paislee went into her room, closed the door, and got dressed, hoping she hadn't broken her toe. She gingerly tugged on jeans. Her toe was bruised and sore, so she put on a snug ankle sock and sneakers to keep it secure.

After a light application of tinted sunscreen and mascara, Paislee was ready enough for the day and went downstairs for breakfast and to make Brody's lunch. Lydia had texted her to check in about last night's committee meeting.

It wasn't last night's meeting that had Paislee so upset. It was a certain DI who'd butted his nose into her business, and now she couldn't stop second-guessing her decision.

Lydia knew Calan Maxwell. She knew what had happened and had supported her through thick and thin. Through maternity clothes and the fresh shortbread that she couldn't get enough of.

"Mum, did you hear me?" Brody'd come downstairs dressed and ready for school, and she hadn't noticed, lost in her thoughts. The pups were outside in the back garden.

"Uh, no. Sorry." She blinked, poured herself a mug of strong tea and then put bread in the toaster. Four slices.

"You're far away this morning, lass," Grandpa chuckled. He brought the paper to the table. "And I ken I didnae keep you up coughing—the medicine works wonders."

"That's true. So tell me again Brody?" Paislee said.

"I was wondering if the DI wanted tae come over this weekend tae be goalie for me. I have a hard time calling him Mack, like he said, but he was pretty guid."

Zeffer, here, without the buffer of Lydia and Corbin?

After what he'd done? The boundary he'd pushed?

Paislee wasn't unreasonable and could even see Zeffer's side, but there was no getting around the fact that he'd crossed a line. Bumping her tea, hot water spilled over the side and burned her thumb. "Ouch! Again."

"I must get my klutziness from you, Mum," Brody said sagely. "Well?"

"I'm not sure." Paislee closed herself off to the possibilities of a relationship. "Don't you have a practice on Saturday?" She pointed her chin toward the calendar on the wall that had Brody's games and practice schedules. Coach Harris was very organized.

Brody flipped his hair off his forehead. "Yeah. Emma wants tae come watch me play."

"You should see what Coach Harris thinks aboot that," Grandpa advised. "He's going tae want you tae concentrate on the game, not girls."

Brody scowled but nodded.

Paislee, glad that Grandpa had taken on that advice so that she didn't have to, knew she had to call Lydia and see what her best friend thought about the Zeffer situation. Was he right to warn her, or was he being pushy? It could be that Brody would forever go along with what Paislee had decreed at eighteen, not knowing how else to handle the situation.

She needed to call Lydia. Even when her friend moved to Germany, she would always be a phone call away.

"Mum!" Brody said again.

Grandpa rose from the table to turn off the toaster oven. "You burnt the toast, lass. What has you so frazzled?"

"I'm not. I have tae call Lydia about something, that's all." Paislee swallowed and checked the too dark bread. "You need tae write a thank-you card tae Aunt Lydia and Uncle Corbin this evening."

"All right," Brody acquiesced, without an argument. When he'd been ten, it had been a nightmare. He was older.

He was older, and things changed. Maybe it was time. She'd been waiting, really, for him to question her—it wasn't like she'd planned to keep Calan a secret forever. Had she been?

"Brody, would you like tae get an ice cream tonight after dinner?"

Her son scowled with suspicion. "Why?"

"No reason! Can't your mum take you out for no reason?"

"You usually have a reason," Brody said.

She was bungling this whole thing. "Never mind, it doesn't matter."

But it did.

Grandpa searched her face and then offered a side hug without a question but sensing that she could use one. "Say hello tae Lydia for me."

"I will." Paislee skipped toast for breakfast and grabbed a granola bar instead. "Let's go, Brody, the vehicle is leaving for school."

She had to go back for her mobile that she'd left on the table. Grandpa was outside in the back garden with the pups and didn't notice, but Brody teased her the whole way to school.

Her plan to call her bestie was thwarted by a phone call from Rhona, who had a flat tire on her bicycle and hoped that Paislee could pick her up and bring her to work.

Rhona wasn't speaking to her mum.

Paislee easily located the frustrated teenager and pulled over to the side of the road. Parking, she got out and saw that the flat tire had a nail through it and would need to be replaced. "Rotten luck, Rhona. It's been that kind of day!" Her toe throbbed.

Together, they folded the bike and put it in the back of the Juke; then Paislee and Rhona climbed inside and buckled up. It was good they were both in jeans.

"I love Artie, and Mum doesnae understand that I cannae just turn off my feelings for him because she doesnae like him." Rhona dropped her handbag by her feet. Her helmet was in the backseat.

"That doesn't seem fair, true. What does your dad think?" Mc-Dermot Smythe was usually even keeled.

"He always takes Mum's side. He thinks she is always right." Rhona's brunette hair was in braids on either side of her oval face, a good style for cycling.

That was splendid parenting, and perhaps someday Rhona would appreciate it, but it was hard to swallow right now.

Would Calan want to jump into Brody's life and offer suggestions or rules? Would he want to hang around and be part of things, or would he be content to never participate?

Paislee's stomach churned.

"Mum says if Artie is cleared of all charges, then she'll be more understanding, but right now, he looks guilty. It doesnae help that he doesnae remember what happened. The police have his mobile, though it was smashed, they're trying tae retrieve data. Gemma seems tae regret giving permission for them tae take it."

If the phone was considered evidence, Paislee thought, they probably didn't need permission. "When was the last time you talked tae Artie?"

"I rode my bike tae the hospital last night. Ross is super sweet and gave me a ride home. Artie still doesnae remember anything, which the doctor says is normal. I could only stay for half an hour, and we werenae allowed tae talk aboot the investigation or what happened tae his da. They might release him tomorrow or the next day, as he's healing so fast."

"He'll need your support," Paislee said. "Artie and Gemma both. What a disaster."

Rhona glanced at Paislee as they arrived in the back of Cashmere Crush and Paislee parked. "So Gemma is back at her house now. She has Joseph's phone."

Paislee's brow rose. "The police didn't ask for it?"

"Well," Rhona hedged. "Gemma wasnae clear on that point."

"There could be clues in there." Paislee turned off the engine, but they stayed looking at one another across the console.

"Gemma is afraid that what's in that phone will prove Artie's guilt," Rhona admitted. "She's trying tae figure oot Joseph's password but so far, it's defeated her."

"Rhona! That's a big deal." Paislee could just imagine Zeffer's response, and it wasn't positive.

"But is it illegal?" Rhona shrugged. "It might be a gray area. Joseph was Gemma's husband. His stuff is her stuff, and she will inherit all their joint property, right?"

"What will she do if she does find evidence? It feels wrong."

"Because it's sneaky," Rhona said. "You and I arenae the type of people tae not play by the rules. Somebody killed Joseph, which is against the law. So, I dinnae blame Gemma for trying tae find the truth however she can. I ken Artie isnae guilty, but I'm worried for Gemma aboot the other things she will find."

"Confirmation of Joseph's affairs, and his steroid connections," Paislee said.

Rhona smoothed her braids. "Gemma says she knew aboot the affairs and never asked aboot the doping. It was best for their marriage for her tae be quiet. I could never live like that."

"Me either." Rhona's view of Paislee as a rule follower was correct, except for the time she hadn't followed the rules and ended up pregnant.

She would never regret the consequences of her actions, but she wasn't as nice a person as Rhona thought either. "Let's go inside."

They entered Cashmere Crush at ten. "Sairy tae have made you late, Paislee." Rhona unlocked the front door while Paislee prepared for the day.

"It's fine. I'm glad I was able tae help."

"Elspeth will be in today, right?" Rhona asked. "I told Aibreann that she could come by and continue learning tae knit. Is that okay?"

"Of course. It makes it look like we are busy, which is great. And maybe we can train her on the register just in case."

"Aibreann would love that—she's brilliant—and Paislee, we have been super busy. When do things slow doon?"

"Tourist season is over in October," Paislee said. "Gran taught me that there will be ebbs and flows in business and tae enjoy the wave while saving for that lull."

"Practical advice I didnae learn growing up." Rhona flipped on the electric kettle. "Tea?"

"Yes, please." Tea was almost always a wonderful idea.

Constable Monroe ambled in around half past ten. "Hello. I've got some questions for you both aboot what you saw on Monday, last week."

"All right," Paislee said. "Where is Constable Payne?" She wouldn't care where Zeffer was—she couldn't. He had to be cut from her mind and heart so that she could get through the day.

"He's checking the area for places Cam's car might have been stashed. Gemma said she hasnae seen it since before the accident and assumed it was taken tae a junkyard. Joseph was handling all of that, since she could hardly get oot of bed. We talked tae some of the local auto thieves tae see if they'd broken it doon for scrap metal or parts, but it's not ringing any bells. Zeffer's been watching footage around that time tae see if somebody took the car oot of the

country. Another dead end. He thinks there's a chance the car is
here in Nairn."

"Really?" Paislee's brow furrowed.

"Anything is possible," Constable Monroe said. "The DI wants
tae do due diligence. Joseph hadnae pursued it, but now that Joseph
is gone, Zeffer is pressing for answers with Gemma's blessing.
Things get fuzzy after two years though."

Rhona's phone dinged a notification, and her eyes lit up.
"Artie was able tae walk on his own. He might get tae go home
tomorrow."

"I see how much you care for him," Constable Monroe said.
"Is that wise, considering?"

"Artie is innocent," Rhona said emphatically.

"I will be the first one tae apologize for doubting his innocence so long as you are cautious, Rhona," Constable Monroe
said. "Got it?"

Rhona sighed. "Fine. You sound like my mother."

Constable Monroe's mouth twitched. "She a sensible woman,
then?"

"Dinnae get me started," Rhona quipped.

"We are doing everything in our power tae find oot what happened tae Joseph Whittle." Constable Monroe left the shop.

Paislee brought out a piece of scrap paper and grabbed a pen.
"Rhona, could you give me Fern's phone number? I had a question
I wanted tae ask her about Cam."

"Sure." Rhona rattled off Fern's number, and Paislee jotted it
down. "Why?"

"Sandi is friends with one of the ambulance medics that
brought Cam in the night he died. He was already dead, and Joseph
signed a statement that Cam had been drinking heavily, but there
was no evidence of that. The doctor didn't press, probably as a favor
tae the family. Why add more grief when it wouldn't change the
outcome?"

Rhona leaned her elbows on the high-top table. "What are you thinking?"

Paislee pulled out a scarf project as they were simple to do and difficult to keep in stock. She'd do a matching tam and fingerless gloves. "What if Cam and Joseph were arguing over something big, like Cam not winning the competition that weekend? We've seen Joseph's temper ourselves, so it wouldn't be out of line. One of the side effects of steroids is rage."

"Like, Joseph might have killed Cam by accident and was covering it up somehow?" Rhona's eyes widened.

Paislee thought that scenario had merit. "That would explain why Joseph hadn't pushed the authorities tae look intae Cam's death and why he'd had him cremated so fast. No proof of how he'd died."

"We should talk tae Gemma aboot what else she remembers." Rhona called but had to leave a message. She would be at Cashmere Crush until six.

Gemma did better than call back—she showed up at noon with Lachlan Felling, on Elspeth's heels. Gemma's eyes were shadowed, her blond hair in a loose clip off her face. Lachlan, in a Felling Construction cap, seemed very solicitous of her, as if trying to anticipate her every move as he stayed in her orbit.

Lachlan had sabotaged Artie the day of the games. Dyana revealed he had feelings for Gemma and a broken engagement. Could he have taken out Joseph to get Gemma for himself?

Gemma halted abruptly next to Rhona. "I was walking by the beach tae clear my head when Lachlan bumped intae me and we got tae talking."

Paislee and Rhona turned to Lachlan. Paislee didn't believe Lachlan was just out walking for one hot second.

"Rhona, lass, Lachlan mentioned needing part-time help in his office at the construction company, and I remembered you were interested in making extra money."

Rhona immediately nodded. "The only day I have left is Sunday."

"That wouldnae work," Lachlan said. "The position is during the week." He tapped his chin thoughtfully. "But there might be something on the weekends for a sales position. I'll talk tae Dyana."

"Dyana?" Gemma queried in a sharp tone. "You didnae mention that she would be involved."

"I'm sairy, Gemma. I wasnae thinking." Lachlan removed his cap and crushed it in his hands.

"No, you werenae," Gemma said. "I cannae stand that woman. I ken Dyana was one of many that Joseph slept with, but with her, it's personal." She placed her fingers on his arm. "We were friends once."

"I ken." Lachlan put his hat back on. "I remember."

"What happened?" Rhona asked.

"Dyana and I went tae the same secondary school. Thought we'd be best friends forever, until she slept with Joseph before Joseph and I were married just because she could. She's an awful person." Her eyes narrowed at Lachlan. "Have you, em, slept with Dyana?"

"No! Absolutely not." Lachlan raised his hands. "I hated what she and Joseph did tae you."

Paislee's empathy for Gemma built at the same time she feared what Lachlan might have done to win her heart. He'd admitted to being jealous. He'd sabotaged Artie.

"Then how can you work together?" Gemma demanded.

"It's business, Gemma. That's all. She's got an idea tae sell homemade organic products, giving me a percentage withoot me having tae do any of the setup."

"Where?" Gemma asked.

"Well, the council wasnae amenable tae a kiosk at the park, so I thought she could set up a kiosk in the car park at Felling Construction."

"I cannae abide it," Gemma said. "We cannae be . . . friends, if Dyana is in your life. Rhona, lass, I'm sairy I suggested anything."

Lachlan seemed genuinely devastated. "Wait! Gemma, just wait a minute. I havenae signed a contract or done anything official. I would do anything tae make you happy."

"Would you?" Gemma batted her damp lashes.

Paislee was drawn in by the unspoken emotion between them.

"What is Dyana selling?" Rhona asked.

"Organic green juice that has incredible health benefits and almond flour chocolate chip cookies that taste like the real thing," Lachlan said.

Gemma's mouth pursed.

"But it doesnae matter!" Lachlan declared. "I willnae hurt you, not now. Do you think—? Of course, it's too soon. I never gave my grandmother's Luckenbooth tae another."

"Joseph's killer is oot there somewhere," Gemma said, pink settling in her cheeks. "I owe whoever is behind his death gratitude." She gave Lachlan a sideways glance. Was she wondering too if he could be that savior? "Dinnae think me cruel, ladies, but you ken he wasnae faithful. I never cheated a day of our marriage. I stopped loving Joseph a long time ago."

Lachlan clasped his hand on her shoulder. It was clear that he still cared for Gemma and would have taken her up on it if she'd offered an affair, but she hadn't done so. It seemed likely that her integrity would keep her from killing Joseph. Would she keep quiet about someone else doing it for her? She'd taken Joseph's phone in what she considered a gray area.

"Well, thanks anyway, Gemma, for thinking of me. I dinnae like not being able tae drive but I need tae pay my parents back tae get my car," Rhona said. "I swear I will never speed again. I've learned my lesson!"

"If transportation is the problem," Lachlan said, "I have a couple of old junkers at the construction yard. You're welcome tae borrow one for as long as you need. I admire the hard work ethic you're showing. And," the businessman chuckled, "you willnae be speeding in these old hunks of metal."

"Really? I cannae pay you, so mibbe we can exchange hours for the cost of the vehicle?"

Lachlan held up his hand. "It would be a favor tae me, so the engines dinnae go bad."

Gemma looked at Lachlan like Lydia looked at Corbin. It was sad that Joseph and Dyana had come between them so long ago.

"Thank you." Gemma blew out a breath. "Just dinnae trust Dyana, whatever you do, Lachlan. A woman willing tae help a man stray in his marriage is not a person with morals."

So true. It took two to dance, and while Dyana had hooked up with Joseph, Joseph had been the one married and sworn to fidelity.

"I ken her true colors," Lachlan assured them. "She cannae hurt me, but if you dinnae want me tae do business with her and Krissie at all, I willnae."

Gemma bowed her head and clasped his hands. "I've never had such uncompromising support from anyone."

"I'm not perfect, Gemma," Lachlan admitted. "I was jealous of Joseph and exchanged Artie's tree resin grip with one that contained linseed oil."

"You *what?*" Gemma said.

"And then I saw how Joseph treated Artie for my sabotage. I felt even more awful. I am so verra sairy, and I will apologize tae Artie as soon as I am able. How is he?"

"Awake. He doesnae remember anything. Joseph pushed people tae their emotional edge," Gemma said in a harsh whisper.

The pair stared at one another in perfect accord on that point at least. "If Artie accepts your apology, then I will too." Gemma cleared her throat. "I should go tae the hospital."

"I'll drive you, and then I need tae get tae the lumberyard," Lachlan said. He nodded at Rhona. "Come on by."

"I will after six, if that's okay, Lachlan?" Rhona asked. "My friend Aibreann will bring me since my bike has a flat tire."

"I have an air pump," Lachlan said. "Bring the bike too."

"You're amazing," Rhona said. "But I honestly need a new tire."

Gemma seconded this emotion and slipped her hand into Lachlan's. "You really are, Lachlan. I made a verra big mistake all those years ago."

"It's nothing at all—a blink in the eye of time." Lachlan squeezed Gemma's fingers. "I'm just sairy that I was in Edinburgh at a Highland Council meeting when it happened, or I would have been with you sooner."

Rhona and Paislee exchanged a glance, and Paislee sighed. Lachlan had an alibi.

Chapter 17

Paislee waved goodbye to Gemma and Lachlan as the pair left. It would be nice if something decent came out of this tragedy. Gemma had denied herself in her marriage, because she believed that it was her duty to submit.

Should she share Lachlan's alibi with the constables, or did they already know? She recalled that Krissie had outed Lachlan being at the station, so they probably did. It wasn't their job to tell Paislee and Rhona information.

"Artie never liked the way his da treated his mum," Rhona said during a lull in customers. Elspeth was assisting a browser by the jumpers. "Which is why the constables willnae take him off their suspect list. We need tae find oot who is behind this tragedy tae get him oot of the hotseat."

"What do you think happened tae Cam's car?" Paislee murmured. She hadn't had time to call Fern.

"That family didnae have a lot of extra money, and I imagine steroids must be expensive? A car would be an asset. Mibbe Joseph sent it tae the junkyard or sold it for scraps. Artie sometimes pitched in tae pay the bills or groceries. He did well with tips at the golf course."

Paislee patted Rhona's shoulder. "Artie is a sweetheart." Had Fern known Cam was doping? She'd loved Cam.

At four there was a break in customers, so Elspeth offered to cover the front while Paislee and Rhona called Fern from the back room, on speaker.

"Fern! Hi, it's Paislee Shaw."

"Hi, Paislee." Her tone was curious as to why Paislee was calling.

"I'm at the shop with Rhona."

Rhona shared a sad hello.

"Hi, Rhona, hon. How are you?" Fern asked.

"I could be better, honestly. Artie is going tae get oot of hospital tomorrow, but the police still suspect him of being involved with his da's death. Gemma is broken up over it."

"What can I do tae help?" Fern asked. "I'm at the Lion's Mane, grabbing a pint with Delilah. She's convinced Artie did it."

"He didnae!" Rhona said.

"Why does Delilah think so?" Paislee asked.

"Joseph was abusive tae Artie; we can all agree on that," Fern said. Her voice was muffled and then it changed to speaker on their end as well. "Delilah is on."

"Joseph was a doper. Cam was a doper. It is known for causing angry ootbursts," Delilah said.

"Artie was clean," Paislee said.

"Cam never wanted Artie tae take steroids," Fern said. "He stood up tae Joseph aboot that plenty of times and got punished for it. I heard Cam tell Artie not tae do them. It gave Cam verra high blood pressure, but he wouldnae stop. The muscle he built was worth the risk."

"It sounds like Cam protected Artie," Paislee said.

"Aye. That was his little brother," Fern said. "I ken Cam wasnae great, but he wasnae this monster either. He had dreams tae be the best strongman in history. He was willing tae use steroids tae reach that mark."

"Fern, did you know about Cam and Joseph doping the whole time?" Paislee asked. Why hadn't she said something earlier?

"What does it matter now?" Fern sputtered. "They're both dead."

Following her hunch, Paislee asked, "Did Cam call you the night he died?"

Fern sucked in a breath. "What do you mean?"

"You said he was your friend, and that you loved him. Did Cam call you? We are trying tae figure out his actions that night. Do you know what happened tae his car, after the accident?"

"No. I hadnae thought aboot it," Fern said. "Joseph told us it was totaled. It made me sick tae my stomach tae think of it."

"And didnae Joseph hurry up with a cremation? You were upset aboot that, Fern," Delilah said. "Cam never wanted tae be cremated."

"He was twenty! Why would you talk about death?" Paislee asked in surprise.

"We were in secondary school and angsty," Fern murmured. "Joseph shut us oot, didnae he?" She caught a sob in her throat.

"Anything you can remember will help us find the truth," Paislee said. And yeah, she did remember being angsty.

"Cam called me," Fern admitted. "That night. I didnae see him, but he wanted tae hook up, and I said no. I regret it now though. He might be alive if I'd given in."

"Where did he want tae meet you?" Paislee asked.

"My flat."

"So, he was in Nairn," Paislee said. She grabbed a pen and a scrap of paper.

"Aye, I think so."

Pen poised, Paislee asked, "What time was that?"

"Rhona, lass, can I get some help?" Elspeth called to the back room.

"Coming!" Rhona said, albeit reluctantly, as she left toward the front.

Paislee glanced out to the shop. Three customers were browsing and chatting. Her employees could handle it.

"What time?" Paislee repeated.

"I've been going through my messages and notes from Cam, with all of this coming tae light, it's made me nostalgic. It was on a Saturday night. I was home from work at Tesco, so after ten. I'd just broken up with Brandon."

"The eejit with the big truck?" Delilah asked.

"Aye."

"Guid riddance tae him!" Delilah said.

"So, I was . . . available, technically," Fern said, sounding embarrassed. "And Cam and I had chemistry."

"He was your doomed love," Delilah said.

"We texted back and forth, and then he called, and I could tell he was angry and disappointed aboot not winning. Emotional, but he didnae sound drunk. He wasnae slurring at all, just furious. He went on and on aboot how he'd let Ross doon, and his da doon, and then that I'd let him doon by not sticking with him. I had enough. Said he could find some other hen, because it wasnae going tae be me cleaning up his mess. I hung up."

"The right thing tae do," Delilah said.

"It was!" Paislee seconded. So, Fern agreed with Sandi and the ambulance medic that Cam hadn't been drunk like Joseph claimed. She'd talked with him after ten.

"That was the last I heard from Cam, until Artie texted me the next day that Cam was dead. We went right over tae the Whittles' house. Joseph didnae give any of us a chance tae grieve or mourn. Just said that Cam had crashed intae a tree, and they were having him cremated and put in the ocean." Fern cleared her throat. "It never occurred tae me tae push. It wasnae my place—but I did feel bad for Artie, you ken? I let him ken I was there, if he needed tae talk."

"That was sweet," Paislee said.

"He never took me up on it," Fern said.

Paislee saw another customer enter the shop. "I need tae run, but thank you for clearing up a few things."

"Why does it matter?" Delilah asked.

"It might not. We are hoping tae find some closure for Gemma and Artie both."

"Guid luck with that," Fern said. "My last conversation with Cam is burned intae my heart."

Paislee ended the call. Regret was awful. What could she do about it? Fern had made the right choice. Cam's decision to take steroids had been on him.

She scrolled her phone for Sandi's number, which she had because of being on the Highland Games committee.

She sent a text message to Sandi. **Hi—it's Paislee Shaw. Had a quick question about Cam Whittle. What time was he in the ER the night he died?**

There was no answer, so she pocketed her mobile and joined the others, enjoying the busy last hour of business.

At ten after six, Paislee closed up for the evening. "Well done, my friends! What a day. I bet this will be one of the strongest sales days yet. I couldn't do this without you."

Elspeth went into the back and got them each a can of fizzy water, handing them out. "I feel like it was a workoot."

"Too much?" Paislee asked, studying Elspeth's lined face. She was in excellent shape as she walked to and from work, sometimes more often, as she walked with her blind sister.

"No! Just right." Elspeth raised the can of water. "I love that I can combine earning money with exercise."

Paislee laughed. Rhona said, "I do too—and now I get even more with the weans I teach for dancing."

After a refreshing drink of water, Paislee jumped, startled at a knock on the door. She peered out the frosted glass window.

"Aibreann!" Paislee unlocked the door and opened it, pulling her inside. Tourists browsed on the sidewalk and Paislee was tempted to stay open, but she couldn't do that to her employees.

"Hey, bestie," Rhona said, giving her a side hug. "Gemma has hooked me up with a loaner pickup truck from Lachlan Felling."

"The guy from the construction company?"

"Aye. He says I'll be doing him a favor, driving them around so the engine stays in working order. I think he's being nice, because he likes Gemma, but I willnae squabble. Now I just need tae find a job for Sundays only so I can pay Mum and Da off sooner."

"Three jobs!" Aibreann said, eyes wide. "I never realized you were such an overachiever."

"Me either, but I like my independence," Rhona said.

Aibreann laughed. "I wish I could afford tae be more independent. Someday, my own flat."

"What happened with Fern and Delilah?" Rhona asked.

Paislee brought them all up to speed. "So, basically, we know that Cam had tae be in Nairn that night. Fern said he didn't sound drunk, just mad. He had high blood pressure, which is why he didn't want Artie tae get started with the steroids. I should call Constable Monroe," *not Zeffer, never Zeffer,* "tae have her talk with the girls."

Aibreann looked at her phone and scowled at the time. "We've got tae get moving, Rhona. We've got the weans at seven. Where is your bike?"

Paislee was exhausted after her sleepless night, which she couldn't even blame on Grandpa's cough but only her own choices. Possible mistakes. She wanted to test the waters with Brody. "Let's go."

"You're not going tae count the money?" Rhona asked.

"No. I am beat. I'll do it in the morning."

They trooped out the back and to the Juke. Elspeth would walk Susan home, with Rosie, Susan's guide-eye dog. Rhona carried her bike around the corner to Aibreann's borrowed car.

Paislee's phone rang when she'd reached the corner market near her home, and she saw that it was Sandi. She used Bluetooth to answer.

"Hi, Sandi!"

"Paislee." Sandi said her name with disappointment. "Why are you asking questions? I didnae peg you for a bletherer."

Was Sandi actually upset about Paislee gossiping, or concerned that Paislee was still asking questions that might uncover Sandi's deeds? "Gemma was in my shop earlier today. Artie might get out of hospital tomorrow but is still a suspect. I've agreed tae help Rhona find out who really killed Joseph so the police will ease up on Artie, which will help the family."

Sandi exhaled. "Cam was already dead when he was brought tae the emergency room at eleven thirty Monday night, but he hadnae been dead long. He'd had a bloody nose, which could be from the car accident, but it didnae quite track with the other injuries. As I told you, my questions were overruled. After so many years in the ER, you develop a sixth sense."

"How awful for you, tae be powerless."

"Another thing that has always bugged me was wondering why Joseph hadnae taken the keys tae save his son? What if Cam wasnae alone that night, or if he'd hurt someone else? Irresponsible! It was unforgivable tae me, as you can probably surmise from my tone."

It could give Sandi a reason to want Joseph dead, to save Artie from falling into his father's known steroid abuse.

"I heard from Fern that Cam had actually protected Artie from doping, and Joseph."

"I believe that," Sandi said. "Nobody is one hundred percent evil. Though I'd be hard pressed tae find a guid thing tae say aboot Joseph Whittle."

Paislee pulled under the carport of her home but didn't turn the engine off. Sandi had been very helpful, but she had a real hatred for Joseph.

Could the strongwoman have stabbed Joseph to death? As a nurse, she had a high tolerance for blood—on the other hand, she would know where to cut and there had been so much blood everywhere.

It would be too messy.

It seemed to be the act of an amateur, which, unfortunately, leaned more toward Artie, or worse, Gemma.

"Cam had high blood pressure, so he was aware of the side effects of the steroids he was taking and warned Artie against them."

"High blood pressure?" Sandi gave a thoughtful hum over the line. "That would cause nose bleeds. . . ." She exhaled. "I pray Artie isnae guilty and that the constables find somewhere else tae look. What happened tae that carny guy? Kev?"

"I haven't seen him around. Not that I would! It's been over a week."

"Tragic," Sandi said. "Well, let me ken if I can help in any way."

"I will—thanks. Night!" Paislee ended the call, turned off the engine, and exited the Juke. Should she phone Constable Monroe?

She needed the sanctuary of her house and her family to regroup first. The smell of rosemary and sage greeted her as she entered the foyer.

"Hi, Shaws!" Paislee hung up her handbag and dropped her keys into the ceramic dish.

"Oot back!" Grandpa called.

Paislee ambled down the hall toward the back door and the covered porch. Snowball was sitting on Grandpa's lap while Brody and Wallace played with the football and goalie net.

"He's improving already," Grandpa said.

"Tryoots are next week for the school team," Brody told her as he collected the ball. He played right now for an independent league and hoped to make the school team. Coach Harris believed Brody could do both.

She didn't want to stifle him, and so long as he continued with school, she wouldn't complain or create obstacles.

Now that she was looking for signs of Calan Maxwell in Brody, they were everywhere. Calan had been tall and lean. Brown eyes. Large feet. The auburn hair could be from her da and her, but Calan's had held streaks of red in deep brown too.

Where was Calan?

What would she do if Brody decided that he *did* want to know about his da? Where would she start?

Zeffer, damn Zeffer, had offered to help her find Brody's dad. Paislee had let Calan follow Calan's dream of being an officer in the military and escaping small-town Nairn. He'd been stifled by his grandfather, though he appreciated the home; he'd been from . . . where? Edinburgh?

The secret genie was out of the bottle, and there was no putting her back in. All through dinner, Calan's features played over Brody's.

Though Paislee would like to talk to him—*not at all, ever*—away from Grandpa's (possibly) judgmental eyes, she knew Brody could use Grandpa's love and support for what might be a bombshell.

She hadn't been able to eat more than a few bites of dinner.

"How's your toe, Mum?"

"It's fine." Brody was thoughtful. A good kid. Would it be too much? "I'm really glad we've gotten tae ken Grandma Rosanna. I've enjoyed your ideas about a trip tae America. I think it might be fun tae plan together."

Grandpa studied her from his seat at the table where Brody was finishing the last of the watermelon ice cream cake. Paislee crossed her arms over her stomach as she leaned against the counter.

"It's cool tae have family!"

Paislee drew in a deep breath. "I was"—she swallowed and rubbed her throat—"wondering, if you'd . . . like tae know more . . . aboutyourdad." There—it was out and done.

Grandpa whipped off his glasses and stared at her, then focused on Brody.

Brody tilted his head and lowered his spoon to the dish. His lower lip gaped. "You said I belonged tae you. I dinnae have a dad. I tell everyone that."

Paislee's knees buckled, and she leaned against the counter to stabilize herself from falling. "You are mine, Brody, love. That is true and will always be true."

"But?" Brody's face turned red.

"It takes two people tae make a baby, as you learned in school. There are ways around that, with invitro, but the point is, that in the normal course of things it takes two people having—making lo—having sex, tae make a baby."

Brody paled, freckles bright across his nose, and jumped to his feet. "I dinnae want tae hear any more. You lied tae me."

Chapter 18

Brody pushed out the back door to the garden and climbed to the top of the chestnut tree. She could hear his sobs, just barely, over her own. She couldn't stop ugly crying.

Grandpa patted her back and kept the tissues coming as they both gawked out the kitchen window to the tree and Brody's auburn locks visible through the leaves. He climbed higher and higher until he couldn't go any farther.

The tears slowed to hot, salty streams down her cheeks as she sucked in a breath.

"What brought that moment of truth on?" Grandpa asked. "A wee warning would've been welcome. Och, this was why you wanted tae take him oot for ice cream?"

"Aye. He hates me. Brody hates me."

Grandpa handed her the box of tissues, and when that was depleted, went to the pantry for a fresh one. "He doesnae hate you. He is angry, and he has a right tae be, dinnae you think, lass? He isnae in the place right now where he can see beyond the deception."

"When would have been a good time, Grandpa? Huh? Tae raise him with the fact his mum had a wild night and got knocked up at seventeen, then had him at eighteen. Not the life lesson I wanted tae teach him! He has never been a mistake tae me—*never*, ever."

Grandpa patted her back. "Why now?"

"Zeffer said that some of the schools will be offering DNA kits this year. Just another *fun* science project."

Grandpa glanced at her with empathetic eyes. "Lass, I am surprised that Brody hadnae questioned you before now. They had the birds and the bees talk in primary, eh?"

"It's not as straightforward as it used tae be with some girl bees not liking boy bees, and vice versa. Not tae mention bees that want tae be birds instead. Also, he said he didn't want tae think about sex. I didn't press it."

"He's thirteen now, and I'm sure he's changed his mind. I've noticed that he's taking longer in the shower, if you ken what I mean." Grandpa kept his gaze on the chestnut tree.

Paislee was tempted to plug her ears, but that behavior screeched of denial, and she wouldn't do that on top of the rest of her sins.

"We have strong pipes and plenty of water. We'll be fine."

"That we will," Grandpa said. "How aboot a dram?"

"I'd love one, but not until after I talk with Brody."

"He might be up in that tree a while."

"I can wait." Paislee didn't take her gaze from the tree, though she eventually moved outside.

In fact, it was after ten that night when her son finally climbed down the tree. Grandpa had gone to bed, but Paislee wouldn't rush Brody. He had to feel what he was feeling.

She had Grandpa and Lydia; he was up there talking to nobody. Not even Wallace.

Snowball and Wallace were on the porch, curled up by her feet. She wasn't even knitting, her attention solely on Brody.

He scuffed up the stairs and plopped down on the top step. Wallace went to him and licked Brody's face.

"You lied tae me, Mum."

It tore the scab off the wound on her heart, causing fresh pain. "I'm sorry."

"Why? You talk on and on aboot being honest, and this is a big damn lie. The biggest."

Paislee bowed her head. Tears fell to her lap. "I'm not sure what tae say, or if you're ready tae hear the truth now."

Brody stood and picked up Wallace. "I cannae trust you, Mum."

"I love you. I'd like tae explain, if you're ready."

"I'm not."

Brody brushed by her and went into the house.

Paislee cried, accepting that she'd hurt her son, the person she loved the most in this whole entire world.

She texted a single name to Zeffer. **Calan Maxwell.** She poured herself a large whisky and went to bed.

The next morning, she overslept for the first time in years. She'd gone through social media on her phone all night, and Calan wasn't anywhere she could find. Maybe he'd gone to freaking America like her mum and her uncle. The battery on her mobile had died.

She hurried downstairs to see Grandpa reading the paper as if it wasn't nine o'clock in the morning on Thursday.

She wasn't feeling good about herself as a person right now.

"You look rough, lass," Grandpa said. "I was going tae let you sleep until quarter past then shove you in the shower."

"Where's Brody?"

"He got a ride with Sam's mum. Nice lady."

"Yes. I am a terrible mother." Paislee plugged her phone into the charger.

Grandpa rattled the paper. "You are not. Brody and Sam will be working on a science project after school, so you dinnae need tae pick him up. I can do it, since I'll have the car."

"Why is that?"

"You have Knit and Sip."

Her mind was a muddle. Paislee poured herself a very strong mug of Brodies tea. "Okay. I have tae give him space, don't I? I don't want tae, but he is avoiding me."

"You've done your best, and Brody will come around. We have tae believe that when we make mistakes," Grandpa said, his voice gruff. "I've made my share of them."

"Craigh loves you, and you know that Gran forgave you. I hope someday Brody can forgive me." Paislee understood her grandfather's sadness better now.

For the person you love to hate you? It was brutal.

Paislee didn't want to talk to anyone, but that wasn't an option she had in her life, so, she grabbed her tea and her phone with twenty percent and went upstairs to cry in the shower. When she got out, she didn't feel better, and her red-rimmed eyes remained sore.

She put on her sunglasses and decided to tell everyone she had allergies. Another lie? She took off the sunglasses.

Grandpa gave her a to-go mug of strong tea and a hug. "It will be awright, love. Give it time."

Paislee thanked him. "See you at noon."

"That you will." Grandpa shuffled back down the hall to finish reading the paper.

Constable Monroe's police car was outside of Cashmere Crush, and Paislee hurried to park in the alley and open the front door.

"Is everything okay?" Paislee asked.

"Och, aye. Sairy—it's just that you were on my way tae question some others. I'd talked tae Rhona Smythe this morning at her home, and she mentioned that you'd talked tae Fern, Cam's ex."

"We did! I was going tae call you, but you're here now."

"Too busy?" Monroe quipped.

"You have no idea." She'd broken her son's heart. There had been no other way.

The constable studied her face. "Are you all right? You look like you've been crying."

"Sad song on the radio," Paislee said, having put on sad music so that it wouldn't be a lie.

"Opera gets me every time."

Not what she'd picked for the officer, but people were complicated.

Paislee brought her mug to the counter. She was supposed to be early and count in the money. She hadn't been late to open the shop in years. Best laid plans.

"Constable, I am actually running behind this morning, so if we could hurry this along? I have things tae do yet before I can open the store and need fifteen minutes." It was five to ten.

"We'll be quick then. Can I record you?"

"Sure."

Paislee could see shadows on the sidewalk out front. The police car parked at the curb might be alarming.

"I'm ready when you are!" Constable Monroe said.

"Constable, did you know that Cam suffered from high blood pressure?"

"You were supposed tae tell me information, Paislee, not ask me questions."

"Sorry! But I think it might be related somehow. Sandi was never sold on the theory that Cam was drunk that night."

"Sandi?"

"Sandi Peckett, ER nurse and volunteer coordinator for the Nairn Highland Games."

"We've talked with her." Constable Monroe pressed the record button on her tablet. "She was very helpful aboot the steroids found in Joseph Whittle. The amount was extreme, and the point of entry was Joseph's back, not where he could reach."

Someone dosed Joseph with steroids and then stabbed him? A knock sounded on the door. "Maybe that will be Rhona," Paislee said.

"I could have given her a ride if I'd realized she was coming here." The constable shifted her attention from the front door to the recording.

"She's borrowing a truck from Lachlan."

"Lachlan Felling?"

"Aye. I'd wondered if he'd done it out of love for Gemma, but he was in Edinburgh." Paislee's mobile rang. "It's Mary Beth. She's probably worried. I am hardly ever late."

"Slept in?"

"Yes. Listen, Constable Monroe, can you please come back at noon when Grandpa is here? I'll have two extra people on the floor then."

"I never thought yarn would be so popular," the constable said. "Fern dated Cam."

"Right—and Fern talked tae Cam the night he died, at ten thirty, looking for a"—Paislee eyed the tablet—"connection. He wasn't drunk like Joseph said, which matches what Sandi believed. Cam was in the ER before midnight."

Constable Monroe's phone rang, and the recording stopped. She brought the mobile to her ear. "Really? I'm on my way." The constable pocketed her tablet. "They found Cam's car, in the back of the Whittles' property, covered up by branches—hidden. Gemma doesnae ken anything aboot it, as she's at the hospital with Artie."

"He's coming home today."

Mary Beth left a message and then texted Paislee.

Paislee walked Monroe out the front door, where Mary Beth waited with a worried expression. "Are you okay?" her friend asked.

"I am—thank you. Constable, noon, all right?"

The constable nodded but was already unlocking the door to climb into her police vehicle. Probably headed to the Whittle house.

The sound of a pickup backfiring was like a shot and Mary Beth clutched Paislee's arm. "What on God's green earth is going on?"

"That is probably Rhona. She's borrowed a truck from Lachlan. Come in, Mary Beth. I need you for fifteen minutes before I open."

Mary Beth rubbed her hands. "I've got you, but then I want a full explanation."

They went inside, and Paislee shut the door.

"Locked, or no?" Mary Beth asked.

"No. I just need fifteen minutes tae count the cash from last night. I'd planned tae get here early but didn't—anyway!" Paislee put in her headphones to listen to music while she counted yesterday's money and situated the register for the day.

It only took her twelve minutes.

"Thank you, thank you!" Paislee gave Mary Beth a hug and saw that Rhona was already helping a customer.

"No problem. That's what friends are for, right?" Mary Beth placed her hands on her chest. "My heart sank when I saw the police vehicle parked on the curb, worrit that you'd been robbed or something."

Paislee knocked on the wood countertop. "Nothing so drastic."

"Why are your eyes red?" Mary Beth asked.

"I can't talk about it right now. Did Rhona fill you in about Artie? He's being released from hospital today and is still a suspect."

"That's just terrible!" Mary Beth said.

"And they found Cam Whittle's car behind the Whittle house, like, covered in branches, so it was hidden on purpose."

"So?" Mary Beth asked.

"Joseph told everyone that the car had been totaled by Cam crashing intae a tree," Rhona said.

"Oh!"

Constable Monroe was supposed to drop by at noon if she wanted to talk more with Paislee about Fern, but the officer didn't show up until after Grandpa had left at six to pick up Brody.

Brody hadn't responded to her text of **I Love You** that morning. Paislee was glad to be busy, so she didn't put too much pressure on him while he was at school, or at Sam's.

She'd thought she was doing the right thing.

At five after six, Rhona's phone rattled off with a series of messages. "Gemma says Artie has tae stay over another night at the hospital. I'll join her in the waiting room tae commiserate."

"Send my love," Paislee said. "See you in the morning."

"Bye!" Rhona hustled out the back, the borrowed pickup backfiring as she left.

Constable Monroe relaxed on a stool at the high table, accepting a Perrier. The women chatted while Paislee locked the front door and counted the money in the register. She prepped the drawer for the next day, putting the cash in her little safe.

"This was normally what I do at night," Paislee said.

"Being late knocks me off kilter for the whole day," Monroe said. "The information aboot Cam's last movements might be helpful in the event it's reopened as an active investigation."

"Is that even possible?" Paislee asked.

"It's up tae Gemma and Artie, I suppose. That Fern seems like a nice lass—completely in love with Cam." The constable shrugged. "I was never aboot the muscled guys, myself. My exes tend tae be the tall thin type. What aboot you?"

"I don't have a type." Paislee directed the conversation to Gemma. "There is no accounting for love. Gemma and Lachlan were betrothed before Joseph swept her away, but Joseph wasn't faithful tae her. He'd hooked up with Dyana, among others."

"Our officers in the field have a list twenty ladies long that confirm Joseph was unfaithful from Bucharest, Romania, to Nairn and back again." Constable Monroe shook her head. "Dinnae understand why Gemma stayed."

"They were married in the church, and tae her, that meant forever." Paislee reached for a knitting project. There were always several in varying stages. "Dyana and Lachlan were supposed tae

work together for her tae sell her organic green juice at his construction business for a cut of the profits, but Gemma said she
wouldn't be comfortable with Lachlan and Dyana being coworkers,
considering their history. Lachlan agreed tae nix it right away."

"That's just as well," Constable Monroe said. "In our investiga-
tions we've discovered that Dyana's juice is not organic. She willnae be allowed tae sell it anyway."

Paislee's eyes widened in surprise. "How did you find that out?"

"I cannae say," Constable Monroe said. "A word of caution regarding business partnerships that fall through, as it might leave one
of them feeling vengeful."

Lachlan? Krissie? She could imagine Krissie taking revenge—
she'd proved to be less of a team player and more about herself.
"Do you think that Kev could be a danger tae Artie or Gemma?"

Constable Monroe swirled her can of fizzy water. "Kev Sloane
is in jail for a different crime in Glasgow, so no, I dinnae think he's
a risk tae Artie. I dinnae believe he killed Joseph, but someone set
him up tae take the fall."

"Who?"

Lydia arrived, coming in through the back door. "Hey!"

"Dinnae ken. Yet." Constable Monroe finished the water and
tossed the can in the recycle bin. "Thanks again for your help," the
officer said. She nodded at Lydia. "I'll walk tae the station. It will be
nice tae stretch my legs." She went out the back. "The days couldnae be more bonny. Bye, now."

"Well, she seems pretty great," Lydia said. "Does she knit?"

"I don't think so, but I might reel her in tae learn."

Lydia studied Paislee's face and the red eyes. "What is it?"

"An upset with Brody." Paislee's stomach clenched tight.

Lydia wrapped Paislee in a hug, no questions, and Paislee cried
on her best friend's shoulder. A knock sounded at the front door.
Her Knit and Sip ladies.

"Should we skip for tonight?" Lydia asked, searching Paislee's
face for clues to help and support.

"No. They'll know soon enough." Paislee tugged Lydia toward the front door. "I asked Brody if he wanted tae know about his da."

Lydia stopped short. Paislee unlocked the entrance and let Meri, Elspeth, and Mary Beth inside. Blaise was crossing the street.

Once Blaise was in as well, Paislee locked the door. Lydia had gotten the wine out and the snacks on the table. Paislee couldn't even think about the knitting projects to do.

"I can only tell this once, so . . ."

Lydia gave Paislee a glass of pinot grigio. Her friends realized something serious was about to be shared and just listened as she told her story, and Brody's, and Calan's. And Mack Zeffer's warning that had turned out to be the catalyst.

"And Brody still isn't talking tae me," Paislee concluded miserably.

"He will come around," Lydia said.

"You made the best choice you knew tae at the time," Meri said. She squeezed Paislee's hand.

"Not everyone would have done the same," Blaise offered, sneaking in for a hug.

"There were other decisions you could have made that were perhaps easier, but you didnae," Mary Beth said. "That was brave."

"I remember when your granny brought you tae church with the news that you'd moved in with her," Elspeth said. "You were so sweet, Paislee, and Agnes was ferocious in her defense of you."

"I had Gran and Lydia." Paislee's body ached, feeling all of the emotions from then and now.

"We need our friends," Mary Beth said.

Paislee nodded at each of them, grateful for their support. She set aside the wine. It tasted like straw in her mouth.

"This is the worst right now," Lydia said. "But tomorrow is another day."

Paislee ached with remorse. "And what if Brody hates me tomorrow too?"

Chapter 19

Paislee awakened right away when she heard a soft knock on her door. "Mum? You up?" The nightstand clock read six in the morning. Brody had been pretending to sleep last night when she'd gotten home early from Knit and Sip.

"Aye—come on in."

Brody entered, his feet bare, his hair rumpled. He wore flannel pajama bottoms and a black T-shirt.

Paislee patted the foot of her bed where he liked to cuddle with Wallace. This time, he had Wallace and Snowball with him. All three jumped up on the mattress.

She sensed that he was on the edge so didn't push for a hug. It was hard as hell to bite her tongue and let him talk. To listen.

"I'm verra, verra mad," Brody said. His eyes were bloodshot. "I dinnae like it. My stomach hurts. I thought I could trust you. How can you keep a dad from me? I talked tae Grandpa, and he said you had your reasons and that I should give you a chance tae explain."

"I missed you yesterday," she said softly. Not blaming. "You and I have been a team since I found out that I was pregnant. Are you sure you want tae know?"

"Aye. Is it *bad*? Like, were you hurt?"

"No!" Paislee was glad that the room was dim, and that they

had the softness of shadows to cocoon them. "Not like that at all. I was irresponsible."

"I was worried aboot the worst."

"No, no." She blew out a breath.

"What then?"

Secondary school. Her da's death. Her mum's desertion. Gran, always, and then Grandpa too. Lydia. Thank God for Lydia. Who was probably leaving for Germany.

Wallace sprawled on his back between them for shameless belly rubs.

Paislee stroked the soft fur. The pup had offered solace since the day they'd bought him when Gran had died.

"My da passed away when I was sixteen. I struggled in school that year. My mum—"

"Grandma Rosanna," Brody said.

"Aye. She was grieving as well. We weren't close. She worked a lot and found someone online, someone in America. She left my final year of secondary."

"She didnae stay tae see your commencement ceremony?"

Paislee forced herself to look at how it had been and her part in what happened. "No. I told her it didn't matter. That Lydia and I would get a flat, that I didn't need her. I wasn't very nice, actually, when she told me she'd gotten her passport and a plane ticket. I wasn't invited."

Brody's eyes widened. "That's mean of her."

Paislee sighed softly in agreement. "Grandpa reminded me that Mum was young. Her and my da had gotten married right out of secondary school."

"How old?"

"Eighteen."

He petted Wallace's ears, absorbing the information. "Grandpa Bruce and Grandma Rosanna. He died when you were sixteen, and Grandma went tae America when you were—how old?"

"Seventeen. I finished S6, because Gran was a teacher and encouraged education. I was thinking of continuing at university, but I wasn't sold on the idea. I was happy enough working at the market behind the register. I wasn't like you, with a dream tae be something more."

Her mother had paid the rent on their house through August, giving Paislee time to sort things out with Lydia. School in Scotland was only mandatory through the age of sixteen, and Rosanna felt she'd done enough.

On graduation night, Paislee had celebrated with a wee bit of anger in her heart toward her mother and, feeling sorry for herself about her da, had drunk champagne with Calan on the beach. They'd bonded during that last year over their das no longer being with them, feeling that life had dealt them an unfair hand.

Lydia had fretted, but Paislee had decided she was going to lose her virginity to handsome young Calan going into the military to be an officer. He had the next twenty years of his life planned out to the last detail of a glorious career capped by a brilliant retirement raising collies. They'd known the score and had no expectations of more. They'd been close friends sharing a beautiful experience—not love, for either of them. Calan had lived with his grandfather, who would be moving to Dundee with Calan's future sorted.

They'd used a condom the first time. The second time, they'd spun the wheel of fate. By the end of July, Paislee knew she was pregnant. Her mother suggested not making a mistake. Rosanna wasn't continuing the rent on the house. She wasn't coming back to Scotland.

Lydia's parents had decided a move to Edinburgh would be the next stage of their married journey—offering to take Lydia, and Paislee, with them. Paislee and Lydia had strategized and called Gran for her wise advice, fearing condemnation; Gran instead opened her home as well as her heart.

Perhaps Brody got his ability to dream big from Calan? What would Calan say to their son?

Tears dripped hot onto her hand.

"Mum?"

"Sorry—lost in thought. I'm trying tae be fair where I can and just give you facts when I'm so emotional." Paislee scrubbed her cheeks. "Nairn was very old-fashioned, and Gran was Catholic. We're Catholic too, though I'm not as strict. I had celebrated my graduation a little too freely and ended up pregnant. Your father was joining the military and had big plans for his future. He didn't want tae stay in Nairn."

"He doesnae ken aboot me?" The hurt there went straight through to her gut.

"No, son."

Silence pounded like a nail to her heart, then, "Can we call him?"

"If that is what you want tae do, then yes, I'll find a way. I wasn't sure how you would feel or if you'd want tae know him."

"You were alone, except for Gran?" She wouldn't give the rotten details of Rosanna to her son, because it would mean he'd never forgive her mother.

"Yes, and Aunt Lydia. Though, she spent a few years in Edinburgh, married, before she moved back." After Gran died.

"I dinnae remember that," Brody said.

"You were a wean." It was a dark time.

"I dinnae understand why it was a big deal," Brody said.

"Well, our small shire of Nairn, and our church, had people with sharp opinions about an eighteen-year-old single mum. Saying that I would never amount tae much, or that I was taking advantage of the system." Paislee's chest constricted at the cruel barbs lobbed her way. "Gran showed me how tae knit while I was pregnant with you and encouraged me tae take online business classes. I started Cashmere Crush online only until—again with Gran's assistance and encouragement—she said I should be part of our community and live a life tae make the gossipers eat their vicious words."

"People were mean? Who?" Brody asked, his back up.

"It doesn't matter now. What matters, and what has always mattered tae me, Brody, was that you grew up protected and loved."

"You dinnae think my da would love me?"

A groan of angst spilled from Paislee's mouth. "He would if he knew—anybody who knows you loves you for the amazing young man that you are." She reached for his hand and covered it, their fingers entwined in Wallace's fur. "Your dad and I were very good friends but not in love. I knew he had plans that didn't include a family or a wife." A tear dripped. "I made a choice at seventeen, and eighteen, and every day after, tae keep you safe. You were mine—my joy, my responsibility, my blessing. I love you, Brody, and I am so sorry for the mess I've made by doing what I believed tae be right. Can you forgive me?"

Brody launched himself over the pups to hug her tight, crying as much as she was sobbing. "I forgive you," her son said. "You didnae want tae hold him back from his dreams."

"I swear that was always my intent," Paislee said, holding her son's gaze. "I've tried tae be the best person that I can be, the best example for you. I never wanted tae fail you or let you down like I have. I'm truly sorry. It was the ignorance of youth."

They cried and talked for another half hour, as Paislee told Brody about Calan Maxwell. His ambition and drive to be the top. "Kind of like you," Paislee said.

"Why now, Mum?" Brody asked.

She was wrung out by her emotions, but she had to be honest. "DI Zeffer suggested that you might want tae know, now that you're thirteen and growing up. I said that you didn't care about it, but I was wrong. I've pushed people back who wanted tae know more about you, and your dad. It was my secret that I would protect until you asked for more."

"Like the headmaster?" Brody asked astutely. "Why dinnae you have a boyfriend? Emma's mum has two boyfriends. She thought it was weird that I didnae have a dad."

Zeffer had been right to warn her, damn him.

"You are my priority. I love you more than anyone else in the world."

"I ken that." Brody patted Wallace. "But maybe you should date. You're getting older," he teased. "Over thirty."

"Funny."

"So, if I would have asked you point-blank aboot my dad, you would have told me?" Brody held her gaze.

"Yes." Paislee put her hand to her heart. "I swear it."

"That's guid enough for me," Brody said. "I can see why you wanted tae get ice cream. Is it too late?"

"We are not having ice cream for breakfast."

He got up and the dogs jumped to the floor.

"I love you, Mum. I'm glad you kept me, and didnae sell me tae the gypsies."

"Don't tempt me," Paislee said on a sob. "I've asked Zeffer tae help locate Calan. Please, keep your expectations minimal, okay? We didnae stay in touch, and he's not on social media."

"Okay."

Brody left and Paislee pulled the blanket over her face, crying with relief that her son didn't hate her.

After her shower, she saw a message from Zeffer asking her to meet him at the bandstand. He knew how much she enjoyed the sea, and this must be bad news if he had to tell her in a public place, with a view of the Firth.

Chapter 20

Brody chattered the whole way to school about Emma, who was trying out for cheer squad, and about practice for the school football team, on which he hoped to place a position even though he was only in S2.

Chances were slim, Coach said, but it was worth a shot.

"See you at four," Paislee said. "I love you and thank you."

He blew her a kiss after he got out of the car.

Shaking, she called Lydia to let her know what had happened. It was a difficult conversation to get through, and they both were crying at the end.

"Of course, he doesnae hate you!" Lydia sniffed. "You have worked triple-time tae make sure you're not your mother."

"What if Zeffer has found Calan, and he's got a family of four somewhere in France or something?"

"Or what if he's dashingly handsome and still single and eager tae be part of Brody's life?" Lydia lowered her voice. "And yours? Calan is the only man you've had sex with ever. I think I like this Emma, wondering aboot why you dinnae date."

Paislee parked in the lot next to Zeffer's blue SUV. "I'm here. I'll call you after."

"I think Mack's a guid guy, Paislee. As guid as Calan even."

"I've got tae go."

"Chicken!" her bestie called.

Paislee glimpsed in the rearview mirror and gasped. Her eyes were red—not just a little, but she looked like she had a bad case of pink eye in both supposed-to-be-white orbs.

Her hair was a mess and her nose shiny from blowing it so much.

She couldn't think about that or even powder her nose, because Zeffer had seen her and waved.

Dang it.

Rhona texted. **Everything okay? It's almost ten.**

Paislee messaged back. **Something has come up. I'll open at noon. Sorry!**

No problem. I'll visit Artie at the hospital. He will be discharged around the same time.

Paislee exited the Juke and walked toward the bandstand, where Zeffer stood and gestured to the seat on the bench. He had two cans of lemon Perrier. Next to those was a thick manila folder with Calan Maxwell's name labeled on the outside.

Zeffer studied her face but instead of mocking her or commenting, he gestured for her to sit down.

"How did it go?"

Paislee's eyes welled. "Not great."

"Stupid question. Sairy." Zeffer tugged a single hand through his thick russet hair. "I have been tearing myself up inside, imagining what's going on and wanting tae help. I'm so sairy that I brought it up at all."

"You were right, though. Brody is curious and wants tae know his dad. So, now I'm beating myself up because of course Calan will want tae know Brody—he's a good kid! Calan and I were friends, not in love, but he was ready tae join the military and had his career planned. We'd used a condom"—she shrugged, her face flaming—"the first time, and had only brought the one. Brody is fate."

Zeffer's lips twitched at her discomfort. "People have sex, Paislee. It's all right, and a joy in life. You were seventeen, so was he, and going intae the military, as you say. Was there whisky involved?"

"Champagne."

His smile slid at her confession. "You were young, and still are."

Paislee's gaze landed on the folder. "It's thick. Is he married? Is he raising border collies in France?"

"Calan Maxwell died a hero," Zeffer said. He passed her the folder.

"Dead?" She blinked the name on the folder into focus. "He can't die. Brody hasn't met him. I promised Brody that you were looking for Calan tae find him."

More dratted tears burned her eyes.

"I'm verra, verra sairy, Paislee. But Calan did what he set oot tae do and was on track for an incredible career. His sacrifice saved thousands of lives. It was top secret whatever he did—so secret that I cannae uncover it."

"Top secret?"

"Aye. You look through that, and I'll get his effects. His grand-father had them."

Paislee opened the folder to see the standard form a person would fill out for the military, with age, name, birth date. He'd wanted to specialize in espionage. His youthful face was the same she re-membered from secondary, when they'd graduated S6.

He'd never married.

Zeffer cleared his throat and offered her a plastic bin the size of a computer paper box.

"Why did he give this tae you, Zeffer?"

"Just read through it all—we sorted it tae start at the top. Calan knew aboot Brody, Paislee. Mr. Maxwell said that Calan loved you, but his career was his priority."

"I had no idea." Paislee began to read. Calan had written a journal, to her, Paislee. He'd known about Brody through his grand-father, who had been to Nairn to visit friends. He'd seen Paislee with Brody and sent a letter to his grandson. Calan watched from afar, thinking he'd have time to scoop Paislee and Brody up after his time in the military. He'd died last year, and the grandfather was in a nursing home but had brought the bin, with instructions to mail it to Paislee after he passed on.

It took an hour. It was a good thing she'd told Rhona not to come until noon—she had a whopping thirty minutes to spare. She'd finished the Perrier and the box of tissues Zeffer had provided as he waited for her to read without rushing her.

"Calan was proud of Brody," Paislee managed to say.

"And you," Zeffer said.

Paislee exhaled, her gaze on the rippling water on the horizon. "Now what?"

"Are you asking, or verbalizing?" Zeffer asked.

"You know all about me, Zeffer," Paislee said. "My worst shame tae my current predicament. Why do you care?"

"Will you please call me Mack?" Mack scooted the papers gently and respectfully into the bin. He smelled like expensive aftershave, so subtle she leaned closer to him. It was a scent that meant safety to her.

"Mack. Yes, I want tae know—what do you think I should do?"

"Why me?" Mack turned the question to her.

"I respect you," Paislee said. "You've shown kindness, intelligence, and consideration above and beyond the law—or friendship."

Zeffer moved her hair back from her forehead. "I dinnae want tae be your friend."

Paislee's stomach clenched and she pushed him away. "That's all I have until Brody is eighteen."

"Not buying it," Zeffer said. "You are brave. Please be brave now, with me." He didn't grab her or force her to see the truth in his eyes. She was terrified of the truth in his eyes. Love blazed from the seafoam-green depths.

Paislee stood up straight, tempted to bolt. "I don't understand."

"I love you—and God help me, because I've spent a year and a half trying not tae love you—but my feelings willnae go away. I am a wealthy man, Paislee. After my da died because of the crooked Norwegians, there was nobody tae take care of my family. I was a child model. I have enough that my family will never want for a thing. I am a DI, because I care aboot right and wrong."

"Ze—Mack."

"I feel bad for Calan, actually."

"Don't," Paislee said. "It's too soon for me tae unpack everything that Calan felt and was and hid. He had pictures of Brody. Not creepy ones, but he knew he had a son and planned tae reach out after his retirement."

Zeffer's hand rested on her shoulder. "I cannae expect tae understand, as I've never had children."

"You said you didn't want them."

"Brody is different." Zeffer's words reached into her heart, and her soul. "Brody is a part of you."

Paislee crumpled to her knees, the knowledge of his love filling her from the inside out. Zeffer—Mack went with her. They seemed connected by their gazes as they stared into one another's eyes, knees touching, her hand in his hair—his hand at her hip. "I love you too."

Mack rested his forehead against hers. "Why do you sound so miserable?"

"I've never been in love before," Paislee said. "Is it supposed tae hurt?"

Zeffer cupped her head in his hands and kissed her until her mind swam with desire. Her entire body was on fire. He lay them down, facing one another, and gently traced her cheek with his thumb. "Do you really want tae wait until Brody is eighteen?"

A knock sounded on the bandstand and Constable Payne, grinning, cleared his throat as he studied the two of them stretched out on the bandstand floor.

"Not the usual suspects caught making oot in the bandstand," Payne said, with a twinkle in his eye.

"Well, avert your gaze if you're offended, Payne," Zeffer said. "I plan on kissing Paislee a lot."

Paislee cursed the redhead blush that suffused her body while, at the same time, she couldn't wait to be kissed. A lot.

"What is it, Payne?" Zeffer asked, rising up on one elbow.

"We got an update on Cam's car."

"Tell me."

"Cam's car wasnae totaled, and we found his doping kit in the boot."

Chapter 21

Paislee scrambled to her feet. "Joseph lied. Sandi and Fern both said that Cam hadn't been drunk, although he'd been really angry. Going on about the next win, tae be stronger and better with use of steroids."

Mack rested his hand on Paislee's lower back to steady her.

Payne tilted his cap backward and shrugged. "I think Police Scotland was given a line by Joseph Whittle tae cover up a darker deed. Inspector McCleod isnae pleased; he remembers the case though he wasn't in charge. When the father of the deceased young man blamed drinking, and there had been a precedent for Cam getting behind the wheel under the influence, well . . . the other inspector accepted Joseph's wishes."

"And now Joseph Whittle is dead. Did Artie do it?" Mack asked.

"Artie had no defensive wounds on his hands," Payne said. "Everything on his body is consistent with his fainting at the sight of blood and hitting his head on the counter. A guid portion of the blood in the kitchen belonged tae Joseph. The messages they've been able tae retrieve from Artie's smashed mobile match what Rhona said we'd find. He didnae talk tae anybody else."

"Artie comes home from hospital today," Paislee said. "Rhona had mentioned she thought around noon." She read the time on her phone. "In twenty minutes. Gemma prepared his bedroom so that he has a safe place tae recuperate. Ross will drive him home—Rhona offered, and so did Gemma, but if Artie needs physical help, Ross is stronger."

Payne read notes on his tablet. "Ross McCrumb?"

"Yes," Paislee said.

"He was the talent agent that Joseph wanted Artie tae impress," Constable Payne said. "If I'd heard how Joseph was speaking tae Artie, I would have stepped in. Why didnae he?"

"Fear of Joseph? Ross believed Cam had a shot toward being a champion strongman, according tae Fern." Paislee perused the water, the usual sight of the waves not as soothing with so much in flux. "Joseph was over the top. Fern said that Cam had protected Artie's right tae not use steroids, because they'd given him high blood pressure." Sandi had noted Cam's bloody nose that didn't seem in line with the car accident.

"What are you thinking?" Mack asked.

"Well, something you officers have taught me is that people are multifaceted. What if Joseph, by berating Artie in front of Ross, was protecting him somehow?"

Constable Payne gestured that she should continue with her thought. "How so?"

Paislee's nape tingled as she recalled Sandi's words: Nobody was one hundred percent evil. "So that Ross wouldn't pressure Artie tae use steroids, because *Artie was no Cam,*" she repeated. "Joseph gave that message loud and clear. Maybe it was for Ross and not Artie. Who else but Joseph could have cracked Artie's caber?"

"What do we ken aboot Ross McCrumb?" Mack asked Payne.

"I'll run back tae the station and do a search," Payne said. "We never had cause tae do a background check."

"I'll go with you," Zeffer said. "Where is Ross right now?"

"The hospital, I think." Paislee read her phone, but there were no new notifications. "Rhona might still be there if she hasn't left for Cashmere Crush. Ross *offered* tae drive Artie home. He's been there at the hospital almost the whole time."

"Sure he has. Helpful—or controlling?" Payne said. "Warn Rhona tae stall and dinnae let Artie leave the hospital. Not with Gemma or with Ross. Be vague until we get the proof we need. I'll call the constable on duty."

Mack picked up the bin of Calan Maxwell's letters and photos. "Let's go." The three of them walked in the same direction: Paislee to the car park, Mack and Payne toward the station beyond. Her lips stung pleasantly from Mack's kisses, and she tried not to think about what had just transpired.

"No answer," Constable Payne said. "I'm worrit."

Paislee called Rhona. The teenager didn't pick up either. Texting Rhona to call her right away, Paislee let her know she was on the way to the shop.

Mack lifted the Juke's hatch and put the bin inside. He gave her one firm kiss and then looked after Constable Payne. Their destinations were just blocks away.

"Want me tae drop you off?" Paislee asked. Her phone dinged a notification from Rhona.

Sorry to be a pain! Can you come get me please? Truck has a flat tire. Ross offered to give me a ride and is now MIA. Artie still not released.

"I have tae go get Rhona—she said that Ross isn't around. Artie is waiting tae be released."

To her surprise, Zeffer went around the car and hopped into the passenger side.

OMW. "What are you doing?" Paislee asked Zeffer.

TY. Calling!

"Payne can get the information aboot Ross McCrumb." Mack buckled his safety belt. "I'd feel better going with you tae pick up Rhona. Do we trust Gemma?"

"Yes?" Paislee drove toward the hospital and answered the phone via Bluetooth. "Hey! Where are you now, lass?"

"The lobby, looking for Ross," Rhona said. "Gemma finally unlocked the password for Joseph's phone. It was super complicated, and Artie had tae help. I think he's starting tae remember things, because he sounded really scared."

"When was the last time you saw Artie?" Mack asked.

"Hey, DI. Fifteen minutes ago. Ross told me tae go downstairs and wait in his car, but then he disappeared. I'm going back upstairs tae Artie's room. I must have missed him somehow. Lachlan is never going tae let me borrow another truck. A nail in the bike tire, a nail in the pickup tire. I have had the worst luck."

Unless someone was doing that on purpose. "I doubt that. Rhona, please, stay in the lobby. Are there other people around?"

"Two people waiting tae be seen and one receptionist," Rhona said.

Mack used his mobile to call the guard on duty but didn't have any better luck than Constable Payne, so he next dialed the hospital itself, asking for Artie Whittle's room.

It just rang and rang.

Paislee's stomach clenched with fear. "Stay where other people can see you," she instructed. "Don't get in the car with Gemma or Ross. If he forces the issue tell him that the police are on the way."

"What's wrong?" Rhona asked.

"Be careful," Mack said. "I'd feel a lot better if you'd find someplace tae hide."

"Gemma wants tae send us what she found on Joseph's phone," Rhona said, not hearing Mack.

Paislee's phone dinged a notification. "It's Gemma!"

"There's Ross. He has Artie in a wheelchair. Artie's slumped over. What—" Rhona ended the call.

Zeffer cursed and called Constable Payne. "Report a kidnapping at the hospital. Ross has Artie in a wheelchair and possibly Rhona under duress. Artie was getting his memory back, and Ross couldnae have that."

"Done!" Payne's voice was cool and collected. "Monroe is at

the hospital already with two back up vehicles. ETA for your arrival?"

"Four minutes," Paislee said. Thinking of a frightened Rhona, she put the pedal to the metal. "Two!"

Mack calmly braced his hand on the dash. "You can do this, Paislee."

Her phone was sounding off like she'd won the jackpot at a casino.

"Who is it?" Mack asked.

"Gemma! Should we call her?" Paislee didn't have the free hands to do so. "You can."

Mack copied the number on the screen. Gemma Whittle. He dialed and she answered right away. "Who is this?"

"Detective Inspector Mack Zeffer. I'm with Paislee Shaw driving toward the hospital—we dinnae have time tae read the messages, can you tell me what they say?"

"I unlocked my husband's phone, expecting tae find numbers for his floozies, but instead," Gemma sobbed, "it's a confession for covering up Cam's death by making it look like an accident. He'd od'd on the steroids and had a heart attack at twenty years old."

"I'm so sorry," Paislee said. "Is Ross involved?"

"Up tae his ears! The traitor. He and Joseph had a side business selling and delivering anabolic steroids up and doon Scotland through Ross's connections at the gyms he canvassed for potential clients. Ross wanted Artie hooked too, considering him a loose end. My husband was keeping his promise tae Cam tae let Artie choose. Artie wasnae interested."

"That's motive for murder," Mack said, as Paislee turned into the car park.

"I feared Artie had killed Joseph oot of anger, but it was Ross," Gemma said. "Ross knew aboot the cameras in the house, they went hunting together. I trusted him, and so did Joseph. Where is Artie?"

"Ross is trying tae kidnap him," Paislee said. "But the police are here and won't let it happen. Oh, there he is! Call you back."

A wild-eyed Ross held a hunting knife to Rhona's throat as Rhona pushed a slumped-over Artie out of the hospital in a wheelchair.

"Constable Monroe is tae the left," Mack said. "Park and stay here." He got out of the car. Paislee waited inside the Juke at the direct order. She couldn't tear her gaze away from Ross and Rhona. Artie.

Constable Payne showed up with sirens blaring. Two other police vehicles blocked the exits.

"Let us go, or Rhona dies," Ross shouted.

His eyes were wide and red with rage. With steroids? Was he addicted to the product he'd sold?

She prayed that Artie was okay. That Rhona would be all right.

Her phone rang again. Gemma. Paislee didn't answer, too focused on what was happening. If Rhona needed her, Paislee would be there.

Constables Payne and Monroe conferred with Mack. The DI had his weapon free, the only one on the ground to have a gun. A police helicopter hovered over the scene.

"Give yourself up, Ross McCrumb," a voice cannoned down from the copter. "We have the entire area surrounded."

Paislee held her breath as Ross suddenly seemed to realize that he was truly caught.

Rather than drop the knife, he stabbed it toward Artie, but Rhona used her Highland Fling leg kick to toss it away from Artie, toward the car park. Constables Payne and Monroe, with DI Mack Zeffer, had Ross pinned and cuffed in seconds, the knife also seized.

It was sure to match the stab marks on Joseph.

Rhona slumped over Artie, patting her boyfriend, searching for wounds. Paislee, knowing the bad guy was caught, raced from the Juke to Rhona.

"Well done," Paislee said to her young employee. She patted Rhona's back. "You saved him!"

Rhona cried out in pain.

Paislee realized that her palm was bloody. "We need a medic!" she said. "Rhona's hurt!"

Two hospital aides rushed out to assist—one wheeled Artie back inside, and the other helped Rhona by applying pressure on the wound with Rhona's scarf. "Will you call my mum, Paislee?"

"Of course, sweetheart," Paislee said. Rhona was escorted inside. She scrolled her phone but didn't have Petra's number. It would be on the contact information on her laptop at the shop. She texted Lydia for it, and her best friend sent it right away with a question, but Paislee would have to explain later.

A screech of tires sounded as Gemma Whittle barreled into the car park with the family pickup, honking. She spilled from the cab and yelled, "Where is Ross McCrumb? I'll kill him if he's hurt Artie!"

"Artie is inside the hospital being checked out." Paislee stepped toward the angry woman. Blond hair had escaped Gemma's clip, her blue eyes were wild. "Maybe don't say that so loud," she advised calmly, burying the panic racing through her body. "Ross is in handcuffs by the police car with Constable Payne. Let me call Petra about Rhona."

Paislee kept one hand on Gemma's shoulder, and with the other, phoned Petra Smythe. "Hi. It's Paislee—I am at the hospital with Rhona."

"I ken," Petra said in a superior tone. "Artie is getting released. I suppose you have some sage advice regarding my daughter?"

Paislee didn't have time to wade through hurt feelings sure to be the root of Petra's attitude. Gemma had her teeth bared at Ross. "Rhona was injured when she saved Artie's life."

"Hurt? I'm on my way. I'll phone my husband, should I? Is it serious?"

"I don't know, but aye, come, and bring McDermot." Paislee ended the call.

Gemma pulled away from Paislee and bolted toward the police

car. Ross McCrumb was in handcuffs and leaning against the vehicle. Constable Payne had his arm on Ross's about to get him in the back seat. "Murderer! Artie better not die."

The family friend, talent agent, physical trainer, and steroid dealer glanced at Gemma, his jaw tight.

"You killed your partner," Gemma said. "Why?"

He didn't answer.

"I talked tae Artie. He remembers a little aboot what happened when you came tae our house on Sunday. I'd invited you, thinking you would save Artie from Joseph. He heard you and Joseph arguing. He saw Kev but didnae understand why he was there. You must have planned tae kill Joseph all along. He didnae want tae make your steroid scheme bigger. You needed Joseph."

"I did not need him," Ross said, finally reacting to her accusations. "You think you're so smart? Well, you got it wrong. Cam had a heart attack because he od'd on the roids. He wasnae drunk! We had tae cover it up tae protect the deliveries from Romania, where steroids are legal. It gave me the idea tae dose Joseph and make it look like an actual heart attack too, but he realized what I was doing and came at me with the knife. It was self-defense," Ross said. "Joke's on you, Gem." He gave Gemma a sleazy smile.

"No, Ross. It's on you. I discovered evidence of steroid trafficking on Joseph's phone, and the scheme is verra detailed. You're going tae jail for murder and selling steroids. For helping Joseph cover up Cam's death." Gemma hefted her chin, her expression mired in misery. "I called the Nairn Highland Games committee tae warn them aboot steroid use, thinking I was ooting Joseph. I didnae realize it was the both of you."

Ross yanked against Constable Payne's tight hold. "You'd better shut your mouth!"

Constable Payne was unfazed by Ross's outburst and had listened closely to Gemma and Ross's conversation. "Please move aside so I can escort Mr. McCrumb tae the station. We will need that evidence."

Gemma backed up from Ross, and Paislee put her arm around the woman's waist. "I will forward it tae you."

"I'd like tae have the phone, Mrs. Whittle," Constable Payne said.

"I didnae bring it. I was in such a rush tae get here when I knew Artie was in danger." Gemma shook and trembled.

"Let's go inside and get you a cup of tea while we check on Artie," Paislee said. "This discovery has tae be shocking."

Constable Payne gestured toward the hospital entrance. "Tea is just the thing. Let me ken how Artie and Rhona fare? That was some kick. She could be a pro."

Paislee made a mental note to share that compliment with Rhona later. She and Gemma entered the empty hospital lobby. Where was Rhona?

"I want tae see Artie Whittle," Gemma told the nurse behind the desk.

"He's being tended tae, as is the young lady with him," the nurse replied.

"Please let us know what you can," Paislee said.

Paislee had just gotten Gemma settled with a hot tea when Petra and McDermot arrived in the waiting room.

Petra scanned the lobby before narrowing her gaze on Paislee. "I willnae have my daughter working in such a dangerous place. A yarn shop should be safe!" She turned to the nurse behind the desk. "Where is Rhona Smythe?"

The nurse calmly explained that Rhona was being seen by a doctor. One parent at a time could go back and talk to her.

"You go," McDermot said to a very worried Petra. "Come back with an update?"

"I will." Petra gripped her handbag and rushed through the door and out of sight.

McDermot joined Paislee and nodded at Gemma who was drinking tea. "I'm so sairy for all you've gone through, Gemma. How is Artie?"

"I dinnae ken." Gemma raised her bloodshot gaze from her mug. "They willnae let me see him yet. That must mean it's bad."

"Would you like some tea?" Paislee asked McDermot.

McDermot held out his hand, which shook. "It's the worst phone call tae get, that your child is injured and in hospital. What happened?"

Paislee made the man a cup of strong tea and explained how Ross had kidnapped Artie and used Rhona as a shield to get away, but the police had him surrounded, and his daughter's Highland Fling kick had knocked the blade away from Artie as the police tackled Ross.

Gemma's eyes widened. "I hadnae heard the story either. I owe Rhona thanks. And you, Paislee. I cannae think straight! I dinnae ken if Artie is alive or dead."

The parents sat next to one another in misery.

Petra, true to her word, hurried out of the back area where they tended to the emergencies coming in.

"Rhona is all right and will be discharged shortly. She has a wee cut—saved by her shawl." Petra did her best to hold her emotions in check. "She told me it was Ross McCrumb."

"And Artie?" Gemma asked.

Petra glanced over her shoulder to be sure nobody could hear her and whispered, "I snuck intae his room. He was hooked up tae a monitor, and I heard it beeping, but I didnae see much else. I'm so sairy, Gemma. He's alive, I ken that."

Gemma bowed her head. "Thank you." She swiped a tear from her cheek.

"Where is Ross?" McDermot asked coolly.

"He's been arrested and taken tae jail," Gemma said. "Lucky for him or I woulda—" She curled her fist. "I feel ill-used by someone I considered a friend tae the family." She blew out a breath. "Not tae mention my own husband's part in all of this. If Joseph was alive, I would send him tae jail withoot a qualm for what he's done."

"What's that?" Petra asked.

"Joe and Ross covered up my son Cam's death from od'ing tae keep from being discovered. He and Ross had a business selling anabolic steroids along the glassware route from Romania and back." Gemma pursed her lips. "I thought I wasnae guid enough for him, and it's a brutal realization that Joseph didnae really consider my feelings at all. Just himself."

Petra squeezed Gemma's shoulder with compassion. "I'm so sairy, Gemma."

"Your lass saved my Artie's life, and you will have a friend in me for all of mine," Gemma said.

Rhona whooshed through the door to the waiting room. She wore a nurse's scrub shirt instead of the top she'd had on earlier.

"Mum! Da! Gemma!" Rhona hugged them all, saving Paislee's hug for last. "Paislee. You got here in the nick of time. If you hadnae warned me tae be on guard against Ross, I would have gotten intae his car withoot a qualm."

"We have a lot tae be thankful for today," Paislee said, bowing her head to give a moment of thanks. It takes a village, as Gran used to say. Or in this instance, a shire.

Epilogue

One month later, a lunch picnic on the beach, Sunday Funday

Paislee, thigh-to-thigh with Mack on a blanket, lifted her face to the cool sea breeze. The end of September meant the winding down of blue skies and tourist season, and that she could catch her breath.

There were thirty plus revelers on a series of connected blankets with thermoses of hot chocolate or flasks of whisky. Blaise and Shep had been unable to make the impromptu picnic but had sent a basket of treats to be opened later with their love. These were her closest friends, her family, and they were celebrating change.

Rather than it be something to curse, Paislee was learning to embrace it.

Brody, Amelia, and Grandpa flew a kite with Wallace and Snowball alternately chasing the waves or the kite's long ribbon tail.

Amelia had done brilliantly in her classes and was continuing training to be a constable. Her hair was now shoulder length and its lovely natural dark brown. She'd met someone, she'd said, but didn't go into details. And she was not the least surprised by Paislee and Mack together. "It's perfect," she'd said wisely. "And time, my friend."

Lydia and Corbin were to Paislee's left side on an extra-large blanket with Rhona, Aibreann, Artie, Petra, and McDermot. Gemma was spending the weekend with Lachlan, on the Isle of Sky, for a romantic getaway.

Gemma had decided to sell the house and split the proceeds with Artie so that he could have a start at a business or a home for himself. Grateful, and wise, Artie and Rhona were talking about moving to Inverness with Aibreann to open a dancing school. One of the buildings under consideration was a triplex, with each unit one bedroom, one bath. The third unit they planned on utilizing as a rental income. Nothing was set in stone, and it was fun to watch them dream.

Rhona had paid off the money owed to her parents, and they'd given her back the cute sports car that had gotten her into trouble. The teenager had matured so much since Paislee had met her—her boundless joy was tempered now by a wee bit of reality.

Brody had met his Grandpa Maxwell when they'd visited the nursing home two Saturdays ago. It had been really nice, the older man welcoming and warm, and they planned to go again every third Saturday after Brody's football practice. He hadn't made the team but was on the alternate list, so if a player was injured or booted off, he would be called up.

Emma was a love—so down to earth, but with a happy smile, as if anything was possible.

"How's Brody doing?" Lydia asked. "Aboot Calan? He seems tae be in a guid space."

Lydia and Corbin had spent the last two weeks signing contracts for the vineyard in Germany, so though they'd talked, this was the first time she'd seen Brody for herself.

"He framed a picture out of the box from Calan and Grandpa Maxwell and has it on his dresser. He's using this circumstance tae push for America. I was already caving, but he's been such a trooper about this that we are absolutely going. It's on the calendar for next year." She placed her hand on Mack's denim-clad knee. "I've asked Mack tae come along with me and Grandpa."

"I said yes before she could change her mind," Mack said, with a rumbling chuckle that would never grow old.

It felt wonderful, comfortable, and right to have him by her side. He was gorgeous to her, and a fashion plate, so of course he'd been a child model. He and Lydia had so much in common, from their giant generous hearts to their love of *Vogue* magazine. He'd followed through on his plan of kissing her a lot. She longed for more, and it would happen, when the time was right.

"That's excellent news!" Lydia exclaimed. "And what will you do with Wallace? If we're around, we can doggy-sit."

Paislee smiled at her dearest friend. "Amelia's offered tae dog-sit at our house—but thank you."

"Looking forward tae meeting Rosanna," Mack said, with a dangerous growl in his throat.

"You have tae be nice, Mack, or you can't come." Paislee peeked at him from behind a fall of hair. "I need you for moral support." She shared to everyone, "Grandpa's trying tae find a way tae visit the Keys, which are far away from Arizona."

"Dinnae tell me," Zeffer said good-naturedly. "I cannae stop it if I dinnae ken aboot it."

To her surprise, the men in her life all got along splendidly.

Wallace knew that Zeffer was no longer the enemy—perhaps due to Mack's giving the terrier high-end chicken treats; Grandpa was happy to have someone to share a dram with; and Brody, after catching Mack press a kiss to Paislee's lips, just grinned at Paislee as she blushed a cherry red.

Change was no longer the four-letter word it used to be.

"But before Arizona, Germany?" Lydia asked, batting her lashes over her steadfast gray eyes. "You might as well see the world."

"I have a business tae run, Lydia."

Corbin leaned across Lydia from the other side of the blanket. "It's like having a baby," Corbin said.

"Not exactly"—Paislee snickered—"but close enough. You're smart tae be close by. It mattered for me tae have my route with the

house, the business, and Brody's school all within fifteen minutes."
She was thrilled for them to pursue this dream in Germany.

"We cannae wait for you tae see it," Corbin said. "Of course,
Mack, you're welcome too."

"Thanks, Corbin."

"Paislee!"

Paislee turned around to see Jerry and Freya being dragged by a
black-and-white border collie puppy that Freya had adopted after
judging the Nairn Highland Games.

The pup broke loose but went straight for Meri, who had found
the dog in need of a home from the judge who'd called in sick. It
was serendipity.

"Rolly!" Meri said, laughing as the puppy waggled his body
with joy.

"Why don't you get a pup?" Paislee asked.

"Mibbe someday. I'm in no rush." Meri patted the dog and
smoothly picked up the leash as Freya and Jerry reached the blankets.

The Mulholland twins were also flying a kite, and it got tangled
in Brody's. As the dragon was slayed by the pink unicorn, everyone
was laughing. Iona, in green, and Anna, in light blue, raced to their
dad. Arran patted their shoulders, still chuckling. "We won, Da!"
Anna said.

Amelia, Brody, and Grandpa rolled up the injured dragon. "It
was a fair fight," Grandpa said. "I need a wee break for snacks."

"Snacks!" the twins and Brody said with equal enthusiasm.

Wallace and Snowball also recognized the word "snacks" and
joyfully ran back to the blankets. It started to drizzle, but that didn't
stop the party. This was Scotland after all, and they were used to
dreich weather.

"I want crisps," Brody said.

"Us too!" the twins said.

There was plenty of room for everyone to have a seat and share
snacks—not just crisps sandwiches, which she would never in a mil-

lion years understand, but Riesling from Germany for the adults, and homemade shortbread, baked by Lydia, for everyone. Paislee opened the basket from Shep and Blaise. "From the O'Connors, who wished they could be here." She passed out designer cheese and crackers to round out the impromptu feast.

Paislee couldn't be happier.

Mack took Paislee's hand and squeezed, his gaze saying without words how he loved her. It was the first time she'd been in love, and it was worth every heartache to feel this bliss. Brody and Wallace stretched out together at the foot of the blanket, opposite Grandpa.

"The only one missing is Gran," Paislee said aloud.

Grandpa pointed to the clouds parting above the ocean, and a double rainbow through the drizzle. "I think she's here with us, lass."

Paislee felt the love surround them all. They raised whatever they were drinking to the sky. "Tae Gran," Paislee said. "Sláinte."

Acknowledgments

This book couldn't come together without the entire team at Kensington—my thanks to John Scognamiglio for letting me create Paislee's world. To the cover artist—thank you. To the various editors and proofreaders, to Larissa Ackerman, publicist extraordinaire, who helped facilitate the signing in North Carolina, to the Rural Hill Scottish Heritage Centre—thank you. Evan Marshall, best agent ever, who asked if I had Scottish roots . . . it turns out that my grandmother was right and we can trace our ancestry to a Scottish king, through the Boyd last name. My son, Brighton Hall, was able to trace our family's journey. That is a story for another day.

To Mom, for reading a million times to see if I'd ever named Mary Beth Mulholland's twins before this book.

To my daughter, Destini, and granddaughter, Kennedi, and my sister of the heart Sheryl, for falling on your swords to watch the men in kilts and the caber toss. To my husband, Christopher, for getting the best pictures of the caber toss—and Sheryl, video of the duck herding that went awry. XOXO

Visit our website at
KensingtonBooks.com
to sign up for our newsletters, read
more from your favorite authors, see
books by series, view reading group
guides, and more!

Become a Part of Our
Between the Chapters Book Club
Community and Join the Conversation

Submit your book review for a chance to win exclusive
Between the Chapters swag you can't get anywhere else!
https://www.kensingtonbooks.com/pages/review/